BREAKAWAY

The Dartmouth Cobras

By
Bianca Sommerland

Copyright 2012, Bianca Sommerland

ALL RIGHTS RESERVED
Edited by Rosie Moewe
Cover art by Reese Dante

Copyright © 2012 by Bianca Sommerland

Breakaway (The Dartmouth Cobras #3)
Second Edition, Paperback-Published 2013
Edited by Lisa Hollett
Cover art by Reese Dante

License Notes

All rights reserved. No part of this book may be reproduced in any form or by any electronic or mechanical means including information storage and retrieval systems—with the exception of short quotes used for critical articles or reviews—without permission in writing from the author.

This book is a work of fiction and any resemblance to persons, living or dead, or actual events is purely coincidental. The characters are products of the author's imagination and used fictitiously.

Warning

This book contains material not suitable for readers under 18. In also contains scenes that some may find objectionable, including BDSM, ménage sex, bondage, anal sex, sex toys, double penetration, voyeurism, edge play, and deviant use of hockey equipment. Do not try this at home unless you have your very own pro-athlete. Author takes no responsibility for any damages resulting from attempting anything contained in this book.

Dedication

To all the players who held the fort during the 2012 lockout, spending their time playing charity games. I can't blame anyone for leaving, but I respect those who stayed.

Acknowledgements

I thank you in every book, but this time, I need to add a little more. Cherise Sinclair, I was nothing but a fangirl at one point, an aspiring author who looked up to you and respected you so much, who saw you as the perfect example for the kind of writer I wanted to be. And not just by writing characters people would love, but by loving the craft and continuing to grow and thrive no matter where the written road took me. That hasn't changed, but now, I don't just admire you, I consider you a friend and a mentor. You've helped me navigate through road bumps in my career and my personal life. You always push me to find the right words, but there are none that fit for this except I love you and I appreciate you so very much. Keep kicking my ass, darlin'!

We both know I need it! <g>

To Rosie Moewe, damn it, I don't know how you put up with me! You've been with me through every step of this book, you've been a friend, a support system, and so patient while I've gone through my ups and downs. You are so precious to me and I've never known a more giving person in my life. I couldn't have made it through this book without you.

Missy Vogler, thank you for making me laugh, for listening to my drunken ramblings, for being so honest and giving me a shoulder when I needed one. I'm looking forward to chillin' in our matching Dartmouth Cobra PJs! In you I've made a lifelong friend and I can't wait to see what the future brings.

To my beta readers, Jennifer Zeffer, Stacey Price, Maria Alvarez, and Genevieve Trahan, I loved hanging out, and throwing around ideas with you about the book! You have all been so essential in making this series successful, and whether you've been with me from the beginning, or came in later, know that I appreciate you so very much.

Toymaker, thank you for helping me get inside the head of a good, strong Dom, for giving me advice and some wicked ideas to play with. If I ever get a Dom of my own, I want him to be just like you. Loving, understanding, and damn inventive! Lol! Eirocawakening, what can I say other than I love you! In such a short time you've gone from being a great friend, to more of a sister. There's nothing I can't tell you, and I'm looking forward to the days when we can be our weird selves together in a . . . unique setting ;)

My readers, as always, you have given me all the support and strength I needed to bring you more of the characters who are as real to you as they are to me. All the emails and comments I've gotten from you have done more to keep me going than you will ever know.

And a special shout out to the Dartmouth Cobras Street Team! You'll all be getting another visit from the guys soon! You've earned it!

To my family, thanks for waiting for supper, and laundry, and pretty much everything else. Sometimes, all we had was minutes before I had to get back to work, but you made every second count. And in return, I'm bringing you all to Disneyland!

Just one thing…there's a few more books to write. Rain check, okay? ;)

Dartmouth Cobra Roster

Centers

No	Name	Age	Ht	Wt	Shot	Birth Place
13	Sloan Callahan	31	6'1"	210	R	Charlottestown, PEI, Canada
45	Keaton Manning	30	5'11	187	R	Ulster, Ireland
18	Ctirad Jelinek	26	6'0"	204	L	Rakovnik, Czech Republic
3	Erik Hjalmar	23	6'3"	219	R	Stockolm, Sweden
27	Scott Demyan	28	6'3"	198	L	Anaheim, California, USA

Left Wings

No	Name	Age	Ht	Wt	Shot	Birth Place
40	Max Perron	29	6'2"	215	L	Alamo, Texas, USA
16	Luke Carter	22	5'11	190	L	Warroad, Minnesota, USA
53	Shawn Pischlar	29	6'0"	200	L	Villach, Austria
71	Dexter Tousignant	23	6'2"	208	L	Matane, Quebec, Canada
5	Ian White	25	6'1"	212	L	Winnipeg, Manitoba, Canada

Right Wings

No	Name	Age	Ht	Wt	Shot	Birth Place
22	Tyler Vanek	21	5'8"	174	R	Greenville, North Carolina, USA
72	Dante Palladino	34	6'2"	215	L	Fassano, Italy
21	Bobby Williams	33	5'10	190	R	Sheffield, England
46	Vadim Zetsev	26	6'0"	203	R	Yaroslavl, Russia
66	Zachary Pearce	32	6'0"	210	L	Ottawa, Ontario, Canada

Defense

No	Name	Age	Ht	Wt	Shot	Birth Place
6	Dominik Mason	31	6'4"	235	R	Chicago, Illinois, USA
17	Einar Olsson	27	6'0"	200	L	Örnsköldsvik, Sweden
74	Beau Mischlue	25	6'2"	223	L	Gaspe, Quebec, Canada
~~78~~	~~TJ Streit~~	~~39~~	~~6'8"~~	~~244~~	~~L~~	~~Hørsholm, Denmark~~
26	Peter Kral	27	6'1"	200	L	Hannover, Germany
2	Mirek Brends	33	6'1"	214	L	Malmö, Sweden
47	Tony Brookman	24	6'3"	212	L	Winnipeg, Manitoba, Canada
67	Owen Stills	22	6'0"	217	R	Detroit, Michigan, USA
39	Rylan Cooper	23	5'11	198	R	Norfolk, Virginia, USA
11	Sebastian Ramos	29	6'5"	227	R	Arlanza, Burgos, Spain

Goalies

No	Name	Age	Ht	Wt	Shot	Birth Place
20	Landon Bowers	25	6'3"	215		Gaspe, Quebec, Canada
34	Svend Ingerslov	32	6'0"	205		Lillehammer Norway
29	Dave Hunt	20	6'2"	210		Hamilton, Ontario, Canada
~~97~~	~~Giroux~~	~~26~~	~~6'1"~~	~~195~~		~~New York, New York, USA~~

Chapter One

Mid April

Luke Carter trudged up the steps and dug his keys out of his pocket. Goose bumps rose under his dress shirt, and his numb fingers shook as he tried to fit the key in the lock. He had to stop letting his roommates hog his indoor parking spot. And he needed a new spring coat. His shoulders had broadened over the last year and nothing seemed to fit right. A nice thick sweatshirt would've kept him warm, but he'd wanted to look good for his girl. He tightened his grip on the bouquet of clunky flowers, pink and white—Stargazer something or another. They smelled real nice anyway.

Nice enough for her to forgive you?

He made a face at the stupid flowers and thought back on a chat with his good buddy Landon, the Dartmouth Cobras starting goalie. The man had used books to fix things with the chick he'd been into. And that chick was now his fiancé.

Teresa ain't into books. But maybe jewelry—or something pretty. He'd forgotten their... third month anniversary? Which was apparently a big deal. Not that he could've known. He'd never dated a girl this long.

Either way, he knew he'd screwed up. All he had was some flowers. That would have to do for now.

After unlocking the door to the apartment he shared with teammates, Tyler Vanek, and their newest roommate, Scott Demyan—a linemate who'd gotten kicked out of his last two apartments—Luke nudged the door open and stepped inside. Then he blinked and stepped back out.

He had to be fucking seeing things.

Moving slowly over the threshold, he shook his head as his stomach turned and clenched his fist hard enough to break the flower stems in half. Teresa gasped and pushed away from where she straddled Demyan on the coach. She crossed an arm over her bare breasts, using her fingers to comb through the tangled mess of her chestnut colored bob as blotchy red covered her cheeks.

Demyan groaned and leaned forward. "Look, man, it's not what you—"

"Shut the fuck up." Luke tossed the flowers aside. "Shut the fuck up and be a fucking man, you son of a bitch. You're screwing around with my girlfriend? In my house? You've got brass."

"Yep." Demyan sighed and stood, rubbing his palms on his black jeans. "That's me. Stupid enough to mess around with your woman right here where you'd catch us. Have at me if you want, might make you feel better. Then maybe you two should have a little chat."

"A chat? Seriously?" Luke slammed the door behind him. "What's there to talk about? You two enjoy each other. But do it somewhere else. Both of you get the fuck out."

"Carter, please." Teresa reached one hand out to him, her soft hair sweeping over her big, teary blue eyes. "This is my fault. I just thought—"

"Thought what? If you wanted a threesome, I might have considered it." He let out a bitter laugh, the ice in his tone seeping through his veins. "But not like this. Damn it, you haven't spoken to me in three days. I asked you to meet me here so we could work things out and—seriously, what the fuck!"

"If I wanted a *threesome*? What kind of freak do you think I am?" Teresa scowled and grabbed her shirt from the edge of the big denim sofa. "I thought this would be easier, okay? Maybe it was stupid, but I didn't know what else to do!"

Luke threw his hands up in the air. "About what? Me forgetting our anniversary? I said I was sorry! I was ready to prove it!"

"Exactly!" Teresa pulled on her shirt, then moved toward him, speaking low. "I've been acting like a total bitch to you. I figured you'd get fed up and dump me. But you didn't."

"Why would you want me to dump you?"

"Because I didn't have the heart to dump you! Not with everything going on with your mom! But I can't do this anymore! I can't be with a man like you!"

Everything inside Luke went still. His heartbeat stuttered in his chest. He heard Demyan swallow and saw him look away from the corner of his eye.

He took a deep breath. "A man like me?"

"Carter—"

"Luke." He ground his teeth. "Why don't you ever call me Luke?"

Her lips moved. Then her jaw set and she shrugged. "Because you're a hockey player. And being with a hockey player was exciting at first, but you're not the type of man a woman wants to spend her life with. I'm going to school in Ottawa this fall, and I want to keep my options open. I realized this wouldn't work when I went down for a tour last month. There are so many clean-cut guys with normal jobs, guys whose jobs don't make them look like—"

Demyan stood. "I think he gets the point."

Holding out his hand, Luke shook his head. "No, let her finish. Guys who don't look like what?"

"Carter—Luke. I'm sorry. Maybe it sounds shallow, but when people look at you, they see a rough hockey player. Damn it, you don't even have all you teeth and you're only twenty-two! What are you going to look like ten years from now?" She rubbed her hands over her face. "My parents asked to meet you. Can you just imagine what they would think?"

Luke traced the scar that ran down from his lip to his chin with trembling fingers. He touched his partials—which temporarily replaced two teeth he'd lost—with the tip of his tongue. All this time he'd been worried about her finding out about how he craved dominance, how much he enjoyed using ropes to tie a woman, how hot it got him to use a flogger to turn her ass nice and red. He'd stopped all that for her because she was as vanilla as a person could be, even though it meant the sex wasn't all that great for him. But fuck, he loved her. He would have given up everything except the game for her.

Even if he *had* been willing to give that up, it wouldn't have made a difference. He was damaged. Flawed. He saw it whenever he looked in the mirror. It had been pretty stupid to expect her not to.

"How long have you stayed because you felt sorry for me?"

"Luke—"

"How. Long?"

She folded her arms over her stomach. "Two months."

Jesus fucking Christ. He sucked his teeth and nodded. "Get out."

"I'm so sorry—"

He reached behind him and threw the door open. "I said get out!"

Not waiting to see her leave, Luke walked to the kitchen, opened the fridge, and got himself a beer. He drank half while leaning into the fridge. And sighed when he heard Demyan step up behind him.

"I'm surprised you didn't go after her." The bottle hit Luke's teeth as he gave Demyan a tight smile. "She's your type."

"That she is. Shallow, selfish, and stupid. An asshole like me doesn't aim any higher."

"You expect me to feel sorry for you?"

"Fuck no. The stuff I told you while I was fucking plastered wasn't for pity." Demyan shrugged, staring at the wall behind Luke. "I just thought you knew me better, that's all."

Dammit, busting up the man's pretty face would make him feel a whole lot better. But he *did* know him better. And they didn't need this shit messing up the way they gelled on the ice. "She just threw herself at you, didn't she?"

Demyan reached around him to grab a beer. "Yeah, after sitting beside me and telling me how horrible she felt wanting to break up with you while your mom's sick and all. I kinda patted her back and told her she needed to tell you what she was telling me. Then she heard you pull up and just climbed on top of me and took off her shirt."

"Fuck me."

"My words exactly. Hell, with my reputation, I didn't expect you to believe me if I told you I hadn't done anything. And I didn't expect her to come clean."

Luke's whole body ached worse than when their fucking captain, Sloan Callahan, put them through their paces the morning after a bad loss. His heart felt like it had fallen victim to a sledgehammer. Why the hell had he gotten all wrapped up in a relationship anyway? They never worked out; his parents were living proof of that.

"I'm gonna head to the club; I haven't been there in a while." Luke finished off his beer and stepped back to close the fridge. "You wanna come?"

"Sure. As long as I don't need to be packing up my shit?"

"Hey, you know what they say." Luke clinked his empty bottle to Demyan's still half-full one. "Bros before hoes."

"They do say that." Demyan tipped his beer to his lips, not coming up for air until he was finished. Then he belched and laughed. "But *they* never mean it."

"Well I do." Luke set his bottle on the counter and headed for the door. "From now fucking on."

* * * *

Pink and blue flashing lights. The sweet, slick perfume of sex. Two pairs of naked breasts pressed together as red lips met in a passionate kiss. A stage full of lust for a handful of cash.

Luke leaned forward and slipped a hundred dollar bill into the curvy blonde's G-string. She glanced down and gave him a sultry smile before bending down to suck on her "dance" partner's nice big nipples, one after the other. His dick jabbed at the inside of his zipper, throbbing with the kind of pain he craved when he needed to feel enough for his brain to shut the fuck up.

Not enough though. Not yet. He shifted as the women resumed fondling one another.

And I gave this up for her? His lips curled away from his teeth in a sneer. Good thing he'd come to the club on a night when the ladies were scheduled to put on a show. Something Silver Delgado, the club owner's girlfriend and partial owner of the Dartmouth Cobras, had come up with a few months back to up the club's income. And he'd missed out on all this while trying to be the relationship kind of guy.

Not because he suddenly wanted to settle down. No, it was for his mom. She'd just found out she had an inoperable brain tumor. Since his dad left them, all they'd had was each other. She was scared that she'd die and he'd be alone. His father's daughter and all the rest from that side didn't count as family. So she'd asked the impossible of him. She desperately needed to live to see him get married, and her doctors said she only had a year or two left. His shock had changed her tone pretty fast, and before he had a chance to say a word she'd whispered "Can you at least find a girl who you might want to marry, one day?"

He'd thought he could. He'd thought he had. It hadn't been horrible either; Teresa had been cool to have around when he wasn't on the road. She'd met his mom who absolutely loved her.

I loved her.

His stupid brain was going into overdrive. He shook as he pictured her all over Demyan, as he heard her telling him his fucked-up face disgusted her—fine, not in exactly those words, but—

Shut up!

He smashed the bottle in his hand against the side of the stage. The neck snapped off in his fist, cutting his palm. He drew in air and pain and shoveled the depressing thoughts into the back of his head. Teresa didn't matter. All that mattered was his mom, what she expected from him.

Sitting on the edge of her hospital bed at the end of the All-Star break in January, Luke had held her cold hands between his. "I don't have to go, Mom. They can bring up someone else to—"

"They need you. You won't do any good hanging around here while I'm getting tests. I'm not going to stop living, and I don't want you to either." She brought her hand up before he could argue. "My sister is coming to stay with me. I'll be fine."

"I ain't gonna be able to play good."

"Lucas Isaiah Carter, you better play well." She laughed when he winced at her use of his full name. Then she touched his cheek and whispered, "Don't dwell on this. Give me a reason to cheer each and every game. I'll be watching you."

His mom didn't ask him for much, and this was something he could do. At first he'd felt guilty, acting all normal with her still in the hospital, but every time he called, she seemed stronger, and finally she got to go home. And the act became real. Hell, people lived longer than doctors said they would all the time. Maybe she'd get better.

She still wants to see me happily married though.

Well, she didn't need to know he wasn't with Teresa. Not yet anyway. He could do that much for her, let her live with the illusion that her only child would one day give her grandbabies.

The heat from the cut on his palm spread, and he frowned as blood dripped on his shoe. Then glared at Demyan who was shaking him, snapping out nonsensical words.

Fingers raked into Luke's hair and his head was jerked back. Hot, minty breath flowed over his face as Chicklet, his mentor at the club, moved in close. "Come with me. Now."

He didn't even consider arguing with her. Then again, no one argued with Chicklet—not even Dean Richter, the Cobras general manager and owner of the club. She was the kind of Domme that could make even the most dominant man submit to some extent.

Not that Luke would *ever* submit to *anyone*.

She shoved him onto a leather sofa near the bar and went to the bar for a towel. After wrapping his hand tight, she straightened and put her hands on her hips. "What's up with you? You wanna hurt, you know I'll hurt you." She jutted her chin at his hand. "And I won't fuck up your stick handling when I do it."

Luke clenched his fist around the towel and shrugged. "It was an accident."

"Maybe so. But you took your sweet time taking care of it. And you weren't hearing Demyan when he told you you were bleeding all over the place." Her eyes narrowed as she studied him. "Where's your head at, kid? You completely zoned out."

"Just broke up with my girlfriend—no big deal." He gave Chicklet his most charming smile, even though he knew it wouldn't work on her. She had two subs—one of them his roommate, Tyler Vanek, and even that angel-faced SOB got the Full Metal Jacket treatment when he pissed Chicklet off. But he had to try. "You wanna know what I was thinking? Tyler's gone for a little while, trying to get his brain fixed." Wiggling his eyebrows, he let his gaze roam over her curvy, leather-clad body. "He won't mind if we have some fun while he's gone, will he?"

Chicklet's lips drew into a hard, mean line. "No, I don't think he'll mind at all. Stand up, boy."

Boy? He rolled his eyes and stood. "Chicklet, I ain't a sub—you know that, right?"

She smirked and glanced over to the right. "Wayne, you mind holding him for me?"

"Not at all." The huge bouncer came up behind Luke and shackled his wrists in big, beefy hands, jerking them back until his shoulders ached from the strain. "Where do you want him?"

"Get him in the upright stocks. The steel ones."

Twisting his wrists, Luke stared at Chicklet. "Whoa, wait a second—"

"You know the club safeword, boy." Chicklet arched a brow. "Ready to use it already?"

"No, I'm not ready to use it. I'm also not letting you put me in the fucking stocks."

"Not letting me?" Chuckling, Chicklet motioned for Wayne to go. "Try to stop me. It'll be fun to watch."

Ignoring Luke's snarling protests, Wayne dragged him to the stocks, twisting his arm when he refused to bend down to them. The stocks were T-shaped, with metal cuffs built in at the ends which were quickly snapped around Luke's wrists, spreading his arms wide. At the end of the V base, shackles on short chains welded into the steel were set up to restrain his ankles. He fought harder to keep Wayne from getting them on him, but the man muscled him into position easily and slapped his thigh when he tried to kick him.

"Behave, boy," Wayne said in the same tone he used with his slave.

Rage pooled up from Luke's guts to his throat, lava hot and thick enough to choke on. "Don't call me boy, you big ugly gorilla."

The brisk click of Chicklet's boot heels drew his attention just long enough for Wayne to lock the last shackle. Chicklet used the end of a riding crop to tip Luke's chin up. "Wayne gets five in for the insult, *boy*. I suggest you think before you open your mouth again."

Eyes narrowed, Luke watched Chicklet set a big white medical kit on the floor. "What the hell do you think you're doing, woman?"

Chicklet straightened. "Mistress."

"Are you serious? You've never made me call you Mistress before."

"Very observant."

How the hell was he supposed to have a reasonable conversation in this ridiculous position? He tugged until his wounded hand, still wrapped in the towel, pulsed as though he had his heart in his fist. "So why now?"

Lips pursed, Chicklet paced in front of him, checking his restrained wrists, running her hands over his shoulders and testing the muscles with her fingertips. Finally she stopped in front of him and squared her shoulders. "Because you need it. I feel like an idiot for not seeing it before, for easing off after giving you a little taste of submission."

"I'm not a submissive." He closed his eyes after another tug and took a deep breath. "Let me go, Chicklet. I get that you're trying to help, but you're wrong about me. I don't need this."

"Don't you?" Leaving one hand on his shoulder, Chicklet leaned close enough for her lips to brush his ear. "Let go for a moment and let yourself feel the restraints. Stop thinking about being a Dom. About what you *should* need. You don't get to decide that now."

Her soft tone soothed him, and he almost relaxed, almost admitted that not having to decide anything felt kinda good. But then he opened his eyes and saw people staring. Demyan, who'd given up watching the dancers. Wayne's slave who distractedly served the people at the bar. Laura, Chicklet's sub, who knelt by a bar stool with a calm expression on her face as though she saw her Mistress handle men like this all the time.

Which she did. She saw Chicklet handle Tyler like this.

But Tyler *was* a sub.

Gritting his teeth, Luke glared at Chicklet. "Let. Me. Go."

Chicklet clucked her tongue. "You worry too much about what others see when they look at you. Use the safeword, or shut up and let me take care of you."

He continued to glare at her, but didn't say a word.

"That's my boy." She looked over his shoulder. "Master Wayne, please take care of his hand. I'm going to fetch a few things from behind the bar."

As she walked away, Wayne came to his side and unwound the towel from his hand. He took out a flat gauze and covered the slowly oozing cut with it, then wrapped a bandage around Luke's hand. After taping it in place, he rose and folded his arms over his chest.

"What's eating at you, boy?" He took hold of Luke's chin when he tried to look away. Somehow he looked less ugly and more... powerful, standing over him. "You know, most good Doms submit at one point just to see what it's like. I've done it."

Luke's brow shot up and he lifted his chest off the bar as much as he could to face the man. "*You?*"

"Yes. Me." Wayne grinned. "Wasn't my thing, but I gave it a shot. Won't hurt you to do the same."

Snorting, Luke looked over to where Chicklet was approaching with her whole toy bag. "With Chicklet? I'd be disappointed if it *didn't* hurt."

Chicklet smiled. "That's the most honest thing you've said tonight. Don't worry, boy, I'll hurt you."

Luke's eyes went wide. He shook his head. "That isn't what I meant."

"That's exactly what you meant. You're not fooling anyone, Carter." She knelt, unzipped her toy bag, and pulled out a blindfold. "What you felt when you cut your hand is nothing compared to what you'll feel when I'm done with you. You wanna negotiate, you better do it now, because after I put this on you, I don't want to hear another word."

"Negotiate?" Luke let out a nervous laugh. "Come near me with a strap-on, *Mistress,* and you better never take these restraints off."

"So noted. I planned to keep this scene non-sexual anyway."

He swallowed and went still as she put the blindfold on him. Non-sexual. Which could only mean one thing as far as he knew.

Darkness stole the last of his resistance. He couldn't see anyone staring, so it was like they weren't there. "You *are* going to hurt me."

He heard Chicklet, and possibly Wayne, moving around him. Someone rolled his shirt up to his shoulders. Someone else undid his belt and slid his jeans and boxers down enough to bare his ass.

"I will, but only after Wayne does." Chicklet—it must have been Chicklet, because the lips were soft and her voice sounded close—kissed his cheek. "Count for me."

The *Snap!* came with a hot lick of fire across his ass. He clenched his butt and sucked in air as the sensation travelled down to his balls. *Holy shit!*

He groaned and whispered. "One."

Four more, harder, without pause, and he was panting against the urge to come. Forcing himself to count helped him hold back, but when smooth hands caressed his burning flesh he shuddered as the tip of his dick moistened with pre-cum.

"You're doing good, boy. Very good." Chicklet's approval made him feel bigger somehow. Stronger. Like he wasn't completely pathetic for letting her do this to him. "I'm going to play with you for a bit, put you in a good place. And you will not come."

"This won't make me come." He almost added "bitch" because being told what to do irked him, but he knew what kinds of toys she had in that bag. And he liked his nuts just as they were, thank you very much.

Clicking heels. A long body, both soft and hard in all the right places, pressed against his back. "You're so close, pet. I can tell. But if you're good, I'll let you go with your buddy, Demyan, and fuck one of those strippers. The redhead on stage now is an old favorite of Sloan's. She'll take good care of you both."

Luke groaned. And nodded. That sounded like a good reward. Not that he needed her permission to fuck anyone, but somehow, getting it, made it seem more . . . appealing.

Chicklet moved away from him. He heard a familiar *Whoosh* and braced himself. A sharp biting pain spread over his ass, snapping at the end. He grunted as the pain flared out, and his eyes watered as she hit him again and again. His balls ached with the need to come, but he focused on the heat, absorbing it, allowing it to consume him.

A woman's screams pierced his skull. The kind of screams he got off on drawing from a woman using the exact same tools Chicklet was using on him.

The steady strokes eased off. And his brain snapped back into place and everything that had brought him here came to him at once. He couldn't be a good boyfriend. He was a lousy Dom. Maybe all he was good for was getting beaten on. He was so fucking weak.

The blindfold was torn away, and he blinked as the dim lights of the club blinded him.

"Carter, look at me." Chicklet held his face between her hands. "You stiffened up. What's wrong?"

"What's wrong?" He laughed and clenched his wounded hand

over the bandage until he could feel the moisture of fresh blood. But it didn't hurt. Nothing hurt, and goddamn it, he wanted it to. "I'm weak. You wouldn't have me here like this if I wasn't. I'm disgusted with myself, okay?"

"Damn." Chicklet shook her head. "I've never had a sub drop *during* a scene."

"This isn't a fucking drop! I need more! It felt good. Too good. And it shouldn't."

"It shouldn't? Is that what you're going to tell your next sub? That she shouldn't enjoy what you're doing to her?"

Luke blinked. "My next sub? But I thought you'd decided I was—"

"Take him down, Wayne." Chicklet massaged her temples with her fingers. "Honestly, I can't figure out what you are, Carter. You don't have the confidence to be a good Dom. You enjoy receiving pain, but you can't submit completely. And since you don't know what you want, you obviously can't tell me. I'm not a fucking mind reader. I just hope this helped you a little."

"It helped." His legs felt rubbery as Wayne freed him and helped him stand. But nausea almost floored him. He was such a loser. At least Tyler knew what he wanted. He embraced it. No one could call him pathetic for kneeling to Chicklet because it seemed so natual. And the Doms on the team all welded their power with unwavering confidence. Chicklet was right; Luke didn't have that. Not as a Dom, not even as a fucking man.

His eyes burned and he wrenched away from Wayne.

"Can I go now?"

"Not yet." Chicklet nodded to Wayne, and the man latched an arm around Luke's neck and wrestled him across the room to a sofa. He held Luke until he stopped struggling. Chicklet brought him a bottle of water from the bar. And a piece of chocolate. "We'll let you go when you're stable again."

"Chocolate?" Luke let out a rough laugh and took the water bottle. He gulped it all down and eyed the chocolate. "You gotta treat me like a chick now, too?"

"You think only chicks like chocolate?" Chicklet asked.

"I know they love it when they're on the rag. Are Domme's like that too?"

"Just eat the fucking chocolate, Carter." Chicklet shoved the brown chunk at him and glared at him until he ate it. "This didn't turn out the way I wanted it to. You're too stubborn. If you need a Dom, man or woman, I hope they're up to the challenge. You're a pain in the ass."

"Thank you." Luke grinned, actually feeling a bit better—not that he'd admit it. He was the good kinda sore, like after a hard workout. And that put everything in perspective. Wayne was an honest guy. If he said some Doms did this, then they did. And either way, he'd earned his reward. When Wayne let him go, he stood and did a seductive dance to the stripper music to prove to Chicklet he was good. "You ready to let me off the leash now, *Mistress?*"

"I'd be an idiot to put you on my leash, kid. But yeah, you can go." Her lips twisted as she studied him. "I like how quick you pop back though. But it might not last. Give me a call if you start feeling shitty again."

"Will do." Luke tugged the sweaty clumps of hair over his brow like a cowboy tipping his hat and sauntered away, He slapped Demyan's shoulder when he stepped up to his side. "You into sharing? Apparently the redheaded stripper likes it."

"Yeah, I don't mind sharing." Demyan scratched the golden scruff on his jaw. "Hey, you okay? That was—"

"Hey, you wanna be a Dom here?" Luke laughed at Demyan's hesitant nod. The man had been coming to the club for months but hadn't committed to anything. "Well, you might want to keep this in mind. Apparently a 'good Dom' learns about submission before he learns about control."

"All of a sudden, being vanilla doesn't seem all that bad." Demyan eyed the redhead who stood to the side of the stage, talking to Chicklet, as though wondering if vanilla would be enough for the woman. "I'm cool with fucking her if she wants it, but besides that . . ."

Luke chuckled and made a come hither gesture with his hand when the redhead glanced over at him. "Why make things complicated? She's hot. She's willing. You need more than that?"

Demyan paused, then shook his head. "Nope. That works for

me."

They took the woman, whose name was Roxy, back to their apartment. And enjoyed her all night long. In every way possible.

And Luke almost managed to convince himself *he* didn't need more. After the third time, driving deep into her cunt while Demyan rammed into her ass, he almost believe it.

Almost.

* * * *

The metallic grind of the skate sharpener sliced through the chattering and giggling about the "drool-worthy" Dartmouth Cobras. Mission accomplished. Jami Richter clicked off the power to the machine and glanced over her shoulder at the crowd of perky blonds and busty brunettes sitting on the benches in the locker room, gawking. "Sorry about that." Damn, she almost sounded like she meant it! "Just got one more."

Ignoring the irritated muttering, Jami let her dark blue hair fall over her face and focused on getting just the right edge. She'd need it here, and not just at the bottom of her skate blades. All those girls knew she had no business trying out to be a Dartmouth Cobra Ice Girl—and worse, that she'd been given an unfair advantage by being bumped into the top 100.

"Hey." A petite Asian girl, one of the few girls who hadn't been giving her dirty looks all morning, slipped up to her side and picked up the skate Jami had just finished with. "I like your skates."

Bullshit. Jami tongued her upper lip and stifled the urge to snatch her skate back. Her skates were black vintage with yellow happy face laces. Everyone turned their noses up at them, but they'd been her grandmother's—they made her feel lucky. Like her grandma was still around instead of back in Halifax. And with Grandma around, she was less likely to fall on her ass.

Not that she'd admit that to this cutsy little dollface. But she *would* be polite until the girl gave her a reason not to be. "Thank you."

"You're great on the ice, though. Why aren't you working on the dancing? I haven't seen you with any of the choreographers yet."

Testing the edge on her blade with her thumb, Jami shrugged. "I'll get to it."

"Akira, I wouldn't be getting all friendly with her if I were you." The only redhead in the group set her curling iron on a metal table by the lockers and smiled sweetly. "She's probably the reason you'll be heading back to Hong Kong this summer."

"My parents are from Japan." Akira ducked her head, speaking too low for anyone but Jami to catch a word. "And I was born in Calgary."

"What did you say?" Red stood and smirked at the snickering twits around her. "Speak up, girl! They need to hear you out on the ice when you're cheering the team!"

Their uniforms—black and gold mid-drift halters with the Cobra logo and black short skirts—might make them all look pretty much the same to some, but they couldn't be more different. Obvious because not one of those bitches called Red on her shit.

But I'm not one of them. Jami pressed her thumb down on the blade until it cut her thumb. The sharp bite of pain sent a cool, calming rush through her veins. She jutted her chin toward Red, then winked at Akira. "This is what happens when inbreeding becomes obvious."

Akira covered her mouth with her hands. Her porcelain features lost the little color they had.

Red's face looked like every blood vessel in her cheeks had exploded. "She said that?"

"No. I did." Jami set down her skate. "Want to make something of it?"

Please say yes.

"As if." Red snorted. "Your daddy and his fuck friend run the team. I'm not stupid."

Brow arched, Jami looked her over. "So you just wear the mask to impress people?"

Tugging at her arm, Akira muttered under her breath, "Please don't fight with her. She's the most popular girl in the group, and the judges already love her. Everyone knows why you're here, but no one can argue that you have skills. If you can dance, you're a sure bet."

"What if I can't dance?" Jami winced when she realized she'd said that out loud. Not a good thing to share with the competition. She frowned at her bloody thumb, then stuck it in her mouth. Warm copper slicked her tongue. *Yuck.* A bit too much. She looked around for somewhere to spit and nodded her thanks when Akira handed her a towel. Mouth relatively clean, pressure on her thumb, she studied Akira, trying to figure out her angle. "Why do you care if I make it or not?"

"Honestly?" Akira managed to maneuver her out of the locker room and into the hall before Red came up with a good comeback. Something about DP that was muffled by the closing door. The tiny girl released her once they were well out of hearing. "You're interesting, and so far, you're not mean. I'd rather be out there, at the end of all this, with you than her."

Fair enough. "So you don't resent me for butting in?"

"Not at all. I think you would have made it anyway." Akira's smile faded away as three huge men strode toward them. She half hid behind Jami as they paused, side by side, completely blocking the hallway.

Jami ducked her head as Dominik Mason, the Cobras big black defensemen, reached out to ruffle her hair.

"I didn't know you were back, kid. How are you?"

"Not bad. Just getting settled in." Jami couldn't tell him more. Not until she had a chance to talk to her father. He knew she was back, but that was about it. They'd argued enough about her moving into her own place—her grandmother saved her on that one by pointing out that *she'd* found the apartment and loaned Jami the money for first and last month's rent—and she really wasn't up to getting into why she was back just yet.

Dominik's lips drew into a thin line as he studied her face. "May I ask you something?"

"Sure . . ."

"Are you opposed to me telling your father we saw you here?"

Okay, that was just scary. How the hell had he figured that out? She eyed the other two players, Sloan Callahan, the freakin' team's captain, and Max Perron. These men, and several others on the team, had become like older brothers over the last five years, ever since her father had taken over as general manager. They saw her around the forum and treated her like she was still that awkward fourteen-year-old girl they'd first met. She didn't see Max telling on her. He had this sweet cowboy thing going for him, and she didn't buy that he was a "Dominant," but Dominik and Sloan . . . ?

She let out a sigh and rolled her eyes. "I'd like the chance to tell him myself."

"See that you do," Sloan said.

Max remained behind for a moment as the other men continued down the hall. He put his hand on her shoulder and squeezed lightly. "Stay out of trouble, you hear?" He grinned when she nodded and glanced over at Akira. "Don't look so scared, hon. Not one man on this team will touch you unless you want him to. Any try and you come talk to me. Understand?"

Akira must have done something besides tremble behind her, because Max inclined his head and strode off to join the others.

Jami turned around and laughed when she saw the stricken look on Akira's face. "Haven't you met any of the players before?"

Lips moving soundlessly, Akira shook her head.

"Well, as you can see, they're pretty cool—"

"They're so big." Akira hugged herself and stared down the hall. "Oh God . . . I don't know if I can do this."

At first, Jami had assumed that Akira was just overwhelmed because, like all the other girls, she idolized the players. But Max was right. She was scared.

"What is it, Akira? Is it the tryouts that scare you? Or . . ." Or what? Big hockey players? Not one girl here didn't love the game. Except Jami. But she was good at faking it. "You just said you'd rather be on the ice with me. Don't be ditching me now."

"I'm not." Akira didn't speak again until they were at the doors to the forum's workout room. Then she pressed her eyes shut and put her hand on her throat. "I just don't like men getting too close. I love watching them out there, but . . ."

Aww fuck. The poor kid. Jami gave her a one-armed hug. "You want to talk about it? We can take off for a bit, grab something to eat and chat?"

Akira shook her head. "No. I have to do this. It took forever to talk my parents into letting me try out. I'll get over it. I *told* them I was over it."

"You came all the way from Calgary by yourself?"

"Yes. But it's okay, I'm used to travelling alone." Akira wrinkled her nose. "And dealing with people like Amy Drisdain—the redhead," she added at Jami's blank look. "I've been all over for figure skating competitions, but my parents couldn't support my dream of going professional anymore and I wasn't winning any medals. Thankfully my father *loves* hockey, or he wouldn't have given me this last shot at a career on the ice. I'm hoping to use the prize money to open my own school in a few years. Help other girls succeed where I haven't. I *can't* give up now."

Jami inhaled deep. "Damn girl, you are my new idol. I wish I had half your dedication. I'm doing this because I thought it might be fun. Pretty shallow, right?"

"Is that really the only reason?"

Making a face, Jami pushed open the door to the gym and shrugged. "I've never supported my dad. Never cared about what he was doing. I figured maybe this was a good way to show I've changed."

Straightening to her full height of five foot nothing, Akira faced her. "Well, I don't think that's shallow at all."

Jami laughed and stepped into the gym, deciding that she'd made a new friend and she'd knock some teeth in if anyone else dissed her. Inside, a dozen girls stretched out on the mats, eyes fixed on the tall woman in the center of the room wearing a black leotard.

And the massive, muscular, drop-dead gorgeous stud beside her. Sebastian Ramos, the new Cobra defenseman. She might not pay much attention to hockey anymore, but she'd snatched up the magazine with him on the cover and shamelessly drooled over his photos for weeks. And he was even more mouthwatering in person. Her pulse beat double time. Her palms dampened. His black hair, done up in a low ponytail, flowed over one broad shoulder, thick and glossy as the mane of a prize stallion. His white tank top and black shorts revealed thick, tanned arms and thighs which couldn't possibly be as hard as they looked. The urge to test their solidity with her teeth made it so she couldn't even voice an apology when the dance instructor frowned and waved her and Akira into the room.

"As I was saying, please don't take it personally if you're not chosen for the pictures. The magazine has been very specific as to what they're looking for. And posing does not guarantee anyone a spot in the final round. Make sure you look your best out there and forget about the silly promo." A blush rose high on the woman's cheeks as she looked over at Sebastian. "No offense."

Silly promo? Are you kidding me? Jami took a quick look around the room at her competition. One of them would be chosen to take pictures with *him*. Unless she got herself noticed. Or . . . *Who do I have to kill to get picked?*

"No offense taken, Madame." Sebastian clasped one hand to his wrist behind his back and strolled around the room in a wide circle. Jami and Akira scrambled to the empty mats at the back of the room, barely managing to compose themselves before he reached them. His gaze didn't stay on Akira long as she cowered on her mat in a half-crouched position, but they locked on Jami as she knelt. "*Eso se ve bien, preciosa.*"

Is it horrible that I don't care what that means? As long as he kept looking at her like she was the only woman in the room. Kept talking to her in that voice that languidly melted through her like hot caramel drizzling into her core. If he did all that, he could say—*or do*—whatever he wanted to her.

The workout room had turned into a sauna. The instructor was showing the other girls a routine, but they all faded away as Sebastian moved closer to her. Her lips parted as he reached down and brushed a lightly calloused fingertip along her jaw.

"Very pretty, *mi cielo*." The edge of his mouth tilted up as he lifted a strand of her hair. "You are different than the other girls. I will position you how I like."

The heat from his single touch spread everywhere. Her eyes widened and she barely avoided squeaking. "Position?"

His brow furrowed slightly. "I am sorry, that came out wrong. Your instructor and I have chosen you for the photo shoot. With me." He took his hand from her hair and gave Akira a tender smile. "You have been chosen as well."

Akira looked ready to pass out.

Sebastian took a knee in front of her. "Little one, take a breath for me." The alluring quality in his tone seemed to have been toned down, releasing Jami from its thrall and calming Akira. As the small girl obediently took a breath, Sebastian's smile broadened. "Very good. Now, you will not do this since it makes you uncomfortable."

"But—"

"No. We will find someone else. Stay here and dance, *pequena*." He rose to his feet and held his hand out to Jami. "You will come with me."

Her hand was almost in his before she caught herself. Her body might be willing to go wherever he took her, her brain kicked in with a great big "Slow down." She was here to prove something to her father. And herself. If she didn't learn the moves, getting bumped ahead of all the hopefuls wouldn't count for anything. It was all on her now.

Ugh. Can't you save the dedication for another time?

The naughty little voice in her head wasn't gonna win this time. Besides, she *had* changed. Last year she would have flirted shamelessly and made it clear he just had to say where and when. She'd been wild and reckless. Grandma called it stupid.

"You can have fun without getting yourself in trouble, girly," Grandma had said after Grandpa Fred found her in the old shed behind their house with the boy next door. "Make the boys work for it; you'll both enjoy it more."

No one would consider Sebastian a boy, but hell, if he wanted her, why make it easy for him?

She withdrew her hand slowly.

"I'm sorry, Mr. Ramos, but I haven't learned the routine yet and this is my last chance." Okay, she'd need more than one session to learn the moves and do them without coming across as a clumsy, two-left-footed monkey, but he didn't need to know that. "Can I meet up with you after you're finished with the other girls?"

His brow furrowed slightly, but he nodded. "You may. Fourth floor, office 409."

"All right."

"And, *mi cielo*?"

She shivered as that alluring timbre seeped into her skin, heating her blood enough to evaporate her token resistance. She put some pressure on her cut thumb and looked up at him. "Yes?"

"Don't make me wait too long."

Chapter Two

Sebastian rolled his shoulders and let the photographer's assistant spray him with oil, hardly breathing as the man rubbed it in, putting a bit more pressure than necessary into his stomach muscles, inches above his stirring cock. More than once... Henry, yes, that was his name, had moved in so close his breath stirred the curly, dark hairs above Sebastian's shorts. Sebastian gave the man a heavy lidded once-over. His mouth was nice and soft, his bottom lip plump, wet from licking it again and again. Sebastian didn't tolerate teasing.

"Go lock the door." Sebastian put his hands on his hips as Henry froze and gaped up at him, cheeks crimson under the dusting of black scruff. He gave the man a slow smile. "I apologize. Perhaps I've misread your intentions."

"No, I just..." Henry fisted his oil-slicked hands by his sides. "It would be unprofessional of me to—"

"What is it you want to do to me, Henry?" Sebastian let the *r* roll off his tongue and smiled as the man shuddered. "You're here to prepare me for the last set of photos. You've tested my endurance, hovering around my cock, practically drooling, making it clear you want me to shove it down your throat." He grabbed Henry by the back of the head and pulled him close to whisper against his lips as he ground his dick into the smaller man's stomach. "This photo shoot is important for the team. I won't do the last set with a hard-on. If it pleases you, consider this part of your job."

Henry groaned and panted into his mouth. "I'm not gay."

"I never said you were." Sebastian traced his tongue along Henry's bottom lip. "Now go lock the door."

Seconds later, the lock clicked. Henry tripped forward, dropping hard on his knees and pulling Sebastian's shorts down past his hips. So clumsy. So abrupt. Not what Sebastian was used to. But he had to get himself in hand before *that* girl arrived.

"Do you have a condom?" His jaw clenched as he caught the ice in his tone. He never treated even casual lovers this callously.

Henry simply nodded, breathing hard as he pulled a condom

from his back pocket and quickly covered him. At least the man came prepared.

Hot lips closed around his dick, but all he could see was the girl's big eyes, fresh spring green and blue with tiny flecks of gold like the first light of dawn around her wide pupils. Strange colored hair, like the night sky lit by the glow of LA, more blue than black, but it suited her somehow. She reminded him of a rare piece of art, something risqué and original. He collected rare pieces, always finding a way to possess them, no matter the price. But possessing a beautiful man or woman didn't usually cost him a thing. They could be purchased with the right words, the right touch.

If I had any interest in wasting my time with shallow affairs.

A sloppy suck brought a growl from him, and he put his hand on the back of Henry's head to guide him. If it hadn't been so long since he'd gotten off with anything but his own hand, he wouldn't have bothered with Henry. He had played with submissives at the club for a while because they were discreet. Right under the noses of his own teammates he could take a man and a woman into a private room and fuck them both with none the wiser. But it had become more and more difficult as he grew to like the other players, and hiding brought shame that made it impossible to even get hard. He had stopped wasting his time over two months ago.

The way the sky-haired beauty had knelt and stared up at him made him feel pure, raw lust for the first time in what seemed like forever. He could already see his marks on her lightly tanned flesh, from his belt, his whip, his fingers digging into her hips . . .

Teeth grazed him and he sucked in a deep, calming breath. "Don't move."

Thrusting hard, Sebastian let his mind latch onto taking the girl and grunted as the pressure built up in his balls and exploded through his cock. He threw his head back as he came.

Henry was on his feet before Sebastian's dick stopped throbbing. "Fuck, that was . . . just seeing you getting off because of me . . ."

Too easy. The man hadn't found his own release. Sebastian shook his head and went to the supply table between the black curtained windows, removing the condom and using a wipe to clean himself. He disposed of the wipe and the condom, then pulled up his shorts. "I am not a selfish lover, Henry. Give me a few moments and I will—"

"Fuck man, I would, but..." Henry scratched his jaw. "My boyfriend won't mind me sucking you off, he'll get it. But if I let you fuck me... well, that would bother him."

Boyfriend? Sebastian laughed. *Eros estupido, Ramos.* Had he really bought the "I'm not gay" line? It wasn't the first time a man had used it and likely wouldn't be the last. He got off on seducing straight men, and there was the added bonus of discretion—perhaps word was getting around...? No, the tabloids were still speculating about his preferences, and none of the men on the team had mentioned it. And they would if they thought he was gay. A man on his team in LA had come out, and the players never treated him the same. No one spoke of it. Or really spoke to him. The man had looked relieved when he was traded. Sebastian hadn't felt the same when the Kings had made no effort to keep him. Apparently suspicions were enough. He knew very well he wasn't being traded because he didn't help improve the team. His agent told him not to worry about it, but how could he not? He'd proved himself, damn it. But his personal choices were enough to ruin him.

"Hey, could I have something of yours as... you know, a souvenir?" Henry dropped his gaze when Sebastian's eyes narrowed. "Just for me. I won't tell no one."

Letting out a sound of disgust, Sebastian went to his abandoned pile of clothes, a white tank top and dress shirt, and tossed the sweat-stained tank top to the man. "I suggest you don't."

His teammates would likely be surprised to know that puck bunnies weren't exclusively female. Bile rose in his throat as he imagined Henry and his boyfriend discussing how he'd done someone on his "list." Using his tank top in their fantasies. Any guilt he'd had over his rough usage of Henry disappeared. Nothing he'd done would make Henry feel cheap.

A soft rap on the door spilled hope over his bitterness. Maybe it was her. And now that he wasn't trapped in a haze of lust, he would be able to handle her with the delicacy she obviously needed. Loose women never made him wait. Perhaps, for once, he had found a woman worth more than a brief interlude on a day that didn't have a game to stir his blood.

Anyone worth more would be a nice change.

"I would like a moment to acquaint myself with the girl before we start, if you do not mind." Sebastian considered his rumpled dress shirt, wondering if he should put it back on so as not to intimidate the girl. His size seemed to scare away the sweet ones.

Henry nodded distractedly as he pulled his cell from the pocket of his slacks. "I'll tell Chantelle to give you two a bit before she comes in."

Sebastian picked up his shirt as Henry opened the door. His "*cielo*" stepped into the office, her hands clasped over her tiny black skirt, her head bowed. Shy, perhaps?

"I did it!" Henry shouted as he slipped out and slammed the door behind him.

The muscles in his jaw ached as he ground his teeth. He moved to pull on his shirt, then paused as the girl whispered, "Don't bother."

He dropped his shirt and turned slowly. "*Mi cielo—*"

"Jami."

"Jami." A soft smile curved his lips. "Come. Sit with me." He drew two chairs away from the table and turned them facing one another. Held his hand out for her to sit.

She moved toward him, her gaze brushing over his bare chest, darting down, then snapping back up. "You're all shiny."

"Yes." He chuckled when a charming, pink glow spread over her cheeks. The girl was reacting to him physically—probably in a way she didn't fully understand. He had to be very, very careful not to let it frighten her. "For the cameras. They will put some on you as well."

"Why?"

He waited until she settled down in one chair, crossing her legs and smoothing her skirt over her thighs. Her hands flattened over the hem of her skirt as though she didn't trust it to stay in place. He reached out and ran his fingertips lightly over the back of her hand.

"To give you a wet look."

Her eyes widened and her blush deepened. "Did they do that to the other girls?"

"They did. But you have nothing to worry about. The

photographer is a woman, and she will slick the oil over your flesh herself. I have told her how I want you positioned with me. I will hardly touch you at all."

The pulse along the curve of her throat quickened. "Where will you touch me?"

Standing, he moved behind her, slowly, very slowly, and curved his hand around the nape of her neck. "Only here."

She drew in a rough inhale. "And how will I be positioned?"

Smiling, he leaned down to whisper in her ear. "On your knees."

* * * *

"On your knees." Jami shuddered. Damn, what the hell was she supposed to do with that? Or with the fact that she could already see herself, kneeling before Sebastian, waiting for . . .

Waiting for what? Since when did she wait for what she wanted? Did she really want to grovel to the man just to get a taste of him? No freakin' way. She wouldn't rush anything, but she wasn't a damn shrinking violet. At very least she had to show Sebastian that he didn't have to treat her like an innocent virgin. Or a sub.

God, please not that. She wasn't supposed to know much about what her dad did at his club, but she knew enough. People talked. And the whole BDSM thing kinda freaked her out.

Twisting from his light hold on her neck, she rose, and knelt up on the chair. Her lips curled into a provocative smile. "I never get on my knees before a nice steak diner, big boy."

His brow lifted slightly. Then he smiled. "Steak sounds like an excellent idea. I will take you out to dinner after the photo shoot."

She pursed her lips. "Are you asking me out?"

"I don't believe I worded it as a question."

A sharp laugh escaped her and she shifted position to sit sideways on the chair. "That's just rude."

"Is it?" He folded his massive arms over his bare chest. "You made a proposition. I accepted. I do not see how that's rude."

Licking her lips, she let her gaze drift over his bulging pecs. His attitude made her feel reckless, and she lifted her hand to touch his slick, lightly tanned flesh. "You think that was a proposition? I'll show you—"

He caught her wrist. "No."

Her eyes widened. "What?"

"There is no hurry, *mi cielo*. If you do not want to be on your knees for the photo shoot, we can try something else." He moved away from her as the door inched opened with a hesitate tap. "We are ready, Chantelle."

Jami stood and straightened her skirt. Chewing on her bottom lip as the tall, pinched-faced woman clucked her tongue at Sebastian and applied more oil to his flesh, she tried to figure out what to do with the man. She knew what she *wanted* to do with him; hell, her panties were already uncomfortably damp. And playing hard to get was not working for her. Apparently, it wasn't even necessary. *He'd* already decided to set the pace.

And you're going to let him? Yeah, right. She hid a smirk behind her hand and quickly schooled her features as Chantelle approached.

"Mr. Ramos tells me you're not comfortable with the initial setup. I want this to look as natural and . . . —" Chantelle's thin lips pressed together "—sexy, as possible. So here's my suggestion. Mr. Ramos will pose by the window, and you will take whatever stance works for you. We already have one set with the redhead that is rather sensual, but it's missing something. I think you have just what I'm looking for."

The woman seemed so stiff, like a teacher she'd had in high school who went on and on about how girls were "proper" and "refined" a century ago, moaning about how girls today were crass and had no values. But unlike the teacher, Chantelle didn't look at her like she was some punk. She looked at her with an artist's eye, making Jami feel like she wasn't a freak. Like she was . . . well, at least interesting.

Sebastian looked at her like that too. But his steady regard, even now, was somehow both carnal and reserved. Damned confusing.

Jami nodded at Chantelle, thinking about the pictures with the redhead—probably Amy. "So just do what feels natural?"

Chantelle nodded and pointed at Sebastian, then at one of the large windows near the back of the room. "Over there, hands on your hips. We'll try a few shots, and I'll tell you if I want you to change your posture. For now, I'd like to see you as almost aloof. If you can manage it."

Giving the photographer a curt nod, Sebastian took his place. Hands on his hips, strong, sharply angled jaw held high, like a Spanish conquistador standing over his vast holdings. He followed instructions well for such a dominant man. Jami smothered a giggle with her hand and caught a wink from Chantelle.

"Go ahead," the woman said.

A few quick steps brought her right in front of him. His size—fuck, he was so much bigger than her!—made her pause for a second before she splayed her hand over his chest, sliding her palm over his slick flesh, exploring the hard slopes of muscles as she'd wanted to since she'd first laid eye on him months ago in that magazine.

His eyes narrowed slightly, but he didn't move.

She took a deep breath and eased her body against his, one knee bent over his thighs, her arm around his waist, her hand gliding down until it rested right over his simple, silver belt buckle. As she gazed up at him, her lips parted at the warning in his eyes. She'd gone too far.

"Try not to look so mean, Mr. Ramos. You have an adoring woman clinging to you, doing exactly what every woman who sees this picture would *love* to do. There we go." Chantelle picked up her camera as Sebastian's expression softened. Almost tender, except for his eyes which darkened with lust. A flash. Then another. "Perfect! Now, Jami, press against him so he can feel every inch of you. You've taken a seductive pose. Own it."

Jami nodded and wet her bottom lip with her tongue. She let her fingers slip just under the waist of his jeans, curved her other hand over his side. Her lips hovered close to his chest as she continued to stare up at him.

His stomach muscles tensed and his jaw ticked.

Chantelle didn't see it. More flashing and murmured approval. From a distance, then up so close purple dots spotted Jami's vision.

"All right, we're done!" Chantelle sounded exhausted, and relieved. "I must say, I'm happy there's so much chemistry between you two. The redhead sitting on his lap was a disaster. It was obvious he wanted to dump her on the floor—"

Laughing, Jami dropped her hands to her sides and gave Sebastian some space. "Did you?"

"I may have considered it." Sebastian went to the sole table in the room and grabbed the plain, white dress shirt he'd abandoned earlier. He pulled it on and turned to Chantelle. "So you are finished with us?"

"Yes." Chantelle put her camera in its case and waved them on. "Enjoy your night."

Jami left the room ahead of Sebastian, not sure why she suddenly felt nervous. She spun around, walking backward, watching him, trying to figure out whether or not her teasing had pissed him off. But he was unreadable. They rode down on the elevator in silence. She made it to her car, ready to give up on him, when he came up behind her.

He held the door to her classic, pale blue Beatle shut and spoke softly. "Where do you think you're going?"

She couldn't help but squeak a little as she turned to face him. "Home?"

"Oh no, pet. You suggested dinner." His smooth, alluring tone dropped to a growl. "I'm hungry. Aren't you?"

Suddenly, she was starving. But they weren't talking about food, were they? She certainly hoped not anyway. "Yes, I am."

"Good. Then come with me." He took her hand, glancing back when she hesitated. "You haven't decided to play shy with me now, have you?"

"I never play at anything." She jerked free, hating the way she half wanted to follow him around like a little puppy and beg for whatever scraps of attention he felt like giving her. Even her frown felt forced over the simpering smile trying to take its place. This wasn't like her. "I'm pretty upfront. You good with that?"

He kept his hand out, palm up, and regarded her calmly as though to say "are you done yet?" But out loud he said, "Yes, Jami. I am 'good with that.' What confuses me is why you are so reluctant to let me hold your hand when you were so eager to touch me before."

"Because you weren't being grabby then." She took his hand and stepped up to his side. "You may take me to dinner now."

His eyes twinkled with amusement. "May I?"

She gave him a regal nod. "Yes you may."

He chuckled and led her to his car at the other end of the parking garage. She stopped. Released his hand. And approached it with a sense of reverent awe.

The Aston Martin One-77. A silver masterpiece in a modern tear-shaped design, constructed to fly across the road with little resistance from the wind. Very few modern cars were this beautiful. This magnificent.

"This is impossible." She shook her head and scowled at him. "Do you know how much this car is worth?"

One brow arched, he inclined his head. "As a matter of fact, I do."

"The insurance alone must be insane!"

"Perhaps, to some." He stepped up to her side and watched her as she went back to drooling over his car. "But I've always wanted a Porsche."

Her jaw almost hit the pavement. "Are you retarded? This is an *Aston Martin*! You dump over a million dollars into a car and you don't even know what it is?"

"Of course I know what it is, *mi cielo*." He tapped under her chin and smiled when her jaw snapped shut. "I was curious to see if you were just admiring the pretty car. I'm pleased that you know enough to appreciate it."

Appreciate it? Fuck, I want to have its babies! She held her breath and inched closer to it. "You're crazy, but you've got damn good taste."

"Yes, I do." He put his hand on the small of her back and propelled her toward the passenger side. His breath flowing over the nape of her neck as he leaned around her to unlock the door made all the tiny hairs rise. "In cars and women."

"Then you should have hooked up with the redhead."

"I could have. Just as I could have bought a Porsche, but that wasn't what I wanted, *mi cielo*. I wanted a car with soul. I want a woman with spirit." He pressed a soft kiss on the back of her neck. "I want you."

****

A jazz band played on the huge stage in the center of the classy restaurant as Sebastian led Jami to his regular table, close to the windows overlooking the harbor. Both the music and the view added a little something special to dinning out, but he usually indulged in the alluring atmosphere, and fine cuisine, alone. There were other nice restaurants to bring the women who expected five star treatment because he was rich. He'd never wanted to ruin the experience for himself by bringing them here. But for some reason, he wasn't concerned about that happening with this woman.

His only concern was that she was too young to truly appreciate it. A girl who dyed her hair blue most likely listened to some kind of grunge music and didn't often—if ever—eat in places where knowing the right fork to use for shrimp or salad was required. This would have been a better choice for a later date, after she'd had a chance to dress up and prepare herself for the high class patrons who might judge her.

But he hadn't thought of that before bringing her. To him, she looked perfect. Fresh and so full of life. Nothing seemed to intimidate her, and he hoped this would be no different. He couldn't care less if she ate with her fingers and talked with her mouth full. This place was part of his lifestyle, and he wanted to see her in it. Too soon for such crazy thoughts, but she intrigued him, drew him in, and it would be better to lay it all out now than to wait until she burrowed herself deep inside him and he began changing things about himself he had no desire to change just to hold on to her.

If they weren't a good match, best to find out before it was too late. Perhaps he was setting her up for failure to protect himself.

He certainly hoped not.

After settling herself gracefully into the chair he pulled out for her, Jami shook out the pale pink napkin she took from beside her plate and laid in over her lap. "This is not what I expected when we talked about having steak."

Sebastian shrugged and made himself comfortable in the seat across from her. "I've never found another place that serves steak just the way I like it. You were very specific in what you wanted to eat. Au Port is the best."

"We'll see about that." She rested her forearms on the table and leaned forward. "My father is an excellent cook and he taught me well. I'm willing to bet I could fix you up a nice, juicy T-bone just as good, if not better, than they can."

He sat back and rubbed his jaw. "You surprise me, Jami. You do not seem like the type of woman who would cook for a man, but you would cook for me?"

"Mr. Ramos, I've made it pretty obvious that there are—" she paused and her tongue swept slowly over her bottom lip as she looked him over "—a lot of things—" the edge of her mouth crept up as her foot—shoeless for some reason—found its way between his thighs "—I'd like to do to you, for you, whatever." She studied his face as she massaged his hardening cock with her toes. A grin flashed across her face as he ground his teeth. She sat up straight and moved her foot. "But cooking for you? We'll have to work up to that."

"Jami." He reached across the table and took both her hands in his. His tone dropped to the dangerous low that made most subs tremble. "You will pay for every time you tease me. I suggest you consider that before you do it again."

"What, are you going to spank me?" She scoffed, even though she looked a bit nervous. "You're missing a little thing called consent. I'm not your sub. This is our first date. Save the threats."

"I'm not your sub." Apparently, she thought she knew a little about the lifestyle. Kinky sex had become quite mainstream. One day soon he might teach her the difference.

Lifting her hands up to his lips, he kissed the back of each one, then smiled at her. "I believe in the punishment fitting the crime." He released her hands and straightened as the waiter came to take their order. "We will discuss this later. I take it you'd like to order for yourself?"

"Yes, thank you." Her demeanor changed completely as she spoke pleasantly to the waiter. "A T-bone steak, medium rare, with a salad, French dressing on the side. Bacon bits and sour cream on the potato, please. No chives. And sparkling water if you have."

"Yes, ma'am." The young waiter seemed impressed by Jami's manners, and Sebastian couldn't blame him. At first glance, Jami came off as rebellious, and he had noticed she could be

31

objectionable, but not in a way that demanded attention. She wasn't "sticking it to the man" with her appearance or her attitude. She was just being herself.

And herself could be both bold and timid, from what he'd seen already. No. Not timid. Submissive. He hadn't misread that, no matter how much she tried to hide it. But she caught her reactions to his natural dominance and masked it as quickly as she could. Many submissives struggled with their natures, and she wouldn't be the first one he'd eased into accepting it. However, he couldn't recall ever looking forward to the prospect quite so much.

He waited until they were served, until Jami took her first bite of steak, chewing into it with a little sigh of bliss, before he spoke. "You are aware that being a submissive doesn't make you weak?"

She finished chewing, swallowed, and nodded slowly. "Yeah, sure, I get that. But exploring that BDSM stuff doesn't interest me."

"I see." He filled his mouth with a chunk of juicy meat and leaned his forearms on the table as he studied her. "Are you under the impression that exploring would involve more pain than you can handle?"

Her fork dipped into her potato, came up almost empty, and jabbed her bottom lip. She blushed. "No. That's not it."

Very interesting. The pain didn't bother her—in fact, if her reactions were anything to go on, she would enjoy that part of play very much. She was already somewhat aware of how pain could be pleasurable then.

"Then what bothers you? Have you found the missionary position so thrilling you're unwilling to try anything else?"

"Has anyone ever told you you're really blunt?" She stabbed her potato, scooping out the white innards as though gutting it, glaring as though she'd like to gut *him*. "I pegged you for a Dom, okay, but I was kinda hoping you weren't a one-trick wonder."

He froze with his fork halfway to his mouth. "A what?"

She leaned forward and spoke low. "Can you get hard without tying a woman down? Without a flogger in your hand? I've always wondered that about 'Doms.'"

Chuckling as she shoveled some potatoes into her mouth, he reclined and rested one elbow behind him on the back of his chair.

"*Mi cielo*, just watching you eat gets me hard."

"Really?" She sliced a piece of meat, brought it to her mouth, then tore into it with her teeth. Smirking at his wince, she set her fork down and spoke around the meat. "How about now?"

"That depends." He had to be quick to stay a step ahead of her. Thankfully, he hadn't touched his wine. And didn't plan to. He needed his wits about him. "How would you feel if I used my teeth on you? Not quite so viciously, but with enough pressure to hurt you, just a little."

Her fork clattered on her plate. Her lips moved soundlessly as she squirmed in her seat. "You're a bad, bad man, Mr. Ramos. My daddy warned me about men like you."

"Did he?" Sebastian calmly cut another piece of steak, then brought it to his lips. "Why do I get the impression you go after the very kind of man your father warned you away from? That if he told you to stay away from me, you'd find me irresistible?"

She shook her head and let out a sharp laugh. "Damn it, I already find you irresistible."

"And you consider me blunt? Where is your teasing now, Jami?"

"You told me I would pay for teasing you."

"I did. But I'm surprised you took heed to my warning, since you are not a sub and couldn't care less about punishments."

"I'm also not stupid. You don't turn it off, do you? Or maybe you can't. If you didn't think I was a sub, you wouldn't even be interested in me." She finished the last bite of her steak and sighed. "Listen, I don't mind things getting a little kinky. This isn't your average date. We both know exactly how this is going to end."

He frowned, set down his fork, and placed his hands beside his plate. "Do we?"

"Yes. So, the question is, your place, or mine? Let's skip dessert, okay? One hot night and we can both move on. You can find the sweet sub you're looking for, and I can . . ."

The lost look on her face tugged at his heart. He took her hands in his, searching her face for a clue that would tell him how to proceed as he laced his fingers through hers. But he found nothing. So he proceeded, blindly. Carefully. "You can what, Jami? Please, don't think up another witty remark to throw me off. Why are you so determined to let me use you for one night and walk away?"

She tugged at her hands, but not hard, not like she really wanted to be free of him. "I didn't say that. I'm just clear on what you want."

"You have no idea what I want. Nor what you want, I think." He took in a slow, measured breath as she dropped her gaze to the table. "Shall we finish our meal and move to another topic? Something beyond 'the lifestyle.'"

Nodding jerkily, she glanced up at him. "What do you want to talk about?"

"Do you like the music?"

She surprised him with a smile. "Oh, I love it. The saxophone most of all. I played a bit in high school, but I wasn't any good. The woman is a bit stiff, like she's tired of playing the same stuff. When we first came in, and I heard the way she was playing, I almost wanted to make a request to see if it would loosen her up."

"What would you have requested?"

She didn't hesitate. "'Baker Street' by Gerry Rafferty."

"So why don't you? Go ask if they know it while I order us some dessert."

"But I said—"

"Jami." He dropped his tone, leveling his gaze with hers, firm enough to get through to her, but not enough to cause her to balk. "The night will not end as you expect it to. Let's enjoy it while it lasts."

Thrusting up from her chair, her chin jutted up, she gave him a curt nod, then strode to the stage. Her hands were fisted at her sides as she spoke to the drummer who'd stepped down for a drink. He moved in close to her, as though he couldn't hear her, but with the band on a break that obviously wasn't the case. Sebastian had to force himself to stay where he was and not join them to lay his claim on her. It was too soon. Much too soon.

His presence obviously wasn't necessary. Jami slid past the drummer when the female band member took interest in the conversation and spoke to the woman. She'd likely been very direct because the woman hugged her saxophone and drew up as though insulted. But by the time Jami was done, she looked determined. The song began as Jami returned to the table. And the woman was playing her heart out.

He'd never noticed how mundane the music had become until Jami had pointed it out. And the change was startling. Listening to the soulful rendition, it almost seemed a shame that the talented lady had settled for playing here rather than pursuing something bigger. He wondered if Jami's words would push her to do just that.

"Oh, I love this song." Jami speared the last of her potatoes, peel and all, from her plate before the waiter could take it away. After finishing the mouthful, she rested an elbow on the table and cupped her cheek in her palm. "I wish I had talent like that. I wish I could do . . . something worthwhile."

"You're auditioning to become an Ice Girl. Surely you believe your skills on the ice, or your dancing, is worthwhile?"

She shrugged. "I can skate. I've done figure skating and played hockey a bit. I'm good on the ice. But I can't dance. Not when someone's telling me how to move." She bit her bottom lip. "And I don't love it. Not like some of the girls do."

"Then what do you love?" He needed to know, needed her to tell him all her vitality, all her passion, wasn't going to waste. "What drives you?"

Her shoulders slumped. "Nothing. I have no idea what I want to do. I want to be an Ice Girl to show my dad I care about the game, even though I hate it."

She hated the game? Nothing she'd said so far shocked him, but this did. "Why do you hate it?"

"It's like . . . I don't know, maybe like a sibling that got all the attention? All my life, that's all my dad talked about. And I tried to get into it, but all I saw was my mom trying to get away because she couldn't compete—" She covered her face with her hands. "No, that's not true. My mother didn't want to settle down, with a kid or a husband. She wanted to travel and experience life without anything holding her back. Sometimes I'm afraid I'm just like her—"

Lips pressed together she glared at him as though she'd said too much and it was all his fault.

He chose not to react to the accusation in her eyes. To instead draw her out from a different angle. "Do you enjoy travelling?"

She made a face. "I hate travelling."

"Really?" He shook his head, for the first time certain he was starting to understand her. "With your reaction to the music, I figured you might have a cultural leaning, that perhaps I would take you to a museum for our next date—"

"You're assuming we'll *have* a next date?"

"—or a musical. *Wicked* will be playing in Halifax in a few weeks." Sebastian paused as the waiter laid out their deserts, two large pieces of chocolate cheesecake with two tall glasses of frozen hot chocolate topped with whipped cream and tiny marshmallows. He thanked the waiter and grinned as Jami stared at the plate. "I hope you like chocolate."

Without answering, she brought a forkful of cake to her mouth, rolling her eyes with pleasure even as it crossed her lips. Licking the fork clean, she let out a little sigh. "Oh, you evil man. I can't resist chocolate. One look from you and I knew I was a goner, but now you're feeding me chocolate and offering to bring me to see *Wicked*—my favorite musical after *Cats* by the way. Damn, I'm done for. Take me any which way you want me."

Dios mio! His blood abandoned his brain as his dick swelled with it. Her offer nearly undid him. The way she devoured the dessert, with the tip of her pink tongue sweeping over her lips, the way she sucked at the straw—he wanted to ask for the check and take her home. Ravish her all night—no, longer. Once he got her in his bed, he'd never let her leave.

But he wouldn't take her to his bed tonight. She would write him off as a one-night stand if he didn't force them both to slow things down. He turned his focus to his plate, keeping his tone light as she questioned him about his career, showing a lot of interest for a girl who "hated hockey." She even remarked on his play during recent games, praising him on a goal and tearing apart a few sloppy plays. Her knowledge went beyond that of a fan.

"Does your father play hockey professionally?" he asked abruptly, her knowledge of the Dartmouth Cobras in particular beginning to concern him. What if her father was one of his teammates? Few were old enough to have a daughter her age, but it was possible.

"Umm, no. He's never played professionally."

Her response set off alarms in his head. He'd never played professionally, but he must be involved in some way if she didn't want to divulge anything else. There had been several scandals with the Dartmouth Cobras over the past year—the kind of drama he avoided to the best of his ability. He participated in charity work, like the team visit to the children's hospital Christmas day and promotions, without question, but avoided gossip, lest he somehow be drawn into the center of it.

He should ask her straight out who her father was, but he feared her response would end things between them before they'd even begun, and he wasn't ready for that. Not yet.

Across the table, she fidgeted, avoided looking at him, giving him even more cause to question her. Inhaling deeply, he forced a smile. "Are you finished?"

"Yes. Unfortunately." She sighed, gazed longingly at her half-eaten piece of cake and slouched back, rubbing her stomach. "That was sinfully good. I'll have to come back here one day."

"I'll have to" not *"We'll have to."* He ground his teeth as the waiter came over with the check, handing over his credit card and signing after adding a generous tip to the total. Jami sweetly asked if the rest of her cake could be packed to go, and they waited as the waiter took her plate, returning moments later with a small pastry box tied with a pale pink ribbon.

Jami winked at the waiter. "I know what I'm having for breakfast."

The waiter looked enchanted with her and lingered until Sebastian caught his eye. Then he cleared his throat and wished them a "pleasant evening."

Sebastian stood and held out his hand. "I must take you out of here."

Laying her hand in his, she nodded, her cheeks flushed and her eyes glazed with desire. "Please do."

They made it to his car before she pulled away and hugged herself. As he reached for her, she held up her hand and shook her head.

"I have to tell you, Sebastian. It's not right if you don't know.

You'll regret it later." She took a deep breath. "My father—"

"No." He silenced her with a kiss, pressing her up against the door of his car, savoring her lips, sweet chocolate and wine, tender and soft. He spoke with his lips a breath from hers. "Don't tell me. I don't want to know. I don't care who he is."

She clung to his shirt, rising up on her tiptoes to kiss him before whispering. "You will."

* * * *

The wind picked up as they drove, slashing against the car as the rain burst from the black clouds above. What a crappy ending to an amazing night. Never in her life had a date turned out so well. Her main goal, which had been to get this big, hot guy in the sack, had wavered as the night progressed. He listened to her, showed interest in everything she said. He didn't go on and on about hockey like she'd thought he would. He didn't treat her like a kid. They shared similar interests—

All right already. He rocks. He's still not going to stick around when you tell him your dad is the Cobras' GM. Which she should do—would do . . . soon. Holding out wasn't even an option anymore.

He'll hate you if you let him fuck you, then he finds out . . .

Let him hate her. It wasn't as if this could last anyway.

"What has you thinking so hard, *mi cielo*?" He caught her eye with a sideways glance and put one hand on her bare knee. "You are very quiet."

"Sorry, I'm just deciding—" She pressed her eyes shut as his hand drifted up her thigh. "What are you doing?"

"I warned you that you would pay for teasing me." His fingers stroked, feather-light, down to her knee and back up again, just under the hem of her skirt. "You were saying?"

Sweet liquid heat spilled between her thighs. She crossed her legs and struggled to get her brain working again. "Yes. I was saying . . ." A soft touch just under her skirt made her insides clench and she moaned. "Oh, please stop! I can't think with you doing that."

He chuckled, eyes on the road, and left his hand half under her skirt. "I apologize. Go ahead."

Her legs unfolded. Parted slightly. She held her breath and fisted her hands by her sides, waiting for his hand to slip lower.

His hand didn't move, but his thumb stroked idly along her inner thigh. Little zings of pleasure caused her clit to swell out past her damp folds. Pressure from his fingers caused her insides to throb. She panted, wondering if she could actually come from just his hand on her leg.

The car stopped. His hand went away and a low, pleading sound escaped her. She stared at him.

He nodded toward the window. "You may need your car tomorrow."

My car? She shook her head and frowned at the darkness. Finally realized they were in the parking garage at the forum. Her tongue felt thick in her mouth, but she somehow managed to speak. "Are we going to your place?"

"No, *mi cielo*. You are going home."

"Home . . . with you?"

"No."

"But—"

He pressed his fingers over her lips. "Will you have coffee with me in a day or so? When I return from the game in Pittsburg?"

She nodded. Then took hold of his wrist and pulled his hand down so she could speak. "But what about tonight?"

Gently twisting his wrist from her grasp, he leaned forward and cupped her cheek. "The night is over, but there will be many more."

"But there can't be. It can't be like that with us, Sebastian." She had to make him understand. Somehow, he'd managed to go this long without hearing about her, but now that she was back, someone was bound to mention her. "Seriously, I wish it could, which is weird because I went into this with one thing in mind, but—"

His lips covered hers and his fingers raked into her hair, holding her in place as he claimed her mouth, giving her a taste of his strength with the bruising pressure. She melted into him, digging her fingers into his forearms as his tongue thrust into her mouth. He stole her strength, her willpower, with his kiss, letting out a warning growl when she scrambled for the slightest bit of control. Once she surrendered to him, he smiled against her lips and drew away.

"You cannot rush me, *mi cielo*, but your patience will be rewarded." He ran his thumb over her swollen bottom lip. "This is nothing compared to what I will do to you when you're ready for me."

"I'm ready for you now!"

"Are you? Are you ready for me to restrain you and take your body any way I please? Do you trust me that much after knowing me for less than a day?"

Yes! The crazy, reckless part of her screamed. But the rational part of her brain, the one she'd spent the last eight months strengthening so she wouldn't fall into the dangerous habits that had put her in the hospital after an overdose, took over. Letting him tie her up would be safer than sniffing coke, but it would be stupid to give him that kind of trust this soon.

Her eyes burned as she shook her head and reached for the door. This fucking sucked. Why did he have to be a Dom? If he wasn't, she would at least have tonight. But he couldn't enjoy himself without taking control, and she wasn't ready to give it. She might never be ready.

And even if she was, even if she wanted to try, who she was would ruin any chance they had.

What if you're wrong?

There was only one way to find out. She stepped onto the pavement, slammed the door, and strode around to the driver's side. Leaning into the open window, she rested her forearms on the ledge and faced him.

"I might eventually be ready, but I have to tell you one thing first."

He shook his head. "Jami—"

"My name, Sebastian. Just my name."

He inclined his head.

"Jami Richter." She straightened and folded her arms over her chest. "Now you know. I don't expect you to call me. Or talk to me ever again."

Spinning around, she moved toward her car, a big fat lump of regret almost choking her. She fumbled with her keys, waiting for the sound of Sebastian driving away.

Instead she heard his car door open. And close. Heard his heavy footsteps coming up behind her. He took her keys and unlocked her door for her.

"Thank you," she whispered as she latched onto the door handle.

He put his hand over hers. Used the other to tip her chin up. Then he smiled. "I cannot call you if you don't give me your number, *mi cielo*."

She bit back a sob, feeling pathetic and weak for getting so worked up. Slumped against him, she let out a strangled laugh. "This isn't a very smart career move, Mr. Ramos."

"The next time you call me 'Mr. Ramos,' I will spank you, *gatita*."

"*Gatita?*"

"Kitten."

"Ah." She sighed again. "Almost as bad as 'pet'. Whatever. Give me your number too. If you don't call me after all this, I reserve the right to call *you* and give you shit."

He laughed and rubbed her back. "I'll keep that in mind."

They exchanged numbers and he held her for a bit longer as she tried to process everything. As if he knew she just wasn't ready to accept it. He didn't seem surprised when she grabbed hold of his shirt and gave him a hard look. "You really don't care?"

The edge of his lip crept up. "I really don't."

And damn it, she believed him.

Chapter Three

Dean pulled out a few files he wanted to work on while on the road and smiled over at Silver as she slipped into his office. Her slightly rounded face usually glowed with health since she was taking such good care of herself for the baby, eating plenty even though she grumbled over almost every bite, but for some reason, her skin had an almost green cast today. Since she wasn't going on the trip with him, he'd suggested she sleep in, but she'd insisted one of them needed to be at the office. Thankfully, Oriana would be here as well and could be trusted to keep Silver from stressing out too much over the details that needed to be handled as the Cobras worked to cinch the sixth spot in the playoffs. And she would keep their bastard half-brother from upsetting her little sister.

Or she would try anyway. Ford Kingsley—now Ford Delgado since he'd officially changed his name to the delight of his biological father—spent every day at the forum making a pest of himself. If Oriana didn't spend an equal amount of time here trying to keep him in line, Silver would insist on doing it herself. But today, Oriana was enjoying the morning with her men before they headed out. Which meant Ford had probably used the opportunity to mess with one of Silver's many projects. He usually only managed to irritate her, but maybe this time he'd done some real damage. Dean couldn't think of anything else that would make Silver look this sick.

Unless she was actually sick?

"Sit down, pet." He gave her a hard look when she shook her head. "Landon will be here in a moment, and if he sees you looking like this, I might as well tell Tim to leave him here and put in the backup goalie."

She dropped into the chair he held out for her and covered her face with her hands. "You're going to be so mad at me."

This can't be good. Moving forward, he lowered to one knee to put them at eye level. "Try to relax. You scared both yourself and Landon the last time you fainted."

She mumbled between her hands. "The doctor says that's

normal when I stand up too fast."

"Yes, but he also said he would agree with Landon's suggestion of keeping you in the hospital for observation if you faint again." Overkill perhaps, but the doctor understood the situation and tended to indulge Landon. Which, as sympathetic as she was, drove Silver crazy. As usual, Dean had to be the calm, reasonable one. "Your blood sugar has been very low."

"Not since you've been controlling *everything* I eat!"

"True, but let's not take any chances. Tell me what you've done. I promise, I won't even raise my voice."

She snorted. "You *never* raise your voice. You don't have to."

He grinned and drew her hands away from her face to kiss her knuckles. "Well then, what are you afraid I'll do? Really, Silver, you haven't been at the office long enough to cause any trouble. Did you confront Ford again? One would figure, after two hundred lines of 'I will avoid the asshole who shares my DNA,' you would know better."

Her shoulders hunched. She didn't even accuse him of giving her carpal tunnel syndrome as she had the last few times he'd threatened to use the same punishment. "This has nothing to do with Ford. It's about Jami."

Releasing her hands, he straightened and took two quick steps away from her. Clenched his jaw. Counted to ten in his head. Did his best to keep his promise not to raise his voice. His tone came out level, but rough. "Why would I be angry about anything involving Jami? You swore to me you would never try to handle anything concerning my daughter without consulting me first."

Silver's whispered something.

He took a deep breath. Let it out very slowly. "Excuse me? I didn't catch that."

"She asked me not to say anything until she has a chance to talk to you herself."

Hooking his fingers behind his neck, he paced to the window, staring out as he spoke. "She's been back less than a week. Please tell me she's not doing drugs again, Silver. If you kept that from me—"

"No! Oh no, Dean, it's nothing like that!" The chair scraped the floor as Silver stood, and he watched her cautious approach through the reflection in the window. "It's nothing bad, not really. I think she wanted to surprise you, but with the pictures I thought—"

He spun around and glared at her. "Pictures? What pictures?"

She winced and glanced at his desk. "Well . . ."

He didn't wait for her to finish. Striding up to his desk, he looked over the folders his assistant, Bolleau, had left for him. He found one folder with the label "Dartmouth Cobras Ice Girls," the only one with pictures inside it. He recalled Silver telling him Sebastian Ramos, one of the team's leading defensemen, acquired at the beginning of the season, had agreed to photo shoots with a few of the girls for a magazine. The Ice Girl tryout had been going on for months. How the hell could this have anything to do with Jami?

Spreading the photos out on his desk, he studied them carefully, avoiding the last few because he couldn't begin to face what he thought he'd seen. The first photos showed Ramos with a redhead perched on his lap. The next had him with blond twins, one under each arm. All appealing, all good for the team because, much as he hated to admit it, Silver's ideas of ramping up the team's appeal to the younger crowd had increased ticket sales and had networks showing more games in response to higher ratings.

He swallowed and pushed the other photos aside. Focused on the set with his little girl, dressed in a flimsy matching skirt and . . . fuck, that shirt barely covered her chest! His jaw ticked as he observed the way she clung to Ramos. The way she stared up at him.

And the hungry way the son of a bitch stared back at his baby.

He finally managed words. "Why is my daughter wearing an Ice Girl uniform?"

Silver came up beside him and touched his forearm. "She wanted to try out."

"The tryouts ended last month. You told me we were down to a hundred hopefuls."

"Well . . ." Silver fidgeted with one of the discarded photos. "One of the girls bowed out because she was accepted to a national figure skating team. When Jami showed interest, I kinda slipped her into the empty slot."

Resting his hands on the desk, he scowled at the pictures. "You knew very well I wouldn't like the idea."

"Dean, she's a big girl! And she wants to prove that she supports the team! Supports you!"

Jabbing at the photo with his finger, his calm demeanor snapped. "Like this?"

The office door swing open and hit the wall. Landon stormed in and immediately cut between him and Silver. "I can hear you two from the hall. I don't know what's going on, but someone better tell me now."

Dean had no patience for Landon's overprotective bullshit. He glared at the man he shared a woman and a bed with. "This has nothing to do with you."

"As long as she's carrying my child, anything that might upset her has something to do with me."

"Where's that fucking trust, Landon? Do you really think I'd do anything to jeopardize the baby?"

"It's hard to trust you when you're acting like a fucking psycho."

With a harsh laugh, Dean straightened and stepped up to the bigger man. A few inches taller, maybe fifty pounds heavier than him, yes, but he wasn't intimidated. If the young man needed to be pulled down a few notches, he was just the person to do it. "You need to back off."

Landon's eyes narrowed. "Make me."

Silver let out a heavy sigh and stepped between them, slapping both their chests. "Put away your clubs, boys. Dean, tell him why you're pissed off, then he can yell at me too."

If Silver is the one being sensible, we have a serious problem. Dean shook his head and retreated a step. He and Landon were essentially on the same page, both trying to protect their children in a situation where they were pretty much helpless. Landon couldn't keep Silver in bubble wrap until she gave birth. And Dean couldn't control his adult daughter.

Of course, that didn't mean he couldn't make Silver pay for not telling him what Jami was up to. She'd promised not to keep anything from him regarding his daughter. She'd broken that promise.

Hopefully, Landon would agree that this was not acceptable.

He gestured from Silver to Landon. "You are perfectly capable of telling him yourself, pet."

Silver didn't say a word. She simply picked up one of the pictures and handed it to Landon.

Landon stared at the picture. Slapped it facedown on the desk as though just looking at it was wrong. He opened his mouth. Paced away from Silver. Paced back. Pointed at the chair behind the desk until she sat. Then turned to Dean. "Writing lines ain't gonna to cut it."

Dean inclined his head. "I agree."

"How the hell did Jami end up in the top one hundred?"

"Would you like to take a guess?"

"*Mon dieu. C'est incroyable! Qu'est-ce que tu penses?*" Landon slapped his hands on the desk. "Silver, you promised not to do this again!"

Impressive. The man, for once, seemed to have recalled that being pregnant didn't make Silver too delicate to be taken to task for her actions. Dean often let the man take the lead in punishments since Silver *was* carrying his baby, but Landon usually asked for suggestions since he had a hard time coming up with "safe" punishments.

Dean had a very safe idea in mind and was pleased when Landon sighed and turned to him. "What do you suggest?"

"Speech restrictions for a week." He smiled when Silver gaped at him. "I will inform Oriana so she can keep an eye on her, but if she can't talk, she can't very well make any more bad decisions while we're gone."

"Works for me." Landon pulled Silver up from the chair and nuzzled her neck, whispering. "Before the punishment starts, tell me one last time that you love me so I can hold onto that while I'm trying to win every game for you."

Silver scowled. "Speech restriction? Screw that! I hate you both!"

"Such sweet last words." Dean touched her cheek, not feeling much pity with the image of his daughter draped all over the most dangerous man on the team sitting in front of him. Some would think his daughter hanging onto Scott Demyan, renowned, immoral playboy, would be worse, but Dean had seen Ramos in action. He could tempt a nun, or—unless he was getting pretty damn rusty in reading people—a saint.

Despite knowing this first hand, Silver had the audacity to give him a dirty look.

"You basically asked me to make sure Ramos stayed away from you because, even with two men who love you, he tempts you. And you've inadvertently sicced him on my daughter. Look at these pictures." He held one up, refusing to look at it again himself. "Do you really expect me to feel sorry for you?"

"No." She stared at the floor, looking utterly miserable. "But I am the primary owner of this team. How can I run it while you're gone if I can't talk?"

He did, finally, feel a bit of compassion. A very little bit. "I'm sure we can both agree Oriana can handle things while I'm gone?"

"She can. Better than me, we all know that." Silver ducked her head as her eyes teared. "You don't need to rub it in."

"I'm not, my little dragonfly." He smiled as the sadness faded from her eyes in response to his tender, personal nickname for her. "I tell you, almost daily, that you are one of the best things that has happened to this team. But that doesn't change what you've done. I don't break promises to you. Think about it. How would you feel if I put your son in the hands of a woman like . . . like Hayley? I can think of no other woman you are wary enough of to understand where I'm coming from."

He could see Silver chewing on that thought, probably thinking that Hayley, the journalist that attacked her in every article she wrote about the Cobras, would be about thirty years older than her son, which made the situation entirely different. But Silver was smart enough to get what he was saying. She would protect her child from anyone who would try to take advantage of him. And she knew, firsthand, how dangerous Ramos could be to a girl as impressionable as his daughter.

"Sir, I'm sorry. I really am. I never thought Jami would be chosen for the pictures. Chantelle is awesome, more professional than any of the photographers we've had so far. I never expected her to choose Jami. Actually, she didn't. And I thought Jami would have a chance to tell you about wanting to be an Ice Girl herself."

"Wait." Dean glanced over at Landon. By his wide-eyed stare, he'd caught it too. But Silver didn't seem to realize how horrendous what she'd just said was. "The photographer didn't choose my daughter?"

"No! She didn't know who she was until she mentioned it and I told her. All she said was Sebastian made a good . . ." Silver cut herself off and covered her mouth with her hand. "Dean, I'm so sorry. I didn't even think about it. Oh, god. Sebastian *asked* for her. Specifically!"

"Shit." Landon wrapped his arms around Silver as though to protect her from her own ill thought out actions. He lifted his head and stared at Dean. "She knows she messed up. She knows she should be punished. I'm sure she accepts it. But she couldn't have expected that."

"No, I'm sure she didn't." Dean's jaw steeled as he gathered the photos and hid them in the folder so he wouldn't have to see them anymore. "But what are the chances that Ramos didn't know he was messing with my daughter?"

Landon paled. "Hey, man. It's not like we talk about her in the locker room."

"Are you saying he didn't know? That he thought she was just another cheerleader exposing herself for—" His throat clogged up. Jami wouldn't go that far. Not without someone urging her on. Sebastian had pushed her to do this. Either ignorant that she was he daughter or not really giving a fuck. His jaded self edged toward the latter. "Is the team really that disjointed, Landon? Is it possible he doesn't know she's my daughter?"

Squaring his shoulders, Landon moved away from Silver. "If he doesn't know now, he will shortly, *I* can promise you that."

"Thank you, Landon."

"Okay, you two need to back off." Silver folded her hands over her big belly and frowned at them both. "Jami won't thank you for getting involved."

"Silver," Dean tried to be as gentle as he could, considering his daughter was the center of the discussion and Silver just didn't get it. Silver's father hadn't cared enough to protect her from men like Ramos. Or even men like him. Of course, it was too late for that. "You do not have permission to speak. To me or anyone else. Landon supports my punishment. If you'd like to safeword out, do so now, otherwise be silent until we return and think about what you've done."

Silver's chin jutted up. "Yellow. We *will* discuss this before I start with the stupid speech restrictions. I should have told Jami, straight out, that she had to talk to you right away. I get that. But *you* have to respect that Jami is an adult. She did her time in rehab. Your mom even agreed her getting involved in something like this would be good for her."

Oh, this just gets better and better. He scratched his jaw and arched a brow at Silver. "My mother knows about this?"

"Yes." Silver smirked. "You gonna tell her off too?"

Landon snorted and Dean was tempted to punch him. Instead he straightened his tie and sighed. Punishing Silver for something his own mother had kept from him seemed ridiculous. As much as he hated the entire situation, there wasn't *much* he could do about it. As far as the women were concerned anyway. "I suppose I'm outnumbered then. Jami may continue the tryouts, and I'll do my best to act surprised when she tells me."

"I'd appreciate that, but what about this thing with Sebastian? It's just a picture, Dean."

She knew him too well. "You can't honestly expect me not to—"

"Stay out of it? Yes, that's *exactly* what I expect you to do. You know Sebastian won't hurt her. You trusted him enough to make him a DM at the club."

"Monitoring scenes at the club is *much* different than . . ." Damn it, than what exactly? He didn't even want to think about what Ramos would do with his daughter. He rubbed his eyes with his fingers and thumb. "At least, with the playoffs, he won't be around very often. But he may have a problem with the other players if they see him with her. Actually . . ." He put his hand over the picture Landon had laid facedown and made a rough sound in his throat. "Seeing this might be enough to agitate a few of them. Many still see her as a little girl."

"But *you* won't make an issue of it?" Silver looked over at Landon. "Either of you?"

Landon mumbled his accord.

"Good." Silver grinned and leaned back in Dean's chair, arms folded over the top of her large belly. "Now, just one last thing—"

"No." He held up his hand and shook his head. "I've reconsidered. No speech restriction."

"What?" Both Landon and Silver said at once, both staring at him.

"You heard me." He squared his shoulders. "It pleases me that my daughter felt comfortable enough to come to you."

Silver's hand drifted up to her throat. "But I promised . . ."

"Extenuating circumstances. Don't worry about it, Silver." He reached out to cup her cheek with his hand. "I'm sorry I came down on you so hard."

Thrusting out of her chair, Silver stepped up to him and poked him in the center of the chest. Her eyes shimmered with fresh tears. "Fuck you! I made a mistake. I know I did and I said I was sorry!"

"There's nothing to be sorry about, dragonfly—"

"There is too, you asshole!"

"Silver." Landon put his hand on her shoulder and frowned down at her. "That's enough."

Dean studied her face, all blotchy and tight with frustration, her eyes red with unspilled tears. He realized something then and had to fight to hold back a smile. His poor little sub felt guilty about breaking her word, and, whether it was right or wrong, she couldn't let it go without feeling that she'd made amends. If he wouldn't punish her for keeping this from him, she'd push to get punished for something else. He could count on one hand the number of times she'd sworn at him in the last few months. That she was doing so now told him everything he needed to know.

"I stand corrected. Speech restrictions then, pet. A few days considering what you should, and should not, say to me, will do you some good." He smiled at the relief in her eyes. She nodded and leaned against Landon. "What was the one last thing?"

She drew in a long, shuddery breath. "I want a nice, long kiss from both of you. Before you get all scruffy."

Landon laughed and turned her in his arms, giving her a deep kiss before rubbing his smooth cheek against hers. Eyes hooded, he whispered in her ear. "All that scruff will feel nice and rough when I bury my face between your thighs, *mignonne*. You may never want me to shave again."

Silver ducked her head and moved to Dean. He pulled her close and gave her a tender kiss, chuckling at her surprised look. He nipped her bottom lip and spoke quietly. "GMs don't grow playoff beards, sweetie. And if I hold you too much longer, I'll be sending our goalie off on his own so I can remind you how smooth cheeks feel between your thighs."

"Arg!" Silver pointed at the door. "You two are horrible. Get out of here before I decide not to let either of you leave."

Dean grinned and pressed a finger over her lips. "Your punishment has begun. Any more and I'll have to add a spanking when we return."

She fixed his tie, smoothed it down, and gave him a look so full of love he was tempted to cancel his trip just so he could stay with her. But she nudged him toward the door. "I can't wait."

* * * *

Ford flipped through the photos on his desk, the scrape of his teeth grinding causing the ache in his throbbing skull to take on a sharp edge. He massaged his temples and looked up as Lee walked into his office, his doughy face slick with sweat.

Did you run all the way from the elevator? He rolled his eyes as Lee collapsed into the chair at the other side of the desk, panting.

"Did you get the ticket?"

"Yes, sir." Lee fumbled inside his briefcase and slapped a plane ticket on the desk in front of Ford. "First class. I also reserved the best suite in the hotel—on the same floor as the players so you can—"

"So *I* can?" Ford frowned and pushed the ticket across the desk. "I'm not going anywhere. You are."

"Me?" Lee squeaked. "But I thought you'd want me to watch Jami!"

"Why the fuck would I want that?" *Idiot.* If Lee wasn't his dad's—Kingsley, not Delgado, Delgado was just a convenient sperm donor—most trusted employee, he'd get rid of him. It made him feel dirty that this man had seen him with Jami—and countless others before her. His father claimed it was for his own protection, which he'd believed when he was too young and stupid to question it. But now he knew he could protect himself better than this tub-of-lard could.

Lee's lips curled away from his crooked teeth. "Because if your dad finds out she's still a distraction, it may be a problem."

"She's not." Ford pushed the photos away from him and stood. "You know I'm not into cokeheads."

"True." Lee's thick lips twisted into a sneer. "But she's all cleaned up now, isn't she? Except for being a whore."

"Don't call her that!" Ford turned away from Lee, realizing too late that he'd just given the man the upper hand. Bile rose in his throat. His own man, Cort, who handled his bar, "The Office," for him, had found out that Jami's new "friends' were getting paid by his father to mess her up. Not long before, Dad had told him the truth about his biological father. Dad would have gotten rid of Jami if she hadn't dumped him. And strange as it sounded, overdosing was probably the best thing that could have happened to her. She'd gone to rehab and moved away, which meant his father wouldn't bother with her anymore.

Ford didn't want to give his dad any reason to turn his attention to Jami again. But the photos had pissed him off. What the hell was Jami thinking?

What the hell was *he* thinking? He should have called Cort. Cort would have gotten something on Ramos, clean and easy, no questions asked. But he'd figured, under the pretense of wanting a way to blackmail the defenseman, he could get his dad off his back about fixing the games.

And still keep Jami safe.

She wasn't for him. The things she needed, he couldn't give her. But he cared about the kid.

You should have cared enough to stay out of it. Too late now, fucktard.

He closed the folder on his desk when he caught Lee staring at the pictures and leaned forward. "Jami is useless to us. Ramos, however, is in the spotlight, messing with the GM's daughter right out in public. If we're lucky, he'll be on the outs with his team. He's new, but he's an important player, and if we can get to him, right before the playoffs..." He watched Lee's pudgy face take on a hungry, greedy expression. The man had made a shitload the last time they'd rigged a game. Hopefully he'd stop thinking about Jami and start thinking about the money that would be coming in if he pulled this off. "He's hiding something. Find out what it is."

Lee frowned and his pudgy neck swallowed his chin. "What makes you think he's hiding something?"

Ford opened the folder, hoping to confuse Lee's small brain with some facts as he held out a photo of Jami with Ramos. "He ain't stirring up this kind of controversy for nothing. Man like him isn't interested in a kid like her. Out of all the Ice Girls, he chooses the GM's daughter? Come on. He's diverting the press."

Taking the picture, Lee held it up and licked his lips. "She's a very pretty girl, Ford."

He fought not to snatch the picture away and let out a harsh laugh. "I've had prettier. And so has Ramos. Trust me, he's using her."

"Like you were?" Lee smirked and arched a thin brow. "Sometimes with a few of your friends."

"Yeah, exactly like that." Ford scowled and plucked the photo from Lee's sausage-like fingers. "What is it, Lee, you still bitter that I never shared her with you?"

Lee shook his head slowly. "No. I was never interested in sharing her." He took the plane ticket and stuffed it in his briefcase. "I'll shadow the man. Find up what he's up to. But I'm not stupid, boss. You can't pretend you don't care that he's got her. And since I'm such a nice guy, I won't say anything to your father. But stay away from her."

Ford laughed uneasily. Maybe Lee wasn't as stupid as he seemed. "I plan to."

"Good." Lee mumbled something to himself and nodded. "Very good."

A chill crawled over Ford's flesh as the man left his office. Something wasn't right about him. He needed to have a talk with his dad. If he had to have a handler, he'd rather someone else.

Anyone else.

Chapter Four

Luke crunched on an apple and stretched his legs out as far as he could in the confines of his seat on the charter bus that would bring the team from the airport to the hotel. His pulse beat hard inside his cotton-stuffed skull, and he hoped eating something healthy would make the aftereffects of tying a few on before lunch go away. If Coach found out that he'd been drinking on a game day, he'd take him out of the lineup. Leave him at the hotel with nothing to do but think about what a loser he was, a feeling he couldn't seem to shake ever since the night Chicklet . . .

You let her top you, you wimp. You're lucky the guys don't know. You'd never live it down.

He suddenly wanted another drink. Worst thing was, he couldn't decide what made him want one more—having his girlfriend throw herself at another man to get him to break up with her, or having his mentor decide he needed his ass beaten. He used to give subs a knowing smirk when they shifted in their seats for days after a good caning, but never again. Hell, the nagging pain had him rock hard. Too freakin' weird.

Doms don't get off on getting hit. They get off on doing the hitting.

But he hadn't gotten off.

You wanted to.

Sitting forward in his seat, grateful for the grey suit jacket that covered the erection straining against the zipper of his pants, he took another bite of his apple and glanced over at Landon Bower, the team's starting goalie, his road roomie, and best friend. They talked about stuff—maybe he could ask him what he thought about the whole thing with Chicklet. See if he'd ever subbed to anyone.

Not a question you can just blurt out. And not something to ask on the bus. Fine, a lot of the players were into kinky stuff, but not all. They could shoot the shit back at the hotel.

Besides, Bower looked distracted. Luke followed the direction of his glare to the back of Sebastian Ramos' head. Ramos was a big guy. A damn good defenseman. He and Bower got along pretty well, but Ramos had some history with Bower's fiancée. Had he made a play for her?

As Bower's buddy, Luke wouldn't stand for a teammate fucking with him. But he had to make sure before he put the Spanish giant on his hit list. So he elbowed Bower in the gut.

"What did he do? Silver's knocked up with your kid. He didn't try to fuck her, did he?"

Bower sat up straight and blinked at him. "What?"

"He covers you good while you're between the pipes. I can't see you being pissed at him unless he dipped his wick in your lady's cunt. Or tried to." Luke ran his tongue over his teeth. "Say the word and I'll deal with him for you. Get under his skin, you know? He'll look like an ass out on the ice when I'm done with him."

Laughing, Bower smacked his shoulder. "Kid, that man could destroy you. Leave it alone."

"Fuck that." Luke stood and stumbled across the bus aisle, vision a little blurry from less than two hours sleep in the last twenty-four hours. And maybe a tad too much to drink. He chewed an apple chunk to pulp and latched onto the back of a seat as he made his way to Ramos.

You don't fuck with the goalie, man. 'specially not when he's my friend.

He caught Demyan's eye as he passed him and shook his head as Demyan made a drinking gesture. "I's all good. Just gots to deal with something."

They were about to start up the playoffs. Just one more game. Bad time to start up drama.

Coach scowled over at Luke as he tripped and jarred his knee against a seat. "Will you sit down, Carter? The bus is about to—"

The bus jerked to a stop, spilling Luke to the floor. A few guys laughed behind him. He scrambled to his feet and managed to block Ramos just as the man was stepping out.

Luke retreated a bit so he didn't have to strain his neck looking up at the man. In an Italian suit that probably cost more than anything Luke owned, long black hair all slicked back nice and neat, Ramos didn't come across as someone who'd bust in a man's face on the ice. Until you met his eyes. He could trap a person in those rich earthen depths even as he beat them to a pulp. The chicks all thought he was mysterious, but he was dangerous. No one really knew what he was capable of.

Not like I'm scared of him or anything. Luke squared his shoulders and cleared his throat.

Ramos frowned at him. "Can I help you?"

"Need to talk." Luke slurred, ignoring the grumbles from the men crowding the aisle. He stuck his thumbs in his pant pockets. "Gots to clear up a few things."

"Do we?" Ramos' lips slanted with amusement. "Right here?"

Umm, yeah. Here might not be the best place to have it out. Luke jerked his chin in the direction of the door. "'nside the hotel be fine."

Inclining his head, Ramos gestured Luke forward. "Lead the way, *hombrecito*."

"Buddy, you best not have just called me a fucking pussy." Luke strode to the front of the bus, took the first step—and almost face-planted after the next few vanished out from under him. A firm hand on his shoulder saved him. He shook his head to clear it and wrenched away from Ramos as the man tried to propel him to the curb.

"I'm good. Lemme go."

Arms folded over his chest, Ramos studied him with his eyes narrowed into dark slits. His lips drew into a tight line and he leaned forward, speaking low in Luke's ear. "You're drunk. I suggest you head inside before the coach figures it out and scratches you from tonight's game. I'll get your bags—"

"I don't need you to—"

"Do as I say, Luke, or I'll make you."

Laughing, because the guy was just fucking funny, Luke moved toward where the team's luggage was being unpacked into the horde of exhausted players. "You can't make me do—"

Ramos' hand latched around the nape of his neck. Rough fingers dug into his skin and his breath lodged in his throat. A strange buzzing rushed through his veins, and he had to lock his knees so his legs wouldn't give out.

He laughed again, this time almost hysterically. "That bitch broke me!"

"Stop." Ramos gave him a rough shake which immediately shut him up. His next words came out in a growl. "Get ahold of yourself.

You're causing a scene."

The command in Ramos' tone brought on the same sensation of Chicklet's flogger biting into his flesh. Mind-numbing white-hot rush of pain and pleasure shooting from his brain to his balls. The world spun around and around as though his brain was a wind turbine on the roof of a barn in a storm. He wanted to sit on the ground to make it stop, but Ramos held him up.

Shoes scuffed the pavement. Luke squinted toward the sound, expecting to see Bower. Instead, Demyan stepped up to Ramos' side and grabbed his wrist.

"We got a problem here?"

Shaken to the core by his weird reaction, Luke quickly shook his head, needing to get away from both men so he could screw his head on straight. Ramos had released him. Which made it a bit easier to think.

"Everything's cool, Demyan. We're cool." He swallowed and glanced over at Ramos. "Right?"

"Yes." Ramos arched a brow and looked pointedly toward the hotel. "We will speak in private."

At that moment, Luke couldn't think of a damn thing he wanted to say to the man. *Ever.* But since the guys were starting to stare at him, he simply nodded. And bolted for the door.

* * * *

Sebastian waited by the window in his hotel room, staring out at the city skyline. Lack of sleep weighed on his body. He wanted nothing more than to stretch out on the bed for a nap to refresh himself before the game.

But not yet.

His lips curled as someone pounded at the door. "Come in."

The door hit the wall. The rookie who had confronted him, Luke Carter, stormed in and pointed at his suitcase, which sat on the floor by the TV stand. "What the fuck, man? Why'd you take my shit?"

Without turning away from the window, Sebastian replied calmly. "Close the door, Luke."

Luke reached for the door. Then stopped and fisted his hands at his sides. "I ain't staying."

Sebastian glanced at Luke over his shoulder. "Didn't you have something to discuss with me?"

The young man gaped at him, blinked, and nodded as though suddenly recalling what he'd wanted to say. He raked his fingers through his already mussed up, dirty blond hair. "I did. Stay away from Silver. She's Bower's woman and she's having his kid. You missed you chance. Deal with it."

"Your loyalty is admirable, Luke—"

Swaying a little, Luke made a grab for his bags. "Hey, the guys call me Carter."

"I know that." Sebastian sighed as Luke tripped over his bags and knocked his forehead into the open door. "Leave the bags, Luke. I will bring them to you later. You need to sleep this off."

Luke kicked the bags and glared at him as he tipped off balance. "Hey, stop trying to fucking Dom me, man. I'm not a fucking sub."

Crossing the room in three long strides, Sebastian towed Luke away from the door by his wrist, kicked it shut, then shoved him toward the bed. His words came in a low growl as he loomed over him. "Don't move."

Utterly still, pupils dilated, Luke rested half on the bed. And sprang up with a snarl. "Like hell!"

Sebastian caught the fist aimed at his face and deftly flipped Luke over, twisting his arm behind his back to hold him still. He shifted so his hardening cock didn't press against Luke's ass and inhaled deeply to regain control of himself. For a moment, he'd almost forgotten the man was his teammate. Which made him off-limits. All he saw was the submission Luke fought so hard to bury. The dominant in Ramos roared for him to latch onto it, drag it out.

Reason took over. They had a game in a few hours. Luke had to be fit to play.

But damn it, if he had to "Dom him" to see that he was . . .

Then that was exactly what he would do.

"Listen to me, rookie." His lips brushed Luke's ear and he felt the smaller man shiver. "This game will decide whether we play the Sabres or the Devils. And we need to be the ones to take out the

Sabres, don't we?"

Luke panted into the gold, floral-patterned comforter and nodded.

"I am . . . very happy that you agree." His accent thickened as his skin heated up. He had to focus not to lose the English words that sometimes slipped from his vocabulary in times of anger. Or passion. He would allow himself to feel neither. "Return to your room. Sleep. I will see you on the ice."

Luke growled something into the mattress.

"Excuse me?"

"Get. Off. Me."

It took every ounce of strength Sebastian had to loosen his grip on Luke's wrist. To push away from him. To put distance between them. He rubbed his face with one hand and pointed to the door with the other. "You may go."

With a hard laugh, Luke stood. And crossed the space between them to give Sebastian a hard shove. "May I? You seriously think I'm going to let you get away with that shit? What the fuck is wrong with you?"

"I am tired and running out of patience. You approached me with violence. I merely restrained you until you regained control of yourself."

"Oh." Shaking his head, Luke tripped backward. "Oh. Yeah, I guess I kinda flipped out a bit. Sorry about that. But you've got to stay away from Silver. That's all I wanted to say."

"And you've said it. But I have no interest in Silver. We are friends, nothing more."

"Really?" Luke's brow furrowed. "Bower was shooting daggers at you. Wonder why."

Sebastian had an idea, but he wasn't about to discuss it with Luke. More than anything, he wanted Luke out of his sight. The man stirred his blood and tempted him. He hadn't had a good fight in a while—not the kind of fight that ended in mutual pleasure. And he had a feeling he could have that with Luke. If only the man wasn't struggling with the very idea of being submissive. If only he wasn't a teammate.

A bottle clinked and Sebastian's brow shot up as Luke knelt in front of his liquor cabinet.

"You don't mind if I help myself, do you?"

"I wouldn't suggest it."

With a snort, Luke uncapped a bottle, then drained it.

Rage clouded Sebastian's vision. His hand was suddenly fisted in Luke's shirt. A wild punch caught him in the throat. He swung back and connected with Luke's jaw. Luke grunted and slumped over his arm.

"Stupid boy." Sebastian hefted Luke up and went to drop him on the bed. Sitting beside him, he watched carefully to make sure he hadn't done any real damage. Other than a thin trail over blood on the young man's bottom lip, he was well enough. He grabbed a tissue from the box on the night table and dabbed at the tiny cut. Took a moment to remove the cheap clip-on tie Luke wore and undo the top few buttons of his shirt.

Light, golden hair trailed in a line down Luke's chest. Sebastian fingered the remaining buttons, tempted to undo them all. Instead he worked the blanket out from under Luke, covering him completely. And went to take his nap in the hard chair in front of the desk. There was plenty of space on the king-sized bed for him, but he couldn't lie down next to Luke. He didn't dare.

He didn't trust his control to stretch that far. He'd tested it too much already, and he couldn't afford for it to fail him now.

* * * *

Well into the third period of play, Luke let out a shout as Bower gloved a top shelf shot and hopped over the boards at Coach's nod. His ice time had been limited—Coach wasn't stupid, he and the whole team knew Luke had gotten drunk—but he hadn't gotten scratched. Thanks to Demyan and Bower, who'd spoken up for him a couple of hours before the game. During the first two periods, he'd made every second count, getting in on two assists and blocking a shot after a rebound. His game was top-notch even after a few drinks.

And it'll be even better during the playoffs. I ain't touching that shit again until we get this done.

Waking up in Ramos' bed had sobered him up pretty quick. He couldn't remember a damn thing besides wanting to talk to the man about Silver. But after both Ramos, and Bower, confirmed that Silver wasn't an issue, he'd dropped it and gotten ready to play. Out here, on the ice, everything made sense. The mess of his life beyond the rink didn't matter. All that mattered was moving fast and getting the puck in the net.

Crisp air rushed around him as he cut across the rink, scooping up a pass on the blue line. He snapped the puck to Demyan and skidded around a big body coming at him for a late hit. Got behind the defense and took a shot as the puck hit his stick.

Red lights flashed. Someone slammed into him. Demyan. He practically knocked Luke over as he shouted and bodily handed him over to Zack Pearce, a gritty forward who'd earned himself a spot on the second line over the past few months. Pearce thunked helmets, then let Bower punch and hug him.

"You did it, kid." Bower laughed at Luke's blank stare. "Hell, didn't you hear me say there was like seven seconds left? We would have had to win this in overtime, but you took it home!"

"Fuck yeah!" Luke grinned as the rest of the team crowded around him, thumping him and squeezing his shoulders. In a daze, he took his place in the hall just past the benches and then did a brief skate around the ice as they announced him as the first star. Back in the locker room, he got a few more shoulder punches, some hair ruffles, and a few "Way to go!"s

A hard slap on his shoulder after he peeled off his shirt finally cleared his head from the victory buzz. He glanced over to see ripped abs and a slack dick. Snapped his gaze up to meet Ramos' deep brown eyes and broad smile of approval.

"Well done, *niño*."

Luke nodded and chewed on his inner lip as the big man disappeared into the shower room. For some reason, even though every man on the team had given him props, it felt like more coming from Ramos. He vaguely recalled somehow pissing Ramos off. Of course, he'd pissed everyone off by drinking before such an important game, but he liked knowing he and Ramos were cool.

Removing the rest of his gear, he grabbed a towel and headed for the showers. Demyan snapped a towel at him as he passed and caught the back of his thighs. Fire spread over the bruises still healing from the cane strokes Wayne and Chicklet had left on him.

His legs shook as he forced out a laugh. "I'm gonna get you for that, you fucker!"

Jabbing his shoulder into Demyan's gut, he drove him into the wall. Demyan hooked an arm around his neck and gave him two fake punches in the side.

"Hey!" Sloan Callahan, the team's captain, grabbed them both by the arms and jerked them apart. "Will you two stop screwing around? I don't need either of you getting hurt before the playoffs even start. If you're that hot for each other, take it back to the hotel."

"What do you say, pretty boy?" Demyan bared his teeth in a wolfish grin. "Wanna rim my ass?"

"Sure, right after you suck my cock, pussy lips." Luke almost fell over laughing as Callahan pushed them away with a disgusted grunt. "Sorry, Captain. You want in on this? What do you suggest? K-Y or Vaseline?"

Callahan rolled his eyes. "I don't know, Carter. I imagine anal with a guy is pretty much the same as anal with a woman. If you know they're clean and aren't using a lubed-up condom, a bit of spit works just fine. Can be painful, but some people prefer it that way." He looked pointedly at Luke's thigh. "From those marks, I imagine you like it rough."

"Shit, man, that's just—" Okay, joking around was one thing, but Callahan didn't seriously think he was gay, did he? "Wayne told me good Doms gotta take if they're gonna dish out. I'm not into guys, hear me?"

"Was Chicklet with you?" Callahan sounded a bit worried.

Awful sweet of him. "Yeah, she was the one who . . . well, you know I want to be a good Dom."

Nodding gravely, Callahan turned a shower on and stepped under the spray. "I get that, kid. And Wayne's right. Hell, I've had pretty much everything I do to Oriana done to me."

"You've been whipped?"

"Yeah, you haven't noticed?" Callahan turned to let them all—

Luke, Ramos, and Demyan— see his back. The other two men were hardly breathing as they took in the faint scars on Callahan's flesh. Nothing compared to the one on his face, but bad enough. "I found out pretty quick that I'm not a masochist, but I was too fucking proud to safeword out. The Domme who whipped me got really into it. Mason is the one who stopped her."

"Holy shit." Demyan's eyes narrowed as he inched closer to Sloan. "I kinda freaked when I saw Carter getting beaten on, but neither Wayne or Chicklet did anything like this. I think I would have lost it."

"If you want to be a Dom, you *never* lose it at a club. Or when you're with a sub who's trusting you to take care of her." Callahan moved so his back was to the black tiled wall and squirted some shampoo in his hand from one of the many bottles on the floor beside him. He frowned at Carter. "Be careful with Wayne. He's a hard-core sadist. Worse than me."

Luke rolled his shoulder and nodded. "Yeah, well, I don't scene with men, so there's nothing to worry about."

"You *did* scene with a man, kid. Maybe it wasn't sexual—"

"You're damn right it wasn't sexual!"

"All right, relax. I'm just saying." Callahan's brow furrowed. "Richter owns the club, and he trusts Wayne, so I hate saying anything bad about him, but . . . he likes his boys nice and young. Not sick young—just . . . inexperienced. He and his boy aren't exclusive. He might see you as fresh meat."

A metallic creak filled the room as Ramos turned off his shower hard enough that it seemed like the faucet might come off in his hand. He shook water from his hair, the long strands slashing at his face as he approached Luke.

"You don't go to the club alone." His harsh tone made it unclear as to whether he was asking or telling. But he squeezed Luke's shoulder and spoke quietly. "What you are doing is good. It is right to want to learn. But you will not be too proud to say red if you must."

"I bet you anything he will be." Callahan rinsed off and scowled. "But I'll be watching you, kid."

Demyan nodded. "We all will. I'm not sure I want to be a Dom after hearing all this, but I ain't letting you go there alone. We all get enough scars on the ice. You're not getting more being a tough guy while someone's beating on you."

Damn, it felt good to know they were looking out for him. His girlfriend—*ex-girlfriend*—might not think he was worth much, but these men did. And what they thought was all that mattered.

Cut the tension. This is getting weird. He choked out a laugh and wiped under his eyes. "Aw man, I'm all teary. You guys rock! Group hug!"

Callahan shook his head and walked away. Demyan snickered and slugged Luke in the shoulder before following.

Only Ramos didn't seem to get the joke.

"You will learn to say red." Ramos glared at him until Luke had to look away because it was freaking him out. A rough hand caught his chin and forced him to face the man. "Even if I have to teach you myself."

Chapter Five

In her comfy little apartment, sprawled out on her orange and pale blue patchwork sofa, Jami watched Akira go over the dance moves for what seemed like the thousandth time and tried not to sigh as she glanced over at her cell. Akira was awesome for trying to teach her, but Jami just couldn't focus. She'd really, really hoped Sebastian would have called by now.

It's only been two days.

True, but the team was back. He'd said he wanted to go out for coffee when they got back.

Playoff time. He's probably too busy.

Akira slapped her hands on her hips and frowned at Jami. "Will you just call him!"

"Ha! As if!" Jami sat up and grabbed her phone to stuff it between the sofa cushions. "He's hot and all, but I'm not that desperate."

"Just hot? The way you talked about him last night, I thought he was someone special."

"Special? After one date?" Jami laughed. "Akira, what you heard last night was me being antsy. It's been *months*."

"Since that boy in the shed?"

Jami groaned. Damn, she'd really over-shared while drinking those strawberry daiquiris. But Akira had gotten all depressed after telling her about being raped by two of her father's coworkers when she was only sixteen. They'd stolen her virginity and left her with a fear of men that practically paralyzed her when any came close. She'd wanted to hear about how it could be good. Strangely enough, Jami found herself talking about Ford. Things had been *amazing* with Ford in the beginning.

Before Jami had turned into a freak.

"The boy in the shed—damn, I can't even remember his name. Sad, eh? Anyway, we only kissed and groped a bit. It was like being back in high school with a clumsy boy who doesn't know what he's doing." She sighed. "Ford was the first *man* I was with. And, well, I told you how it was. He was gentle. Tender. He always made sure I enjoyed myself, but..."

Taking a seat beside her, Akira hugged herself and leaned forward. "But what? You made it sound so wonderful last night. I still can't understand why you broke up with him."

"Well, we both got drunk one night and—" Jami wasn't sure she should tell Akira any of this. The girl was so broken from the things that had been done to her. She couldn't possibly understand. And yet... talking to Akira was so easy. After just a few days, they were pretty much best friends. Not just from lack of options. They'd clicked. "He had some friends over. Things got hot and heavy and— I was totally willing. Not so drunk that I didn't know what I was doing. Anyway, one of his friends got really worked up and called me their little slut. Ford got pissed off, but I got him to relax. And I told him... I told him I liked it. Things were weird after that. I wanted more. Ford didn't."

"That's when you started doing drugs?"

"We were already smoking pot, but Ford didn't like the harder stuff. I met a new crowd at his bar and they came to a few parties. The women were all over Ford. I didn't mind, it was like one big orgy. But at one point, Ford gave me this look, like he was disgusted with me." Her throat tightened as she recalled that look. It came back to her how she'd suddenly realized something was wrong with her. Some guy held her while she cried and gave her some pills. She took them and everything was all better. More than better. Shiny, erotic. Pure pleasure with no regrets.

Until the next day. But her "friends" were around to give her more pills. To listen as she ranted about Ford. He'd caught her popping pills during another party and kicked everyone out. Restrained her as she completely flipped and told her "No more."

Nobody told her what to do. He'd even gone so far as to tell her she couldn't see her friends anymore.

He'd been right to do so. But she hadn't seen it then.

As she told Akira everything, she watched her face for disgust, for any kind of judgment. To her relief, she found neither. Actually, Akira looked fascinated.

"The drugs—the drugs were bad." Akira took a deep breath. "But everything else... *God*, Jami! I don't think I could let that many men touch me—or any man, at this point, but it's all so exciting! So crazy!"

"Crazy is right!" Jami gave Akira a one-armed hug. "And you'll get past this one day, sweetie. I won't let those bastards permanently fuck things up for you. No gang bangs for you, but we'll find you a man that can make you feel so good, you'll tell me about it and *I'll* be jealous!"

"That would be cool." Akira ducked her head and blushed. "Since you've told me so much, I should probably tell you something."

"I agree."

Slipping off the sofa, Akira went to fetch her overnight bag. She hugged it tight and bit her lip. "You have to promise not to laugh."

"Akira, I swear, I will *never* laugh at you." Jami folded her knees under her and held her breath, wondering what in the world her sweet, shy friend was about to show her. When Akira didn't move, Jami groaned. "Come on! The suspense is killing me!"

Closing her eyes, Akira reached into her bag, pulled out a book, and handed it to Jami. The book's cover was faded, creased, obviously read often by its condition. But the title was clear enough.

Jami's eyes widened. She gasped. "Oh my God, Akira! *The Story of O*? Wow!"

"Yeah." Akira stared at her bare feet, her black hair covering her face like a sleek, black veil. "*I'm* a freak, aren't I? Reading this after what happened to me—"

"No way! Damn, girl, don't you get it?" Jami set the book aside and took Akira's hand. "This tells me you're going to be okay. That maybe, just maybe, you're almost ready to explore, you know? Not to this extreme . . . unless this is what you want?"

"Oh no! Nothing like that!" Akira giggled, her hands hovering over her throat. "But sometimes I wonder what it would be like. Giving up control. I read a lot. Other books that make me feel like maybe it would be nice. Not to have to worry. To have someone taking care of me . . ."

Nodding slowly, Jami held her tongue between her teeth. "You know it's not like that in real life, right?"

"So you know what it's like? Have you ever, like, let a man take

69

over?"

"I've let several!" Jami laughed, then wrinkled her nose. "But not like in your books. We could find out though, if you want. My dad owns a club where people do that stuff."

Akira gasped. "Stuff like that? Really? You'd go even though your dad might be there?"

"Not while he was there, no. That would be weird. But he's going with Silver and her husband to visit my grandparents this weekend."

"So no one in the club would know you?"

Jami made a face. "Umm, well, considering a lot of the Cobras go to the club . . . *but* I have a key to the back door. My dad gave it to me in case of emergencies."

Akira's brow shot up. "This isn't an emergency."

"Yeah, well, he doesn't have to know we were there. We sneak in, watch from the stairs or something—if we're dressed right, no one will even notice us."

"Your hair is *blue,* Jami. I'm sure someone will notice that."

"With all those kinky broads I doubt I'll be the only one with funky hair."

"I don't know . . ."

"Well, you don't have to decide tonight. My dad isn't leaving until Friday, and the club is only open on the weekends, as far as I know anyway." She gave Akira a mischievous smile and went to the shelves under her wall mounted TV to grab a movie. "You staying over again?"

"Sure."

"Cool. I got a movie you might like. Want to get some snacks while I set it up?"

By the time Akira returned with the popcorn and drinks, the movie was paused on the title. Jami grinned as Akira fell onto the sofa laughing. *The Secretary* was the perfect movie after their little chat.

At one point, while the secretary was being spanked, Akira leaned over and whispered, "You ever wonder what that would be like? Has a guy ever done that to you?"

"No." Jami clenched her thighs as she drew her knees up to her chest, Sebastian's threat coming back to her as she watched. It had been made so offhandedly, but still, she wondered how it would feel to have his big hand coming down on her bare ass, over and over. "But I will try it one day."

Akira winced at a rather hard smack but still nodded. "Me too."

* * * *

The next morning, all freshly primped and suited up in their Cobra Ice Girls uniforms, both excited about the day ahead since they would be showing off their skills on the ice for the judges, Jami and Akira took Jami's car to the forum and had a quick breakfast in the locker room. Akira was called in first, and Jami paced the halls, waiting to find out how her friend had done. Not that she doubted her in the least, but Akira was so shy . . .

A man cleared his throat and Jami froze as he spoke. "You're looking good, babe. Not so skinny."

Jami took a deep breath and turned to face Ford. Her skates put her almost at eye level with him, but she avoided his steady gaze, instead focusing on the shine of his Italian leather boots. "Thanks. You're looking good too."

"You haven't even looked at me." Ford sighed and touched her cheek with his fingertips, drawing away when she jerked out of reach. "Hey, I'm sorry."

"For what?" Jami wrapped her arms over her stomach, feeling practically naked with him in a fancy suit after seeing him so often in worn jeans and a leather vest. "I'm the one who messed up. I went all dopehead and freaky on you."

"I should have tried harder, should have protected you—"

"From what, Ford?" Jami's eyes narrowed. "The drugs? Your friends? Mine?"

"All of the above."

"Really? That's funny, because when things got all wild, you were into it. Then you made me feel like shit because I enjoyed it too." All her self-recriminations came back, but she realized, for the fi[rst time] that he hadn't been innocent. "Would you have felt [bad if I] screamed and cried and begged you not to let your fri[ends touch me?]"

You handed me off, so I assumed you were cool with it."

"Maybe I wasn't."

"Then maybe you should have thought about that before you let it happen."

Ford hung his head and nodded. "You're right. I should have. But I can't change what happened any more than you can. I wish I'd treated you better. That's over with though, Jami. You've cleaned up, right? What are you doing with a man like Sebastian Ramos?"

After spending yet another night doing her best not to think about Sebastian, Ford bringing him up really pissed her off. They'd broken up over half a year ago. Who she got involved with was none of Ford's business.

"I'm clean. I worked my ass off to prove it. But what does that have to do with Sebastian?"

"I saw the pictures."

Already? Jami swallowed hard. If Ford had seen them, maybe her father had too. But he hadn't mentioned anything on the phone yesterday. And he would have.

She hiked up her chin a bit more. "They're just pictures, Ford. They don't mean anything."

"Bullshit." Ford lifted his hand, fingers curling as though he wanted to grab her. But he let it fall to his side. "You were looking at him the way you—"

"The way I used to look at you?"

The muscles in Ford's jaw hardened. "Yeah. Exactly."

"I'm good at putting on a show. All kinds of shows actually. The man I lo—the man I'm with might make me feel nasty about it the morning after, but while it's happening I feel sexy. Worth looking at."

Ford dropped his head back. "*Fuck,* Jami! Why can't you get that I hated them calling you a slut. Hated you acting like you were one. You're better than that."

"Maybe I wanted to be *your* slut."

"I would *never* have treated you like that."

She got it. Kinda. Sex in public, in front of a crowd, hadn't bothered Ford. Even the sharing hadn't been a big deal. But the name calling, the degradation . . .

Could she really blame him? Most men wouldn't be okay with it. She wouldn't have gotten into drugs if she'd been totally okay with being turned on by being treated like that.

"I guess you were too good for me, Ford. And like you told me, I needed to grow up." She planted a strained smile on her lips. "And I think I have."

Nodding slowly, Ford reached out and took her hand. "If things were different, I'd want to try again. Hell, I'm tempted to—"

"No offense, but that's sooo not happening." Jami grinned as he dropped her hand, stepping back like she'd slapped him. "Aww, babe, you're not going to take offense, are you? You really think a girl can forget you telling her 'That's sick' when she begs you, in the heat of the moment, to call her your nasty little bitch?"

"You caught me off-guard."

"Several times." Jami inclined her head. "But your reaction never changed. And that's okay. I've accepted that you and me wanted different things."

"All right, but what about Sebastian? You're not seriously going to tell me you have anything in common with him?" Ford glanced around at the empty hall, as though worried that someone might be listening. "I've heard things about him. Trust me, he's not for you. If anything, he's using you to cover up—"

"Damn it, Ford. Did you have him followed?" Her palm itched to slap him when he looked away. "Why? Because of me?"

"He's using you."

"Not yet he isn't." Jami smirked at Ford's shocked expression. "What would you say if I told you I was planning to use him?"

"I'd say you're full of shit. He's a Dom. You don't like giving up control unless you're drunk or stoned. And even if you did, you're built all wrong to interest him."

"*What?*"

"He's into guys, Jami. He spent two hours in a hotel room with Luke Carter."

"Ford, that's a stretch. All the players share rooms on the road."

"Luke shares a room with Landon Bower."

"So what? If every time the men were alone together, it meant they were fucking each other, they'd all have asses too sore to skate.

And either way, even if he's doing guys, why does that mean he's using me?" She smirked. "You fucked other girls while we were together. Were *you* using me?"

"Yes." Ford met her eyes. His face went hard. "I was using you. You're the GM's daughter. I was hoping you'd give me some access. But since I ended up being the owner's son, I didn't need you."

Her stomach lurched. She ran her tongue over her teeth and inhaled. "Really? So how does this confession fit into the part where you want me back?"

"I thought you'd appreciate some honesty. Sebastian won't give it to you."

"That's just awesome, Ford. So what is it? You think I've got to choose between the two of you?" She stepped up to him and glared up into his handsome, hard-edged, bad boy face. "I. Don't. Need. Anyone. Got that?"

"I got it. But I could give you—"

"What exactly, hot stuff?" She flipped her hair over her shoulder as she spun on her skate blades. "Did I ever tell you I'm not into reruns?"

"I could treat you right, Jami."

"You had your chance. I wasn't impressed." She gave him one last long look over her shoulder. "Good luck, though. I don't hate you, so I really hope you can find someone nice. A clean-cut chick who can watch you fuck other woman and still curl up in your arms at night and tell you you're all she needs."

"You *were* all I needed, Jami. I just didn't know it," Ford said quietly.

"Well, you weren't all *I* needed. Goodbye, Ford."

She rounded the corner quickly as her composure snapped. Tears streamed down her cheeks and she cursed under her breath. She'd loved him. In that young, I-don't-know-better way, but it had been real at the time. And seeing him brought it all back. Her intense attraction to Sebastian hadn't changed that. She'd thought she was over Ford, but with rehab, and living away from everything that had pitched her into a free fall, she hadn't really had a chance to get over him. They'd had some good times. She remembered sitting in her car, out by the pier, her head on his shoulder, talking about how they both wanted more than what their parents wanted for them. Her dad thought as long as she stayed in school, she'd eventually figure it out. If she stayed in school for the rest of her life, he'd write that off as doing *something*. Ford's father wanted him in the family business. And nothing else would be enough.

They'd made love in that car more times than she could count. It had been in storage while she'd stayed with her grandmother, and when she'd gotten it back, she hadn't thought too much about the memories it held. But now, she had the sudden urge to go out and total it in a ditch. Her loved for the old, funky thing had died with her love for Ford. Or was dying.

Fuck, it hurt.

She paced up and down the hall, and after what seemed like forever, Akira burst through the doors that led to the rink. She squealed, then cut herself off.

"What's wrong?"

"Nothing." Jami went to Akira and hugged her tight. "How did you do? After that reaction, I'd say you did good?"

"If them standing up and cheering is anything to go by? Yes!" Akira giggled. "One of the judges said, 'I would come to see the game just for that performance. You can do better than being an Ice Girl, and I really shouldn't be telling you that!'"

"Wow! Oh, sweetie! You're a sure bet!" The dejection that had seized her like a cold iron fist around her heart loosened its grip. She kept hugging Akira and decided, then and there, that she would make the team. She would do this with Akira.

The door opened and a baby-faced blond waved to her. "Jami? Come on. You're the last one up."

Last? Damn, how had she not noticed that no one else was out here waiting? Going last meant all the judges had probably chosen their favorites. Yeah, she was good on the ice, but was she good enough to make an impression? Getting in had been easy, but Silver couldn't help her any more than she already had. From this point on, it was all on Jami to prove herself.

Akira must have caught the uncertainty in her expression, because she squeezed her arm and said firmly, "You can do this."

"I'm just one out of a hundred girls, Akira. And they're going to want to show they're not taking it easy on me because of who my dad is. How can I make them forget that and give me a chance?"

"Make an impression, Jami. Go out there and put on a performance they won't be able to pass over."

Jami nodded and followed the blond through the long hall that led to the rink. The woman gestured to some shovels and trash cans, set up beside a rack of hockey sticks and asked Jami if she wanted to use them in her performance. Scraping snow off the ice was a big part of the Ice Girl's job.

The sticks drew her attention as she shook her head. She hadn't played hockey in years, but she remembered going to the outdoor rink near their old house with her dad where he taught her how to skate, how to hold a stick, how to control the puck. She suddenly had an idea. A crazy idea.

Looking over the sticks, she paused by the ones in the #11 slot. Sebastian's sticks. She grinned and grabbed one. Hopefully, he wouldn't mind if she borrowed it.

Nice weight. A little long for her, but Dad's sticks had always been too big and they were all she'd ever played with. She looked over at the blond who stood with the door to the rink open, waiting for her.

"Can you get me a few pucks?"

"Sure . . ." The blond went into the equipment room and came out with a small stack. Her plump red lips twisted slightly. "You do know that the Ice Girls don't play hockey, right?"

Really? Damn, and I thought I'd get a chance to put my name on the Cup! Jami resisted the urge to roll her eyes and smiled sweetly. "I know. But the cameras will be rolling for clips for the show, right? I was kinda hoping to put on a performance worth the reel, you know?"

"All right, but . . ." The woman laughed and shook her head. "I usually tell the girls to just smile and make it clear they can captivate the crowd. I have a feeling I should tell you not to miss whatever you're shooting at."

"Good advice." Jami took a step forward, then paused and glanced back at the blond. "Are you one of the judges?"

"Not for this, no. I'm a veteran Ice Girl for the Islanders. A bunch of us signed up to judge the next round. You'll be heading off against us in the final showdown." She held out her hand. "The name's Sahara. I hear you're the GM's daughter?"

Jami shook Sahara's hand and cringed as she nodded. "Yeah. Me getting into the top hundred wasn't really fair."

"No, maybe it wasn't. But you've got to work twice as hard prove you deserve this as much as the rest. They're looking to cut you, to tell you the truth. A few of them are worried that your dad won't like seeing you out there." Sahara jutted her chin toward the stick in Jami's hand. "Give them a reason to keep you around."

"Will do." Jami sucked in all the air she could fit in her lungs and strode out to the ice. She set the pucks on top of the boards by the benches. The music she'd requested, "I Wanna Be Bad" by Willa Ford, started up. She slid out, stretching her legs as she sped up, holding the stick like any hockey player would. Then she spun and skated backward, letting her hair sweep over her face as she smiled provocatively at the judges. Skidding to a stop, skates spitting up snow from the ice, she held the stick between her thighs and twirled around it like a stripper pole dancing. Down low, she dipped back, bracing one hand on the ice as she thrust her hips up, once, twice, before spreading her thighs into the splits even as she slid forward. Her hair whipped over her face as she leapt up.

Murmurs from the judges. She didn't know what to make of them. But she didn't stop as she danced over to the boards, jutting out her chest and grinding down without slowing. As she rose again, she struck out with her hand so the pucks waiting for her went flying. She did another quick spin and took a shot. The puck hit the goal post with a loud *clang*. She giggled and shrugged, dancing some more before taking another shot. Right down the middle. She pantomimed using her stick as a bow and shot an invisible arrow at the judges.

Two more goal posts, just because she liked the sound, then a smooth shot in the top corner. She lifted the stick over her head and dropped to one knee as the music stopped.

Silence.

She held her breath.

Finally, someone spoke up. "Thank you, Miss Richter. That was very nice."

Very nice. She headed off the ice, blinded by the stinging tears filling her eyes. *Very nice.*

They weren't impressed.

Very nice.

"Jami?" Akira caught her by the shoulder. "Oh no. What's wrong?"

"They hated it." Jami swallowed a sob. Damn it, why had she fooled herself into believing she could do this? Why had she put herself out there? They must think she was some kind of joke, flaunting herself like that, after they'd already decided they didn't want her. "Ugh, it wouldn't be so bad if I'd just gone out and skated around a bit. But I tried. I tried so hard to make them see that I have what it takes."

"Stop it! Right now." Akira pushed her against the wall and put her hands on her hips. "This isn't over. You still have the dance tryouts."

"But I can't dance!"

"Oh yes, you can. And I won't let you sleep until you can do the routine."

"Have mercy, girl! I need to sleep!"

"Jami..." Akira glanced down the hall and cursed under her breath. "They want me to do an interview for the show. I hate being in front of the cameras!"

Jami swallowed back her own insecurities, feeling much better dealing with Akira's. At least the girl would make it. And *she* deserved to make it. "You'll do fine. Just be your adorable self. Pretend you're talking to me when you answer their questions."

"I can do that." Akira took a step forward, then paused. "Are you going to be okay? Do you still want me to come over tonight?"

"Hell yeah! I'm planning to drown my sorrows in a bowl of ice cream with chocolate sauce. You in?"

"Absolutely." Akira took her hand and gave it a little squeeze. "You going to hang around or should I catch the bus?"

"No, I'll wait for you." Jami forced a smile to her lips. "I'll go see if my dad's around, chill with him until you're done. I'll be on the fourth floor."

"I'll meet you there."

The air seemed tar thick as Jami made her way to the elevator. She went to her father's office, but it was locked. He was probably with Silver and Landon. Good thing. She wasn't really ready to tell him about the Ice Girl thing. Especially since it seemed like she wasn't doing anything with it. Because she was his daughter.

In the elevator, she realized, for the first time, that she was still carrying around Sebastian's stick. It was about time she brought it back, but for some reason, just holding it made her feel better. The weight in her hands was nice. Familiar. She held the stick against her chest as the elevator went down. Maybe she should think about doing something like what Akira planned to do. Teach kids. She had no idea where to start, but she knew the game good enough to show young girls how to play. And there were girls who wanted to learn. Of course, she had nothing to recommend her, other than being the daughter of a pro team's GM, but rather than let it hold her back, maybe she could use it to her advantage.

Being "Miss Richter" doesn't have to be a bad thing. Maybe it was now, but for girls with dreams of making the pro women's league, they'd figure she—or her dad—had connections. She wanted nothing more than to show her father that his team meant something to her, but she still had to look to her own future. And she didn't have a goal of her own. Maybe this could be it.

She got off the elevator at the basement level, stopped by the equipment room to drop off Sebastian's stick, then headed toward the parking garage. Akira knew where she parked, she could wait for her there, listening to music and drinking one of the cans of Dr. Pepper she kept in a case in her trunk. No need to get all depressed. She'd figure things out.

As she pushed on the bar handle for the garage door, a thick arm crossed her chest. She let out a shocked scream. A hand covered her mouth.

"You did well, *mi cielo.*" His hot breath stirred her hair and she shivered. "I do not understand why you looked so sad before you left the ice."

"Hey, you." Jami leaned back into Sebastian's chest and sighed. "You were watching? I thought you'd forgotten all about me."

"No, *mi cielo,* I hadn't forgotten about you. I have not slept yet. I needed to see you first—we have not spoken in days."

"Why didn't you call?"

"I tried. A lady answered and asked me for my order. I assumed you gave me the wrong number on purpose, but your question makes me wonder if it wasn't a mistake."

She winced and glanced over her shoulder at him. "What number did I give you?"

He told her the numbers and she winced again. The last few were all mixed up. That happened to her sometimes. It had happened to her all the time when she was in high school during math class. She wrote the numbers all screwy and failed test after test. She still hadn't told her dad that her math scores made it so she'd had to take an extra course to get into college. She'd barely passed. One look at the books for the accounting course she'd signed up for to make him happy had her dropping out. Only when she'd been stuck in a bed after an overdose had she admitted to him that college wasn't going to work for her.

And now Sebastian knew she couldn't even write her own cell number right. She hated people knowing that she was stupid. So she tried to laugh it off.

"You had me pretty distracted. Sorry I gave you the wrong number. I'll text you the right one now." She quickly dialed, then waited for Sebastian's phone to buzz, or ring, or whatever it did when he got a text. Her stomach sank when nothing happened.

Sebastian shook his head and moved close to her, backing her into the wall by the door. His lips skimmed her throat and he spoke. "Always in such as rush. Take your time, *cosita*. Tell me the numbers. *Slowly*."

His fingers skimmed up her sides, over the bare flesh between her tiny shirt and the waistband of her skirt. Little jolts of pleasure caused all the fine hairs on her skin to stand on end. His scent, fresh ice and the exotic spice of his cologne, intoxicated her. Drawing enough air to whisper the numbers took more effort than actually remembering what they were. Every time she paused, he gently nibbled and kissed along the length of her throat. So she didn't feel the need to hurry.

She moaned when she said the last number and his lips left her, almost wishing she'd gotten it wrong so they could do that again.

He took out his phone and called her phone, chuckling at her frown when it rang. He caught her chin in one hand and pressed his body against hers. "Perhaps a reward now, *mi cielo*?"

"Mmm." She smiled as he kissed her and brought her hands up to touch his hair, which wasn't black as she'd first thought. It was a deep, dark brown and incredibly soft. She stroked the length as she teased the tip of his tongue with hers, giggling when he pulled away and gave her hair a little tug.

"Naughty girl."

"No, Sir. I am quite well behaved." She slid one thigh between his legs and pressed her breasts to his chest. "Are you ready to take me home yet?"

"We will discuss that after you answer one question." He kissed her again before easing away from her. "What had you so sad?"

"Oh, that." She shrugged and rubbed her arms. The hall felt cold without him holding her. "I was hoping for more than a 'very nice'. But maybe I'm just overly sensitive because the day's been pretty crappy so far."

"How so?"

"Well, my ex came to talk to me. It was weird, and he was asking me about you, and he told me—" *Okay, you're not seriously going to tell him what Ford said, are you?*

Sebastian's eyes narrowed and he gave her a look that said he'd make damn sure she told him everything. "What did he say, Jami?"

"That you're using me. Just like he was."

"Like he was . . ." Sebastian nodded slowly. "Does this have something to do with who your father is?"

"With Ford, it did, but with you . . . I guess it has more to do with the rumors—" She put her hand on his forearm. "Listen, I don't care about the rumors. Even if they're true. I don't think you're faking with me to cover anything, but I want you to know, if you need something that I can't give you . . ."

"Such as?"

"*Anything.* I can't submit to you yet. I need to figure out how I feel about that stuff first." She crossed her arms over her breasts. "Just so we're clear, we're not at the exclusive stage yet. Okay?"

He studied her for what seemed a very long time. Then inclined his head. "We are clear, *mi cielo*."

"You're not mad, are you?"

Shaking his head, he pulled her close and kissed her forehead. "Not at all. I must earn your trust. And there are things I must tell you that require trust as well."

"So we're cool?"

"Yes."

"But you're not taking me home now, are you?"

"No. As eager as I am to have you naked and bound to my bed, completely helpless as I use my hands—" His hands drifted along her outer thighs, up to her ass. His fingers dug into her flesh as he pressed her tight to him so the hard muscles of his thigh rubbed her through her panties. "My mouth." He caught her earlobe between his lips and sucked. Then bit down hard enough for her to moan and wiggle against him. She dissolved into pure liquid heat as he whispered in her ear. "And my cock to make you come over and over again, you are not ready."

She licked her lips and stared up at him. "Fuck, Sebastian. That sounds . . ."

"Yes?"

Amazing. She wanted nothing more than to go with him, to let him have her any way he wanted her. Hell, she wouldn't mind if he took her right here. But the bound and helpless thing . . . "You're right. I'm not ready."

"That will come. We will go out again." He smiled at her. "Are you free on Sunday?"

Sunday? It's only Thursday! She clenched her jaw to keep from scowling and made her expression as pleasant as possible. "Sure, I can fit you in. Just give me a call and we'll meet up somewhere."

Before she could slip through the garage door, Sebastian caught her arm and spoke low. "Keep one thing in mind until we meet again, *mi cielo. En mis sueños, tu ya eres mia.*"

She shivered and her eyes went wide as he released her and walked away without looking back. She had no idea what he'd just said. But she did know one thing.

No matter what, she'd find the strength to submit to this man.

Because if she didn't, someone else would. She'd been okay seeing Ford fuck other woman, but for some reason, she had a feeling that even seeing another woman kneel at Sebastian's feet would tear her apart.

Despite what she'd told him about not being exclusive, the same words repeated, over and over, in her head.

He's mine.

Chapter Six

"Make sure he behaves himself."

Sebastian arched a brow at Chicklet, resting his elbow on the bar, his muscles tense under his black T-shirt as he looked over to make sure they were discussing the same person. He shook his head when he saw her concerned gaze trailing Luke as he sauntered across the club with Demyan. His leather pants rasped against his stool. "The only way I can make sure he behaves is if I collar him and attach his leash to my belt."

"Is it sad that I wouldn't object to that?"

"Not at all, but I imagine he would."

Chicklet groaned, spreading her thighs to expose one fully from the slit in her long leather skirt. She petted her subs, kneeling at either side of the stool she perched on. One, a dark haired beauty who seemed content to hover quietly in Chicklet's shadow. The other a young man who had the appearance of a William Bouguereau's cherub all grown-up. Most of Chicklet's attention was on him tonight.

"I promised Tyler a scene. He really needs it after . . ."

Lips pressed into a thin line, Sebastian inclined his head and caught Tyler's eye. "I was sorry to hear that the procedure was unsuccessful."

Tyler glanced at Chicklet. Once he had her permission to speak, he took a deep breath and forced a smile. "Thank you, Sir. But I'm not ready to give up yet. My doctor's looking into other treatments."

"Good. We could use you out there."

"You've got Demyan and Carter." Tyler smirked. "Together they're *almost* as good as me."

Callahan joined them at the bar with Oriana Delgado, the elder sister of the team's owner, and ruffled Tyler's hair. "I can see cracking your skull didn't affect your ego, kid."

"Hey, hands off my sub, Sloan." Chicklet looped an arm around Oriana's neck. "Unless you want to swap for the night?"

"You might want to ask her husband," Callahan said.

Oriana frowned. "Umm, how about asking me?"

"Or me!" Tyler swallowed hard at Callahan's dark look.

"You don't want to play with me, boy?"

"Hell, no!"

"Manners, pet," Chicklet said, obviously trying very hard not to laugh. "Sloan *is* a Dom here."

"Sorry, Mistress." Tyler shifted on his knees. "Hell no, *Sir*. You're way too fucking hard-core for me."

"Aww, and I reckon Sloan would've had fun playing with him for the night." Max Perron came up behind Oriana and kissed her bare shoulder before curving his hands under her breasts, barely covered by the low V of her black halter top. "And I could've had you all to myself."

"One." Callahan yanked Oriana away from Perron so roughly Sebastian wondered if he should intercede. But Oriana melted Callahan's arms as he took her lips in a brutal kiss. Dark eyes locked on Perron, he bared her breasts. "You sure you don't want me to play, Max?"

Perron groaned as though just watching Callahan toy with his wife turned him on. "Fuck, man . . ."

"Two." Callahan smirked as he teased Oriana's nipples into hard little nubs with his thumbs. "I don't do men. Though I sometimes wonder if you'd get off on seeing that too."

"That don't do nothing for me one way or the other," Perron said.

"Three." Callahan framed Oriana's chin with his hand, speaking to her now. "I have a knife with your name on it."

Oriana's lips parted and a pretty pink blush rose high on her cheeks. She didn't hesitate as Callahan led her away. Perron looked eager as he followed them.

Sebastian rose from his stool and glanced over at Chicklet. "I'll have to supervise this scene—please don't tell me how good a Dom Callahan is; I've never seen him do knife-play. But I'll keep an eye on Luke."

Gesturing for her subs to rise, Chicklet shot him a grateful smile. "I won't tell you. And thanks, I'd appreciate that. I'll take over the second shift so you can play if you want to."

He nodded, but he doubted he'd be playing tonight. The men

joked around with one another, both here and in the locker room, but "I'm not into men" was constantly repeated, as though they all wanted to make sure everyone knew it. How would they react if they found out he *was* into men?

Other than Jami, he hadn't met a woman who interested him since... well, since Silver Delgado, the team's current owner. And that was long before she'd become the owner or met the men she was now committed to. Of course, his interest hadn't gone far beyond introducing her to the lifestyle. He'd like to believe his interest in Jami went further, but it was hard to say.

As the music—something by Marilyn Manson, a singer not at all to his tastes—started up, Sebastian made his way to the knife scene through the small crowd filing in. He paused once to check on an erotic piercing scene. The sub on the table didn't even wince as her Dom threaded a black ribbon through the rings in her back. She smiled dreamily as the man stopped to pet her hair with one gloved hand and questioned her, not continuing until he got a response. The redness around the top four piercings, of the sixteen running up either side of her spine, showed they were new. The Dom checked them, cleaning tiny droplets of blood with an alcohol swab before leaning down to kiss her. Very attentive. She was in good hands.

A whip cracked. Screams filled the room in a lovely chorus, drowning out the dreadful music. Sebastian rounded the roped-off area where Callahan had Oriana cuffed to the bondage frame. Oriana whimpered as Callahan cut through her shirt, but her cheeks were flushed with arousal. As Callahan moved around behind her, he handed the knife to Perron, who stood nearby, and pulled out his wallet. He took out a credit card and sliced it down Oriana's back.

She screamed. Callahan laughed.

"That's just... twisted."

Sebastian glanced over to where Luke had stepped up beside him. His lips quirked. "Callahan is a sadist."

"I know, but..." Luke glanced over at the knives displayed on a small, white folding table. "Not sure I get it. He never actually cuts her. What does she get out of it?"

And you would get it if he cut her? Sebastian had a feeling he understood Chicklet's concern. Luke wasn't asking what Callahan got out of the scene. He was curious about the sensations of the submissive. And he was reckless enough to go for the experience on a whim. Wayne had given him an easy way to do just about anything without admitting he was submissive. If he wanted to be a "good Dom," he would try it himself first.

From the corner of his eye, Sebastian saw Wayne watching the scene—no, *watching* Luke. He hovered close to the door to keep an eye out for anyone who didn't belong here, but he, like Sebastian, would be relieved at some point so he could enjoy the latter half of the night.

But he wouldn't be enjoying it with Luke. Not if Sebastian could help it.

He's a teammate. You can't play with him.

Of course, he wouldn't actually be playing. He would keep things strictly educational.

Picking up a long knife with a curved blade, Sebastian moved close to Luke. His lips slanted up as Luke's dark blue eyes widened. "A certain amount of trust is necessary for knife play. We've been teammates for months. Can you give me that trust?"

"Yeah, but . . . hey, we're starting the playoffs in a few days." Luke retreated until his back hit the wall and held up his hands. His throat worked as he swallowed. "Might be a bad idea for you to—"

"I won't hurt you." Sebastian let his tone drop as he reached out and fisted his hand into the front of Luke's shirt. "Lace your fingers behind your neck."

Luke obeyed, and Sebastian studied him for a moment, taking note of the way Luke's dick had swelled in the confines of his leathers. He smiled as he ran the blunt side of the blade down the curve of Luke's throat and pinned him to the wall with the press of his hips. Their dicks rubbed together through the layers of leather.

"I haven't cut you, haven't done much to you at all, but you're already reacting to the threat of having the knife touch your flesh."

"Oh, God." Luke's eyes fluttered shut. "I think I get it now."

"Do you?" Sebastian slipped the blade between them, and Luke went perfectly still. He gave himself enough space to cut the top two buttons off Luke's shirt. "Imagine me using this knife to cut all your clothes from your body. Then I may or may not use something else on your skin. You wouldn't know, because I wouldn't let you see. I'd only let you feel."

"Ramos . . ."

"Sebastian."

"Fuck, Seb—" Luke's breath came out in hot little pants. "Stop. Please stop."

Sebastian let out a harsh, cruel laugh. He would stop before things went too far. At this point, he could still play it off as having taught the young man a lesson. But the way Luke's lips parted tempted him to do more. So he spoke loud enough for everyone around them to hear. "Stop is not a safeword, Luke. Say it or I *will* hurt you."

Luke shook his head. Then scowled. "Red. Happy?"

The boy was much smarter than people gave him credit for.

"Yes. You were very good, *niño*." Sebastian moved away from Luke and placed the knife on the table. He grinned at Callahan when the man chuckled, then waved Luke away. "I believe Demyan has taken a couple of waitresses to the classroom. Why don't you join him?"

"Why don't you go home and teabag your mom." Luke shoved his hands in his pockets and stalked away.

Staring after the young man, Sebastian shook his head. He hated leaving Luke like that. Likely confused by his own reactions. Possibly angry at himself for having them. But it would be better for him to find a woman to slake his arousal with. Safer if he proved to himself, and to Sebastian, that he was a heterosexual man with no interest in experimenting with his own sex.

Because Sebastian didn't know if he could restrain himself again if Luke gave him another opening. And he didn't want to put the young man in the same position he was in, having to hide who he was from his teammates. Being submissive was hard enough for him to deal with, but if he found a Domme, the others would accept it as they had with Tyler.

Unfortunately, he would likely look for a sub. A young woman who he could Dom because that would make him feel more like a man.

A damn pity. For him and the woman. Neither would be satisfied, but there was nothing Sebastian could do about it.

For a while, he wondered aimlessly around the club, trying to distract himself by doing his job monitoring the many scenes. He caught sight of Luke from time to time. First at the bar. Then observing a whipping. Something drew him away and Sebastian sighed with relief. His relief died a quick death as he spotted a girl with dark blue hair slipping out the back door with Luke close behind her.

Mi cielo. He ground his teeth as he checked his watch. Ten minutes before he could leave. He wouldn't abandon his post, but as soon as it was over...

I'll be damned if I lose them both.

* * * *

Jami had never seen anything so fucking... *hot.* From the shadows of the stairwell, she watched all the scenes going on around her in a daze, not sure where to look because everything fascinated her.

I wish Akira was here. She'd lost her nerve at the last minute, at first trying to convince Jami it was a bad idea, then making her promise that she'd call with each and every detail. Not that *any* amount of details could really get across what Jami had seen or how she felt just being here. She wanted to try it all and that scared the hell out of her. Not so much the needles, or the piercings, or the whips—if they weren't safe, Dad wouldn't let people do it. But the longing, deep within, when she saw men and women submit, saw them kneel to be stroked like a pampered pet, or strapped up to be beaten, made her very, very afraid.

You're freakin' weird, Jami. You'd rather be whipped than kneel? Your therapist would have a field day with that one.

The thing was, the idea of kneeling for Sebastian didn't bother her. She could see herself slowly lowering to her knees, pulling the zipper to his leather pants down with her teeth, taking him in her mouth to taste and tease him with her tongue. Only, if she knelt like those subs did, it would mean more than getting in position to suck cock. There was something... vulnerable about the position, about the way a sub gazed up at their Dom, surrendering so much more than their bodies.

Of course, a person could surrender with a look alone. Luke Carter, a guy who'd flirted with her a time or two at the forum, had done just that as Sebastian had held him against the wall with a knife to his throat. No one else had made much of the little scene, but Jami saw the chemistry between them. At one point, she could have sworn Carter would kiss Sebastian. Which aroused her and pissed her off all at once.

Maybe Sebastian was just teaching him something. Her dad taught people. She'd overheard Silver and Oriana talking about how well her dad had taught Sloan to use a whip.

Silver never sounded jealous about what her men did at the club. *I'm not jealous.*

Okay, that wasn't *entirely* true. But why should she be jealous? *They're hockey players. They can't be gay.*

What a stupid thought. Just because no hockey players in the league had come out, that didn't mean there were none either attracted to, or in a relationship with, other men. Denying what she'd seen wouldn't help matters. The fact was *she'd* told Sebastian they weren't exclusive. *After* hearing about him and Carter sharing a room from Ford. She'd pretty much *given* him to the competition.

So what was she going to do about it?

Before she could decide, she felt the skin-crawling sensation of someone watching her. She glanced over and spotted Carter heading toward her.

She bolted for the exit. Had he recognized her? Damn it, if he called her name out in here—her breath lodged in her throat as she spun to shut the door and saw Sebastian over by a needle play scene, frowning right at her. She gulped as she tugged the door shut.

Her car was parked a block away. She could probably make it there before Carter caught up with her; she was pretty fast, but the urge to run left her as she pictured the look on Sebastian's face. He'd probably be a step behind Carter, demanding to know why she'd come here.

She would answer with the truth. She'd wanted to find out if she was ready.

I am. But is Sebastian?

Well, he'd taken the opportunity to explore his options. Maybe Luke could give him something she couldn't.

Maybe I should find out what.

* * * *

The girl hadn't been all that hard to catch. Not that she'd made any real effort to get away. Luke trapped her against the brick wall in the alley behind the club and grinned as she struggled to catch her breath. She shook her messed up, dark blue hair away from her face.

He stared into her wide hazel eyes, barking out a laugh. "Jami Richter. You been back long?"

"I got back last week." She panted, gazing up at him as though seeing him for the first time. "You should go back inside before someone catches you out here with me."

"Do you want me to leave?"

Her throat worked as she swallowed. "I don't know."

He pressed a little closer to her, carefully running his thumb down the side of her throat to feel her racing pulse, watching the way her tongue darted over her bottom lip. "What were you doing in the club? Does Daddy know you're here?"

"No, so don't be an asshole and tell him, okay?" She ducked her head. "I was just . . ."

"Curious?" He smiled as her pale cheeks got nice and pink. He'd caught sight of her from the corner of his eye, all long legs and a tight ass barely covered by a cut-off jean skirt, perky breasts in a black studded bra. Kick-ass five strap knee boots. Rocker-chick style, but not tough looking. Sweet. Submissive. Just the type of woman he liked to play with.

She's the GM's daughter.

He snorted.

So what?

"I wanted to see what all this shit was about." She wrinkled her nose. "I came, I saw, I'm bored now."

"That's because you've got no one to play with, cutie."

She bit her bottom lip, giving him a look torn between pride and need. "You'd play with me? I thought you'd . . ."

"I'd what, Jami?" He cupped her cheek, searching her face for some clue as to what was bothering her. "Hey, you don't seriously think I'd rat you out?"

"You might think you were doing what's best." She dropped her gaze. "Most of the players still see me as a little girl."

"Not me." He tipped her chin up. "But I need to know how you want to play. It's a little too nippy to flip up your cute little skirt and spank you out here."

Giggling, she glanced toward the door, then trailed her finger down the center of his chest. "Is that what you want to do to me?"

Holy fuck. This girl was trouble. He would do anything she wanted, but that wasn't the point, was it? She wanted a taste of what she'd seen, and damn it, he wanted to give it to her. "Will you do anything I ask?"

"You mean, like, submit to you?" Her hair drifted over one eye. She shivered as he tucked it behind her ear. "I don't know if I could do it straight up, but . . ." She batted her eyelashes. "Maybe as a game."

"A game?"

Her impish grin, the way her eyes lit up with mischief, made her absolutely irresistible. His gaze locked on her lips as she whispered, "Blackmail."

He blinked at her. "Umm . . ."

"Say you *were* mean enough to threaten to tell my daddy you'd found me here. Because you want me so bad you'll do anything to have me. What would you say to me?"

He chuckled. "You're beautiful, baby, but I hate that outfit. Take it off."

The dim light in the alley caressed her face as her chin jutted up. Her eyes were bright with humor as her tone sharpened with feigned defiance. "A cheesy line? Oh, please. You think I'll get naked for you? Strip and call *you* 'Sir'?" Her lips curled in a sneer. "I may be a bit kinky, but I'm not a sub."

Luke snorted, getting right into the game. "I've heard that one before."

"I'm sure you've heard them all. I'm not a sub. I'm a lesbian—anyone every try 'I'm just not interested'?"

Feisty. This is going to be fun. "No, actually, that's one I haven't heard before."

"Well." She tossed her head in a way that slapped her hair across his face. "Now you have. I'm warning you, Luke, if you don't move on your own, I'll make you. And that could ruin your night."

"Make me? How will you do that?" He blocked her knee jab and grabbed her wrists before she could take a swing. For a split second, he worried that she'd forgotten that they were just playing around. But her pupils dilated as she flattened her tits against his chest. She didn't test his loose grip on her wrists. So he kept going. "Come on. You can do better than that. Why don't you scream? There are at least ten guys in there that will come to your rescue and kick my ass."

She held her breath, glancing toward the door to the back of the club again. "You know why I won't."

"Because then Daddy will find out. Damn, you're pretty stuck then." He bent down to press his cheek to hers and whispered in her ear, "So what are you going to do?"

"Shit, Carter, what do you want?" Her tongue wet her bottom lip. "If I suck your dick, will you keep your mouth shut?"

Fuck, yeah. But he wasn't sure she was ready to go that far, so he shook his head slowly. "That's the going rate, but since I like you, I'll cut you a deal. I'll kiss you, touch you a little, and stop when you ask me to. Sound fair?"

Her eyes narrowed with suspicion. "Kissing and a bit of touching? That's it?"

"You sound disappointed."

"Bite me."

"That wasn't part of the deal." He lowered his lips to her throat. "But I can be generous."

As his teeth closed on her soft flesh, she squirmed, whimpering. He bit harder until a gasp escaped her and ruffled his hair. Moving up with tiny nips, he clasped both her wrists with one hand, latched onto her chin with the other, and slowly slid his lips across hers, teasing her with the tip of his tongue. Fuck, she had to be the sweetest thing he'd ever tasted. His eyes drifted shut as he leaned into the kiss, dipping deep with his tongue, forgetting to hold her wrists as he lost himself to her response. Her fingers laced behind his neck and she wiggled against him, as though trying to contain herself. And failing.

They didn't need the game anymore. He opened his eyes and she was looking right at him, at his mouth, like she wanted more. And hell, his mouth wasn't a pretty sight, so he must have done something right.

"Jami, you need to tell me when to stop." He kissed her again and slid his hand into her bra. Her tiny nipple hardened as he circled it with his thumb. He pushed the material off her breast and dropped down to suck that hard nub into his mouth. "Tell me or I won't."

She made a sound that seriously didn't sound like "stop." Not even close. His dick throbbed as he slid his hand between her thighs and rubbed the swatch of damp, silky cloth over her clit.

"Tell me."

"I can't!" Her thighs quivered against his hand and she moaned. "Carter—"

"Luke."

"Luke!" She let out another whimper and spread her thighs farther apart. "Please!"

He bared her pussy and slipped one finger inside her. "What you saw in there turned you on, didn't it? Would you like to try that with me? A little bondage—or maybe I *will* spank you. I bet you'd get off after just a few smacks."

"No . . . I don't know." Her warmth clamped around him and her nails raked at his scalp. When his fingers went still, she thunked her head against the brick wall. "I want to try."

"Good girl." He rewarded her by adding another finger, which he could only push in to the first knuckle. "It's been a long time, hasn't it, cutie?"

"Yes!"

A bit more pressure and he managed to get both fingers inside her. But she was so tight, his dick was out of the question in this position. Of course, there was always the backseat of his car.

Sucking in a deep, deep breath, he withdrew his fingers and straightened. "Come with me, baby. I don't want to fuck you in an alley." *Okay, I do, but it's not happening.* "We'll go somewhere where we can get comfortable."

She hesitated for less than a second before nodding. He grinned and took her hand.

His back hit something hard. Maybe another brick wall? Not that they had a habit of sprouting out of pavement.

"This 'price' for silence—who pays it for you?" A heavy hand dropped onto his shoulder, and the smooth accent drizzled down his spine. Which would be cool if it was another chick. But there was no mistaking Seb for a woman. The big man slapped his hands against the wall, caging both him and Jami. "I stood back, ready to let this go at the 'kissing and a bit of touching' you asked for. But what kind of man would I be to let you take advantage of Mr. Richter's daughter?"

Luke swallowed and looked down at Jami. The lust-filled haze that had stolen her away had faded. She looked nervous—not that he blamed her. Seb must have gotten some flak about those pictures. What if he told Richter to get on his good side? To protect his career?

No. Seb wouldn't do that.

You sure about that, Carter?

"Seriously, man. We're teammates." Luke gave Seb a weak smile. "That's got to count for something?"

Seb's lips slit into a cold smile as his hand curved around the nape of Luke's neck. "Yes, it does. I'll stop before you ask me to. You're not ready for all I want from you, but I'm patient."

Before I ask him to? Is he fucking high? Blocking Jami with his body, just in case the man *had* lost it, Luke turned to face him. "Look, buddy. I don't know how they do things in LA, but here, straight men don't suck cock. *Comprende?*"

"Can you look me in the eyes when you say that, Luke?" Seb took hold of Luke's collar and used it to jerk him forward. "Tell me a 'straight man' would react the way you did when I touched you inside the club. That he would hold still as I rub against him and make it clear how I want to use his body."

His dick was already hard. Because of Jami. And it stayed that way because she was right behind him, wet and ready. His balls tightened because he wanted to get rid of this guy and continue where he'd left off. Seb didn't turn him on, he . . . he freaked him out. But, damn it, he had to do something to shut him up.

I know who I'm into. If the guy wants to get his rocks off by groping me again, what-fucking-ever. Seb was pretty big. He wouldn't be able to stop him from doing whatever he wanted. Like . . . his ass clenched. A total no-go-there reaction.

"A straight man would tell you to go fuck yourself. And I'm telling you exactly that." Luke reached back and Jami grabbed his hand. "But you've got me, so do what you've gotta, man. Squeeze my fucking ass and get it over with. But I ain't putting your dick in my mouth."

"You will do as I say, Luke." A swift motion and Seb had his hand in Luke's hair, jerking his head back painfully, his dark eyes narrow as he leaned down. "We can start with a kiss."

Luke twisted and winced. The man wasn't letting go. "I'd *rather* suck your dick."

Seb smiled. "Well, I am willing to negotiate."

* * * *

"Maybe I should leave the two of you to discuss this." Jami tried not to sound bitter, but she was woman enough to admit defeat. Sebastian wanted Luke. Not her. She'd almost felt guilty when Sebastian had stepped up behind Luke, but he hadn't looked jealous, like most men would when catching another man with their woman. Hell, he hadn't looked at her at all. She slipped out from behind Luke, tossing back, "Don't worry. Sebastian won't say anything."

"*Mi cielo.*"

Her knees locked. Her spine went stiff. She fisted her hands by her sides and kept her back to the men. "What?"

Steady footsteps behind her. Fingers slipped through hers as Sebastian spoke quietly. "You didn't truly believe I would let you go so easily?"

Spinning around, she stared at him. "Why would you want me when you have him? I saw you together in there! You—"

"You told me you did not want to be 'exclusive.'"

"Yeah, but—"

"From what I saw out here, you obviously meant it." His brow furrowed slightly. "Should I assume that you are no longer interested in me?"

"No!"

"What the fuck! You two are together?" Luke's sharp tone cut through the silence of the alley as he moved toward them, stopping close enough for her to catch the glare of the streetlights in his narrowed eyes. "Were you fucking playing me? What are you, bait? Giving him a way to blackmail me into letting him fuck me?"

Jami sneered. *In denial much?* "He doesn't need to blackmail you for that."

"I'm not a fucking fag—I mean, not that being queer or . . . fuck, whatever's PC, is a bad thing. No offense." Luke's cheeks were blotchy red as he glanced up at Sebastian who simply gave him a blank look. "You're gay. And you don't want people to know. I'm good with that. And flattered, really, but—"

"*Niño.*" Sebastian's jaw hardened when Luke opened his mouth. Still holding on to Jami, he crowded Luke back toward the wall. "Be. Silent."

Luke drew in a noisy breath and clamped his lips together.

"I am about as gay as you are a Dom. No, perhaps slightly more, but that is irrelevant. Think carefully before you argue." Sebastian turned to her now, and his grip on her hand tightened. "Why are you here?"

She winced. He obviously wasn't thrilled that she *was* here. And she didn't think it was because he'd caught her with Luke. "I needed to see what this was all about. To see if I was ready . . ."

Sebastian nodded slowly and reached out to tuck a strand of hair behind her ear. "Are you?"

"Yes."

Clearing his throat, Luke slowly moved away from them. "Glad you two worked that out. I should go."

"You are no longer interested in Jami buying your silence?" Sebastian didn't physically block Luke's escape route, wasn't really holding Jami in place anymore, but something in his stance made either of them budging an inch seem like a bad idea. "I would hate to think I ruined things for you both tonight."

"You didn't—I mean, it was just a . . ." Luke scuffed his shoes on the pavement and rubbed his hands on his leathers as he met her eyes like he wasn't sure she'd want Sebastian to know about their game. "You know that, right?"

Fuck. Playing with him had been a bad idea on so many levels. "Dammit, Luke. You seriously think I'm going to let him believe any of that was real?"

"I don't know."

"Give me some fucking credit." Her face heated up as Sebastian arched a brow at her. "We were playing a game and . . . we got a bit carried away. But after seeing the two of you in there, I needed to . . ."

"You needed to be part of it, *mi cielo.*" Sebastian kissed her throat and eased her back against the wall. "You still do."

She shook her head, but he put his finger over her lips before she could speak.

"I want to see you as you were—so close to complete surrender." He moved to the side, head tilted slightly as he studied Luke. "Can you bring her to that point again, or are you so eager to leave?"

Luke's tongue trailed his bottom lip. "She's your woman—"

"Tonight, she is *our* woman." Sebastian's tone changed, taking on an alluring quality, pacing her pulse, seeming to control the way she drew in each breath. As Luke approached her, his inhale and exhale matched hers. Sebastian caged them together once again, and they both stopped breathing as he whispered in Luke's ear, "Get her ready for us, *semental.*"

Hot lips covered hers. Bricks dug into her back as Luke pressed against her. She couldn't help but respond to the wild passion in his kiss, even though it was so, so wrong. The man she wanted had given her to another. Was guiding his hands to her breasts, to her cunt, curving his fingers into her. She whimpered as two fingers thrust deep, one Luke's, one Sebastian's. She could feel how Sebastian's was slightly longer, thicker, while Luke's was rougher. And they touched all the right spots. And she knew it was because of Sebastian.

For a moment, it was almost as though Luke wasn't between them at all.

"Sebastian . . ." She moaned as the sizzling pressure built up within, reached out, needing to touch him.

A gruff sound escaped Luke as he raked his fingers into her hair. He stared into her eyes as he sucked on her bottom lip. His finger thrust in deep as he bit down hard. The metallic taste of her blood came with the flick of his tongue.

He smiled against her lips. "A little kinky?"

"Mmm." She let her lips part and arched up to him, loving the feral way he kissed her, as though he'd lost all control. "Just a little."

"I want you, Jami. I want to fuck you so bad—*God!*" He kissed her again, moving so he was flush against her, so she could feel Sebastian's hand sliding down over the bulge between them. She cupped his face in her hands as he groaned and his eyes snapped open. "I can't—"

"Stop thinking about it." She panted as the thrust of his finger became erratic and Sebastian's slick finger slipped over her clit. Her thighs shook as the sensations pooled into a fiery undercurrent of pleasure. As Sebastian stroked Luke's cock, she felt tension in his kiss. He shook his head and his lips left hers.

"Can't. Wrong—"

"No, it's not!" Jami dug her nails into his shoulders as his head dropped back. Her eyes met Sebastian's seconds before he claimed Luke's lips. Everything within clamped down and her eyes teared as Luke's fingers went still. The dull throb of denial was almost painful, but she held in her protests. Something had changed, and suddenly, it didn't feel like Sebastian was sharing her with Luke. It felt like . . . like she was sharing Luke with Sebastian. He could have her easy; she'd made that much clear.

But Luke . . . he couldn't have Luke without her. And he wanted them both.

Her lips curved as she brought her mouth to Luke's throat and slid her hand up over his chest.

* * * *

Luke groaned into Seb's mouth and fought to resume the steady pumping of his fingers into Jami's snug, wet slit, but the pressure on his lips and his dick stole any control he had over his own body. The gentle kisses running up his throat made him shiver, such a fucking sweet contrast to the almost violent way Seb was kissing him.

Damn it, *Seb* was kissing him. He should stop him. Should knock him on his ass and beat the shit out of him—or at least get in a few good shots before Seb had a chance to get back up—but not just yet. No one had kissed him like this in a long time. Sometimes it felt like he was that guy with the hooker in *Pretty Woman*. His money made him good enough to fuck, but not to kiss.

You're letting a dude kiss you, Carter! His brain kicked into high gear, and his hand fisted at his side.

Soft, slender fingers worked his fist open. Jami's hips dipped forward, urging his thick, clumsy fingers in deeper. Torn between mind-numbing desire and self-loathing, nothing he did seemed right. What would a girl like Jami want with a guy like him when she had a guy like Seb?

Hell, he couldn't even figure out why *Seb* would want him. Or why he gave a shit either way.

A low growl rumbled from Seb's massive chest, ripping Luke from his wandering thoughts as it vibrated straight down his spine. The man tasted like some kind of dark, foreign beer, which Luke never liked until he learned not to guzzle it down just to see how fast he could get wasted. Those bruising lips were slightly salty with sweat. And hot. So goddamn hot.

The kiss gentled just as Seb drew away, and Luke made a rough sound in his throat as he latched onto the collar of Seb's shirt. No matter how messed up this all was, he wasn't ready for it to end.

"She's close, Luke." Seb took ahold of Luke's wrist and nodded toward Jami. "We should make her wait."

After drawing his wet fingers from Jami's pussy, Luke sucked them clean, smirking when Jami clenched her thighs together and rasped out a curse. He smacked his lips and focused on Seb. "Why make her wait?"

"If she was your sub, would you reward her for coming here on her own?" Seb smiled at Jami's stare. "You did say you were ready, *gatita*?"

Jami licked her lips and nodded.

"Good. Then Luke and I will show you what happens when a

naughty sub goes to a club alone and two Doms decide to steal her away to play with her."

Now that sounds like fun. Luke grinned. "Yeah, she's lucky it's us."

Seb arched a brow. "Is she?"

The way Jami paled at the implication in Seb's tone made Luke even harder. Props to the place where he'd bought his leathers—his dick would have ripped through cheap stitching.

Rubbing her arms to warm her chilled flesh, he spoke softly in her ear. "Last chance to back out, boo."

"You think you scare me, stud?"

Luke winced. Right. She didn't know about the stupid scene with Silver, when *he'd* called "red" after letting Silver push him too far. Nice fucking control for a Dom. "I scare most subs."

"I'm not most—I'm not a sub." She rolled her eyes and sighed. "Can we skip the labels? I have a feeling you'll have a problem with them by the end of the night."

Shaking his head, Luke caught her wrist before she could move away from him. "What's that supposed to mean?"

Her lips curled as she stepped up to him and poked him in the chest. "*You're* not a sub. You're not gay. All the things you're not are going to make getting kidnapped by you two pretty boring."

"*Mi cielo.*" Seb curved his hand around the back of her neck and locked his arm across her chest. "I promise you, being kidnapped by us will not be boring." He wrapped her hair around his hand and tugged so she was forced to look up at him. "But it would be wise to be a little afraid. Luke, I've seen the way you handle ropes—you are quite skilled. You will find a new hemp rope in my bag." He nodded toward a small black sports bag on the ground by the back door of the club. "Please use it to bind our pretty little captive."

"I'm not a big fan of hemp—not unless I have a chance to treat it myself."

"They can be bought preconditioned."

"Yeah, I know. But it's not the same." Luke shrugged as he went to fetch the rope. He unwound it, somehow feeling more powerful, more comfortable with the whole scene, as he played the smooth length through his hands. He hadn't gotten a chance to tie anyone up in a while. Getting the chance to do so again was like picking up a stick for the first time after an injury. Using Seb's rope kinda felt like using someone else's stick, but all that mattered was it was in his hands again. A lost limb returned, functioning as it should.

The heavy weight of Seb's eyes on him brought his head up.

Seb motioned him over. "Something simple. Before she's tempted to escape."

Suddenly, Jami was free, and Seb was watching her, a hint of amusement on his face as she tripped sideways. Her gaze snapped to Luke and she inhaled over a laugh. Right before she bolted.

Luke snorted and surged after her, rolling the rope from his hand to his elbow as he ran, his long strides eating across the distance before she reached an old blue Beetle at the end of the block and started fumbling with the keys. She giggled, then screamed when he latched onto her wrists, using his weight to hold her against the car as he looped the rope around them and bound her nice and tight. He looked toward the club. No one was outside, and the street was empty, so there were no witnesses to their little game, but the risk of getting caught thrilled him. His heart pounded as he hauled Jami up and slung her over his shoulder.

Now they just had to decide. Seb's car or his?

"Where are your keys, Jami?" Seb asked as he came to stand at Luke's side. "Your car will have to be moved if we don't want to draw suspicion—it is fairly unique."

"In my left boot." Jami gasped before pressing her face against Luke's back. "Please, please just get me out of here before someone comes out. If anyone sees me . . ."

"Yes, *gatita*, I know." Seb's lips thinned. "I told you I do not care who your father is, but we're both well aware of the risk to my—and now Luke's—career if he learns of any of this. Consider that before you do anything so foolish again."

Luke heard Jami swallow. Felt her nod. Her body went slack as she whispered, "I'm sorry."

Seb nodded, then got the key out of her boot. He gave Luke directions and slapped his shoulder before climbing into the car.

Jami didn't speak again until he had her buckled into the backseat of his own car, parked the next street over. Before he closed the door, she bit her lip and looked up at him, her eyes pleading. "Don't think I'm a freak, 'kay?"

He blinked and reached out to touch her cheek. "Why would I think that?"

"Normal chicks don't do stuff like this."

A wide grin spread across his lips. "A normal chick wouldn't interest me. Or Seb, I think. And listen, either of us start analyzing things, and we might as well call it a night. I'm trying not to think too much. The morning is for regrets."

She smiled. "Very true."

"But if you want to go home, just say so. No hard feelings."

"I don't want to go home." She took a deep breath. "Just drive. Get me to Sebastian's place before I change my mind."

"Yes, ma'am." He leaned over to give her a quick kiss and spoke against her lips. "I should say all kinds of pretty words, but I can't think of anything but spreading your thighs and putting my mouth on your cunt. A nice guy would take things slow, but I'm not a nice guy, Jami."

Her teeth caught his bottom lip. She tugged lightly on it, then teased him with her tongue, backing away with a laugh when he groaned. "If you were a nice guy, *I* wouldn't be interested."

Hell, he could fuck her, right here, right now, and she probably wouldn't object. Why he held back freaked him out a bit, but he managed to get behind the wheel and drive straight to Seb's place without being too tempted to pull over and have his way with her. He wanted to see what Seb had planned. For them both.

Which was pretty messed up. But he couldn't find it in him to care.

Chapter Seven

Sebastian made himself comfortable on his brown leather sofa, heavy black bathrobe parted to reveal his bare chest and black boxer briefs. His lips curved slightly as he pictured the looks on Jami's and Luke's faces when he'd found them in the alley. At first, he'd been furious. The game had seemed so real. But Luke coming quickly to her defense, Jami being so honest about her feelings, had him seeing them both in a very different light. They were beautiful together, Passionate and playful.

But they need me.

The way they touched, and kissed, was wild, desperate, like the starving served a feast. He'd arrived just in time to stop them from devouring what should be savored. They had a spark between them that would flare up and burn out untended, leaving nothing but smoke and tears.

He couldn't be sure a relationship between the three of them wouldn't end the same. But he could make sure no one was hurt tonight.

As a car pulled in on his quiet street, he steepled his fingers under his chin. Laughter preceded them to the front door of his house. A knock and the door swung open. He smiled, pleased that he'd read Luke right. The young man knew he was welcome here and didn't hesitate before carrying Jami over the threshold.

Jami's lips parted as she caught sight of him. She tugged at her bound wrists as Luke set her on her feet. "Sebastian, I want to—"

"Quiet." Sebastian shrugged off his robe, letting it fall to the sofa. "You do not speak unless you are asked a direct question." He arched a brow as she gaped at him, then continued when her mouth snapped shut. "Luke, our prisoner is rather overdressed."

"I agree." Luke turned her to face the wall and undid the ropes. He kicked them aside when they fell and raked his fingers into Jami's hair, using it to keep her in place. "You have a choice. Either strip on your own, or I'll cut your clothes off. Which means you'll be naked for as long as we have you."

"I'll take them off." Jami sagged against the wall when Luke released her. "Just... I need to call my friend. Akira. I promised I would when I got home. I don't want her to worry."

Sebastian inclined his head and sat back as Luke joined him on the sofa. Jami pulled her cell phone from her boot and paced as she spoke to her friend in a hushed voice, nodding and giggling before hanging up. He took a moment to admire her, standing there before them with her feet shoulder-width apart, tough in stance and wardrobe, her eyes filling with uncertainty as he and Luke waited.

Luke, for his part, didn't remind her of the choice she'd made. Slouched back on the sofa, he rested his ankle on his knee and absently scratched the golden stubble on his jaw. He showed a great amount of patience for one so young. Then again, Sebastian had seen some of that patience on the ice, when the man held on to the puck to make a calculated shot or pass. He had the qualities of a good Dom. Only lacked the self-assurance.

They could work on that together.

Letting out a long-suffering sigh, Jami put her hands on her hips and frowned at him. "What are you waiting for?"

"You were told to strip, *gatita*." Sebastian gave her a slow, indulgent smile. "Do you require assistance?"

"No, I just thought..." She glanced over at the door. "This whole scene—"

"Try for the door and I will hurt you." Sebastian rose and prowled toward her, languorously cutting off her escape route. "I assumed you would do as you were told to save yourself some pain. Was I mistaken?"

She shook her head, taking a step back for each one he took forward. Her hand hovered over her throat. She didn't seem to notice that Luke had slipped up behind her until her back hit his chest. With a little yelp, she spun around.

"You're in a lot of trouble, little girl." Luke's eyes took on an evil glint. "Do you have any idea what we're going to do to you?"

"N-no." She reached around blindly and exhaled loudly when Sebastian took her hand. Her light laugh sounded relieved. "Sorry, this is suddenly a lot more intense than I thought it would be."

Sebastian smiled, pleased that she found reassurance in holding on to him. He stroked her knuckles with his thumb. "The game can be very intense, *mi cielo*, but you can end it with 'red' if you need to."

"I know." She squeezed his hand, then squared her shoulders. "I promise, if you let me go, I won't tell anyone. Please, *please* don't hurt me!"

Her acting skills left much to be desired, but it didn't matter. She was ready for him to go back "in character". "I don't think we can take your word for it. If I am going to risk being traded somewhere like Columbus—" He pressed his lips together to hold in a laugh when both Jami and Luke shuddered. "You are going to make it worth my while. You have five seconds to remove your clothing."

"Or what?"

"Or I will let Luke cut them from you as he said he would. Then I will tie you to my bed and we will take turns fucking you." His lips curved as her eyes widened. "Once we're done for the night, I will lock you in a cage and we will see if you are more cooperative in the morning."

She licked her bottom lip as though considering her options. Which, strangely enough, made him even harder. Few of the women or men he'd played with in the past enjoyed such extremes. Then again, part of the attraction was that Jami was different.

But she wasn't ready for that.

"Think carefully, *putita*." He growled close to her ear. Her pulse sped up at the insult, and her short breaths became a shallow pant. His words excited her. "You will be locked in the cage without food or water until we decide to give it to you. We will control everything you do until we decide to release you."

Luke had paled slightly, but he nodded as he moved to Jami's side and framed her jaw with his hand. "You'll have to beg just to take a piss."

"Fuck." Jami held her breath, then lowered her eyes. "I don't want that. I'll cooperate."

Sebastian folded his arms over his chest. Luke stepped away.

Jami tugged at her bottom lip with her teeth as she unzipped her short jean skirt. She eased it down, then crouched to unbuckle her boots. A flush spread over her cheeks as she straightened and unclipped her bra. Her small breasts were pale, with tiny rose colored nipples, nice and erect either from arousal or from the chill temperature of his house. He liked the air indoors somewhat crisp and had opened the windows a crack as soon as the snow began to melt outside.

But Jami would be warm soon enough.

Her bra hit the floor. Her black lace panties followed after she stepped out of her boots. He expected her to cover herself with her hands, but instead her chin hiked up. "Whatcha gonna do with me now, big boy?"

He gave her a hard look. "I will gag you if you speak again. On your knees, *puta*."

"Hey." Luke frowned as Jami lowered to her knees. "Maybe she doesn't know what it means, but I don't like—"

"I know what it means." Jami ducked her head and her blush darkened. "Believe me, if it bothered me, I would say so."

Luke nodded slowly. "Pause on the gag thing—I need to clear this up." He glanced at Sebastian, then took a knee in front of Jami. "Verbal humiliation turns you on? Anything not work for you? Cunt, whore, bitch—"

"It's all good. Still don't think I'm a freak?"

A freak? Sebastian's fist clenched at his side. He wanted to meet whomever had made her think that of herself. It took all his strength not to demand a name. Thankfully, Luke took her words in stride.

Grinning, Luke touched her cheek. "I think you're a dirty little slut. *Our* dirty little slut. I can't promise not to kill anyone else that calls you that."

Well done, semental.

"Depends *why* they're calling me that. My 'Master' will decide who to share me with." She shot Sebastian an uncertain look. "Is it too soon to call you that?"

Sebastian reached out to take her hand, squeezing her fingers, his tone steady despite the impact of her words. "Yes, but you may refer to me as Master tonight if it makes you more comfortable with what we're doing." He turned to Luke. "Anything else?"

"No. I'm good." Luke went to retrieve the rope. "Where do you want her, boss?"

Hand clasped to his wrist at the base of his spine, Sebastian circled his sofa, which jutted out across the end of the living room, dividing the space from the wide hall. Thick wood feet at the base of the sofa provided the perfect anchor for ropes. They had no scars from it yet, but he looked forward to putting several on them tonight.

"Sit her on the sofa. Tie her legs apart at the knee." The edge of his lips quirked up at Jami's gasp. "Bind her wrists in front. I want her as comfortable as possible."

Luke helped Jami to her feet and propelled her toward the sofa. Her bottom hit the smooth padding and she almost sprang right back up. Her blush had vanished and she squirmed as Luke held her down.

Unsure whether she was still playing, or genuinely afraid, Sebastian latched onto her wrists with one hand and tipped her chin up with the other. "What is your safeword, *mi cielo*?"

"Red." She gave him an impish grin. "I don't need it. You didn't expect me to make this easy, did you?"

Naughty, gatita. He chuckled and stretched her arms out over her head, tipping her off-balance as Luke cut the rope in three pieces: one short, two long. Jami seemed fixated on the knife, not fighting as Luke held the blade between his teeth and swiftly bound one knee to one sofa leg, then the other, spreading her open.

Sebastian released Jami and leaned on the back of the sofa as Luke tied her wrists together. "I do believe I mentioned a gag?"

Jami stared up at him, clamped her lips together, and shook her head.

"Can you be silent while he's licking your cunt?"

She nodded.

"Even when he refuses to let you come? Because he will. You must be punished for forcing us into this situation. We may not let you come until we both do."

Her second nod was hesitant.

He smiled and positioned her arms over her head once again, letting her wrists rest on the back of the sofa. "Keep your hands here. If you move them, or speak, there will be a penalty."

The muscles in her arms tensed, but she kept her wrists where he'd placed them. Her breasts quivered as she pressed her eyes shut and arched her back. He could practically taste the anticipation flowing from her. Her skin took on a rosy glow. *Lovely.*

He walked around the sofa to stand behind Luke, then patted his shoulder.

"If you want her, you will strip as well, *semental.*"

Luke stood and stripped down to white cotton boxers, the material thin enough to show the darkened head of his fully erect cock. His clothes were tossed across the room, and he dropped to his knees with a *thunk.* His entire focus was on Jami, but something about the way he reacted to Sebastian's commands made it obvious he was very aware of his presence. He focused so intently on Jami, it was clear he wouldn't acknowledge Sebastian any more than he had to.

So close to naked, and he was still hiding.

And I will let you, niño. For now.

Bending forward, Luke ran his hands up the insides of Jami's thighs, his eyes locked with hers as he spread her pussy open with his fingers. He brought his lips close, then lifted his head to press light kisses on the slight curve of Jami's belly. He used his teeth along the shallow indent by her hipbone, teasing her by moving closer and closer to her mound, letting his chin brush the very top. She shivered and moaned.

Sebastian trailed his fingers over her thigh, up her side to the underside of her breast. He licked his finger, then circled her rosy areola, avoiding her nipple until she bowed her body as far as the ropes would allow, seeking more.

He pinched her nipple hard as he bent down to kiss her, swallowing her breathy scream. "How does it feel, Jami? Having us both tease you?" He pressed his fingers over her lips before she could speak. "I don't need words. Answer me with your whimpers, your sobs, your screams." He kissed her long and hard, then let out a cruel laugh. "*You* didn't think I would make this easy on you, did you?"

****

Evil man. Jami whimpered as Sebastian lifted her breast to his lips. A moan escaped her as Luke rubbed his scruffy chin right over her clit before drifting down to finally give her pussy a long, slow lick. She dropped her head back into the sofa, hips quivering as sweet sensations melted through her. Part of her knew this was so bad. But being naughty made it that much hotter. And when Sebastian had called her *"Puta"* . . .

Damn, he had no idea how wet that made her. And Luke accepted her liking it. This couldn't be more perfect.

Sebastian sucked on her nipples until they ached and throbbed, so sensitive his breath sent sharp jolts down to her clit. Luke's tongue hardened and slid inside her. His whole mouth covered her cunt and everything inside tightened up. Another thrust and she'd come. She'd never come so fast, but she was so, so close . . .

"Stop." Sebastian knelt beside Luke and cupped the other man's face between his hands, holding him still as he kissed him. The way he sucked her juices from Luke's lips made heat surge into her core, but his next words had her shaking her head. "Don't let her come."

"I'm trying not to." Luke swallowed, leaning closer to Sebastian as he licked his lips. "But I can feel her, right on the edge . . ."

"Shallow thrusts, long strokes of your tongue." Sebastian patted Luke's cheek. "Avoid her clit as you feel her tense up."

Fuck that! "Please, Luke! I need to—you're so good—"

Sebastian smacked her inner thigh. The stinging pain made her eyes water. The look Sebastian gave her froze her words in her throat. "This is not the time for begging. The next time you do it I will put you in the cage with a chastity belt and you will find no pleasure at all tonight."

His threats brought her even closer. Her thighs tensed and her hips shook. *Oh God!*

Sebastian pinched her clit so hard she screamed. Heat pierced the swollen flesh. The urge to come buckled under the pain, as though she'd been thrown back from the edge of a cliff, still within reach, but too far to fall over. The ropes chafed her wrists as she twisted them, but he held her firmly in place, using his other hand to grab a fistful of her hair.

Luke thrust his fingers inside her.

She groaned, simmering, but kept her mouth shut.

"Be a good little *puta*. You will get what you need soon enough."

She whimpered as Luke withdrew his fingers and nodded, tears streaming down her cheeks. Using her safeword occurred to her for a split second, but she wanted this. She loved that Sebastian wasn't shying away from treating her rough. She needed him to use her. For him to let Luke use her.

She just hoped they wouldn't both be disgusted with her when it was over. Ford had been, and he'd never gone this far.

"Please continue, Luke." Sebastian stroked his hand down Luke's back as his mouth covered her once again. But his eyes never left her face. The way he paid such close attention to her reactions made her feel safe.

As Luke gently licked and sucked, she let herself sink into the pleasure but fought to hold back as erotic tremors carried her back to the edge. Luke dug his fingers into her thighs, his own moans adding vibrations to the already exquisite sensations. Her grip on control slipped, and she cried out as a violent orgasm ripped through her, shredding her control like wet silk. The disappointment in Sebastian's eyes drew a sob from her chest which lodged in her throat. She should have—

She jumped as Sebastian laid a solid slap on Luke's ass.

Luke roared, red flaring on his cheeks as he sat back on his heels. "What the fuck!"

"What is *your* safeword, *hombrecito*?" Sebastian bared his teeth in a sneer. "Did you not understand my instructions?"

"I understood." Luke wiped his mouth with the back of his hand. "But—"

"Either use your safeword, or bend over and try again."

The muscles in Luke's jaw ticked, but he took his position and carefully ran his tongue between her tender folds. His eyes met hers, as he teased her, dark with defiance barely reined in. He'd chosen to take it, to give Sebastian control, much like she had. And there was nothing weak about the way he submitted. She couldn't see him doing it for someone he didn't respect, which made her feel like she finally understood him.

Until his eyes narrowed and he grazed her clit with his teeth.

Another hard smack.

Luke grunted and pressed his forehead against her thigh. Jami watched Sebastian peel down Luke's boxers and slap his ass twice. Then he pulled Luke up by the hair.

"I don't reward defiance." He shoved Luke away. "Kneel there, out of my way. You may use your hand, jerk off while I fuck her. But if you come, you won't touch her again tonight."

Sebastian seemed to dismiss Luke as he stood and went to the clothes folded neatly on a chair by the window. He pulled a condom from his wallet and rolled it on even as he returned. Jami swallowed as he leaned over her.

He cupped her cheek and whispered in her ear. "I will not have him ruin this for you. But we will both take care of him, won't we?"

She nodded.

"But first, I will take care of you." He kissed her lips and smiled. "You will come for me, *puta*. Come again and again until you can't stand it anymore. Until you're begging me to stop. But I won't until I feel you've had enough. Until you've learned your lesson."

In a way, she felt sorry for Luke, but not enough to deny herself from getting what she wanted. Hell, what she *needed*. No experience in her life compared to this. She'd expected Sebastian to spank her, tie her up, then make love to her. But she had to admit, if he'd done that, she would have been disappointed. Everything with him seemed like it could be—should be—more.

He held her gaze as he slid into her with one long, slow stroke. As she stretched around his hot, hard cock, he massaged her inner thighs and ran his fingers along the ropes around her knees. He drew out, one inch at a time, and she whimpered at the languid, torturous pleasure. Then he slammed in and covered her mouth with his, drinking in her soft cries as he continued to pump in and out, dragging over a spot deep within that triggered another orgasm before she even saw it coming. She tugged at the restraints and screamed into his mouth.

His breath came out in a humid gasp as he continued at the same pace. "More."

Her inner walls were tender. Every slick slide of his dick kept her on the verge of another climax. But she had already come twice, so it seemed impossible. The edge became painful, and she made a low sound in her throat as it evaded her again and again. That one word became part of a chant in her head. *More! No more! Moremoremore!*

Circling his hips so his dick hit the spot within from a different angle, Sebastian V'd his fingers over her clit.

"Come for me, *gatita*." Sebastian bent down and closed his teeth around a nipple.

The pain pitched her up until she was falling and falling and screaming with the undulating ripples of heat, drowning in it until she couldn't breathe.

"Another." Sweat slicked Sebastian's chest as he pressed against her. The dark hairs rubbed her nipples, and he pushed in so hard the sofa creaked beneath them. He let out a roar that resounded within. Her clit felt like it would burst between his fingers.

She couldn't though. Not again. But then her pussy wrapped around him and she let out one last strangled scream. She felt him pulsing within and it was too much. She tensed, hoping he'd stop moving. It hurt. In a good way. So long as he didn't move.

He held still, his eyes searching hers. As she inhaled, he smiled and kissed the tears from her cheeks. "You are very sensitive. Tell me when you're ready for me to draw out, *mi cielo*."

I'll never be ready. She pressed her head again his shoulder and let her arms fall over his neck, pretty impressed that she'd kept them where he'd told her to for so long. She felt him going slack within and shifted her hips. She was okay. In one piece.

But the leather felt gross under her ass which was just as slick with sweat as his chest. She made a face. "I'm ready. Please get off me."

With a gruff laugh, he drew out, disposed of the condom, then went to work on the ropes. They fell away and he pulled her into his arms, sitting on the floor with her in his lap. The way he stroked her hair was an odd contrast to the rough way he'd used her, but right somehow. Because she'd trusted him enough to show him this side of her. And he seemed to be telling her, without words, that there was nothing wrong with her needs.

Only, he wasn't the only one there.

Luke knelt on the floor, a few feet away from them, pumping his dick in a way that seemed painful. His face was red, strained, as though he was holding back. Which was exactly what Sebastian had told him to do. She pictured herself in his position, having to watch him getting off with Sebastian when she didn't dare because then she'd get nothing. Hoping that if she pleased him, the torture would end.

"Master—" She made a face as she looked up at Sebastian because addressing him that way felt weird. "May I . . . ?"

Sebastian inclined his head. "You may. He's done well."

She slipped off Sebastian's lap and crawled to Luke, wincing at the ache between her thighs. Still on hands and knees, she glanced up at Luke. Then slipped her lips over the head of his cock.

He moved his hand and groaned as she took him into her mouth. "Fuck, Jami. You're fucking gorgeous."

Why did him calling her that make her feel so good? She kept her eyes on him as she tasted the slick, salty slit at the tip of his dick. He caught her eyes on him as his tongue touched the scar splitting his bottom lip and turned his head slightly so she could only see the unmarked part of his face. Suddenly, she knew why the word meant so much. The way he said it was reverent, like he couldn't believe she'd want him.

His scars were sexy to her, but bringing that up now wouldn't help anything. And she used her mouth to prove how much she did want him. Sucking hard, she lowered her head until he hit the back of her throat. Then used her tongue on the underside of his dick as she eased up. His fingers tangled in her hair as he tried to pull her down faster, but Sebastian knelt behind him and caught hold of his wrists.

"Don't rush her, *semental*. This could be the last time I let you use her mouth." Sebastian's words were followed by the slick sounds of wet lips, and she tipped her head back so she could watch them kiss. Watch Sebastian wrap his hand around Luke's throat. "She's mine."

Luke groaned and his dick twitched between her lips. His salty pre-cum coated the top of her mouth as she dipped down, then up, moving faster and faster. His balls hit her chin every time she lowered. But as his cum spurted down her throat, her chin hit rough knuckles. She swallowed and rose up, letting Luke's dick slip from her lips as Sebastian held Luke tight, his huge arm barred across his chest as he massaged Luke's balls, then gave his cock one last stroke so a bit more cum oozed out. She bent down to lick up every salty drop, grinning at the way Luke shuddered.

Scowling, Luke pressed her head against his thigh. "Bitch."

Jami snickered and circled her finger over the top of Luke's dick, still trapped in Sebastian's fist, loving the way he cursed and squirmed. "You have no idea."

"Up with you now." Sebastian helped Luke to his feet, then pulled Jami up as well. "Would you like me to drive you home, Jami, or would you prefer to stay?"

"I can drive her," Luke said.

Sebastian's brow rose slightly. "I don't recall giving you the option to leave."

"Listen, buddy, what happened here wasn't me signing up to be your sub. Or your fuck friend." Luke combed his fingers through his mussed up hair. "It was one wild night and it was pretty awesome, but that's it."

Asshole. At least he wants you to stay. Jami hugged herself. "My car's here; I can drive myself."

Rolling his head to crack his neck, Sebastian let out a heavy sigh. "Luke, you live with two other players. If either questions you tonight, you may say the wrong thing. Jami, I would like you to stay, but your dancing will be judged tomorrow—"

"The dance tryouts are on Sunday. And I don't even know if I'm going." The very idea of embarrassing herself in front of the judges again made her feel sick. At least she'd been confident about her skating abilities. "I can't do the routine, so what's the point?"

"With the way you move on the ice, I find it hard to believe that you cannot learn a routine."

"Yeah, well, I can't dance."

"How come?" Luke put his hand on her shoulder. "Dancing is easy. Hell, I can help you with that if you want to give it a shot."

Jami's lips twisted as she looked him over. He wasn't as muscular as Sebastian, but he still had enough bulk that she couldn't picture him dancing. Male dancers were long and lean. "I would pay to see you dance."

"Babe, being a male stripper was my backup plan." He winked and turned to Sebastian. "I'll give it to you; you have a point. Tyler won't say shit, but Demyan? He'll wonder where I took off to, and I've gotta think up a good cover story. How about we both stay?"

Sebastian nodded, then took her hand and brought it to his lips. "Yes. That would please me. I must admit, I'd prefer not to let you leave me so soon. Most assume subs are the only ones that need aftercare, but after treating you so roughly, I would very much like to hold you while you sleep."

Her cheeks heated as she moved away from Luke and let Sebastian wrap her up in his arms. He *did* want her to stay. Which made her feel special. No one, besides her dad, had made her feel special in a long time.

"Hmm, let me think. Go home to my empty bed or stay here and snuggle with you." She pressed her face against his chest. "Your next game is on Tuesday. You're gonna have a hard time getting rid of me before then."

"You might rethink that after tonight." Luke pressed against her from behind. "I can't promise you'll get much sleep."

"She'll sleep well tonight, *niño*." Sebastian kissed her hair and rested his chin on her head. "I have not decided how much of her I am willing to share. But we may discuss it after you give me the blow job you promised me."

Luke stuttered and she giggled as she glanced over at him. "Sounds fair to me."

"You're a little pain in the ass, you know that?" Luke stepped away and put his hands on his hips.

Jami shrugged and batted her eyelashes at Sebastian. "Gag him if he snores, 'kay? Doesn't matter with what."

Sebastian's lips curled with amusement. "I will make sure he does not disturb you." He swept her into his arms and carried her up the stairs to his bedroom.

Following them, Luke gave her a dirty look.

She smirked and snuggled close to Sebastian. Whatever Luke was to him, he wasn't competition. What had happened between them was more than "one wild night." Luke wanted it to be more. So did she.

With them both.

117

Chapter Eight

In the king-sized bed, a dark green comforter tangled around his legs, Luke folded his hands under his head and stared at the ceiling, grey in the darkness. Beside him, Jami slept, curled up on her side, her body flush against Seb's. Her head had been on Luke's shoulder, her hand on his stomach, until he'd shifted away so she wouldn't feel his erection. Or see it tenting up his boxers. Not that she'd notice while she was dead to the world—he grinned as he rubbed her drool from his shoulder—but he didn't want to chance her waking up and figuring out that not only her touch made him hard.

He'd been fast asleep when rough, calloused fingers had grazed his thigh. He'd woken up and froze, knowing that those fingers belonged to Seb, holding his breath because they were so close to his cock and if he made a sound they might move closer. Or away. He'd watched Seb's face for the longest time, sure the man was awake, messing with him. But Seb's face remained still. Breaths steady. If he was awake, he would have done more because Luke hadn't made a move to stop him.

Sick thing was, Luke wanted Seb to wake up and take over. Force him to accept his touch the way he'd forced him to accept his kiss and his hand on his dick. Not sick because he had a problem with gays—hell, he was a modern kinda guy. Who people fucked was their business.

But I'm not gay.

He groaned out a laugh as he rolled off the bed. Jami had been right. The labels were really screwing with his head. He called himself a Dom, but he'd gotten off on being caned by Chicklet and Wayne—and being . . . *spanked* by Seb. The man had slapped his ass when he made Jami come and damn it, he'd wanted more. When Seb gave a command, he almost obeyed automatically—had to stop himself every time.

But I'm not a sub.

As he'd told Jami, he heard that all the time. From men and women who showed up at the club thinking, since they were tough, they would be the dominant in any relationship they ended up in. He rubbed his face and sighed as he slipped out of the room and crept down the stairs. He paused in the living room, eyes on the sofa where sweat stains still marred the rich brown leather surface. The furnishings in the white-walled room were sparse. A sofa, a matching armchair, and a heavy, wrought iron coffee table. A few plants. No TV. Actually, he hadn't seen a single TV in the two-story house so far. Not that he'd seen much beyond the living room and bedroom.

In the wide hall, some cool art hung on the white walls. He couldn't name a single painter, but he could tell it was quality. Seb was a classy guy, but everyone knew that. He drove a car worth more than some of the players earned in a lifetime. There were pictures of the "mystery man" in the tabloids at museums and stuff. With actresses and models, yeah, but it said something that he did more with them than go to movie premieres.

He tried to picture Jami at those places and shook his head. One, Jami didn't fit the image Seb's agent was fixing him up with. Two, he didn't see her being into all that. Not that he knew her well enough to say, but punk rock and Michelangelo didn't mix.

Me and a gay dude don't mix.

He opened a door between the living room and the kitchen and snorted as he took in the walls of books. A man that didn't have a TV had to be a reader, and that fit Seb perfectly. He made his way around the room, trailing his hand over the high back of the black leather chair near the center, picturing Seb sitting there with one of those big books on his bent knee. Smart guy, athletic, all the things a quality chick looked for in a man. And even though Jami had the rocker thing going for her, he knew she was quality. She'd want a guy who had more going for him than what he laid out on the ice.

Why do you care? You don't really know this girl!

But he wanted to. He'd teased her a bit when he'd run into her at the forum, but until he'd caught sight of her at the club, they hadn't really connected. Dating a woman who didn't do kink for months made Jami damn appealing. And she wasn't scared of him. She didn't even seem to care that he was a hockey player, which was damn refreshing.

Yeah. Perfect rebound material.

The scar on his lip, running in a jagged line down his chin, seemed bigger as he rubbed it, recalling how Jami had gazed up at him as though she didn't see it. She'd probably been too worked up to notice. And even if she had, she was too young to really think about the impact of having a man like him in her life might have. Not like she was thinking about long-term with him anyway.

Not like he wanted her to. She was a good kid. She deserved better.

We can have fun for a little while though.

If Seb let them.

Shaking his head, he moved toward a bookshelf and picked up the first familiar book, *Strangers* by Dean Koontz. On another shelf he found a bottle of Jamaican rum and a tumbler which he filled before bringing the book and the glass to the chair.

"I have sports books."

Luke arched a brow as Seb slipped into the room. He gave Seb a dry smile. "No picture books? With real big words?"

"I'm afraid not." Seb came to stand in front of him and lifted the book to see the cover. "I wouldn't have taken you for a fan of Koontz. This isn't one of his best."

"It's my favorite. All those people trying to piece together the weird shit that's happening to them. Lots of suspense. Couldn't put it down once I picked it up. Shocked my mom and read it in just three days."

"So you haven't read it recently?"

"Naw, when I was thirteen." Luke took a sip of rum, then gestured to Seb with the glass. "I hope you don't mind that I helped myself?"

"Not at all. I'd tell you to make yourself comfortable, but you've done that already."

"Yeah, sorry, bad habit." He grinned. "Bunnies hate it when they bring me home and find me checking out their Vagisil and shit in the bathroom. I figure, once I've had my tongue up your ass, 'privacy' is kinda a moot point."

Seb's eyes widened. Then he chuckled. "Well, since I haven't had *that* pleasure, should I assume you won't invade my privacy?"

Choking on a mouthful of rum, Luke stared at him. "You had

your hand on my balls—*aaannnd,* umm, yeah, let's not talk about that. Want to talk about the playoffs? Think Mason's knee is solid enough?"

"I never discuss the playoffs until twenty-four hours before the game. It's superstitious nonsense, like—" he grazed Luke's scruffy cheek with his knuckles "—not shaving during the playoffs. I noticed you started early."

"Yeah, well, I shaved twice as often before, hoping it would help my beard grow faster once I stopped." He swallowed, unable to help leaning into Seb's touch. "You think it will work?"

"It's hard to tell." Seb crouched to eye level and traced Luke's jaw with his fingers in a way that made him shiver. His thumb brushed his bottom lip. "The growth is pretty even, no patchy spots that I can see. I doubt you'll make the rankings for worst playoff beards."

"Thanks."

"So, why was your mother so shocked that you finished the book quickly?" Seb straightened and leaned a muscular forearm on the back of the chair. "She must have seen you read like that before?"

Luke grinned and shook his head. "Nope, not unless it was for school, and I grabbed the movie for reports every chance I got. My grades were sucky, and my mom threatened not to let me play hockey anymore if I didn't get them up. My English grades were the worse, so I made her a deal. I would write an extra report, and if I got an A, she'd let me play. My English teacher agreed, under one condition. I had to choose a book over four hundred pages."

"You took that as a challenge?"

"Damn straight, I did. And I got my A. My mom was so happy, she nagged my dad until he got me two new sticks. And not the cheap ones." He thumbed the pages of the book and smiled, recalling how every single one of Koontz's books had sat in a box beside the sticks on the kitchen table. "You see, my dad played hockey most his life—only made it to the minors though. He didn't finish school and had no other plans. So when he got injured, he couldn't get a good job. My mom was scared I'd do the same thing. She cried when I graduated high school and cried some more when I got a scholarship to the University of Minnesota. Made her happy that she didn't raise a dumb jock."

"And your father?"

Finishing off his rum, Luke shrugged. "He didn't care whether or not I was dumb, so long as I played good. He showed up when I was drafted—five years after filing for divorce to chase some young tail, walking out on my mom and me—telling me he was so proud. I wanted to deck him. My mom worked her ass off as an orderly in a local hospital to pay for all my shit. Me making it had nothing to do with him."

"But you had your mother's support. Which is all that matters." Seb squeezed his shoulder. "Would you like another drink?"

Lips pressed together, Luke handed over his glass. "You gonna get me drunk so you can take advantage of me?"

Seb laughed. "I will *never* take advantage of you when you are drunk, *semental*. Whatever we do, you will have to face sober."

"Remind me to keep a flask on me at all times."

The dark look Seb gave him stilled his heart. He inched back into the chair as Seb returned, glass in hand, and loomed over him. "You may drink tonight. And tomorrow night. After that, you *will* be sober, *niño*. At all times. To be otherwise will disappoint both me and the team, and you are better than that."

Yeah, I am. But I don't need you telling me what to do. Luke took a long, burning gulp of rum and scowled. "Are you under the impression that I give a fuck what you think?"

Placing his hand over the glass, Seb leaned over him, lips close enough to kiss. His accent thickened his tone as he spoke. "I know you care what I think, Luke. And I know you are fighting, very hard, not to. When you're done fighting, let me know."

A brief, hot brush of lips and Seb moved away, leaving the room without looking back. Luke pressed his fingers to his lips and ground his teeth.

I. Don't. Care.

It took an insane amount of effort to choke down what would no doubt be one of his last drinks for a while.

But that doesn't mean I care. Just means he's right.

****

Jami hummed as the rich scents of bacon, breakfast sausages, and fried sliced ham surrounded her. She fixed up scrambled eggs and sunny side up, not sure which the men liked best. Then she put the hash browns—which her dad told her she made even better than him—on a plate with paper towels to soak up the grease.

Her idea to make the guys breakfast had started out simple and, well, expanded a little when she saw all the food Sebastian had in his fridge. More than half would go bad within the next few days if it wasn't used, and she figured two big men probably ate a lot. Her stomach growled as she glanced toward the hall. Hell, they'd probably be surprised when they saw how much *she* ate. Her mother used to grumble about how it wasn't fair that she didn't get fat. Every time Dad was home, and they spent the morning cooking up a nice big breakfast, she'd bitch about how they were going to spoil her diet. And she'd always been on some kind of fad diet. Which Jami never understood because her mother had beautiful curves. Curves which her dad always said he loved.

Smoothing her hands down her sides, over her trim waist and very small hips, Jami let out an aggravated sigh. She might be slender, but she had the body of a teenage boy, which her mother had pointed out whenever she was in a mood. Which was pretty often. At least Jami had finally grown some tits. And Sebastian seemed to like those—Luke certainly did. If they didn't, she might have wondered whether they were interested in her *because* she looked like a boy.

Oh, stop it. They definitely won't like you acting like some insecure chick.

At the soft padding of bare feet on the tiles, she spun around and smacked on a bright smile.

Luke lifted her up and planted a hard kiss on her lips. "Damn, woman! If this is what mornings are like with you, I'm gonna have to kidnap you more often! This looks amazing!"

Sebastian came into the kitchen, eyeing the full table with a frown. Without a word, he went to serve himself some coffee, drinking it black as he stared out the window over the sink.

"Sebastian?" Jami wiggled away from Luke and approached

Sebastian, fiddling with the bottom of the big white T-shirt she'd borrowed from his dresser. Without asking. Just like she hadn't asked to raid his fridge. "I'm sorry. I wanted to surprise you, and there was so much I figured you'd want to cook it before it went bad. I should have—"

"No, *mi cielo*. It's fine." Sebastian cupped her cheek and his lips curved up slightly. "I always buy more than I need—I bring it to the local shelter before I head off on a road trip so it doesn't go to waste. I was a little surprised, that's all. I hope you and Luke are very hungry because I dislike throwing out food."

"I'm always hungry." Luke came up behind her and gave her hair a little tug. "This one probably eats like a bird from the look of her, but I'll clean her plate after I have a few helpings of my own." He paused and cleared his throat. "If there's not enough left for the shelter, I don't mind pitching in for more."

"I can manage." Sebastian turned away from them, back stiff as he made his way to the table. "But thank you."

Jami bit her lip and brought the rest of the plates to the large oval, mahogany table, her stomach turning as all the food she'd prepared took up most of the space, leaving just a bit of room for the three of them to eat. Maybe she'd overdone it. No, she *had* overdone it.

I should leave before I piss him off any more.

Dragging his chair away from the table, Luke sat, faced Sebastian, and scowled. "What the fuck is your problem, man?"

"Excuse me?" Sebastian went still, a serving spoon full of scrambled eggs hovering over his plate.

"She made us a nice breakfast, and you're acting like a dick. Being all charitable doesn't give you the right to be an asshole." Luke dumped a pile of bacon on his plate, followed by some sausages and ham. Then hash browns and two eggs. He grabbed a piece of toast and used it to annihilate his egg yolk. "If you're grumpy in the morning, have some coffee, shovel in your food, and shut the fuck up."

"*Niño*—"

"Don't '*niño*' me. That's 'boy' isn't it? You gonna play Dom now? *Seriously?*" Luke crammed the toast into his mouth and spoke around it. "You might have *the look,* but you're still a dick."

Jami's chest ached, but she had to cover her mouth with her hands to keep from laughing. It wasn't funny. Not really. But Luke was on a roll.

Sebastian pushed away from the table. "Luke—"

"Is 'thank you' too complicated for you? How about *'muchas gracias'*? I can translate if she—"

Slamming his hands on the table, Sebastian stood. "Stop. Talking."

Luke pressed his lips together. Frowned. Then took a deep breath as though preparing to continue his rant.

"It will be rather difficult to enjoy all this food while wearing a gag, Luke." Sebastian's searing gaze locked on Luke until he lowered his eyes. Then he sighed and raked his fingers into his hair, ruining the sleekness of the tightly bound strands. "He's right, *mi cielo*. And I am sorry. I reacted without thinking beyond the potential waste. Can you forgive me?"

Shaking her head, Jami eased closer to him, working his hand free from his hair so she could lace their fingers together. "It's my fault for assuming I could do what I wanted in your kitchen."

"No." He pulled her into his lap and wrapped his arms around her waist. "I wouldn't have allowed you to stay if I didn't want you to feel comfortable here. It was very thoughtful of you to prepare all this for us. I do hope I haven't ruined your appetite?"

Yes. But it's my own fault. But Luke had made him feel bad enough to apologize. She wasn't about to make it worse by dragging this out.

"Not at all." She kissed his jaw, loving the way his dark morning stubble felt against her lips. Then she slipped off his lap and plunked herself down on her own chair. Tried to keep a happy face on. And choked down the first few mouthfuls of food, hardly tasting a thing.

For a while, they ate in silence, clearing their plates and taking seconds. Luke stabbed each bite with his fork, grumbling under his breath. Sebastian ate as though savoring every mouthful. Jami tried not to let them see her watching them.

Suddenly, Luke dropped his fork onto his empty plate with a clang and sat back in his chair. "We've got to do something to break the tension. This is driving me nuts. You wanna fuck?"

Jami sputtered as a piece of toast lodged in her throat.

Sebastian patted her back and let out a strangled laugh. "Do you ever think something and not say it, *niño*?"

"Not that I recall." Luke grinned and took some more hash browns. "If we can't fuck, would you freak if I made myself a sandwich?"

Eyes wide, Jami looked over the table, with all the empty plates that had been piled high. "You can't still be hungry?"

Luke patted his stomach. "I'm a growing boy. And I'm hoping to gain a few pounds before playoffs so I can throw my weight around."

Sebastian gave him a wry smile. "Maybe I should force you to fast so you'll keep yourself out of trouble."

"Hey, I get myself in too much trouble and you'll bail me out, right?"

"I always do."

The men's exchange made her feel left out. She didn't want to talk about the goddamn game. She didn't want to be around two more men who thought the stupid game was more important than her.

Dad never made you feel like that. Stop being a baby.

No, Dad hadn't, but her mother's words poisoned her memories. If Dad couldn't be there for a checkup with the doctor or a holiday, then he cared more about hockey than them. It didn't matter what he did when he was home, every day away was resented.

"*Mi cielo*, tell me why you look so sad."

She lifted her head and blinked at the two men staring at her, Sebastian with his intense, dark eyes, and Luke with his lips pressed tight and slanted as though he was holding in a great big joke. If she was alone with Sebastian, she would have told him everything. And maybe it would have felt good to get it off her chest.

Then again, maybe not. Sometimes talking about crappy stuff just made her feel crappier. She liked the way Luke managed to keep things light, and she wanted more of that after the way the morning had started.

Letting out a dramatic sigh, she flipped her hair over her shoulder and shrugged. "Oh, it's nothing. I was just wondering what other playoff superstitions you both have. No shaving, no shop talk, no—"

Luke burst out laughing. "I knew it! She's worried that she's not gonna get laid for the next couple months. Boo, you've got nothing to worry about. I'll take care of you if Seb's gotta abstain. No way will I be scruffy and sober *and* sporting monster-sized blue balls."

Sebastian scrubbed his face with his hands and left the table to finish off the coffee. "*Hombrecito*, you may have missed it, but I believe Jami is tired of the . . . 'shop talk.'"

"Yeah, I got that." Luke rolled his eyes. "Anyhow, what are your plans for the day, Jami? When do we start your lessons?"

"I *was* planning on chilling here—hey, what lessons?"

"*Dancing*." Luke stood, spun toward her, and pulled her into his arms for a smooth dip. He bent over her, brushing his lips over hers, his eyes hooded as he murmured, "I'm going to make damn sure I get to see you in that cute little outfit at every home game next season. I'll show you how to move, how to make all the judges want you so bad that they won't be able to turn you down."

She giggled and pushed on his solid chest as she tried to straighten. "Most of the judges are chicks."

Luke grinned and nuzzled her neck. "That's hot."

The muffled sound of music from the living room cut off her moan and her eyes went wide. She scrambled away from Luke and bolted to her boots. The special ring tone, "Papa Don't Preach" by Kelly Osbourne, had almost reached the chorus by the time she got her phone out of the inner pocket of her boot. She looked up once, finger over her lips, as Sebastian and Luke stepped into the living room.

After a deep, deep inhale, she answered. "Hey, Daddy!"

"Daddy?" Dad's tone was already sharp with suspicion. "It's been 'Dad' since you were thirteen unless you were in trouble. What's wrong?"

"N-nothing." *I'm such an idiot!* She scrambled for an excuse that would keep him from going off the deep end. "I, umm, kinda have something to tell you—nothing bad! I stopped by your office the other day to talk, but you weren't there."

"Tell me now."

"Probably be better if I tell you in person."

"Probably would have been better if you had—*what*, Silver? As you can see I'm on the . . ."

Jami grinned as the sound cut off on the phone, as though her father was covering it. Silver would keep him from doing his smothering father bit.

Sebastian took a seat on the sofa behind her and put a supportive hand on her shoulder. She rested her cheek against the back of his hand.

A deep sigh in her ear let her know her father was back. His tone was strained, but light. "Fine. I'll head back today. We can have lunch."

"Ah . . ."

"What?"

"I kinda had plans today, Dad. Don't cut your visit short. We'll get together Monday, before you leave for Buffalo."

"Maybe it would be better if you just told me, Jami. I swear I won't get mad. I'm more worried than anything. You've only been back a week, and I have no idea what's going on with you."

"All right, here it goes." She took a deep breath and turned to press back against Sebastian's knees. "I'm trying out to be an Ice Girl."

Silence. Then an offhand, "Was that so hard?"

Damn. She slumped and shook her head. If he was being *this* calm about it, he'd already known.

His next words confirmed her suspicions. "Since that's out of the way, let's talk about the pictures."

Shit.

* * * *

Dean's teeth clinked together as his jaw hardened in response to his daughter's prolonged silence. When had he ever made her feel like she couldn't talk to him? If it was just promo, if it didn't mean anything, why couldn't she just come clean?

He heard the accusation in her voice when she finally spoke. "If you know about the pictures, you knew about everything. Why'd you pretend you didn't?

Massaging the ache between his eyes, he turned away from Silver—and his mother. And tried to sound as reasonable as possible. "I needed to hear it from you, sweetheart. To be honest, when I saw the pictures, I wasn't happy. Sebastian Ramos is as bad, if not worse, than Ford Kingsley. I don't know what I would do if another man took advantage—"

"You *did not* just compare Sebastian to Ford." She let out a bitter laugh. "You have no idea what you're talking about, Dad. More importantly, you don't get to choose who I get involved with."

Her words were a cement block dropping right onto his guts. He fisted his hand by his side. "So you're seeing Sebastian."

"That's none of your business."

"You're last boyfriend put you in the hospital with a cocaine overdose! How is this none of my business? The things Sebastian does—"

"The things *he* does? Oh my God, you're such a fucking hypocrite! It's okay for you to do that with a woman just a few years older than me, but there's something wrong with me doing it? Are you serious?"

"Silver knew what she was getting into."

"So do I! And *if* I decided to do any of that stuff, I would figure you'd be happy I chose a guy you trusted enough to be a dungeon monitor at your club!"

"The people he monitors aren't naïve nineteen-year-old girls acting out to piss off their fathers!"

She didn't respond for a very long time. But when she did, she wasn't screaming. She was very, very quiet. "I can't believe you just said that to me. I joined the Ice Girls because I wanted to support the team. *Your* team. And I still want that. But now I'm not doing it for you."

The dial tone cut off anything he could have said, but that was probably for the best. He should have waited so he could speak to Jami in person, as she'd asked for in the first place. Instead, he done it in a way that would leave her vulnerable to the very man he wanted to protect her from.

He let his phone fall to the table and dropped to the hard

wooden chair in his mother's kitchen, banging his elbows on the table as he covered his face with his hands. All he could hear was Silver telling him how Ramos had scared her away from the scene with his intensity, with the way his words, his presence, made her feel like she could give up control without a second thought. All he could see was his little girl, who he would have kept in pigtails with a sticky, chocolate covered face and angel smile forever if he could.

Then he closed his eyes and he could see her, the first time he'd put a pair of skates on her, all of three years old, clinging to his hand and shaking her head.

"I'll fall, Daddy!"

"Oh no, you won't. Not this time." He'd eased his hand free from hers and hooked both under her arms. *"I won't let you go."*

Eventually, he'd had to let go. And watch her fall and get back up. He'd watched her from farther and farther away, taking bigger and bigger strides. She was strong. Smart. But then he'd stood back too much, constantly reminding himself that she needed to slip up, make mistakes, and learn from them. And one slip had almost taken her away from him for good.

He couldn't go through that again.

"Dean." Silver came up behind him, sliding her arms down his chest as much as she could with her big belly pressed against the back of the chair. "You were right when you told me not to worry about Sebastian. He's a good guy."

"If he was a good guy, he'd stay away from my daughter. He's almost ten years older than she is."

Silver laughed. "Umm, excuse me Mister Just Turned Thirty-Nine. How much older than me are you?"

"And if your father really cared, he would have killed me for even looking at you." Dean winced as Silver drew away from him and shifted sideways in the chair. "Hey, I didn't mean that way."

Landon, who'd been watching them from where he leaned on the thick, pine-plank counter, scowled and went over to pull Silver into his arms.

Dean's mother made a sharp sound in her throat and picked up a wooden spoon from the counter. She smacked Silver's thigh with it, then pointed it at her. "None of that drama, little girl. We all know your father is an asshole. You have two good men taking care of you." She turned to Landon, jabbing the spoon close to his face. "And you, stop coddling her. A tough woman has healthy babies. You can't push out that baby for her, so you're going to have to start letting her handle some things on her own. Like how she deals with her other man."

She came toward Dean, and he ducked as she swung the spoon at his head. His mother had never been abusive, but that spoon had been used on her men, and her children, for several decades. He was pretty sure it had never been used for anything else.

"Do you think I would have let that girl leave my home if she didn't have the sense to stay away from the kind of people that got her into trouble in the first place? It's a scary world out there. She has to live in it." She planted her fists—one still holding the spoon—on her hips. "And you have to let her, whether you like it or not."

Standing, Dean faced his mother. From a safe distance. "Do you expect me to stand back and do nothing while my daughter is hurt by another man who may be using her?"

"Yes." His mother shook her head and sighed. "Dean, honey, I understand. I couldn't stand your wife. I hated the way she treated you and that little girl. You were my baby boy, but I knew no woman would be worthy to my mind. So I treated her decent when she came around because she was your choice. I raised you to be a good man, and I respected you enough to accept that. Respect your daughter the same way. She's made her mistakes, but you raised her right. Just you. I don't see any of that bitch you married in her."

"She mentioned the club." Dean needed his mother to understand—he knew he was grasping, but maybe . . . "What if he goes too far?"

His mother frowned and looked over at Landon. "Do you know this man? He's on your team, isn't he? Do you think he'll abuse my granddaughter?"

Landon opened his mouth. Frowned. Then shook his head. "No. When we were on the road, I was thinking about talking to him, but I knew it wasn't my place. I mean, if he hurt Jami, I'd bury him, but . . ." He groaned. "Hell, I've seen the way he treats his subs. He's a good Dom."

"Fuck!" Dean turned his back on them all. "I don't need to be hearing this! I don't want to picture my daughter—"

"Then don't. What she does in the bedroom has nothing to do with her daddy." His mother pursed her lips. "And it was damn wrong of you to suggest it did. I don't know how you can expect her to come to you about anything after that."

"I know." Dean paced the floor, wishing again that the conversation had happened differently. At another time. In person. But wishing wouldn't change a thing. "I just hope she has someone she can talk to if she can't come to me. When this goes bad . . ."

His words trailed off, and even his mother didn't have any harsh wisdom to offer. They all knew he was right. This thing between Jami and Sebastian—and from the way she defended him, there was obviously something between them—would end badly.

And there was absolutely nothing he could do about it.

Chapter Nine

After slicing an apple, an orange, and some melon into small pieces, Sebastian put the fresh fruit in an earthenware dish and brought it to the kitchen table where Jami sat, staring sightlessly at the wall. The coffee he'd poured for her almost an hour ago hadn't been touched. The newspaper she'd pretended to read while he'd cleaned the kitchen lay open on the same page. Her hands were hidden in the sleeves of his white T-shirt and her hair curtained her cheeks. She didn't react to his approach.

He couldn't recall ever seeing her so quiet and still.

A faint scuffing sound brought his gaze downward and the edge of his lip crept up. Her bare feet were moving restlessly, toes tapping on the floor, gripping those of the other foot, stretching out, then squeezing in. There was something adorable about her fidgety little feet. Something that made him want to shackle her ankle in his big hand and tickle the soles of her feet until she squealed and laughed— or at very least smiled.

Before Luke had left for his morning run, she'd managed a smile, but it hadn't reached her eyes. He knew the conversation with her father had not gone well, but she didn't give the impression of wanting to discuss it.

Perhaps she needs a distraction. He curved his hand around the back of her neck, gently rubbing the tense muscles with his fingertips and thumb until she let out a soft sound very much like a kitten's purr. He smiled and spoke quietly. "Come with me, *mi cielo*, I have something to show you."

Casting a curious glance at the bowl of fruit in his hand, she followed him to a door across the hall from the kitchen. As soon as he opened the door, she gasped and took a few quick steps into the room on tiptoes, eyes wide as she spun in a circle to take it all in.

"Sebastian, this is . . . wow." The sunlight spilling in from above and around lit up her face. She giggled and shook her head. "I have no words. Just 'Wow.'"

The Georgian-styled conservatory, with dark stained wood accents and huge windows, specially designed to keep the elements and the sun from affecting the temperature of the room, was his favorite place in the house—the reason he'd bought it, actually. His vast collection of plants flourished in here. No sound came in from outside, which made it easier to focus on the sounds within.

An excited, ear-piercing screech came from the side of the room, and Sebastian laughed as Jami jumped backward, slamming into him. "What the fuck!"

"Be calm, *gatita*." He steadied her with an arm around her shoulders and pointed out the large wooden cage behind a huge, potted palm tree. "Pit and Cherry are simply greeting us."

Jami's lips parted as she inched toward the cage and watched him open it. "You have *lovebirds*?"

"Yes. They were my mother's." Sebastian reached into the cage. Pit, the black-masked male, let out a happy peep and hopped onto his hand. "I brought them to the States with me after I came back from her funeral." He shook his head when Jami opened her mouth, sure she'd offer unnecessary condolences. "It has been four years. I'd planned to find them a good home with someone who knew more about birds, but I grew attached to them. Learned enough to care for and train them."

"Like . . . they can do tricks?"

Sebastian nodded and brought Pit and the fruit to the small glass table in the center of the room. Pit chirped and stepped onto the table. He approached the bowl, but stopped when Sebastian made a clicking sound with his tongue and waited as he took a seat on one of the two wicker armchairs.

"Pit." Sebastian smiled when Jami knelt by the table, holding her breath as she watched the bird. He tapped his finger on the table until he had Pit's attention and made a circling gesture. "Roll over."

Pit rolled onto his back, wiggled slightly to shift his balance, then popped up to his feet.

"Good boy." Sebastian fed Pit a piece of melon. Then he whistled a three-note tune. "Come, Cherry."

The peach-faced female bounced from her perch to the open door of the cage, chattering noisily. She cocked her head when he whistled again, sang back to him, and took flight. After landing on his shoulder, she began preening his hair, tugging lightly at the strands when he moved, making fussy little chirps.

"That's so cool!" Jami's eyes lit up. She reached out toward Cherry, then hesitated. "Can I touch her?"

"Not her—she's very possessive and she may bite." Sebastian picked Pit up and placed him in Jami's cupped palm. "He's friendlier and he enjoys showing off. Hold your hand flat."

Jami flattened her hand, looking nervous, as if she thought Pit would fall off.

Sebastian grinned and made a gun with his finger and thumb. "Bang."

Pit flopped onto his back on Jami's palm, lying still until Sebastian clicked his tongue.

"He's just like a dog!" Jami smiled at the bird and offered him a piece of apple. "This is . . . this is not what I pictured you doing with your free time. I totally expected there to be a piano behind that door."

"A piano?"

"Didn't you know?" Jami's tone became matter-of-fact. "All sexy, brooding, mysterious men play piano."

Gently lifting Cherry from his shoulder to the table so she could help herself to the fruit, Sebastian regarded Jami seriously. "No, I wasn't aware of that. Nor did I know I was brooding or mysterious."

"But you knew you were sexy?"

"I've been told often enough. I see no point in arguing with the masses." He smirked when she rolled her eyes. "I apologize, *mi cielo*. Should I claim to be a beast?"

Crawling toward him, her movements sensuous, cat-like, Jami slowly licked her lips and purred. "You were a beast last night."

He shook his head and pulled her between his parted thighs. "I was actually quite gentle last night, *gatita*. I thought it best to consider your lack of experience." Bending down to kiss her parted lips, he spoke softly. "I plan to teach you to take more."

She swallowed audibly, gasping into his mouth. "More?"

"Yes, but not today. Today I hope to teach you something else." He stood, drawing her to her feet. This could be a mistake, but he didn't think so. "If you are willing to learn."

"Sure." She shrugged, fiddling with the hem of his shirt. "I did tell you I was ready."

Ready? Ah, she thought he meant to teach her to submit. He shook his head and tucked her hair behind her ears. "Not that kind of lesson."

Placing his hand on the small of her back, he guided her to the other side of the room where a small, gilded cage sat on a metal stand. The baby bird within, whose coloring matched his father's, bounced on his perch and sang softly.

"He's almost four months old. He had two siblings who are now with my neighbor. Most people believe lovebirds must be in pairs, which simply isn't true. They need to be socialized. Need attention every day. I have a housekeeper who comes in every day when I'm on the road to care for Pit and Cherry." He left Jami with the baby bird and went to put Cherry and Pit back in their cage. "She cares for him as well, but he needs a home of his own. A person he can bond with."

Jami cooed to the bird, then looked over at Sebastian as he returned to her side. "Me? You'd let me have him?"

"If you want him, he's yours." Sebastian chuckled as she squealed and jumped up to hug him. "I will show you how to train him, how to handle him once he matures, but you must be sure you have the time for him. Unless you pair him with another lovebird, he will become very attached to you."

"I'll make the time." She bit her bottom lip as he took the baby bird out and cupped her hands to hold him. "What's his name?"

"I've been calling him Peanut."

"Hello, Peanut." She whistled as Sebastian had to Cherry and Pit and laughed, delighted, when Peanut chattered back to her. "You are the sweetest thing."

Sebastian watched her nuzzle the little bird to her cheek and felt a tightness in his throat as he remembered his mother doing the same when he'd brought her Cherry and Pit. In the end, she'd taken better care of the birds than of herself. But for the first time in his life he'd seen her truly happy. Which made the birds precious to him.

Jami leaned against his chest, still cuddling Peanut. "I think I'm in love."

He kissed her hair and closed his eyes. *So do I.*

* * * *

Luke lowered into a half-pushup stretch on the mat in the workout room which the Ice Girls were using for practice—empty now, since at 6:00 p.m. on a Saturday night even the most dedicated girls were done for the day. Except for Jami and her friend, Akira. Jami didn't know the routine well enough to practice with him alone, and Akira was just as determined as him to get Jami through to the next round. Only, as soon as she saw him, she balked and made a dozen excuses to leave. Apparently she had appendicitis. Or was about to start her period.

He *really* hadn't needed to hear that.

Right outside the door in the hall, he could hear Jami trying to convince Akira to help her with the routine. He shoved up to his feet and approached the doorway. The poor little Asian girl looked damn scared. And catching sight of him made her chalk-white.

"Hey, everything cool?" He leaned on the doorframe so he didn't loom over them.

"Yeah, Akira's just . . ."

"I don't deal well with men." Akira hugged herself and took a step back. "I'm sorry."

"All men, or just men who might come on to you?" He took a deep breath and told himself he had to do whatever it took to get Akira to help out. Jami needed to be an Ice Girl, if for no other reason than to prove she could do what she'd set out to do. So he looked at Akira, straight-faced, and told her what he'd deny being to anyone else no matter what he and Seb did. "I'm gay, so you've got nothing to worry about."

Akira's eyes widened. She swept her slick black hair away from her face. "You are?"

"Yep. Jami didn't tell you about last night?"

She shook her head.

"Well, I don't fuck and tell, but I had fun. And not with her." He gave her his patented I'm-harmless smile. "How many straight guys do you know who can dance? Watch me move, then you can decide."

"Okay." Akira inched into the room, keeping a distance, but not looking scared anymore. She smoothed her hands over the sides of her leotard and pursed her lips at Jami's skirt and black silk button-up shirt—one of Seb's. "You didn't even stop to get a change of clothes after spending the night with that guy, did you? Ugh." She swung a small, black canvas bag off her shoulder. "Good thing I came prepared."

"You're a doll. But hey—" Jami took the black leotard Akira handed her and headed out the door, tossing back. "Don't seduce my *gay* friend. 'kay?"

Luke frowned. Hell, so much for being nice. She had to put it that way? If he wasn't sporting a stiffy half the time at just the thought of getting to fuck her, he might've made a play for her friend. He adjusted his shorts and turned away from Akira, sliding into another stretch so she couldn't see his semi, barely hidden by his blue and white Bermuda shorts and white wife-beater.

"So . . ." Akira skirted around him and went to stand by the weight set pushed against the wall. "This guy, Sebastian . . . was he good to Jami?"

Besides calling her a slut in Spanish and ramming her like an animal? Luke shrugged, hopped to his feet, then laced his fingers together, turning them so his palms faced the ceiling and raising his arms under he felt a nice pull between his shoulder blades. "Seb's a great guy. Yeah, I'd say he was good to her."

"And you and him are . . ." Akira's porcelain cheeks went bright pink. She ducked her head. "Lovers?"

Luke felt heat spread over his own cheeks. "Hey, don't start telling people that."

"Oh, I won't! I just want to make sure—I mean, Jami's been hurt before. Not that she'll really admit it, but her ex made her feel bad about herself. If Sebastian is with you—I mean . . . you aren't jealous?"

Aww, fuck. I should have told her I was becoming a priest. Taking vows and all. He tugged on his collar even though it wasn't tight enough to account for the strangling sensation. "I'm not the jealous type. Me and Seb do our own thing. It's all good."

"You see other men?"

Someone please shoot me. "Ah . . . if you don't mind, I'd rather not talk about my sex life."

"I'm sorry!" Akira pressed her hands over her mouth. "This is really none of my business."

"It's okay." *Not.* "It's cool that you're looking out for your friend. You two known each other long?"

"Not really. We met during one of the prep classes. Just last week. But it's like we've been friends forever."

"Meaning you're close?" He lowered his voice and glanced toward the door. Gay guys got some perks, right? Like all the juicy details from their female friends? He might as well have some fun with it. And if they let him watch, this would all be worth it. "You have sleepovers and stuff?"

Akira smiled. "Yes. I've spent every night except last night at her place."

"Do you share a bed? Help each other . . . *relax* after a rough day? You can tell me, since—"

"Luke!" Jami swung the door open and stomped up to him. She gave him a sharp shove and waved her finger in his face. "You are such a perv."

"Who me?" Luke made his eyes big and spread his arms wide. "It's just a bit of girl talk. Harmless, since I don't like girls that way."

"Jerk." Jami mumbled, fiddling with her black leotard, first the straps, then discreetly stretching the part covering her ass. She let out a little growl when he wiggled his eyebrows and moved to help. "You're supposed to be teaching me. Behave yourself."

Poor little Akira looked so confused. "Am I missing something?"

"No. Let's just get this over with." Jami pulled a bright yellow elastic from her wrist and swiftly twisted her blue hair into a tight bun. "I'm telling you both now, I'm hopeless."

Over an hour later, Luke had to agree with her. He already had the simple routine down pat, and Jami was still going through the motions with all the grace of the tin man from the *Wizard of Oz.* Before his rusty joints were greased up. Every move she made was stiff, jerky, and she spent more time watching their reactions to her movements than focusing on doing them. She collided with everything in the room at least once when turns had her tripping over her own feet.

He had to stop himself from asking her how she managed to walk without hurting herself. No one could be *this* bad of a dancer. And apparently she could skate?

"I give up." He picked up a towel from the supply table and draped it over his face. "This isn't working."

"Thank God!" Jami grunted and he flipped the towel over his shoulder to watch her drop hard on the mat. She smiled at him, but her eyes shimmered with tears. "I'd prefer honesty from you two, rather than the judges. I suck. Just say it."

"Oh, you're not getting off the hook that easy, boo." He grinned at her open-mouthed stare. "That's right. You're still learning the routine. Just not like this."

"Then how?"

"Let's go get something to eat. Then I'll show you."

Her doubtful expression made him even more determined. The girl had braced herself for failure.

He didn't know the meaning of the word.

* * * *

Strobe lights flashed, making it seem like all the people on the dance floor were set on slow-mo. Jami fidgeted with the skirt of her red plaid mini-dress, then traced her fingers over the zipper that ran all the way up to the wide black folded collar. They'd stopped off at each of their places to change after a quick supper at a burger joint, and she'd chosen one of her favorite, funky outfits. If people were going to be staring at her, at least she'd feel like herself.

A drink—or five—might help too.

But before she could ditch Akira and Luke and head to the bar, Luke hooked his finger to the thin black belt riding low on her hips and clucked his tongue.

"Oh no, you don't. One dance first. And if you don't move like a constipated robot, you can have a drink. My treat." He propelled her to the dance floor with a hand curved around the nape of her neck. Then paused to frown at her clunky red Doc Martins. "You *sure* you can move in those?"

"Yeah, they're more comfortable than those flat shoes we have to dance in."

"All right, babe." He motioned for Akira to follow and dragged her to the center of the crowded dance floor. He chuckled in her ear as she cocked her head and wrinkled her nose at the song. "Till the World Ends" by Britney Spears. "Oh get over it. I'm sure you'd prefer Avril Lavigne, but she doesn't have many sexy songs."

Jami rolled her eyes. "Oh please. Avril? Really? Try Sick Puppies or—"

"Sick Puppies? Are you making that up?"

"Nope."

"Huh." Luke put his hands on her hips. "All right, enough talking. Just move with me. Don't think about anything else."

His muscles moved under her hands, and her breath caught as his arms framed her body and took control. She shot a glance at Akira, but she'd already let go, her simple, frilly black skirt flipping off her thighs as she wiggled her hips. She didn't seem to notice the men watching her. Or that there were any men at all. Jami had been a little scared for her, knowing how nervous she got when anyone male was in the vicinity since the crowd she would be dancing and cleaning the ice in front of would be primarily men, but at the moment, it was as though Akira was aware of nothing but the music.

Suddenly, she understood why Luke had brought them here. With the music so loud, the entire atmosphere pulsing with the beat, she didn't have to think about how to move her body the *right* way. She just had to let herself go. Let the rhythm move her.

On the ice, she felt in complete control. Whatever song she chose might change things a little, but it was all about the ice under her skates, about the spins and speed, and she knew she could do it all. Without skates, she felt as though something was missing. She *wasn't* in control. And worse, she had to follow a routine that someone else set out for her. Her body felt like it belonged to someone else.

But not now. Not with Luke's hands on her hips and his hard chest flattening her breasts, making them throb, making her so aware of every hot inch of flesh and muscle and bone. Every part of her became liquid, fluid, part of the rhythm, following it, and him, without any need for her brain to intercede. Even when he eased away from her, she flowed into each movement as easily as she did with each smooth glide on the ice.

"There you go." The warm approval in Luke's tone as he slid behind her and pressed his lips to her throat filled her with confidence, making her bold. She ground back into him, tipping her head to kiss him. His breath was a summer breeze stirring a bonfire, and she trembled as his hand stroked low over her belly.

She hardly noticed when the song ended.

"You've earned a drink." He cupped her cheek and jutted his cheek toward Akira, whose eyes narrowed slightly as she watched them. "And I'm thinking we need to come clean with your friend."

Pressing her lips together, keeping her expression as serious as possible, she hooked her arm to his and trailed Akira to the bar. "About what? I think we've been pretty honest."

He smacked her butt hard before lifting her up to an empty stool. "You're horrible. We both know I'm not gay. Are you going to tell her, or should I?"

Pointing out that he was likely bi seemed cruel, since he was clearly still torn about it, but he was right. It was technically a lie, and Akira deserved better from her after the way they'd opened up to one another. She waited until Akira had taken a few sips of her rum and Coke, then turned on her stool to face her friend.

"I have to tell you something."

"Ooo-kay." Akira frowned and fiddled with her straw. "What is it?"

"Luke's not *really* gay."

Akira took another sip and scowled at Luke. "So you and Sebastian—"

"We're just teammates." Luke draped his arm over Jami's shoulders. "You have nothing to worry about, though. I like you, and I'd do you if you showed any interest, but I've got my sights set on this one, and it's just not classy to do your girl's friend—*unless* they're into that."

"We're not." Akira eyed Jami as though making sure. When Jami nodded, she took a deep breath. "You know, this really sucks."

Luke blinked. "What?"

With her lips in an amused slant, Akira shrugged. "I've always wanted a gay friend. You were so perfect; I thought all my dreams had come true."

Jami laughed and leaned over to hug Akira. "So you're not mad?"

"No, I get it. And to tell you the truth, I was only fooled until I saw you two together on the dance floor. After that, I wasn't worried about him coming on to me. He was so focused on you that he didn't even see that drunk chick flash the crowd."

The bartender came over to see if they wanted a refill. Luke waved him away and leaned closer to Akira. "Which chick?"

"The bouncer dragged her out." Akira shook her head. "And maybe I was wrong about you. Why are you still looking when you've got her?"

Biting her bottom lip, Jami took Luke's hand and gave it a little squeeze to let him know she got it. It would be wrong for her to expect him not to look when he knew she was with Sebastian. For fuck's sakes, Sebastian had told Luke before they left his house—he couldn't come with them because his cousin was coming down early to attend the team's first playoff home game—that if he and Jami wanted to do anything, Luke had to call and ask first. If Akira didn't have an issue with men, she wouldn't have blamed Luke for wanting to go home with her. She would have hated it, but that was selfish beyond words. He had too much pride to ask Sebastian's permission to fuck her.

But Luke shook his head and slid his arm around her waist. "I'm not looking. Not anymore. I play real loose, but when I want a woman, all I see is her. And, right now, all I see is Jami."

His statement obliterated her filter and she spoke without thinking. "Lovely. Do I get to be the rebound?"

Luke let his arm fall to his side. His hand drifted up to cover the scar on his lip as he spoke. "Guess you heard about my breakup."

Jami winced. She had heard. The Ice Girl locker room was full of gossip, and most of the girls were all worked up about Luke's "available" status. But she'd assumed the breakup was something he'd wanted.

"That was really thoughtless of me. I just . . . I mean, everyone talks about how quick you find a new girl. Apparently this was your longest relationship ever. I should have considered that she was special."

"She wasn't." Luke took a step back. "All right, finish up your drinks, ladies. I want to see Jami dance to a few more songs, then I'm requesting the one you guys have to do during the auditions. She can move now that she's got the stick out of her ass. Maybe the routine won't be so hard anymore."

On the dance floor, Jami managed to lose herself to the music once again. And when Luke requested the audition song, "I Know You Want Me" by Pitbull, she did every move perfectly. But she wasn't as into it as she could have been. All she could think of was Luke's last words.

"She wasn't."

Luke was lying. That girl had meant something to him. And Jami had ruined the night by bringing her up.

Or maybe not. He didn't seem to have *her* on his mind when he led Jami in a slow dance as the club was about to close. And all Jami could think of as they left was how his body responded to hers.

All that was on her mind as they directed the cab to drop Akira off at her apartment was that this man wanted *her*. And maybe, just maybe, that made her special to him.

She hoped so anyway. Because he'd showed her she could do what she'd thought was impossible. She could surrender to the music, loosen up just enough to be graceful, and beautiful. To forget who might be watching. There were so many ways she could give up control with no regrets.

But she regretted what she'd said. And hopefully, he'd give her a chance to take it back.

*****

Luke wandered out to Jami's balcony, only four floors up, but perfectly situated for a clear view of the Bedford Basin, all sparkly with the city lights of Halifax reflecting off the night darkened water in the distance. His place with Tyler and Demyan actually wasn't too far from here, but he hadn't been looking for a great view when he'd signed the lease. His biggest priority was having a landlord who let him out at a moment's notice. Setting down roots in any city was a sure way to end up traded—which sounded weird, but had been proven too often for him to take chances. Sharing the apartment made that less of an issue, but he kept to the tradition of never having more stuff than you could pack up quick.

Jami's place looked well settled into even though she'd only been here a couple of weeks. And it was so . . . *her*. A funky patched up sofa, multicolored shag rugs, an eclectic collection of graffiti-style art. Sometimes, he went to a chick's place and was afraid to touch anything, but Jami's place was fun. Welcoming. Comfortable.

He smiled as she came up behind him and wrapped her arms around his waist. "I thought you were gonna hide in the bathroom all night."

Jami pressed her forehead against his back, and he felt her shaking her head. She had been awfully quiet since they'd dropped Akira off at her apartment on the other side of Dartmouth. Something was eating at her.

"Hey." He turned and eased her back as he leaned against the balcony railing. She stared at his socked feet, so he tipped her chin up with a finger. "What's up? You nervous about tomorrow?"

"No, it's just . . ." She scraped her bottom lip with her teeth and gazed up at him. "Are we cool?"

Her question caught him off-guard. He blinked at her. "Why wouldn't we be?"

"I shouldn't have said that about being a rebound. That was stupid."

"Damn, Jami! Is that all?" He laughed and gave her a one-armed hug. "I forgot about that like two seconds after you said it. You're a girl, of course you'd be worried. I'm not sure what to tell you though 'cept that if I was looking for a rebound, it wouldn't be with a girl into another guy."

Letting out a snort, Jami drew away and shook her head. "*I'm* not the only one into him."

"Hey, start with that again and we *won't* be cool."

"Whatever. Guess that's between you and Sebastian."

"I'm more interested in what's between you and me." He

brushed her hair away from her face with one hand and curved his fingers behind her neck. "When we were dancing, all I could think about was taking you home so that I could touch all those sweet curves. You drove me nuts the way you moved once you relaxed." He dipped down to taste her lips, hot and sweet from the two rum and Cokes she'd earned. "I want you. I don't care right now if I have to share you with him."

"But, you have to—"

He kissed her to shut her up. "I know what I have to do."

She stared at him as he pulled out his phone. As he dialed Seb's number. And it looked like she was holding her breath as he spoke.

"I take it you know why I'm calling?"

Seb didn't say anything for a bit. It sounded like he was moving to another room. A door clicked shut over the line, and Seb spoke quietly. "Yes. And I'm impressed. I thought your pride would have you seducing her without a word to me. You did not look pleased when I gave you my instructions."

"Well, it's not every day I have to ask permission to be with a woman." Luke shifted, the hard-on that had been plaguing him all night throbbing painfully, already wet at the tip. "Fuck, I hate that she's yours. I hate having to ask. But she's worth it."

"You're both mine. Admit it, and you'll never have to ask again."

The sea-sweetened air thickened as Luke slowly inhaled, absorbing that word that shouldn't mean anything. *Mine.* Shouldn't feel good having a man say that. Not when he wanted Jami. His lips parted and he almost told Seb what he wanted to hear.

But he caught himself just in time. "No. The way I see it, if you're good with sharing, I'm good with asking."

"I see." Seb went quiet. His tone was neutral when he spoke again. "Enjoy your night, *semental.* Tell Jami I will call her tomorrow."

Luke stuffed his phone in his pocket and stared out at the horizon. The muscles in his jaw ticked. He forced out a laugh. Then reached back to drag Jami in front of him. He fisted both hands in her hair and kissed her, far more gently then he thought he'd be able to, but the softness of her lips made his restraint worth it. He slanted his mouth and traced the crease of her lips, diving in as they parted, enjoying each delicate flick of her tongue. He didn't release her until her nails clawed his chest and she let out needy little whimpers.

"Right here, boo." He kissed her throat as he turned her to face the railing. "Right here looking out at the bay. Hold on to the railing. Don't let go."

"Someone might see us." She wrapped her fingers around the railing and threw her head back as he peeled her panties down and let them fall around the top of her boots.

He plucked a condom from his pocket and tore the wrapper with his teeth. "Does that bother you?"

"No. I've just never done this before—and I've done a lot."

"So I get to be the first at something with you?" Luke unzipped his jeans, then rolled on the condom. His own hand tested his endurance as he positioned himself between her thighs. "Anything else you haven't done, my dirty girl?"

Jami gasped as he slammed in. Her inner muscles tensed, making her so tight he held still and pictured Ingerslov's hairy ass so he wouldn't embarrass himself by coming too fast. The backup goalie was a cool guy, but damn ugly. Which he bragged didn't stop him from getting as many bunnies as any guy on the team. Luke had seen him take two at a time to his hotel room, so it was the truth.

He grinned as he regained control of his body. He'd have to tell the man about his trick. He'd get a kick out of it.

"Luke . . ." Jami squirmed and thrust her hips back against him. "Please!"

"I like hearing you beg." He ground into her slowly and scraped his teeth down her throat. Her long hair clung to the scruff on his cheeks, and a light breeze teased him with the scent of fresh fruit and flowers that always drifted around her. Mouthwatering. Every fucking inch of her. "Tell me what else and I'll keep moving."

"Damn you, I don't know." She hissed as he slid his hand between her thighs and pressed on her clit with the tip of his finger. "Ah!"

"Think about it, Jami." He pushed in deeper and his balls bumped her thighs, held close together since her panties were keeping her from spreading her legs. "I've got all night."

Jami groaned and lowered her forehead to the railing. She mumbled something he couldn't make out.

"What was that?"

She spoke through her teeth. "Anal. I've never done anal."

"Mmm." He rewarded her with several long thrusts, slamming in so hard the smack of flesh on flesh echoed into the night. "So you've never been with two guys at once before me and Seb?"

"I have . . ." She moaned and her pussy clamped down on him, telling him she was close. "I've done some nasty things. Just no . . . anal."

He chuckled as he pressed his lips to her hot cheek. "Are you blushing?"

"No."

"Good, I'd hate to think I'd embarrassed you." He brought one hand to her chest, pulling the top of her dress down with her bra to expose her breasts, each barely big enough to fill his hand, but nice and soft and sensitive. The cold air brushing over them made her hiss and tighten around him even more. He licked a fingertip and used it to wet her nipples. "What kind of nasty things?"

She let out a little growl as he circled his hips and teased her entrance. "Two men—once three—" Her words became soft, breathy. "Taking turns. One in, then out, then the other taking his place." She gasped as he filled her, an inch at a time. "Or one after the other . . . I was a complete slut."

"Yes, you were." Luke quickened his pace, breathing hard. "But I've been a slut too. I love that you're so into sex. We wouldn't be doing this now if you were a shy little prude."

"No, we wouldn't." She panted, bracing every time his pelvis hit her ass, then threw her head back. Her lips parted. She shook as her insides tightened like a fist around his cock. "Oh—!"

He covered her mouth with his hand and dropped his head to her shoulder, his cock throbbing as he came. It happened so fast the pleasure hit him like an aftershock, so fierce his knees buckled with the onslaught. His brain hadn't been fully functional while he'd fucked her, but as the blood washed up into his skull, he held her tight, suddenly, insanely possessive. He didn't want anyone else touching her. Not Ford. Not his friends. Not anyone who didn't see how amazing she was. The crude words might get her off, but she wasn't a dirty slut. She was hot and passionate and beautiful. She was . . .

She was all his, but only tonight.

Hugging her against him, he drew out carefully and kissed her hair. "I want to take things slow next time, boo. I want you on your hands and knees, naked on your bed, in fifteen minutes."

A soft groan escaped her, and she clenched her thighs as she watched him remove the condom. "Fifteen minutes?"

"Yeah. Can you wait that long?"

"Hmm. I don't know." She pushed him away and bent down to work her panties over her boots. Then she tossed them in his face. "I'm ready to go now. You mind if I get started without you?"

Roaring out a laugh, he chased her inside, paused in the kitchen to toss the condom in the trash, then met her in her bedroom, and tackled her on her bed. Already his dick was swelling a bit. He'd never met any woman who could go again this fast. Or made him want to go again so soon. He almost wished he hadn't come so they wouldn't have to wait. The things he wanted to do to her—he grunted as she rolled him over, then straddled his hips.

"I want to make you a deal." She flattened her hands on his chest and bent down to kiss him. "If I can get you hard again in five minutes, you can fuck me any way you want."

He chuckled and folded his arms under his head. "I like this deal."

"Yes, but then you owe me a sexual favor. Anything *I* want."

"Works for me." He let his eyes drift shut as she moved down his body and wrapped her hands, then her lips, around his cock. At this point, she could ask him anything and he'd do it.

His blood left his brain before he could consider *what* she might ask.

****

Jami let her wet lips slip off Luke's fully erect dick and smiled up at him as he fisted his hands in her burnt orange comforter. Much as it worried her that he might look at her differently in the morning—even though he hadn't this morning—she felt strangely powerful getting him all worked up and ready for another round. She crawled over him, grazing her lips over his stomach and chest, exploring the rippling muscles, loving the way the barely-there, down-soft golden hair tickled her cheeks as she rubbed against him.

He braced himself on his elbows, his dark blue eyes hooded as he gave her a positively wicked smile. "Strip. Then get on your hands and knees. I'm going to raid your bathroom."

She sat up on her knees as he slid out from under her. "My bathroom?"

"Uh-huh." He stood, his dick jutting out, just begging for her to take it back in her mouth. But before she could reach for him, he pulled her down and laid a solid smack on her ass. "Bad girl. I told you to do something."

Pouting, she practically tore her dress off, tossed her boots, then got into position. The heat spreading over her ass made her squirm, and she couldn't help but think of the movie she'd watched with Akira. She had to press her lips together as Luke left the room to keep from asking him to smack her again. Getting spanked wouldn't be any fun if she had to *ask* for it.

But he'll spank you again if you're a "bad girl." Jami smothered a giggle with her hand, reached out for the book on her nightstand, *The Stand* by Stephen King, and flopped on her stomach as she opened it to the folded page.

When Luke returned, she flipped the page and held the book open with one hand as she glanced over her shoulder at him. "Find what you were looking for?"

He frowned at her. "You don't listen very well, do you?"

"Nope."

"That's going to change." Without warning, he hauled back.

Crack!

She gasped as pain split across her ass. It soaked into her and she groaned as moisture spilled from her already wet folds.

"You okay?" He rubbed her butt and leaned close to her. "If it's too much, you know what to say, right?"

Face buried in her pillows, book abandoned, she nodded.

"Are you going to do as you're told?"

She shook her head.

"It's like that, is it?" He laughed.

Crack!

"Ugh." Her core pulsed as the fiery sensation spread. "Oh, fuck, Luke!"

Crack!

Her hips bucked. She cried out as he hit her again and again, amazed that each strike brought her closer to climax. *Just. One. More.*

He palmed her cunt and clucked his tongue. "I think Seb had the right idea, punishing you by not letting you come. Or by making you come again and again. Should we try that?"

No no no! The very idea of Luke torturing her like that now had her mindlessly shaking her head and scrambling into position. On hands and knees, she pressed her lips together to keep from whimpering as Luke stroked up and down her inner thighs. Need became a different kind of pain, and not one she enjoyed. Not that she'd ever thought that she'd enjoy pain this much.

"You're so wet, Jami." He climbed onto the bed behind her, spreading her juices with his fingertips, slicking it up from her pussy to her asshole. Then he pressed one finger against the one place no man had ever taken her. "I could probably fuck you here, using nothing but this, but I don't want to hurt you." He pushed the tip of his finger inside her and bent down to bite her hip. "Any more than you can take anyway."

She swallowed and pressed her eyes shut, not sure how she felt about the burning sensation of his finger inside her there. Never mind how it would feel with his dick. "Luke—"

"Shh. I'll go slow." He worked his finger in a bit farther. "I have to ask you something. I found some Vaseline in your bathroom. It was either that or conditioner, but I've been told Vaseline is better. The thing is, it could ruin a condom. I'm clean. I got tested after my girlfriend dumped me because I didn't know if she might have— anyway, I won't judge you for how many guys you've been with, but I need to know..."

Oh God. She moaned, just the idea of taking him, without anything between them, bringing her up to the precipice where she hung as she gasped out her answer. "I had all kinds of tests at the hospital after I overdosed. Including... I'm clean. And I want you inside me. I want to feel you come inside me."

"All right." He kissed the small of her back and withdrew his finger. "This will take a bit of work. Try to relax while I stretch you a little."

His finger returned and he spread the thick, slippery stuff around her back hole before pushing it inside again. It went much deeper and the nerves within flared to life. She stiffened as he added another finger, but he petted her thigh and murmured for her to push back against him. Once both fingers were fully seated within, he pumped slowly and she found herself swaying into each thrust. It still hurt, but the slight burning pain was nothing compared to how good it felt.

This time, when his fingers left her, she couldn't stop a desperate whine from escaping.

I need more!

"I know, baby. Fuck, I need you so much it's going to kill me to take my time. I want to slam into this sweet ass." He kissed up her spine as he knelt between her thighs and pressed the head of his dick against her. "Don't move."

A bit of pressure and the head of his dick, slickly coated, made it past the tight ring of muscle. Burning, burning so much she dropped to her elbows and smothered a sob in her pillows. He stroked up her side, not going any deeper, and cupped her breast in his hands, rolling the nipple between his fingers and thumb. Sharp, tingling pleasure rode over the pain, and she moaned as her body relaxed and he slipped in a bit farther.

"There we go. I'm going to push a bit. Breathe in and push back against me."

Tears stung her eyes as she followed his instructions and his dick forced her to stretch around him. Another inch seemed to grate within, and she shook her head and cried out. "Stop. It hurts."

"Do you want me to pull out?"

"No. Maybe. Ugh, I just don't think I can . . ."

His hand left her breast and covered her pussy. His fingers stroked through her wetness and over her clit. "Maybe you just need a distraction."

His fingers teasing her clit, then filling her, over and over again, made her quiver with renewed desire. She wanted him fucking her cunt again; she wanted him deep inside. Another inch and it didn't matter where he took her. Being fucked like this was somehow nastier than anything she'd ever done. Dark and gritty and dirty. All the degrading names, all the ways she'd let herself be used like a mindless toy, didn't come close to how it felt to be taken in the ass. And even though she could have used her safeword to end it at any time, the fact that he hadn't given her much of a choice made it even better. Or worse.

He let out a gruff sound as he dug his fingers into her ass, spreading her open as he rocked his hips. "I'm going to make you my little ass slut."

She arched back and screamed as he impaled her. White flashed across her vision as she buckled under the assault of a violent, fiery orgasm. Longer, more intense than any she'd had before. Too much. Way too much. Like the richest, most divine chocolate melting on her tongue only to reach an exposed nerve. She almost scrambled out from under him to avoid another wave of searing sensations, but he latched onto her hips and held her still.

"Safeword if you have to, Jami." He used one hand to massage all the tense muscles of her lower back, then pressed down there to keep her in place as he drew almost all the way out. "If you don't, I'm going to fuck you. Hard. I think you can take it, but I'll stop if you ask."

Panting, flat on the bed now since her limbs didn't want to work, she mumbled into the rumpled blankets. "I don't want you to stop, I just . . ." She shook her head to right her muddled brain. "I just need you to hold me for a minute while you're inside me. Let me come down. I can't explain, but at this point any more won't be good."

"Okay, boo, I got it." He aligned his body with hers, gently gliding in all the way, and rolled with her in his arms so they spooned on the bed. Whispered sweet nonsense as he played with her hair and kissed her shoulder. Helped bring her down with a tenderness she hadn't thought him capable of.

Inside her, she felt the pulse of his swollen cock, still fully erect, and bit back a smile. Holding back must be almost as painful for him as taking more would have been for her. But he'd done it. She could breathe again. The feeling of him inside her was exquisite, but bearably so.

She was ready to return the favor.

"Tell me again how hard you want to fuck me?"

Luke groaned and his dick twitched inside her. "Damn, woman. I want to pound your ass, but . . . I've never had a woman react the way you did. And I've had a lot of anal virgins."

Oh, thanks. I feel much better now. She rolled her eyes and tried to pull away from him. "Nice to know I'm special."

"Shit." Luke wrapped his arm around her waist. "I shouldn't be bringing up other women while I'm fucking you."

"Ya think?"

"Sorry."

"That's okay, I know you're a jerk." She wiggled her hips and cast a smirk over her shoulder at him. "You can bring up other men if you want. Seeing you and Seb together—"

"You." He dragged her back up to her hands and knees. "Are." He pulled out completely and worked the head of his dick in and out of the sore ring of muscle, reigniting everything within. "A pain." He slammed in and snarled as she tensed and moaned. "In the ass."

Sucking in air through her teeth, she laughed. "Maybe I'll use a strap-on on you one day to return the favor, stud. Or better yet, I'll ask Sebastian to fuck you. I'd love to see him taking *your* virgin ass."

"No." Luke slammed into her, moving faster and faster even as he gasped out his protests. "Not happening. I'm not letting him fuck me."

His palms on her hips grew slippery with sweat. She could feel his heartbeat in her core. No matter what he said, the thought turned him on.

"And while he's prepping your tight little asshole, I'll suck your dick." She pressed her eyes shut as the mental image shot her up to the edge of another climax. Sebastian taking Luke from behind as she used her hands and mouth to help him relax. "You'll come down my throat as he comes in your ass."

Luke cried out and the sensation of him spurting inside her brought on one last orgasm which stole her strength and had her falling face-first onto the bed. She could hardly breathe as Luke collapsed on top of her, but she didn't need to. She just needed to soak it all in. To let her imagination finish off her little fantasy. To figure out a way to make it a reality.

* * * *

Sheets of scoring hot water sluiced off Luke's body. He scrubbed every inch until his skin was red and left the shower, leaving a bit of hot water for Jami. After drying off quick, he dropped on her bed with a groan. Jami shot him a sideways glance before she disappeared into the bathroom. He covered his face with his hands and thought over all the things she'd said. And his weird reaction to the images she'd planted in his head.

Fuck!

He didn't want that. He *didn't!* But his body didn't seem to agree.

Would it really hurt to try it once?

Hell yeah, it would! He could accept Seb being gay. He wouldn't judge him for it. But that same mentality didn't apply to him. He loved pussy. Loved it so much he could have it for breakfast, lunch, and supper. He'd done barely-legal chicks—which Jami pretty much was—and women older than his mother. They were all worth nomming on whether they tasted like peaches or fish. He'd never been picky.

Seb seemed to enjoy women too though. He obviously liked Jami.

So he's mostly gay?

Luke had no clue. He didn't see how someone could swing both ways. If you liked ass, what did you want with pussy?

You like both.

True. But on a woman. Men had never appealed to him. In threesomes, the closest he came to touching another man was when their balls bumped as they fucked a woman from both ends. That wasn't the same. The men never touched him intentionally and he never touched them. Never wanted to.

When Seb touched him, it was different. In the moment, he didn't think about how wrong it was, he just went with it because . . . because damn it, it felt good. But lots of things felt good—didn't mean he should do them. The first time Chicklet had topped him, just to show him what it was like to be tied up, things had gotten a little crazy and her sub, Laura, had stuck a small butt plug in his ass. She might look all shy and quiet to most people, but she was into some freaky shit. He'd hated the way she'd giggled as he came. Tyler had seen, but the guy was cool, he wouldn't tell no one. Luke had almost slipped and told Bower once though . . .

Yeah, Seb was smart not to let me go home last night. I've got a big fucking mouth.

His cheeks heated. For some reason, thinking of his mouth got him thinking of the blow job Seb kept bringing up. He made a face and rolled onto his stomach, squishing his erection and burying his face in the pillow. He needed a drink just to burn the images out of his brain. If it wasn't so close to the playoffs, he'd stay sloshed round the clock just so they wouldn't come back.

"Hey, you okay?" Jami crawled onto the bed and curled up beside him, brushing her fingers lightly through his hair as she studied his face. "If you worried about me, I'm good. A bit sore, but I'll live."

Luke planted a shit-eating grin on his face and pushed up to a sitting position before dragging Jami, still naked and wet from the shower, underneath him. "How sore?"

"Too sore for that." She shoved him off her, then rested her head on his shoulder. "You've got practice tomorrow. I have the dance audition. Why don't we get some sleep?"

Sleep? Hell, he couldn't sleep. He'd keep Jami up all night if he could to remind her, and himself, that a hot, willing woman was all he needed. Which wouldn't be fair.

Easing her head away from his shoulder, onto her pillow, he sat up and pressed a quick kiss to her forehead. "Good idea. I'm gonna head home. Give me a shout tomorrow and let me know how it goes, 'kay?"

She gave him a tight smile and pulled the blanket over herself as he stood. "Sure."

He zipped his jeans and hesitated by the foot of the bed. "Hey, you'd tell me if something was bothering you, right?"

"Nothing is bothering me, Luke. Have a nice night."

"You too." He pulled on his shirt and went to the hall to put on his shoes and socks. He knew she was lying. A good Dom would force her to come clean, but he wasn't her Dom. Seb was. Let him deal with her.

'Cause if he's focused on her, maybe he'll leave me alone.

Chapter Ten

"Fuck, Carter! You're screening me!"

Sebastian frowned over his shoulder as Bower shouted at Luke, and Luke awkwardly sidestepped to the other side of the net. Out of Bower's way and well clear of Sebastian. The young man had been avoiding him all morning and he couldn't figure out why. But it was messing with his play. Fine, this was only practice—a quick two-hour practice the coach had insisted on to keep them sharp without tiring them out—but the coaches and trainers were all on the ice, keeping an eye on who was ready for the pressure of the playoffs. And who was buckling.

Luke looked like he was buckling.

The head coach, Tim, skated over after blowing his whistle and pulled Luke aside. He spoke low, but Sebastian could still hear every word.

"I don't know what's up with you, Carter, but either tell me, or get your head in the game. If what's going on with your mother is distracting you, maybe it's best if you take some time off."

His mother? Why hadn't Luke said something? To him or their teammates? Even Bower, Luke's best friend, looked surprised.

"It's not about my mom." Luke scowled over at Sebastian and Bower. "I know you're listening! My mom's responding well to treatment, since you're so interested." He looked at Demyan, who was too far to have heard anything, but apparently had pissed him off just by skating by at the wrong moment. "And it has nothing to do with my ex either, before you bring that up."

Demyan held his hands up, stick fisted in one, and shook his head. "I wasn't gonna say shit, man."

"If it's not your mother, or your ex, what is it?" Tim sighed and spoke before Luke could answer. "You know what? Doesn't matter. Can you play or not?"

"I can play." Luke snarled. He smacked his stick on the ice and his eyes seemed to challenge anyone to question him.

Tim shook his head and slid off to the side where his assistants and the trainers waited. The mock game continued for another twenty minutes, at which point Tim irritably shouted for them all to go home. Luke wasn't the only one whose head wasn't in it. Bower was snapping at everyone and Demyan was eyeing the door in a nervous way that made Sebastian wonder if he was in some kind of trouble.

Callahan let them all have it once they were in the locker room. "What the fuck was that? You guys ready to hand this series over to the Sabres?"

"Sloan, relax." Perron tossed his equipment in front of his stall and plunked down on the bench. "Might be the guys are a bit nervous. We've all got a couple days to pull our shit together."

"I hope you're right." Callahan rubbed his hand over his face. "Because that was pathetic. Looks like everyone's got some kind of drama going on and I sympathize. Really. But Tim's right. Keep it off the fucking ice."

"Good idea." Perron stood and stepped up to Callahan, putting his hand on his shoulder. "Speaking of which, we need to talk."

Eyes narrowed, Callahan brushed Perron's hand away. "Talk about what? I'm fine."

"We ain't talkin' here, buddy."

"Why the fuck not? You accusing me of something, Max? I did my goddamn job out there."

"Your shot's off again. If your hand is bothering you, you better say something."

The room went quiet. Sebastian looked around at all the carefully blank faces. None of them had been paying attention to the captain. They all had their own things going on.

"My hand is fine." Callahan went to his stall and quickly changed, ignoring all the players who watched him in silence. He walked out without a word, Perron following close behind.

Owen Stills, a rookie defenseman who'd been brought up from the farm team for the second time to replace Mason while he recovered from a knee injury, thunked his head against the back of his stall and groaned. "We're screwed."

Zetseva, a Russian forward whose English was improving almost daily, tossed his shin guard at Stills' head. "We no screwed. You big pussy. Stop wearing mother's panties."

The men broke out laughing and the tension broke. Sebastian grinned and carefully arranged his equipment in his stall before heading to the showers. Luke and Demyan were both there, not speaking as they washed up. Until Demyan's container of body wash slipped from his hand.

Eyes closed, face covered in suds, Demyan laughed and called out. "This is going to sound bad, pal, but you want to pick up the soap for me?"

Sebastian caught the flash of rage in Luke's eyes. The way his muscles tightened. And surged forward to catch his wrist before Luke's fist connected with Demyan's head. He dragged Luke away from the showers and spoke under his breath. "Get out of here. Walk it off."

"Fuck y—"

Tightening his grip on Luke's fist, Sebastian practically growled. "Now, *niño*."

Luke wrenched away and stormed out. Sebastian watched him from the doorway of the showers as he dressed and jerked his chin toward the locker room exit when he paused. After Luke walked away, Sebastian did his best to appear relaxed. Unaffected by all that had passed.

I need to speak to him. Find out . . .

No. He'd done enough. As he scrubbed in the shower, avoiding quizzical glances from Demyan—who apparently took longer showers than most women—he forced himself to admit his first instincts regarding getting involved with another player had been right. Because it wasn't Luke's mother, or a woman, disrupting his game.

It was Sebastian. And that would end now.

* * * *

Sloan clenched his fists at his sides as he stepped onto the elevator and Max followed him in. He didn't need the man's calm bullshit right now. He needed Oriana and everything she could give him. But telling her husband he wanted to be alone with her was still weird. Much as it satisfied them all for him to do a scene with Max watching, sometimes pushing her limits, someone else forcing him to hold back was a pain in the ass. Max wasn't as bad a Dominik, but he had his moments. He still winced when he saw the bruises Sloan left on their woman. The last few times he and Oriana had played together, if Max couldn't be there, he sent Dominik. And Dominik was never content just watching.

They don't trust you.

Which wasn't true, and Sloan knew it. But sometimes he couldn't help but feel like he borrowed his time with Oriana from her husband and her Master. At this point, nothing seemed like it belonged to him. His game was off, and if he told coach his hand hurt like a motherfucker every time he picked up his stick, he'd be sent to the team doctor. And he'd be out for the rest of the season. If he let Max or Dominik know how often Oriana begged him for more—how tempted he was to give it to her—they'd never leave them alone again.

"Sloan, you're all over the men to pull it together," Max said just as the elevator doors opened. "How can you expect them to when you can't?"

Sloan shook his head and stepped onto the fourth floor. "You had some nerve bringing up my hand in front of the guys."

"Hey, I said I wanted to talk to you alone."

"There's nothing to talk about."

"You're fucking full of it. Your hand didn't heal right. You think I don't see you popping them pain pills every day from that crack doctor you're seeing? Fine, surgery might take you out of the playoffs, but if you keep going the way you are, you're going to end your career."

"You're paranoid. TJ's daughter's bones didn't heal right, so now you assume the same thing happened to me?" Sloan lowered his voice as they passed Ford's office. The last thing he needed was that asshole knowing he wasn't playing at a hundred percent. His contract was only good for one year, which ended this summer. Then he'd be an unrestricted free agent. Which meant he could sign with any team and the Cobras would get shit in exchange. He didn't see Richter, or Silver, wanting that, but Ford wouldn't care less. His focus would be on the team winning—or losing—in a way that made money for the

Kingsleys, the team's biggest investors.

And even if Richter didn't want to let him go, he couldn't justify keeping him if Sloan couldn't perform. Sloan wanted a long-term contract. Anything short of a good playoff run wouldn't get him that.

"Sloan, I know that look. You're worried. You're trying to prove yourself, and I get it. But you're not going anywhere."

"Tell me that next year when I'm playing for fucking Boston."

Max grabbed his shoulder to stop him as he lifted his hand to knock on Oriana's office door. "That shit ain't funny, man."

"My agent's gotten some damn good offers." Sloan shrugged away Max's hand, then grabbed his wrist before he could step back. "Admit it. You wouldn't be too torn up if I was gone. You hate what me and her have."

"What the fuck is your problem? You're my best friend. She needs you." Max jerked away and frowned at him. "Since when do you doubt that?"

A door creaked behind them and Ford sauntered into the hallway. "Lover's quarrel? Sorry to interrupt, but I've been meaning to talk to you, Sloan. How does the team look? We got any chance to beat the Sabres?"

Fuck, Sloan wanted to pound the bastard's smarmy face in. Instead, he shrugged. "We wouldn't have made it this far if we didn't."

"True, but we had Dominik then. His knee is acting up. How are you feeling?"

"I'm fine."

"You sure about that?" Ford stepped out to the center of the hall and whipped something at him with an offhand. "Catch."

Max snatched it out of the air before Sloan could even move. It was a stapler. He held it up, then threw it into the wall before striding toward Ford. "Listen, you goat-tit-sucking momma's boy—"

Sloan latched onto Max's shoulder and hauled him back. "Don't."

The door behind them hit the wall. Oriana came out, eyes flashing. "What's going on?"

"Nothin'." Ford leaned on the wall and smirked. "Just wanted to see if our captain's ready to play, but your husband has a problem with my methods. Not good, *sis*. Didn't Dean say we shouldn't make things personal? Is Max going to be watching Sloan's ass during the playoffs? I can't see that going well."

"You two, in my office. Now." Oriana drew herself up, squaring her shoulders, tiny but imposing in her crisp black skirt suit. Then she glared at her half-brother. "You and I are going to have a little chat."

Inside Oriana's office, smaller than both her siblings' since *they* officially owned the team and she only had an advisory position, Sloan and Max stared at each other from across the room. Sloan turned away first and took a seat on the edge of Oriana's desk. He picked up a stained glass framed photo of himself, Max, and Dominik in front of his father's house during the All-Star break in April, holding shovels and laughing as Oriana pelted them with snowballs from the side of the freshly cleared driveway. Things looked right in the picture, but Oriana had spent each night of their visit sharing a bed in the guest bedroom with Max. Sloan had let Dominik take his room and crashed on the sofa. His father knew a little about their relationship, but... not enough for Sloan to feel comfortable flaunting it.

Stealing kisses with the woman he loved had lost its appeal after the first few months, but the media attention made Oriana uncomfortable. After some rather nasty articles, Max had taken him and Dominik aside and asked if they could keep things low key. Private.

Of course he'd agreed. But he fucking hated it.

"What's eating at you, Sloan?" Max stepped up beside him and looked down at the picture. "I know the thing with your hand pisses you off, but there's more."

Sloan's grip tightened on the frame. He set it down carefully so he wouldn't break it. "Yeah, there's more. I'm sick of you and Dominik in my face all the time—of the constant reminders that you're her husband and he's her Master. No one says shit when you take her off by yourself. No one bothers Dominik when he brings her to the club and doesn't want company. But me? Fuck, it's like I need goddamn supervision."

"It's not like that." Max shook his head and took a big step back, holding up his hands. "Hell, man, why didn't you say something?"

"That's what I'd like to know."

Both Max and Sloan's heads shot up as Oriana spoke from the doorway, arms crossed over her breasts. Max ducked his head and brushed his hand through his wavy blond hair.

Sloan pushed off the edge of the desk. "You seem happy with the way things are."

"You think I'm happy? Ugh! You're such an idiot sometimes!" Oriana pressed her eyes shut as she approached her desk, sinking into the chair, anger fading from her face as she covered her face with her hands. After letting out a defeated sigh, she dropped her hands to the desk. "I know how important your games have been—do you honestly think I'd let how I feel ruin your chances to make the playoffs?"

Max let his hands fall to his sides and moved toward her. "Sugar—"

"Don't you *dare*, Max. Both you and Dominik have been trying to keep the peace at home, but you must think I'm fucking blind." Oriana's cheeks reddened, and Sloan had to fight not to grin. He knew very well Oriana avoided confrontations at all costs, that she loved the way Dominik ran the household with an easy structure she could follow that kept her in a submissive mindset whenever they were all home, but he missed seeing her all fired up. Speaking her mind without a care about repercussions. Max leaned a little more toward Dominik's style—except when he was in the mood to keep things relaxed—but Sloan preferred blurring the limits, keeping things fresh. It was more fun when Oriana didn't know what to expect from him.

When he could challenge her and she'd challenge him back.

Some of the tension left him as he braced on hand on her desk and leaned over her. She wasn't being submissive, so Max wouldn't try to speak for her. Somehow, even with Max there, he sensed it was really just the two of them.

"You're not blind, sweetheart. We all know that." His lips curved slightly. He fingered the thick wood ruler on her desk, new because he'd broken the last one on her ass. "But what exactly is it that you think you see?"

Easing back into her chair, lips parted, Oriana stared at the ruler. Then she snapped her lips shut and scowled up at him. "What I see is you being a moody asshole. You have no idea how much I want to slap you when you tell me to talk to you. Tell you how I *feel*. Why should I talk to you when you can't talk to me?"

"You're right." Sloan straightened, giving her space he hoped she didn't really want. Or maybe that was the problem. Maybe he'd given her too much. He couldn't lay *all* the blame on the other men. "I haven't been honest, and it's not fair for me to expect you to open up when I can't."

"Why can't you?"

"I'm not your husband. I'm not your Master. Maybe you haven't noticed, but they make most of the decisions for you."

"Nobody makes my decisions for me."

He arched a brow. "Really?"

She licked her lips and swallowed audibly. "What do you want, Sloan?"

You're going to wish you didn't ask that, love. "I want more of you. All to myself."

Her hands shook as she thrummed her fingers on the desk. She glanced over at Max. "Do you have a problem with that?"

"No." Max pressed his lips together and his brow furrowed. "But . . . damn it, woman, you don't know how to say no to him. He's better at aftercare than he used to be, but still, sometimes it takes me and Dominik days to get you leveled when you drop. I'm not sure if I'm—"

Oriana's eyes flashed and Sloan grinned as she stood and pushed her chair into the wall. "You're not sure if you're what?"

Wincing, Max slowly lifted his head. "He's made you bleed. You have scars from the whip."

Sloan clenched his fists by his sides. There was only one lasting scar. The one he'd given Oriana on her wedding night, the one that was supposed to mean as much as her ring and collar. All the others had faded to nothing with time. He was careful with her, and Max fucking knew it.

Before he could speak, Oriana held her hand up and moved closer to Max. "I treasure every single mark he leaves on me." She tipped his chin up with a cuff of her fist. "I love you. But I love him too. We all share something different. I thought you were okay with that."

"I am."

"Don't you trust him?"

"Yes."

Sloan blinked. He'd expected Max to hesitate. Dominik would have.

Max rubbed his gold scruffed jaw with his knuckles and gave Sloan a cocky half-smile. "That's right, I trust you. And ya know, I reckon I've been a bit overbearing with you two. I'll back off."

They'd been through a lot together, he and Max, but their friendship had kinda gotten lost in sharing a woman they both loved. Sloan trusted Max. He'd have his back, no matter what. He shouldn't have doubted Max would do the same. But it felt pretty damn good to be reminded.

Not that we need declarations or anything. Sloan grinned at Max. "About fucking time."

"You ain't right in the head, pal. Speak up next time," Max said.

"Will do." Sloan chuckled at Oriana's dirty look. "Were you expecting us to hug or something?"

Hands on her hips, Oriana nodded.

"Keep dreaming, sweet—ugh!" Sloan rolled his eyes as Max crushed him in a bear hug. "Get off me, you beefy bastard."

Oriana smiled and petted Max's bicep when he released Sloan. "He has bulked up nicely in the last few months, hasn't he?"

"Yeah, but he's slow as shit lugging his fat ass around on the ice. I think he needs to spend more time at the gym."

"Your whip would be good incentive."

"Oh, *hell* no." Max held his hands up in surrender and backed toward the door. "I'll leave the whips and chains to the two of you. But I reserve the right to kiss every mark better when he's done with you, darlin'."

"Mmm, I can't wait." Oriana followed him and planted a lingering kiss on his lips before shoving him out. "But I have to get them first."

A bark of laughter filtered through the door as Oriana pushed it shut. She was giggling as she turned, but the sound cut off with a gasp as Sloan closed the distance between them in three long strides. He trapped her with the press of his body and a bruising kiss.

"I hope you don't like this suit." He growled as he tore her jacket open, scattering buttons. He didn't stop tearing at her clothes until he had her huge breasts bared, golden in the bright office light. Her brown nipples were already hard, and he dipped down to suck one into his mouth. He watched Oriana's face as he set his teeth into the tiny nub hard enough to make her gasp.

She thunked her head against the door and moaned. "Oh fuck, you are going to hurt me, aren't you?"

"Yes, my love." He attacked the other breast with lips and teeth and tongue until the only noise she made was a long, throaty whimper. Then he undid her skirt and dragged it down to her feet. The way she trembled as he straightened to undo his belt had his blood pumping in a hot, steady flow, straight into his swelling cock. He folded the length of leather in half and gestured toward the desk with it. "You know the position."

"I do, but . . ." She licked her lips and glanced down at his hand. "We're talking about that after."

"Sure we will, pet." He caught her by the back of the neck and put her where he wanted her. Hands on the desk, ass sticking out. Nice, naturally tanned flesh and sweet, sweet curves. A blank canvas because it had been way too long. He tightened his grip on the belt with his good hand, hauled back . . .

And proceeded to make her forget all about the one he'd ruined.

Chapter Eleven

Sunshine blazed through the huge windows, filling the office-turned-audition room with enough light to blind Jami every time she turned. But she didn't need to see the judges or the other dancers. All she needed was the music and Luke's face in the back of her mind, grinning as he watched her nail every move.

Good job, boo.

Her hair stuck to the sweat on her forehead and temples as she took the finishing pose. Her gasping breaths matched those of the nine other girls in the room. The judges were smiling. Sahara, the veteran Islander Ice Girl, gave her a thumbs-up from behind the cameraman. The gesture could have been for any—or all—of the dancers, but Jami knew Sahara was rooting for her.

"Excellent!" An older woman with fuzzy grey hair, who the girls affectionately called Miss Birdy, stood behind the long table where all the judges sat. She clapped enthusiastically, looking pointedly at the other judges until they joined her applause, then slapped the folder with her notes shut. "This is going to be a difficult decision, but I must say you are all so talented you will have brilliant futures whether it's with the team or elsewhere. Please don't ask me or the other judges if you've been picked yet—the final fifty will be posted outside the changing room tomorrow morning at eight a.m. There will also be a list of ten alternates in the event that anyone must bow out before the next cut. There will be tryouts next year, so if you didn't make it this time, you'll have another chance. It's been a pleasure meeting each and every one of you."

After accepting a towel from an assistant by the refreshment stand, Jami joined Sahara in the hall, laughing when the other woman pulled her into a firm hug.

"What's that for?"

"Ugh, I'm sorry. Just feeling a little sappy." Sahara ducked her head as they stepped onto the elevator. "You remind me of myself a few years ago. My grandfather is a legendary hockey player, so everyone thought I'd had an easy time getting on the team, but that couldn't be any further than the truth. I worked my ass off to get where I am, and after seeing you on the ice . . . if they don't take you, they're stupid. You might not be the best dancer in the world, but you did the routine well. If the Cobras are smart, they'll do skating shows with you up front and center and leave the dancing to the others."

Ah . . . okay. Apparently her dancing hadn't been all that spectacular. But it didn't matter. She'd done it and hadn't looked like a fool. Whether or not she made it, she was pretty damn proud of herself.

She chatted with Sahara on the way to the locker room, asking questions about Sahara's younger brother who'd be drafted this summer, and her grandfather who moaned constantly on how the game had changed. Part of her wanted to go find Luke so she could tell him how well she'd done, but . . . the way he'd left her place in the middle of the night, approaching him in any way would make her feel pathetic. Way too desperate for approval which she didn't need from *him*. And, well, she missed Sebastian. She needed to see him, to know that he was okay with what she'd done with Luke.

Granted, he'd given them permission, but that didn't mean anything. He could be regretting it now.

The locker room was crammed full of girls, half of those who'd auditioned before them had waited to see how they'd done. Sahara took out a pen and wrote her phone number on Jami's palm before taking off, and Jami paused by the end of the lockers to carefully type the numbers into her cell, smiling as she remembered how Sebastian had helped her slow down to get them right.

She finally squeezed up to her locker. Amy was there, giggling with two of her cronies as she held up a picture for them to see.

"She's such a slut." Amy elbowed the girl beside her. "It disgusting."

Says the girl who was sitting in his lap? Jami couldn't see the picture, but she didn't need to. Amy was probably just jealous because—from what Jami had heard—the photos of her with Sebastian weren't even being used.

Rolling her eyes, Jami unlocked her locker, nudging the girls aside so she could open it. "I'd say I'm sorry you wasted your time with the photo shoot, Amy, but I'm not. Apparently they were *really* bad."

Hundreds of photos spilled from Jami's locker and covered the floor at her feet. Among them were unpackaged tampons. Jami tripped backward and almost fell over the bench behind her. Hauled acidic air into her lungs as she stared down at the mess. At the photos of her bent over, breasts bared, while Luke fucked her on her balcony. Close ups of her face, slick with sweat, lips parted as she came. In red ink, on every photo, were the words "stuff it up" and "no more, whore."

Her insides clenched around the curled mess of her stomach. Red flashed across her eyes.

"You sick fucking bitch." Jami pushed off the bench and lunged at Amy. Her fist connected with Amy's chin and cut off the bitch's laughter. Several girls dragged her back, and one ran screaming into the hall for help.

The redhead dabbed at her bottom lip, bloody where she'd bitten it. "You're crazy! I'm pressing charges!"

"You broke into my locker and—" Jami gulped back the rising burn of bile. "Why would you do that?"

"It wasn't me, but whoever it was has quite the sense of humor." Amy sneered as she picked up one of the marked-up photos. "'Stuff it up.' A little crude—good idea though. Maybe if you cork it, you won't be tempted to fuck the whole team."

Whispering, all around. The girls holding her loosened their grip. Everyone was staring. At the pictures. At Jami. Repeating those words. *No more, whore. Stuff it up.*

"What's going on in here?" The room went quiet as Miss Birdy made her way through the swiftly parting crowd. She covered her mouth with her hand as she stared at the pictures on the floor. Her face took on a milky cast. "Oh! What is this?"

"Just a stupid prank." Jami knelt and picked up handfuls of the pictures and tampons. She gave a girl who brought a trash can close a weak smile and almost burst into tears as a few others began helping her.

"She blamed me!" Amy pointed at her chin. "Look what she did to my face!"

Miss Birdy squinted at Amy and frowned. "*Did* you do this,

Amy?"

"No!"

"She was holding one of the pictures when we came into the locker room," A tiny brunette said from beside Jami.

Several girls murmured their agreement.

"The picture was taped to the outside of her locker! Don't try to pin this on me—my friends were with me the whole time!" Amy looked frantically to her minions. "Tell her."

"It's true," one said.

As if they wouldn't fucking lie for you. Jami dumped the rest of the photos and grabbed her knapsack from her locker. "I don't care. I just want to go, okay?"

"Of course, my dear." Miss Birdy waved for the crowd to clear a path, then followed Jami to the door. "But perhaps it would be best if you don't come back tomorrow. I'll have someone call you."

Jami kept moving until she reached the garage. The ache in her chest made it impossible to breathe. She wanted to scream.

All for nothing. She locked herself in her car and pressed her forehead to the steering wheel. Hours of practice, days of dealing with everyone but Akira and Sahara resenting her for even being here, putting everything she had into proving herself worthy ... she choked on a sob. They had been looking for a reason to get rid of her from the start. *And I gave them one.*

* * * *

"Luke, honey, I don't understand!"

Luke thumped his fist into his thigh as he paced the parking lot outside the forum, holding his cell phone to his ear. "I don't know why someone would email you that, Mom. I'm sorry they did."

"That's not what I mean. How could you do that where someone could take pictures of you?"

"I didn't see anyone hanging around the balcony with a camera."

His mother hissed out a breath in his ear. "Don't you take that blasé tone with me, young man. *Oh!* If you weren't too old to spank—"

Luke snorted, then coughed hard. "Mom, you never spanked

me."

"I should have! Maybe then you'd be loyal to your girlfriend. That poor girl. Does she know?"

So much for letting her believe whatever would make her happy. "Teresa dumped me."

"Because of the girl you were on the balcony with? What were you thinking? She was such a sweet thing too. Unfortunately, you can't expect her to forgive you for this. You humiliated her!"

"She dumped me before that. Last week actually."

"Why?"

"Because I'm an ugly hockey player."

"Nonsense! Who told you something so ridiculous? If Teresa said that, she was probably upset about something else." His mother sighed in that way she did when all was lost. "I imagine you forgot her birthday or something. In any case, there's nothing you can do about it now. What about this other girl? Apparently, she has a wild side, but is she nice? Do you think you could—"

"I haven't known her that long, Mom." Luke grinned despite himself. Since Mom was so eager to marry him off . . . "I promise, if we make it past two weeks I'll propose."

"You are impossible." She sighed again, then laughed. "Anyway, how about some good news for a change? I met a new doctor, and he thinks he can operate! He's handled other cases just like mine before. And since the swelling has gone down, it could be done as soon as this summer!"

"That's awesome!" His hand shook and he almost dropped the phone. Tears spilled from his eyes, and he didn't bother trying to hold them back. He'd done what his mother had told him to do. He'd focused on the game. But fuck the game. And fuck all the other messed up shit. *Mom's gonna be okay!* "*Swear* you'll tell me when it is so I can be there. I'll bring you your favorite chocolate and those ugly flowers you like. And books. What are you reading now? If you're waiting for something that isn't out yet, maybe I can talk to my agent and see if he knows someone that knows someone that can—"

"Luke."

"Yeah, Mom?"

"I love you. Just bring you and I'll be happy." She let out a girlish giggle. "And bring that girl of yours if you're still with her. Or the next one, I don't care. Maybe one day you'll accidentally give me grandbabies!"

"*Mother!*" He tried to sound scandalized, but his mom joking around meant she was feeling better. And she finally had a reason to hope. "All right, your doctor told me being on the phone too long isn't good for you, so I'm gonna let you go. I'll call you Friday when I get back from Buffalo."

"Make sure you do."

As soon as he hung up, someone touched his arm. Before he could turn, Akira had already snatched her hand back and retreated.

"Hey, what's up?" He put his hands in his pockets and gave her a disarming smile. "Jami send you?"

"No. And I can't find her anywhere." Akira hugged herself, and her eyes shone with tears. "She's not answering her phone. I came to meet her after tryouts, but I missed the bus and I was a bit late—one of the girls told me . . ."

"Told you what?" Luke did his best to keep his tone calm, but if something was wrong with Jami, Akira needed to spit it out. "Come on, Akira. What's going on with Jami?"

"There were pictures of you and her in her locker—hundreds of them. One of the judges saw them."

Shit. The cement floor underneath his feet didn't seem solid anymore. A dull ache pulsed behind his eyes as he pictured Jami, surrounded by those pictures, by all those bitches who were so fucking jealous of her, trying be so strong because that's the kinda woman she was. Something like this could ruin any chance she had to make the team. And it was his fault. He'd been caught by the paparazzi before doing craziness, and there were a couple of pics out there of him naked, sleeping in a hotel room, taken by puck bunnies. But he was a guy. It wasn't fair, but that's how things were.

Jami must be crushed.

"Come on, we'll go see if she's at her place." He led Akira into the garage, glad that she'd gotten over her fear of him enough to help her friend. Jami needed them both.

Or maybe not.

He spotted Jami's car on the way to his. Sebastian was there, holding her steady, kissing away her tears and speaking softly in her ear.

He knows how to take care of her. You fucking know that, Carter. You knew it last night. Luke stopped short, swallowing hard. *There's nothing you can do to make this better for her.*

Akira walked right past Luke, hovering near the car, but not getting too close. Jami slipped away from Sebastian and went to hug Akira. She was shaking so hard, he wanted to go to her, to give her some of his strength and tell her . . .

Tell her what? You really gonna make her look at you after you fucked everything up for her? Luke shook his head. This wasn't about what he wanted. It was about what she needed. And that wasn't him. He backed away quietly. Then froze when Jami spoke up, loud and clear.

"If you walk away from me now, Luke . . . don't bother coming back."

* * * *

Jami had no idea why she'd said that. She almost told him to forget it. If all they'd had between them was some hot, kinky sex, then he could keep going. At least she'd know.

But she held her breath as every step he took echoed loud in the big, virtually empty parking garage. As he came closer, she had to lock her knees to keep herself from retreating into Sebastian. She didn't know what to do with Luke's unreadable expression. The only thing she had to go on was that he hadn't walked away.

"I wasn't sure you'd want to see me," he said.

She nodded slowly and looked down at the plain, flat black dance shoes she hadn't gotten a chance to change out of yet. "Akira told you about the pictures?"

"Yeah, but I'd already heard from my mom."

His mom? She brought her head up, brow furrowed. "How did she—"

"Someone sent her an email. She doesn't know who." He scuffed his sneakers on the pavement. "She was pissed when she thought I was cheating on my girlfriend, but I told her we broke up so it's all good."

"It's not all good."

"Yeah, I know. This ruined things for you, and I'm sorry. I wish I could—"

"No, I'm sorry. This isn't your fault." She reached out to take his hand and shook her head. "I got on the bad side of one of the girls trying out for the team. I'm sure she did this—she denied it of course."

His lips curved slightly. "Of course."

"She's just jealous."

Luke laughed and rubbed his knuckles on his chest. "I'm not surprised. I'm a coveted piece of meat."

And a real fucking asshole sometimes. "Can you be serious for once? I'm glad this didn't shock your mom, but she's not the only one you need to worry about. If my dad sees those pictures—"

"*If* he sees them, and wants to do something about it, I'll deal with it then. I knew the risks of getting involved with you and . . ." His words trailed off as the inner door to the parking garage opened.

They all looked over as Zachary Pearce, who she recognized from the one brief interview he'd done a few weeks back, sauntered over to his bulky black Harley. He inclined his shaved head in acknowledgement to a "Hey" from Luke, then mounted and drove off.

"Antisocial bastard." Luke grumbled. "Coulda stayed to shoot the shit."

Right, because that wouldn't have been awkward. Jami sighed and leaned back into Sebastian. This guy wasn't the one she and Sebastian had been with, or the one she'd danced with. He was the one who'd left her last night. And she didn't have the energy to deal with him. "If you don't want to talk, Luke, just say so."

"I don't want to hear about how bad those fucking pictures will be for me. I'll be fine." He ran his tongue over his teeth. "Actually, I didn't getting much sleep last night. Your fault." He winked. "I'm gonna take off, crash for a bit. Why don't you hang out with Seb and Akira? I'll catch up with you tomorrow."

Yeah, I'm right on that. "Sure. Whatever."

He rolled his eyes. "Stop doing that girly thing. It's nothing against you. Think of it as me wanting to be rested up for round two—or is it three?"

"Enough, Luke," Sebastian said, his tone razor sharp. "She doesn't need this from you now. Or ever."

"Then what does she need from me, Seb?" Luke arched a brow. "Pretty sure you've got it all covered. Give me a shout when you need a spare."

"Neither of us considers you a spare." Sebastian rubbed Jami's arms as she tensed and leaned back against him. "And this isn't about sex."

"So sorry, *Sir*. Guess I got confused without you telling me what to do."

Wow. You trying to piss everyone off, Luke? Actually, she had a bad feeling that was *exactly* what he was doing. But she didn't know why. She inhaled deep and let it out in a sigh as she gazed up at the block lighting of the garage ceiling. "I'm so done. Akira, you want to go hang out? Get something to eat?"

"No, that's okay. The guys are leaving tomorrow, so enjoy yourself while you can. My parents are supposed to be calling sometime today anyway." Akira chewed on her thumbnail as she spoke, obviously nervous and probably eager to get away from the men.

Or away from Sebastian anyway. She seemed almost okay with Luke. Even though he was being a complete jerk.

"You want a lift?" Luke asked Akira, pulling out his keys to twirl them around his finger. "I'm heading in that direction."

"Sure." Akira paused and reached out to squeeze Jami's hand. "Call me tomorrow, okay? If your name isn't on that list, I'm going to . . . to do something. Not sure what yet, but I'll figure it out."

Jami laughed, pulling Akira into a hug, pressing her forehead against her friend's shoulder so she could hide the tears that welled up in her eyes. "Thank you."

Standing beside Sebastian, Jami watched Luke and Akira as they walked over to Luke's red Camaro. Luke held the passenger door open for Akira, then came around and hesitated by the driver's side. He glanced back.

"Take care of her!" Jami called out.

Luke gave a mock salute and climbed into the car.

After he'd driven off, she spun around to face Sebastian, talking fast. "So, what are you going to do to me, now that you've got me alone?"

"*Mi cielo*—"

"Please, Sebastian, I don't want to talk about it. Or think about it." She toyed with his black and silver striped tie. "Help me forget."

"Do you honestly believe you can?"

"With you? Definitely." Her fingers went to his belt, but he gently pried them away from the buckle.

"Not yet, *gatita*. You will not evade my concerns as easily as you did Luke's."

"I didn't evade—"

"Yes. You did. And he let you." Sebastian cupped her cheeks with both hands, using his thumbs to dry the tears that trickled from her stinging eyes. "I will help you forget, but first you will admit that you're angry—"

"I'm not angry!" Not about the pictures. Not anymore. Her anger about the pictures had burned out seconds after she'd punched Amy. But she was . . . frustrated. So frustrated she could hardly breathe. She'd wanted a one-night stand with Sebastian, but she'd gotten so much more. And then she'd ended up having one with Luke, and that had fucked up everything. His being sorry about the pictures didn't count; he'd had no control over that. But he'd had complete control over making her feel used. And not in a good way.

How the hell do I explain that to Sebastian?

"You told me you can no longer be an Ice Girl," Sebastian said slowly, stroking her damp cheeks with his thumbs, "because of the pictures."

"Yeah, because I looked like a whore." She winced at the word. At one point, being called a whore hadn't bothered her, but those pictures put the word in a whole new context. "They made me see myself like other people see me. And that hurts."

Fuck it hurts. Admitting it felt like lancing an infected wound, sharp pain and then . . . it lessened. With Sebastian holding her, it all seeped away. The damage was still there, but she would heal. And he would help her.

His hand stroked from her cheek, along the length of her throat, and settled on her shoulder. "You know I don't see you that way."

"I do know." She let out a watery laugh, sniffling. "Ugh, I'm all gross now. Can I clean up so we can get to the forgetting part?"

"You are not gross." He smiled and handed her the white silk handkerchief from his suit pocket. "Just a little wet."

She dabbed at her eyes, inconspicuously wiped her nose, then gave him the sexiest look she could manage. "A little?"

Dark eyes hooded, he pulled her into his arms, one hand cradling her head as he kissed her. His mouth left hers far too soon, and then the jerk laughed at her pout. "Perhaps I should forget about my surprise if that's how you're going to behave."

"What surprise?"

He smiled. "I thought we could go for a long drive. I know how much you love my car."

His car and hers were the only ones left in the garage. She looked over at his and nodded. Sure. A drive would be . . . nice.

It took a lot of effort not to sigh. To smile sweetly and say the right thing. "Sounds fun."

Chuckling, Sebastian pulled out his keys and pressed them into her palm. "Lead the way."

Her eyes nearly popped out of her head. "You're letting me drive? Sebastian, I swear if you're teasing me—"

"Jami, I promise, if you voice whatever threat you have in mind, I will bend you over the hood of my car and spank your ass so hard you won't be able to enjoy sitting in the driver's seat."

She swallowed. *Fuck, that sounds hot.*

He laughed again, spun her around, and gave her butt a hard whack. "Hurry before I make you choose between driving or being spanked."

That got her moving. She half ran to the car, stroking the sleek side reverently before sliding into the driver's seat. She'd give him a reason to spank her later. For now, she couldn't imagine more of a rush than sitting here with all this power in her hands.

Until she glanced over at Sebastian. His smile lit his eyes like the sun glowing on clear pond in a smooth, brown stone bed. Something in that smile, in the way he looked at her, seemed like it was for her alone.

And *nothing* she'd ever felt compared to the rush of knowing she wasn't the only one falling hard and fast. If she didn't get away from him soon, she'd take a nosedive, which was crazy.

But she had no intention of going anywhere anytime soon.

Chapter Twelve

Sunset caressed the calm ocean in red and gold hues which spread out into the deep blue sky in a fading glow. The salty air was damp and slightly crisp. Cooling rapidly as it drifted up to the cliff where they stood. Sebastian took off his suit jacket and draped it over Jami's shoulders. In that tiny skirt and shirt, she'd freeze out here. It had been a surprisingly hot spring, but the night still held a winter chill. He should have asked her where she was headed sooner, planned in advance.

This wasn't like him. He was always prepared, never did things on the spur of the moment. Not until he'd met Jami. And Luke, but he tried to dismiss the young man from his thoughts. When it came down to it, he might have been able to resist Luke if it hadn't been for Jami. He would find a way now. He had no choice since one night had been enough to affect Luke's performance on the ice, but that shouldn't be too hard since the playoffs were a priority to them both. With Jami it was different. When he was with her, he could forget the game and pretty much everything else. She made it easy to live in the moment.

"I love it here." Jami snuggled up to his side and rested her head in the crook under his arm. "Damn, how is it that you know exactly what I need? Between the drive, and this, and you . . ."

He kissed the top of her head. "I don't know what you need, Jami. All I know is, after your tears, I need to see you happy. If I'm honest, it was a purely selfish gesture."

She hooked her fingers to his belt and buried her face into his chest, muffling her words. "I hate crying."

"Why?"

"My mother turned tears on and off like a faucet when I was a kid. It was disgusting." She tipped her head up and her eyes were hard. "I never want to be like that."

"I can't imagine you ever will be. But you've had a difficult day and I think a few tears helped."

She shook her head. "No, *this* helped. Just getting away from everything for a bit." Her sigh went straight through his thin cotton shirt and stirred the coarse hairs on his chest. "But I'll eventually have to go back and face it."

"Eventually." He rubbed her arm through his jacket, wishing he could give her more time to get away. Keep her far from anyone and anything that could hurt her. It wasn't realistic. But perhaps they didn't need reality now. "For a little while, pretend that you don't."

Spinning away from him, she laughed. "Why Mr. Ramos, are you suggesting we play make-believe? That doesn't seem like you."

"Make believe it is." He lunged forward as she twirled a little too close to the edge of the cliff for comfort and gathered her in his arms. "*Eres la hostia!* Be careful!"

Fingers pressed to his lips, she shook her head. "I'm fine and you're spoiling the game."

Impossible gatita. He kissed her fingertips and let out a gruff sound in his throat as the surge of adrenaline heated his blood and his cock stirred. "I'm not sure I know how to play, *mi cielo*. I had little time for make-believe as a child."

She bit her lip and a shadow of sadness passed through her eyes. "You'll tell me why one day. But for now, I'll teach you."

He took hold of her wrists and bent down to kiss her lips. "I'd like that very much."

"Well, you're doing it wrong already." She twisted her wrists free and ducked under his arm when he reached for her. "We've played you catching me and tying me up already. I say we make believe that I've caught you."

Brow arched, he pointedly looked over her tiny frame. "I'm not sure my imagination stretches that far."

"That's because you're not trying. Close your eyes and feel the ropes—vines actually—wrapping around your ankles and your wrists." She stared at him until he closed his eyes. The soft pad of her footsteps moved in a slow circle around him. "You've walked right into my trap. I can do anything I want to you."

He chuckled. "What if I break free?"

"You can't." Her voice came from behind him. She smoothed her hands down his arms, digging her tiny fingers into his thick muscles. "All this strength is nothing against my magic."

You have no idea how true that is, mi cielo. "So what will you do to me?"

"Answer me first. Can you feel the vines? They're holding you so tight."

Her game seemed silly, but he was willing to indulge her. "I can feel them."

"Good." She moved in front of him and undid his shirt. "Now..."

The wind caught up and goose bumps rose on his flesh as the silence lengthened. He had to fight not to smile. His *gatita* didn't know what to do with him. As fun as the game had seemed to her, she preferred giving up control. He could help her with that.

Eyes still closed, wrists and ankles still in their invisible restraints, he turned his head toward the last place he'd heard her voice. "Make-believe that, even though you've trapped me, even though my strength is nothing against your magic, you are drawn to me in a way you've never felt before. When I speak, you feel compelled to do whatever I say."

Her warmth seeped into the cooled flesh of his chest as she came closer. "Yes."

"Kiss me."

Without a word, she wrapped her fingers around the back of his neck and pulled him down, pressing her lips to his in a hungry kiss. Her tongue darted into his mouth, and she moaned as he sucked it in deeper. He slanted his head and his tongue followed hers into her mouth, hot and filled with the sweetness of some kind of cherry cola. He used his teeth to catch her tongue, then released it and grazed them lightly over her lush bottom lip. She gasped and tangled her fingers in his hair, pulling it loose so the strands drifted across his face in the breeze.

"I want your mouth on my skin, *mi cielo*, your lips, your teeth."

She obeyed and he hissed in the tangy sea air as she sucked and bit down his throat, along his collarbone, moving down his chest to his stomach, then up again as his hips shifted in response. Her mouth closed around his nipple and he clenched his jaw as the jolt of pleasure speared down to his cock. She gave the other nipple the same attention and he suddenly wished there really were vines retraining his wrists. The urge to touch her was driving him mad.

"Release me." His tone sounded feral. His forearms flexed as he locked his arms in place. Every instinct screamed for him to take over, but he wouldn't. Not until she let him. His next words came out softer, breathless. "Release me so I can give you pleasure."

"Not yet." Her fingers fumbled with his belt. "I've been wanting to do this all night. Please?"

"I can't stop you." No. That wasn't true. He certainly could, but he'd always considered himself an intelligent man. She was looking for permission which he had no problem giving her. "I will not stop you."

"And I won't be able to stop you when I release you, Sebastian." She freed his dick and swirled her tongue around the tip. "You're right about me—I always rush things. But I need to take it slow with you tonight. I don't know why."

"There's no need to explain, *cosita*. Do whatever feels right." His eyes fluttered shut as she slowly slid her lips down his shaft, tasting him, stroking him with her hands when she couldn't take him all the way in. The way she handled him felt incredible, but he couldn't help being a little concerned by the temperament of the unrestrained passion she'd shown before. He hoped she wasn't afraid he'd always take her fast and rough. As much as she'd enjoyed it, he knew there would be days—perhaps days like today—when she needed tenderness.

Telling her so would accomplish nothing. By the end of the night he would show her, again and again, how gentle and loving he could be.

Loving, Ramos? Already?

His hands clenched into fists as he fought not to reach out and touch her hair, her cheeks. He needed a way to show her how he felt.

Yes. Loving.

Her soft touch and light sucking tore him away from his poignant thoughts and caused the muscles in his thighs to tense as he struggled not to thrust into her mouth. Despite the cold wind drifting over him, sweat broke out on his flesh. His body and his emotions tore him in two different directions. If he didn't take control soon, he'd lose it completely.

"Release me, *mi corazón*." My heart. He couldn't stop the words from escaping, but he was happy she didn't know what they meant. Calling her "*mi cielo*" from the start had been unwise—he might have scared her away if she'd discovered the meaning—but it fit her perfectly. The endearment came to him at first because of the color of her hair, but it meant so much more now.

"You're free, *mi alma*."

All the invisible restraints seemed to release him at once, as though he'd let himself drift too far into the game to keep a grip on reality. His legs almost gave out. She couldn't know what she was saying. He stared at her, on her knees before him. "Jami—"

"I have Google, Sebastian. I don't know if I'm using the word right, but if I am, it fits." She bowed her head and spoke quietly. "I've never felt this way about anyone. Maybe what you were saying to me didn't mean much—maybe you were just being sweet. And that's okay. Please don't tell me now though. I'm a little fragile."

"Why, *mi cielo*?" He tucked himself into his boxers and knelt in front of her. "Before you answer, know that I mean every word. I am not . . . being sweet. I will not always be sweet. But you are *mi cielo*—my heaven. You own parts of me no one has touched." He shook his head in frustration as the words she would understand escaped him. "I am not saying this right."

"You're saying it perfectly. It's just . . . ugh, my 'needs' are weird sometimes. I get off being used; I know that. But after, I need to know . . ." She shook her head, then leaned against his chest. "I need to know *someone* wasn't using me. And that makes no sense."

"It makes perfect sense." Damn it, had he made her feel like that the last time? He'd carried her to bed and held her most of the night, but she may have needed more. "I am sorry if I—"

"You didn't."

"Then . . ." His jaw ticked. Only one other person could have done it. "Luke."

She shook her head and tried to stand, but he held her down, rubbing her shoulders through his jacket as she trembled and whispered. "We were just having fun. I shouldn't have expected him to—it's just . . . after what we did . . ."

"What did he do to you?" *Why did you trust him, Ramos?* The damn boy didn't know his own mind. How could Sebastian have been so

187

stupid as to give Luke permission take her alone? "Tell me everything."

Once she did, Sebastian felt completely lost. Luke had explored things with her that had made her vulnerable and then abandoned her. And Sebastian had no one but himself to blame. He'd wanted them both and that had made him careless with Jami's emotions.

"Sebastian, listen to me. You and I both know Luke is messed up. I won't hold it against him. I remember what you said." She cupped his cheeks between her hands. "We'll both take care of him, right?"

She was right, he had said that. But in the heat of the moment. "I should stay away from him. You do not see the way I affect him."

She smiled. "I think I have an idea."

"I was not there that night." He took a deep breath as his accent weighed heavy on his tone. "And he is not here on this one. Only you and I. When we first arrived, I thought of him, on how I should leave him alone. But you—"

"Don't leave me alone." She sat on her side and curled into his arms, looking out at the ocean. "Can a sub force her Master to stay?"

"No, but a woman can make a man want to remain by her side. And you've done that." Loose strands of his hair clung to his lips as he looked down at her. She shivered and he shook his head. "But it is cold outside. Come home with me."

"Not yet." Jami slid her hand into his boxers and wrapped her hand around him. "You're still hard."

"That I am."

"I still want you."

"Do you?" He grinned as he drew her to her feet. "I don't suppose you have the patience to wait for the two hours it will take to get back to Dartmouth?"

"Can we save the torture for another time?" She tugged on the collar of his open shirt and kissed him. "Tell me you want me too."

"More than I can possibly say in any language." He raked his fingers into her hair, ravishing her mouth as he guided her to his car, parked just a few feet away. He seated her on the hood and met her eyes as he released her. The world had righted itself again. "Don't move."

He went into his car and started the engine, which would heat the hood of the car and warm Jami. And when he joined her, his body heat did the rest. He laid her out over the hood, bared her breasts, and covered them with his hands. She moaned into his mouth, tugging at his shirt until he shrugged it off and let it fall to the dirt. Her body writhed beneath him, urging him on, but he moved slowly, kissing down her body as he peeled her black cotton booty shorts down, leaving her skirt. The panties joined his shirt as he lifted her calves to his shoulders and lowered his head between her thighs.

"Mmm, Sebastian." She squirmed as he dipped his tongue between her folds. Her hands fisted in his hair. "Oh, please . . ."

He brought his head up and licked the subtle sweetness of her juices slicking his lips. "Hands over your head, *gatita*. Make-believe it is my magic that binds you now."

She stretched her arms up until her fingertips pressed against the windshield. And thrust her hips up. "More."

He let out a gruff laugh and nibbled lightly on the plump outer lips of her pussy. "Good little subs do not make demands of their Masters."

"Do I *have* to be a 'good sub'?" Her calves shifted restlessly on his shoulders. "I'd rather be a naughty one."

"Would you really?" Most Doms would have already started her training, laid out the rules, but his little imp wouldn't enjoy too many restrictions. Better to set limits gradually so as not to stifle her with them. "Did you like your last punishment?"

She gave him a look of feigned innocence. "Which one?"

"Perhaps a reminder is in order." He spread her pussy open and closed his lips around her clit as he thrust his two middle fingers into her moist heat. A slight curve forward brought his fingertips to a spot that had her gasping and clenching in seconds. He sucked the tiny, throbbing nub and quickened the pace of his thrust. His bent fingers hit her pussy lips hard enough to add an edge of pain. As her inner muscles squeezed his fingers tight, he slammed in and held them there.

Her head thunked the hood of the car and her back bowed. Her lips parted in a soundless scream.

He waited until the trembling, bucking motion of her hips stilled and glanced up at her. "Again?"

"No no no! Not yet. I'll be an angel, I promise!"

"My expectations are more realistic than that, *mi cielo*." He shoved his pants and boxers down to his knees and lowered her legs so she could wrap them around his waist. He rested over her, flattening her breasts under his chest. "Obey me when you give your body to me. We will decide together if you need more."

"Yes!" Her thigh closed against his hips. "Yes, *mi Rey*!"

"You have done your . . . homework. I am impressed. My king. I rather like that." He rocked his hips, sliding his dick against her pussy. All he had to do was reach down and he could fill her . . . but his brain caught up with his body. Must use protection. He reached down for his wallet.

"Sebastian, I trusted him without." Jami moaned as he worked his dick over her slick entrance, pressing harder. "I have even more reason to trust you. I'm safe. I've been—"

"I understand." He fisted his dick in his hand, positioned himself, and drove into her. Delicate, wet heat enveloped him. An overwhelming sensation, feeling her like this, wrapped around him with nothing between them. He was usually more cautious, usually insisted on being tested with his partner, but every single one had been a brief, meaningless relationship. He needed this with Jami. Only . . . he needed to know he alone would share this with her. "But no more, Jami. From this point on, you trust no one but me."

"But Luke—"

"No." He wrapped her up in his arms, sinking in all the way as he claimed her lips and her body. "Only me."

****

High above the ocean, surrounded by the heat of the car and Sebastian's body, Jami drowned in pleasure and pure, mind-numbing emotion. Every nerve ignited as Sebastian kissed her and murmured in Spanish, gliding into her with long strokes. His hands on her hips moved her sweat-slicked body on the warm hood of his car, up and down in a slow, controlled rhythm. Her fingertips left streaks on the windshield as she struggled to keep her hands over her head.

Only me.

Nothing had changed, and yet, at the same time, everything had. Sebastian knew what she needed, probably better than she did. Would he find another way to fulfill her desire to be used? To be treated like a mindless little fucktoy?

Or did she really need that? She wasn't sure anymore because this, what he was doing to her right now, was perfect. And normal. It was about time she made an effort to have a normal relationship.

"I am losing you, *mi cielo*." Sebastian leaned his elbows by her head and slowed his thrusts. His eyes were dark, and the light of the moon gave the hair framing his hard face the sheen of polished ebony. "Where have you gone?"

"I'm with you." Her body ached as a violent orgasm closed in on her, but something was missing. The final admission that would close the gap between them. "There are things you don't understand about me. I'm a little weird."

"No more than I am, *gatita*."

He didn't get it. And his slow grind was making it very hard to get the words out. But she managed. "I need to belong to someone."

"You belong to me." A low growl underlined his tone as he rocked into her. The fierceness in his eyes quickened her pulse. "Tell me how I must prove it. If I must keep you all to myself—if I must fight any man that wants you—"

"Is that what you want? When you say 'you're mine,' does that mean you don't ever want another man to touch me?"

"If I allow another man to touch you, he is under my control as well. He may have as much, or as little of you as I allow him."

Her blood surged low and flames licked her flesh. Everything within clamped down, so tight she felt the way the skin of his dick shifted with every motion, felt the thick head of his cock spreading her as it reached her core. *Fuck. Maybe he does get it.* "Sebastian—"

"You've no desire to be a possession high on a shelf only I can reach. You are *mi tesoro*, and I may choose to let others admire what is mine. I may choose to let them look, but not touch. Or touch, but not taste." He gave her a slow, wicked smile as he eased almost all the way out, teasing her entrance with the head of his dick. "To taste, but not to fuck."

She groaned as he slammed into her, arousal unraveling like a flaming ribbon of pleasure deep within. Right and wrong had no meaning. She needed whatever he was willing to give.

"Someday soon I will have you bound and blindfolded, on display for guests in my home. And erotic centerpiece." His tone took on a lulling quality, the one which seemed to entrance any he used it on. And it affected her the same way. He framed her face with his hands, his lips hovering over hers, rolling his hips so his dick circled deep within. "You will never know whose hands are on you, who is kissing you, toying with you."

The ribbon flared up, coiling faster and faster even though his movements had slowed. Her eyes teared as he moved in and out in short half thrusts, anchoring her in the heat until the sensation of endless pleasure made her dizzy. Like being high, only better. Pure.

"I must warn you of one thing, *mi cielo*." He drove in hard and reached between them, scissoring his fingers over her clit, creating a friction which caused the threads of heat to spark and fray. "I will become rather possessive after I share you. It may takes days, even weeks before I am comfortable doing so again." He stretched her clit slightly and she gasped as it ignited like a struck match. He growled against her throat. "I am feeling very possessive now."

He hammered into her, and the bonfire he'd lit inside her burst as though doused in accelerant. All her senses fixated on the roaring fire consuming her. She thrashed as she came undone, riding the flames like boiling waves, clinging to him as one climax, then another, crashed into her. His roar rose over it all as he pistoned in and out, his grip bruising her hips with one last hard thrust. When he came, she shuddered and wrapped her arms around his neck. There was something intimate about the warmth of his cum spilling inside her and she needed to hang onto it, just a little longer.

"*Cada día te quiero más que ayer y menos que mañana.*" Sebastian kissed her cheek, her eyelids, as he whispered. "I love you, Jami. I should not say this, but the words will tear me from the inside out if I do not."

Her heart stopped. Then swelled as she blindly sought his lips through her tears. "I love you too, Sebastian. And I swear I'll say it again when I'm not half drunk on the incredible things you do to me."

"You know how to please a man, *mi corazón*." He brushed her sweaty hair away from her face. Every word he spoke seemed uncertain, as though he'd lost his grasp of the English language in the afterglow. "Let me take you to my home. I will hold you as you sleep. Then I will make love to you again before I must leave."

"I wish you didn't have to go."

His lips flattened. The muscle in his jaw tensed. "I will stay if you ask."

She stared at him, emotion creating a thick, hot lump in her throat. How could he offer that, of all things? She knew how much the playoffs meant to him. "I would never ask you to do that."

Relief stole into his eyes as he smiled down at her. "Which makes me love you more."

Chapter Thirteen

Butter melted on the blueberry muffins, and the scent drifted up to Sebastian as he brought the tray to his room. His stomach rumbled. Rarely did he sleep in so late—he grinned and shook his head as he glanced at the clock. Almost 10:00 a.m. No wonder he was hungry.

But the soft, sweet woman still curled up in his bed, cocooned in his heavy black and gold comforter, had been almost impossible to pull away from. If the Cobras weren't heading out to Buffalo this afternoon, he would have spent the day with her, right here.

Jami smiled sleepily as she lifted her head from the pillow and used the back of her hand to dry her chin. "G'morning."

Sebastian waited for her to sit up, then laid the silver tray on her lap, careful not to spill the coffee. He leaned over the tray and kissed her. "Good morning, *mi cielo*. Break your fast quickly. I have somewhere to take you."

She nodded and drained half the coffee before attacking the muffin. She spoke around a mouthful. "Where are we going?"

"Your manners are better than that, *gatita*." He smiled when she ducked her head and color flooded her cheeks. "It's bad enough that you are getting crumbs all over my bed."

Her brow creased. Then she stuck her tongue out at him. "It's your fault for bringing me breakfast in bed." She took another big bite and hummed her appreciation. "They're so good though! Did you make them from scratch? I *need* the recipe."

"I'll give it to you." Sebastian took a slow measured breath as she pressed her fingers to the plate to get all the crumbs and then sucked her fingertips with relish. "I also made a dozen—you may take half home with you." He set the tray aside and pulled her to her feet, his gaze roaming over her naked body. All the blood in his body converged to the head of his hardened cock. He forced himself to step away from her. "Dress quickly or I won't be responsible for my actions. We haven't much time."

"Now I'm curious." Jami pursed her lips, glanced down to his crotch, then back at the bed. "And you're lucky I am, otherwise I'd so rape you right now."

He gave her an amused half-smile and kissed her forehead. "If it wasn't important, I'd let you."

Downstairs, in the kitchen, the cardboard boxes he'd collected covered every available surface. He emptied the fridge into two boxes labeled "Perishables," then left Jami to empty the cupboards while he went to the basement to empty his huge freezer. They carried all the boxes out to the porch, and he asked her to wait while he went into the garage by his house. He pulled out in his pickup truck and silently loaded it up with enough food to feed a small nation.

Only once they were seated in the cab did he speak. "What I do with this food is an important part of my life. I'd like to share it with you."

She nodded and put her hand over the one he had clenched to his thigh as he drove. "Of course. But you need to talk to me, Sebastian. I'm worried about you."

"I'm sorry, *mi cielo*, that was not my intention." He took a deep breath. "This makes me . . . raw. I debated letting you see me like this, but you should know me. I am not entirely the person I show the world."

Her small hand squeezed his as she rested her head on his shoulder. "I know."

Such a simple response, but somehow, perfect. He didn't feel compelled to speak again until they'd stopped at the shelter in Halifax he donated to once a month. Jami stood in the back of the pickup, handing boxes down to him and two volunteers from the shelter.

He frowned at her when she let out a little grunt and tried to lift the box full of cans. "Leave that one for me, *gatita*."

"I'm fine—ouch!" The box crashed to the truck bed, and cans rolled out of the split side. Jami smacked one hand into his chest when he vaulted up beside her. "Don't panic, I just got a little cut from a staple."

"Let me see." Hand extended, he waited for her to show him where she'd hurt herself. Likely her hand since she'd hidden it behind her back. His eyes narrowed when she tried to step around him. "Are you testing me, Jami?"

Her chin jutted out. "I don't know what you mean."

Moving slowly forward, forcing her to retreat into until she was trapped against the back of the cab, Sebastian spoke low so the volunteers wouldn't hear him. "I prefer to keep discipline private, but I will put on a show for them if you'd like. I'm not sure if your desire to be used and humiliated extends to strangers seeing me spanking your bare ass, but this is the perfect time to find out."

She gulped, bit the tip of her tongue, and shook her head. "No, that's okay. I'll pass."

"You will show me the cut. Once I tend to it, you will wait inside the truck for me."

"I'm sorry, Sebastian." She thrust her hand out, revealing a long, ragged cut on the side of her index finger, steadily dripping blood. "Look, it doesn't even hurt. I just don't like being fussed over. A couple of Band-Aids and I'll be good as new. I can still help."

Sebastian shook his head. He could understand not wanting to be fussed over, but hiding *any* injury from him didn't bode well. He needed a moment away from her to decide how to handle this calmly. "There are Band-Aids in the small first aid kit in the glove compartment. Now go take care of your finger while I finish up here."

"It'll just take a sec and I can—"

"No, Jami."

"But—"

"No."

For a long moment, Jami just stood there, staring at him. Then she nodded and lowered her eyes, blinking fast as she slipped by.

I believe you are truly sorry now, gatita. He picked up all the cans and put them in a plastic cart one of the volunteers—an older man with a head full of grey hair, solid and strong though slightly overweight—brought him. The man's name was Earl and he spent most of his time working at the shelter. A good man—and a fan of the Cobras. Sebastian could tell he recognized Jami.

"Don't be too hard on the little girl, Mr. Ramos," Earl said as he folded the check Sebastian handed him and tucked it into his pocket. "She's only trying to impress you."

Sebastian arched a brow. "I've asked you to call me Sebastian."

"That you have, sir." Earl grinned. "But it don't seem right with everything you put in here. You're practically my boss."

The same old argument. Sebastian let it go. He was accustomed to people treating him as though he was someone important. Because he was a professional athlete. Because he was rich. None of them knew where he'd come from. He'd grown up no different than those who needed the services of the shelter. He slammed the back of the truck closed and leaned against it.

"I won't mention I saw you two together." Earl rested his elbow on the truck beside Sebastian and glanced at the cab. "Her daddy won't like it."

Sebastian gave him a grim smile. "He doesn't."

"But that don't matter a lick to you, does it?"

"No, sir." Sebastian straightened and shook Earl's hand. "You have my number if you need anything else. My housekeeper can provide anything you need while I'm gone."

"Don't even worry about it. You've done more than enough." Earl shook his head. "What I don't understand is why you're so secretive about it. Isn't this kind of thing good for publicity?"

"Yes, but there are parts of my life I'd rather not share with the public." Sebastian shoved his hands in the pockets of his crisp, grey slacks. "The press knows who my grandfather is and believes I grew up wealthy. Let them."

Earl nodded, but didn't comment. He patted Sebastian's shoulder and waved to Jami before disappearing into the shelter.

After climbing into the driver's side of the pickup, Sebastian turned to Jami. She sat with her knees pulled to her chest and was squeezing her wounded finger so hard fresh blood seeped out from under the Band-Aids.

"Stop that." He took hold of her wrist, holding it between his thighs as he opened the glove compartment to fetch fresh Band-Aids and an alcohol wipe from the glove compartment. Once the wound was cleaned and redressed, he kissed it gently. "Jami, I cannot accept this behavior. We must trust one another. When you are hurt—"

Her face crumpled as she pushed up to her knees, climbed into his lap, and pressed into his chest. "I didn't mean to make you mad.

Please . . . you can trust me. I swear I'll be up-front with you from now on. I just didn't think it was a big deal."

He smiled and kissed her hair. "All right, *mi cielo*. I think you've been punished enough."

"Punished? Oh, hell no." She tipped her head back, and her lips quivered as though she was trying not to smile. "What about a spanking? That should work."

"I try not to reward bad behavior."

"Spanking is a weird ass reward."

"For some, perhaps, but not for you. You enjoyed it when Luke spanked you."

She groaned and eased off his lap. "Must you remind me?"

"Does it bother you that you enjoyed it?"

"A little."

"It shouldn't." He took her hand, holding it carefully in his even though she clearly wasn't in pain. "I'd rather you find pleasure in a spanking than in hurting yourself. Do you do this often? Have you ever done it intentionally?"

She shook her head. "No. I mean, when I was a kid, I punched things when I was mad and that helped me relax, but I never cut myself or anything."

"Good. But it is something you need on occasion, true? I expect you to tell me when you do."

"As in, 'Please beat me, Sir'?" She made a face. "I can't see myself asking for it."

"Then I will try to pay attention when you are acting out. I would like it if you'd talk to me though."

"That goes both ways. You had something to tell me." She pressed her lips together and fiddled with the buttons of his shirt. "Did I mess up too bad? I spent the whole time in here feeling crappy because I know I messed up. It was worse than being sent to my room when I was little, and my dad is pretty good at giving you *that look* that lets you know he's disappointed."

Since her father was a Dom he could imagine how well he showed his displeasure. He'd never considered how a child raised in a household with parents involved in BDSM would behave as an adult. Were they more inclined to crave dominance or submission?

He couldn't say for sure, but Jami's need to please reached him on a basic level. And her honesty pleased him very much. He had to give her something in return.

Pulling out of the shelter parking, Sebastian stretched him arm out over the back of Jami's seat, gaze fixed forward as he spoke. "What would you like to know?"

"Whatever you're comfortable telling me. I already know coming here is more than you wanting to give back to the community."

The truck bumped over the curb. He pulled into midmorning traffic and nodded slowly. "It does. I know firsthand what happens when a person is too selfish to give what they can. My mother came from a wealthy family, but she married a man her father didn't approve of. She was only seventeen when she ran away with her high school sweetheart. My father was five years older than her—he worked in a factory and made enough money for my mother to continue her education. Until an accident crippled him and she found out she was pregnant."

"With you?"

"Yes. She considered having an abortion, but she was raised very religious. So she had me. She told me she stopped hating me when she held me for the first time. But the medical bills from my father's injury and my birth were too much for my parents to handle. She went to her father and begged him for help, but he refused." Sebastian ground his teeth and tightened his grip on the steering wheel. "So she managed the best she could, but we never had enough to eat. I can still remember the pain of going days without food, retching up whatever food my mother was able to bring home from the restaurant where she worked. Rent and bills and debt left us with nothing. And that bastard didn't care. He didn't give her a cent until my father died when I was twelve."

Sebastian recalled the stench of death, lingering in the house for weeks since his father had died in his bed, refusing to put them in more debt by going to the hospital. And the way his mother had cried when her father had shown up to bring them to their new home. A big apartment with a fridge full of food—more than they needed. Bitter bile rose in his throat as he remembered how he'd screamed at his mother and told her he wouldn't eat a thing "that man" provided. As if things hadn't been bad enough for her. He'd made it worse.

"With my grandfather covering the rent and the bills, we finally had enough food. Money for nice clothes—for me to play hockey. I'd played in the streets, but until then, I'd never put on a pair of skates."

"You started late. You must have learned fast to make it so far."

"I took to the game quickly. And suddenly my grandfather was interested in me. He came to all my games, and my mother made sure I thanked him constantly for giving me the opportunity." He let out a harsh laugh. "I was sixteen when I introduced my grandfather to my boyfriend. He was disgusted, but he told my mother as long as I was 'discreet,' he'd continue to provide me with all I needed. I refused at first, but it came to a point where my mother's tears were more than I could bear. My boyfriend had pressure from his family as well. We both got involved with girls our families approved of."

"But you weren't really interested in women."

Frowning, Sebastian glanced over at Jami as she toyed with the hem of her skirt. "I have always been interested in women. And men. Part of me instinctively rebels against having who I love being restricted to sex. But it made my mother happy to see me with a woman. Any woman. Her father was cruel to her when I did things that didn't please him, so I learned to keep that side of myself private."

"You're pretty good at it." Jami lifted her head and gave him a sheepish smile. "You're so mysterious. Which makes everyone want you."

The edge of his lip crept up. "Is that why *you* wanted me?"

"At first, maybe. But I want to hear the rest. What happened with your mother? Your grandfather?"

The air in the car filled his lungs like rancid oil. He shook his head and pulled over to the side of the road. His hands were shaking as he brought them up to rake his fingers through his hair. "After I was drafted and moved to the States, my mother refused to accept help from my grandfather. I didn't see it—he told me after . . . " He pressed his eyes shut. "I thought she was lonely. I wanted to stay with her, but she said . . . if I didn't become someone great, everything she'd done had been for nothing. So I bought her the lovebirds. She seemed happy. I came back to the States. A few months later, my grandfather called me to tell me she'd passed away. She was hording food, but eating nothing. She starved to death."

Jami brought one hand to her mouth and put the other on his forearm. "Sebastian—"

He had to finish. Then he had to move past the depths the memories brought him to. He put his hand over hers and hauled in a ragged breath. "I went to her funeral, then cleaned out her house and cut ties with my family. It took years for me to accept calls from any of them. I speak to my aunts, uncles, and cousins now. I finally accepted that they had nothing to do with what happened to my mother. She lashed out at them because of her father. She pushed everyone away."

"So the cousin who came down to see you play . . . are you two close?"

"As close as I am to any in my family. But he read something about Luke and I sharing a room in a tabloid and decided he'd rather stay in a motel. The article made it seem like more happened than—"

"You don't have to explain it to me, Sebastian. I've had sex with Luke—with your permission." Her nose wrinkled and she hugged herself. "I'd actually feel better if you two—I mean, then it's not like cheating."

Cheating? His brow furrowed. "How is it cheating if I share you with a man?"

"I just want you to know—you and him can—"

"It's unlikely, *mi cielo*. Luke is not comfortable being with a man. Unless I'm wrong, just the idea of being with me is affecting his game. Which is unacceptable." He cupped her cheek and leaned close. "I may find another man. How would you feel about that?"

She bit her lip and cast her gaze downward. "I don't know."

He nodded and kissed her. "Thank you for your honesty. I will discuss other lovers with you before anything happens. I expect you to do the same. Then it is not 'cheating.'"

"So you're giving up on him?"

Sebastian sighed and pulled back onto the road. Once they reached his home, he prepared Peanut, the lovebird he was giving

Jami, for transportation. His bags were already packed, so it didn't take long before they were on the road again in his car. Jami stared at him when he handed her the keys and asked her to take care of it. She swore she would.

Then, after walking him to the bus that would bring the team to the airport, she pulled him in for a kiss right in front of all the men. As the catcalls and grumbles broke out around them, she whispered in his ear. "You never answered my question. Don't give up on him, Sebastian. He needs you as much as I do."

In the bus, seated alone in the back, Sebastian watched Luke, Jami's words still fresh in his mind. The way Luke joked with Demyan and teased Bower about taking on the "daddy status" made it difficult to believe that he needed anything or anyone. He seemed content.

I'm sorry, mi cielo. He plugged his ear with music from his iPod and lost himself to the classical music. Bach. His mother's favorite. *You're wrong. And I hope you don't feel for him. Because what he needs is beyond me. And you.*

Chapter Fourteen

Tuesday night, less than an hour until puck drop. And Luke's body had turned into a solid chunk of wood. He sat on the bench by his stall in the locker room, watching Bower juggle four tennis balls and nodded to whatever the man was saying. He couldn't move more than his head. Not just yet.

Just nerves, Carter. Pull yourself together.

A retching sound from the other side of the room made his stomach flip. He hadn't eaten much for supper, but every mouthful lumped up in his gut, ready to come up any second.

Bower shot him a hard look as he stood and tossed the balls into his bag. "You're awfully pale, Carter. You gonna be okay?"

Luke nodded and gulped against the nausea. "Yeah, I'm dealing. You might want to check on Mischlue though. He doesn't sound good."

And if he pukes again I'm gonna need a bucket of my own.

"Maybe you should go for a walk, pal." Bower slapped his back and strolled across the room, saying something in French that drew a snort from Mischlue before he bent down again, gagging and spitting.

A walk. Sure, that'll help. Luke scratched his jaw where the hair was longest and stood, stretching out his legs in long strides to the door. He managed to hold in a groan, followed by a loud belch as his stomach heaved, until he reached the hall.

"Oh, that was attractive."

The unfamiliar woman's voice came from a few feet away. Luke rested his back against the wall and his hands on his bent knees, not bothering to look up as he spoke. "Sorry, it was either that of toss my beef stew all over your shoes."

"I supposed I should be grateful." The woman's tone turned sharp. "You're that rookie, aren't you? The one that pissed off Nelson?"

"Yeah, that's me." Luke brought his hand up to the scar on his mouth, the souvenir Nelson had given him in return for chirping about his wife. Maybe he'd gone too far, but he hadn't expected the guy to go psycho on him. "You might say he was a little pissed."

The woman snorted. "Yeah, well he was suspended for fifteen games because of you. And you fucking deserved—"

"Hey, it's your lucky night, babe. You can have me and Carter all to your sweet self." Demyan laughed and thunked Luke's back. "Got a mint? I think he just threw up in his mouth a bit. Guess he ain't interested in sharing."

Wow. Way to cockblock yourself, man.

"You're an asshole." The brisk *snick* of the woman's heels echoed down the hall, and Luke managed to haul himself straight just in time to get an eyeful of her round ass wiggling in a tight, pink skirt.

He stopped feeling pukey and tipped his head back to stare at Demyan. "You seriously gonna let her walk away? I know you play better when you empty your sack before a game—hell, I'm pretty sure the whole team knows by now."

"Very true." Demyan shrugged and stuffed his hands into the pockets of his dark blue pants. "But bros before and all. I'll just—" He straightened and his lips slanted into his sleazy, playboy smile as he caught sight of someone down the hall. "Hey, sexy. Miss me?"

A woman in a crisp, light grey skirt suit with a press badge clipped to her jacket lapel approached them. Curvy, fine, and right near the top of the "Off-limits" list. Bower's older sister, Becky.

"Of course I did, Scott. The article I did on promiscuous sports stars and venereal diseases got me a promotion, and I have you to thank for it." Becky smiled sweetly. "You inspired me."

Demyan smirked, unfazed as usual. "So you think about sex with me a lot? Because it just so happens I've got some spare time before the game, and like my buddy here was pointing out, I always play better—"

"I heard him. And I think I can help you with that."

What the fuck? Luke glanced over at Demyan who was already sporting an obvious stiffy.

Becky opened her huge leather purse, pulled out a small bottle of Jergens lotion, and dropped it into Demyan's hand. "You can go ahead and keep that. I'm sure you'll need it again."

Luke laughed so hard he choked and almost fell over. He

laughed even harder when Demyan cuffed him upside the head.

"Not funny." Demyan grumbled, turning toward the locker room. Then he stopped and groaned as a big body blocked the wide open door. "Bower, I was just . . ."

Aww, shit. Luke quickly stepped between Bower and Demyan. The two had come to blows at the beginning of the season, but that hadn't big too big a deal. Right before the playoffs though? Could be a problem.

"I'm going to put you on fucking IR, Demyan! They can call me ripping off your balls a groin injury!" Bower tried to move around Luke and snarled when Luke cut in front of him again. "Get out of my way, Carter!"

Before Luke could refuse, Becky was beside him, shoving Bower back mid-lunge. "Stop it!"

"Damn it, what are you doing here, Becky?"

"I'm doing my job. Which is exactly what you should be doing."

"I told you to stay away from him."

"You *told* me? As in you thought I would obey?" Becky's eyes snapped with rage. "I'll have you know, little brother, that I'll do what I want, with whomever I want."

Spinning on her heels, she grabbed Demyan by the collar of his dress shirt. With a tug, she brought him down to her level and slammed her lips into his.

Luke wasn't sure whether to laugh some more or go for reinforcements. Bower looked ready to go postal.

"Damn, woman." Demyan curved his hand under Becky's chin and tipped her head back, moving in for another kiss. "I thought you were submissive."

"I am." Becky put a finger to Demyan's lips before they could touch hers, then slipped away from him. "Enjoy your lotion. Sir."

After shoving her brother out of the way, Becky disappeared into the locker room. The door shut behind her and drowned out the brisk tattoo of her heels. Demyan's gaze locked on the closed door. The muscles in his jaw hardened. He moved to follow Becky.

And almost got cracked by the door as it swung open. Coach stuck his head out. "Bring it in, boys. I want everyone suited up in fifteen minutes."

They all nodded. When Coach ducked out of sight, Bower grabbed Demyan's arm.

"I won't tell you again. Stay away from her."

Demyan wrenched free and stepped right up to Bower. "If the playoffs weren't about to start, I'd tell you to go fuck yourself. But we need you focused on what happens between the pipes. So yeah, I'll stay away from her."

Bower paused by the door, frowning at Demyan as though he didn't believe him. Then he nodded. "Good. Guess we're good then."

For a beat or two, Demyan didn't say a word. He watched the door ease shut behind Bower. Mumbled to himself. And let out a harsh laugh. "Yeah. Sure. We're good."

Damn. Luke followed Demyan into the locker room, shaking his head. Talk about dedication. He knew Demyan well enough to take him at his word. He'd stay away from Becky. He even ignored her furtive glances, completely focused on waxing up the tape he'd wrapped around his stick blade.

Becky moved around the locker room, questioning players and taking notes on her iPad. She spent the most time with Seb, but he didn't seem to be telling her much. Luke watched them as he taped his wrists. Seb hadn't said a word to him since yesterday. And no matter what Luke did, he couldn't get Seb's attention. He scowled as he worked the tape around his fingers, then stuffed his hands in his gloves. Fuck, not like he cared if Seb wanted to ignore him, but it was kinda weird.

Or maybe it wasn't. Maybe Jami didn't blame him for messing up her life, but Seb probably did. Luke cracked his neck and rolled his shoulders. If she'd have just talked to him, let him apologize—not that an apology would fix anything. It wouldn't change the fact that Luke hadn't been able to protect her. Seb had trusted him, and Luke had let him down.

Shit, I wouldn't want to talk to me either.

All the coaches and the trainers gathered in the locker room and the men quieted down. Luke grabbed his cell from his stall and flipped it in his hand as the pep talk started, hardly hearing a word. He'd leave his cell with one of the trainers as usual, just in case his mother or aunt called. They wouldn't unless there was an emergency. Every time he handed his phone over, he prayed it wouldn't ring.

It buzzed in his hand as the men were shouting in response to whatever Coach had said. Luke moved away from the horde of players heading out to the ice and leaned against the wall, inhaling slowly before he checked the number on the display.

He exhaled and laughed before answering. "Hey, Jami. What's up?"

"Not much. You about to get out there?"

"Yeah. Don't have much time to talk." Or any time really, but it was nice hearing her voice. "Something you needed to say? Or you need me to say? About the pictures—"

"I don't want to talk about the pictures."

Of course you don't. Luke sighed. Then did his best to keep things light. "I'm telling you right now, if you're calling to tease me with you and Akira's plans for the night, I'm gonna beat you when I get home."

"Oh, so tempting." She giggled in that cute, fresh way she had. Not a girly giggle really—more like a light, bubbly spring laugh. "Can't stand hockey, but I wanted to let you know I'll be watching my first game in years tonight so I can see you play. You don't suck do you? I'd hate to waste my time."

"I don't suck." He grinned as an odd warmth filled him. Then waved Demyan away when he called out and lowered his voice. "And just to prove it, I'll score one for you. Then I'll do that move you liked—remember when we were dancing?"

"I remember," she said softly. She paused and it sounded like she was holding her breath. Then she let it out noisily. "Hey, Luke, can you do me a favor? I couldn't get ahold of Sebastian. You want to let him know I'm rooting for him too?"

"Assuming I talk to him."

"You'll do more than talk to him, stud."

The room had all but emptied out. Still, kept his voice down. "Boo, he won't even look at me."

"That's because . . . damn it, I shouldn't be telling you this, but he thinks what's going on between you is messing with your game. Prove it's not."

"It's not, but I don't know what you think's gonna happen."

"That's entirely up to you."

"Right." Luke shook his head, not wanting to end the call talking about Seb. He needed to know he and Jami still had something too. But anything he said would sound lame. *Suck it up, Carter.* "Hey, Jami?"

"Yeah?"

"We're gonna dance again. Soon. I had a lot of fun that night."

She didn't answer for what seemed like a very long time. He expected to hear the sound of the game starting without him any second. But he waited anyway.

"So did I, Luke. Just . . . just fix this."

After saying goodbye, Luke hung up and let out a heavy sigh. Fix this. Sure. Because what happened with Seb was entirely up to him. He just had to decide what he wanted from the man.

If anything.

But . . . he didn't have to worry about that now. If Jami was right, the first thing he had to do was prove he wasn't weirded out by what had already happened. Easy enough.

Seb thought he was off his game? As if some kinky sex would change the way he played?

No way, pal. Need proof? Just watch me.

* * * *

Mussorgsky's *Night on Bald Mountain* boomed out as a compilation of the best plays from the Sabres' season played on the huge screens of the Jumbotron. Laser lights painted the ice in flashes of gold, slashing across the faces of the players which covered the ice in large, glowing stills. Luke rocked on his skates as he watched, nostrils flaring as a dirty hit on him from Nelson was shown above, and the crowd burst out in wild cheers. Luke's blood all over the ice and they acted like Nelson was a fucking hero.

Someone squeezed his shoulder, and he glanced back and grinned at Pearce to let him know he was good. Hockey fans in Buffalo hated Luke "The Mouth" Carter with a passion. And they would hate him even more by the end of the first round. Let them. It was quite an achievement to be loathed this much after only two seasons in the league.

The Sabres were all introduced over the speakers to the delight of the packed stadium. Boos met the Cobras when they hit the ice. Everyone stood for the anthems, and from the benches Luke sang as loud as he could for the Canadian one. His face was shown on the Jumbotron, and the crowd booed again.

He grinned. *Damn that's good for my ego!*

Callahan won the face-off. Luke leaned on the boards and shouted Perron on as he accepted a pass and skipped it to Demyan who'd been promoted to the first line. Demyan caught the Sabres' goalie off guard, and the puck skidded toward the goal. A Sabres' defenseman dived behind his goalie and kept it out of the net. The goalie froze the puck.

Another face-off. The Cobras' line spread out and cleanly cleared the puck for a shift change. Luke's skates hit the ice, and he rushed forward as Pearce scooped up the puck and riffled a hard pass in his direction. Energy exploded through his muscles as he cupped the puck and surged forward. Nelson hopped over the boards ahead of him, but Luke jetted sideways, twisting around the defense. He let the puck fly.

The Sabres' goalie gloved it at the last second. Nice save. Luke panted as he took his place off to the right for the puck drop. He caught a swift pass and tucked the puck back to Seb. Seb circled wide and whipped the puck to Luke. Pearce was open and positioned perfectly. Luke saucered the puck to him and roared out a cheer as a swift shot hit the back of the net. He raced up to Pearce and plowed him into the boards in a hug. Sweat spilled into his eyes as he screamed praises to the man. They were on the scoreboard. First goal meant everything in the playoffs. Stats almost guaranteed a win. As long as they didn't get stupid.

Score remained 1-0 until the second period. Refreshed from the break, dry gloves on his hands, Luke strode onto the ice, excitement burning in his veins. He didn't even think when the puck ended up on his stick blade. He just fired.

And the red light made him think of Jami. Watching him. He spun around and rotated his hips as he danced toward the roaring horde of Cobras rushing toward him. The music he'd danced to with Jami, something by Pitbull, played in his head as he held his gloved hand up and counted down. 1, 2, 3, 4. He pointed toward the camera, hoping Jami would know this was for her.

You can't stand hockey, boo? Say that again after watching me out here and I might buy it.

By the third period, with nothing on the boards, the Sabres got desperate. Bower covered the Cobras' net like a wall, spread out like a jointless monster. Luke scooped up a long pass from Bower and zipped across the ice. Nelson drove him into the boards. Luke gulped in air as pain erupted from his back and his muscles seized. He dropped hard and ice melted under his cheek. He was all right. But he needed air.

Air. None came. He pressed his eyes shut and rolled over to his back. Demyan stood over him, lips moving.

His brain fogged with a sharp buzzing, but he finally heard what Demyan was saying.

"Need a hand up? If anything hurts, tell me. I'll get the doc."

"Just a little shook up. Give me a sec." Luke shook his head and rolled over. Got to his knees. The sounds from the crowds had changed. Taken on a bloodthirsty edge. A fight. He pushed Demyan aside. "Let me see!"

Holding his hands up, Nelson skidded backward, but Seb grabbed him and clocked him right in the jaw. He released Nelson and made a sharp motion with his hand, giving Nelson an out.

Nelson didn't take it. Even though Seb was a head taller, and at least thirty pounds heavier, Nelson dropped his gloves, letting the refs know he was in. He took another jab to the jaw, then blocked a punch with his forearm. Threw himself forward to catch Seb off balance and swung his fist.

Seb caught the punch and used Nelson's momentum to toss him over. Skates up, head down, Nelson fell. He tried to shake off the ref, but the officials moved in to separate the fighters. They hauled Seb to the sin bin, then let Nelson make his way to the Sabres' penalty box on his own.

The crowd didn't care much who'd won, but the Cobras hit the boards with their sticks harder than the Sabres, cheering the victor.

Luke inclined his head as he glanced toward Seb. The man had stuck up for him. He deserved some props.

Seb acknowledged the gesture with a stiff nod.

In the final minutes of the third period, the Sabres crowded Bower, blinding him as a defenseman took a rocket shot from the point. Callahan tried to block the shot, but it hit his glove and trickled over the line. Luke frowned as he watched Callahan shake his hand before he hit Bower's pads with his stick, letting their goalie know it was okay. They were still ahead.

But their captain was hurting. And Luke wasn't the only one who noticed.

"He's not right," Demyan said as he leaned close to Luke.

"That puck hit him hard. Probably just bruised up." Luke watched Callahan disappear into the back with a trainer. "They'll check him out, but I bet he's fine."

"He'll say he is no matter what."

Nodding, Luke leaned forward, stretching his arms and his spine. A dull ache settle low in his back. Yeah, they were all gonna get roughed up. That's what happened in the playoffs. Callahan returned after just a few minutes. He was okay.

Last five minutes. Demyan broke away from the Sabres' defense, who were pinching in an effort to even up the score. Luke stabbed his stick into the huddle in the corner and freed the puck. His pass was wide, but Demyan snapped it up and headed in alone. His first shot hit the post, but the goalie was all alone and Demyan snatched the rebound, diving into his shot as the goalie spread out. The shot hit the right corner post. Clipped the goalie's helmet. And dropped between the pipes. The goalie tried to scoop it out and accidentally pushed it over the line. He covered his helmet with his glove and dropped his head as the red lights flashed.

Seb left the box in the next shift and caught Luke's eye. Luke stumbled at the power in his gaze but recovered fast enough to clear the puck. Icing. But it was the last seconds of the game. And Bower covered like he'd grown extra limbs. Sad thing was, he worked harder than he should have because all the Cobras acted like the game was already won.

And then it was. And they all went mad.

The team converged on the locker room and showered and donned their suits. Demyan had a local club in mind, but something Seb had said to Luke stuck with him. He wasn't supposed to drink during the playoffs, but damn, he wanted to. All the guys would be celebrating, so why couldn't he?

Because Seb had said no. And for some reason, that made Luke pause.

"If I get wasted, I'll be shit at practice tomorrow."

His words sounded lame, but Demyan nodded.

"Hey, if you can't handle your liquor, go back to the hotel and catch some shut-eye."

As if I can sleep now?

It was pathetic, but for some crazy reason, Luke needed Seb's okay. He found him in the hotel lobby and stuffed his hands in his pockets as he inched close to the man.

"Hey, Seb?"

"Yes, Carter?"

Luke winced and took a step back. Seb must be pissed if he was calling him Carter. Asking him if it was okay to drink would probably make it worse. "Never mind."

Frowning, Seb put his hand on Luke's shoulder before he could turn away. "Is there something you wanted to say to me, *hombrecito*?"

"Just . . . well, a few of the guys are going out to celebrate. I wanted to know if you were coming."

"I see." Seb's eyes narrowed slightly. "Shall we try the truth now?"

"Fuck, man." Luke rolled his eyes. "Fine. Is it cool if I have a couple'a beers? I won't get plastered, I—"

"Why do you need my permission?"

"You know why."

"No." Seb's hand fell to his side. "I don't."

Those three words felt like a punch in the gut. Seb obviously didn't give a shit what he did.

Good. It's better this way. Luke gave Seb a curt nod and headed out to catch a cab. At the club, he mingled with the guys. Laughed and drank two beers. Then a third. He let some hot chicks drag him to the dance floor and considered going home with a couple. But he couldn't do it.

Near closing, he went back to the bar and ordered another beer. The first sip was bitter, and he couldn't make himself take another. He took his cell out of his pocket and smiled when he saw one missed call from Jami. And a message.

He went outside to listen to it.

"You won!" A whoop and a laugh followed. Then Jami's tone changed, sounding pointedly unimpressed. "Anyway, just wanted to let you know I wasn't totally bored. You played good and that little dance was cocky—and kinda sexy. Wish you guys were here. The things I would do to you . . ."

His cock twitched and he groaned. *Tease!*

"Give me a call tomorrow if you want to . . . you know, talk about anything. I know some of this stuff is hard for you. We're friends if nothing else, right?"

The message ended abruptly, and he found himself grinning like a moron and shaking his head. She would let up, would she? He put his phone away and strolled down the block aimlessly, his mind going over the "if nothing else." He'd given her the impression they had nothing else, and he hadn't really meant to. He was just . . . confused. How he felt about her and how he felt about Seb was tangled together. And he didn't know how to deal with it.

But he had a good idea where to start.

* * * *

With a towel wrapped around his waist, Sebastian stood in the center of the bathroom, combing the tangles from his wet hair. He bound it low in a plain, black elastic, then faced the bathroom mirror and prodded the dark, blotchy red spot over his ribs from a slash in the first period. His stomach muscles bunched in response to the throbbing pain, but he'd had bruised ribs often enough to know it wasn't serious. An ice compress should dull it enough for him to sleep.

He took a small towel to the bedroom, then scooped a handful of ice from the bucket he'd ordered from room service before his shower. He grunted as he sat on the edge of the bed and held the makeshift icepack against his ribs. A few painkillers would be more effective, but he avoided them whenever possible. Early in his career, he'd had a bad case of withdrawal after taking them for a few weeks when he'd fractured a couple of ribs. Minor discomfort was easier to deal with than kicking what could easily become an addiction.

Stretching out on his back, he let his eyes drift shut and smiled as he recalled the message from Jami. He'd left his cell phone in his hotel room out of habit to avoid distractions, and by the time he checked his missed calls—the one from Jami and several from his cousin excitedly recapping every fifteen minutes of play—it was too late to call her back. But he'd listened to her message several times, impressed that she'd managed the whole thing in Spanish. Very bad Spanish, but it was the effort that counted. And the gist of what she'd said.

One part stuck out the most. "I could almost learn to love the game again if it didn't take you away from me for so long."

Sebastian picked up the phone from the nightstand and grazed his thumb over the screen which displayed the picture of Jami and him, taken for the magazine. Once he returned to her, he would keep her with him as long as possible. Make it so she wouldn't resent the game or anything else that kept them apart.

A soft knock at the door made him groan as he forced himself to sit up. A twinge of pain kept him still as he breathed through it. Another knock came, louder this time.

He gritted his teeth. "I'm coming."

"Fuck, Seb. Don't make me talk through the door." Luke sounded impatient. Almost desperate. "I swear, I'll say what I've got to say right in the hall, and I don't give a damn who hears me."

Stupid, niño. Sebastian cut across the room in long strides and threw the door open. "I don't respond well to threats, Carter."

"Luke." Luke stepped in and caught him off guard with a hard shove. "And too fucking bad. You're not ignoring me anymore."

The door slammed as Luke kicked it shut. He hooked his arm around the back of Sebastian's neck and rose up to give him a brutal, angry kiss. The intensity lessened abruptly, as though Luke's strength had left him. His eyes went wide as he released Seb and combed his fingers through his hair.

"Shit. I don't know what I'm doing. Tell me to get lost if you want, but I wanted to tell you—wanted to show you . . ."

Sebastian wrapped his hand around the back of Luke's neck with just enough pressure for the young man to know he wasn't completely in control. He had a feeling that was what caused the uncertainty. Whatever Luke needed from him went beyond curiosity, beyond lust.

But is it enough? Sebastian couldn't say for sure. But now that he had his hands on Luke again, letting him go would be almost impossible.

"What do you need to show me, Luke?"

Luke dropped to his knees. His breaths came out in harsh bursts of air. He curved his fingers around the top of the towel covering Sebastian. "I can—"

"No." Sebastian shook his head and gently drew Luke to his feet, brushing sweat slicked hair from his temples with his fingertips as he smiled. He should send Luke away. Should refuse the offer in his actions. But he knew how much it had cost Luke to come this far. He pulled Luke closer so he wouldn't feel rejected. "You're not ready for that, *semental*. But there are things I want to do to you. Show me you are ready to submit, that you can handle me touching you. Swear to me you will not hate yourself, or me, tomorrow—"

"I won't." Luke swallowed as Sebastian led him to the bed. "But I can't promise I won't be a little screwed up in the head about it in the morning. I'll still be able to play though. Jami—I mean, I get you being worried about that."

In other words, Jami had spoken to him about Sebastian's concerns and asked him not to say anything. He probably wouldn't have if he hadn't given in so completely. At this point, Sebastian could ask Luke to reveal his deepest, darkest secrets and he would.

"I will take you at your word. But this will work much better if you are not so overdressed, *niño*. You have one last chance to walk away. If you want to stay, you will strip and lie down on my bed." Sebastian released Luke and waited for him to obey. His lips quirked when Luke tore at his shirt, eyes pressed shut, jaw muscles hardening with determination. "I do hope you brought more than one suit."

"I brought a few." Luke tugged off his dark blue, clip-on tie and tossed it toward the bed. "Hate wearing the damn things though."

Sebastian picked up the tie and shook his head. "You will not wear this again. I will show you how to wear a proper tie tomorrow."

"But—"

"I will dress you in the morning, Luke. Don't expect me to leave you—or make you leave—in the middle of the night."

Luke winced as if finally understanding the impact of what he'd done. "You're pissed about me leaving Jami, aren't you?"

"I am not happy about it, no. But we will discuss that further at another time. This, tonight, is about you and I." Sebastian folded his arms over his chest, giving Luke a pointed look. "The pants as well, niño."

"Right." Luke tongued his bottom lip and pushed his pants and boxers down to his ankles. He stepped out of them, then straightened and clasped his hand to his wrist behind his back. His dick was fully erect, but by the stiff way he stood, with his chin up high, he was ignoring his own physical reactions to the situation. "So what now?"

"On the bed. Facedown."

Casting a wary look at the bed, Luke repeated. "Facedown?"

"Must I repeat my every command?" Sebastian let a hint of displeasure seep into his tone. "I don't have a cane or a crop on me, but I can improvise with my belt if you require punishment."

"I don't . . . I don't want this to be about me not obeying." Luke made a face and scowled at the floor. "It's just . . . when you had the knife to my throat—and a few other times after—it was like I didn't—"

"Have a choice." Sebastian nodded slowly. Luke couldn't completely surrender control. Not yet. He needed it taken from him. "Very well. Don't. Move."

In his sports bag, Sebastian found some sports tape. He eyed the lube and condoms. He doubted he would need either tonight, but he took them in case . . .

Don't rush him, Ramos. Sebastian crushed the condom in his fist and dropped it back into his bag. He pulled on a pair of black jeans, then returned to Luke's side. Observed him for several long moments, perched on the edge of the bed, fist pressed into the mattress as though he'd rise any second and take a swing.

"I am prepared to hurt you if you fight me, Luke."

"Good." Luke frowned at him. "Why'd you get dressed?"

"To avoid scaring you." Sebastian grabbed Luke's wrists and jerked them over his head, the circle of tape around his hand, the lube dropping to the bed. He held tight as Luke struggled. "Any more than necessary."

"You don't fucking scare me, man!"

"Don't I?" He growled, restraining Luke's wrists with one hand as he pulled out a length of tape with his teeth. He easily overpowered the smaller man, using his weight to pin him as he bound his wrists together. "Say 'red.'"

Luke bared his teeth. "No."

"Say it or I won't stop."

The muscles in Luke's forearms bulged as he tugged. "I don't want you to stop."

Fuck. Showing any restraint after that admission was almost impossible. He let Luke feel how close to losing control he was in a bruising, open-mouthed kiss. And pulled away at the taste of beer. "You've been drinking."

"I'm not drunk."

"How much did you have?"

"Three. Not enough to make this okay if it wasn't." Luke threw his head back. "Please!"

Sebastian used his fingertips to explore Luke's face, the golden stubble on his jaw uneven in a way that made him seem a wild thing. The soft, barely-there curls on his chest showing how young he still was. He grazed his teeth over Luke's ribs. Power surged through him as Luke hissed in a breath and bucked his hips. He flipped Luke over and pressed down between his shoulder blades to stop him from twisting around.

"How is your back?" He braced one hand between Luke's shoulder blades and rose up enough to feel the tight muscles, spotted with dark bruises where Luke had been hit. "I expect you to tell me if the pain becomes unpleasant."

Luke groaned and buried his face in the pillows as Sebastian carefully massaged around the worst of the bruises. "Oh God, that feels good. Don't hurt much anymore. Can't be half as bad as your ribs. Did you get them checked?"

"Your concern is touching." Sebastian kissed the nape of Luke's neck, slowly breathing in the clean scent of soap, a hint of musk and sweat. He stroked down Luke's side, over his hip, then up again. Worked his fingers into muscles wrought with tension. Going slow while relaxing his hold. Giving Luke a chance to adjust to being touched by him. Waiting for him to become aware that he wasn't being forced to accept the attentions of another man. A dominant man. To understand that he had finally submitted.

A shudder went through the solid body beneath him, and he could practically taste Luke's fear as a fine sheen of cold sweat covered his skin. He rose up as Luke panted, then rolled him onto his back. "Stretch your arms over your head. I don't want them in my way."

Luke swallowed and nodded. He lifted his arms, twisted his wrists in the tape binding them, and squeezed his eyes shut.

"No. You will look at me." Sebastian waited until Luke opened his eyes. Stared into them as he moved down. "Don't pretend you are with someone else. Someone who it is not wrong to let do these things to you. I am the one touching you. Tasting you. I am the only one who will until you understand that you belong to me."

"Fuck." Luke trembled and made a rough sound in his throat. "Fuck, Sebastian, what are you doing to me? I still can't believe—"

"Believe it." Sebastian let his breath tease the swollen head of Luke's cock and smiled. "As for what I am doing? Whatever I please, *semental*. And you've no desire to stop me."

"No."

His fingers bit into Luke's thighs as he took his throbbing dick between his lips and arched his neck so the feverishly hot head hit the back of his throat.

"No!" Luke arched his back and groaned. "I should—"

"I will tell you what you should do." Sebastian held Luke down as he teased the pulsing veins along his length with his tongue. "Don't think about what is right or wrong. Feel what I am doing to you. You have no choice but to accept it."

"I already have." Luke tossed his head. His back bowed, and he moaned as Sebastian sucked his length between his lips once again. "I had a choice, though. And I made it."

"Good." Sebastian cupped Luke's balls, enjoying the weight of them in his hand, all too aware of what it meant for Luke to allow him to handle the most vulnerable parts of him. Not only physically, but mentally. Emotionally. He fisted his hand around the base of Luke's cock, increasing the pressure as he ran his tongue over the bead of pre-cum at the tip. "I was willing to let you go, but not anymore."

"Don't ever make decisions like that for me again, Sebastian. God!" Luke let out a sound half between a roar and a scream, like an animal in exquisite pain. He came deep in Sebastian's throat, trembling with each hot spurt. And then he went still and turned his head, staring at the wall. "Don't fucking give up on me. I know I'll give you plenty of reasons to, but just . . . just don't, okay?"

Sebastian nodded slowly as he stretched out on the bed behind Luke, releasing his wrists before pulling him tight against his chest. He spoke softly, barely a whisper, his lips brushing against Luke's throat. "I won't give up on you. I will be here as long as you need me."

Luke nodded and settled into his arms, likely exhausted from the game as well as what had taken place between them. Sebastian knew very well most of what Luke had said came from a pleasure-induced haze, but he wouldn't worry about that now. He would hold on to tonight and hope not too much changed in the morning. Or in the days to come.

Anything more was beyond his control.

Chapter Fifteen

With a happy chirp, Peanut bounced off his perch and onto Jami's hand, wings fluttering as he chatted excitedly. Jami carried him to the sofa where Akira was sitting, stroking under his chin before easing down carefully and holding him out to Akira's cupped palms. Peanut cocked his head and let out a little shriek.

Akira winced and withdrew her hands. "Maybe he's not comfortable with me yet."

Jami rolled her eyes and wrapped her fingers around Akira's wrist. "Don't be silly. He just likes the sound of his own voice."

Peanut whistled softly as he hopped into Akira's palm. When Akira smiled and cooed to him, he made a sound like he was cooing back.

"Oh, he's precious." Akira used her fingertip to pet him. "You're so lucky! Most guys give their girlfriends flowers and chocolate, but you got a bird!"

"I know! But Sebastian isn't most guys. He's . . ." Jami bit her bottom lip and hugged herself. Damn she missed him. Friday couldn't come soon enough. And he had a game on Saturday which meant they wouldn't be able to spend much time together—unless she went to the game. "Hey, what would you think of coming with me on Saturday to watch the Cobras play?"

Eyes wide and bright with excitement, Akira almost jumped off the sofa, but held still when Peanut fluffed up his feathers and scolded her with irate chirps. "I'd love to!" Then she frowned. "But it's the playoffs. The forum's probably sold out."

"I can get us into one of the boxes." Jami pressed her lips together in thought. If she called her dad, she could get them into the press box, but that would mean talking to him. Which she wasn't ready to do just yet. Being all sweet after what he'd said, only to get what she wanted, so wasn't her style. Fortunately, he wasn't the only option. "Give me a minute, I gotta make a phone call. You okay with him or should I put him back in his cage?"

"I'm fine as long as he won't try to fly away."

"He won't; he's a little suck up." Jami grinned. "As long as you're willing to hold him, he won't go anywhere."

Leaving Akira with Peanut, Jami took her cell to her bedroom and pushed the door almost closed. Not that she was worried about Akira listening in, but she had a feeling her friend wouldn't approve of what she was about to do.

What's the point of having contacts if you don't use them?

Not that she made a habit of using people. In this case, it was payback and she refused to feel guilty about it.

Ford answered on the first ring. "Jami. This is a pleasant surprise."

"Isn't it though?" Jami smirked and plunked down on her bed. "How you doing?"

"Not bad. I'm a little disappointed in you though."

Her brow shot up. "Excuse me?"

"Why weren't you at the Ice Girl practice today? You do know the finalists will be putting on shows in groups during the playoffs, don't you? I was hoping to see if you're really as good as they say, but you didn't show. Not very dedicated, are you?"

"Ford, you're obviously way out of the loop. I didn't make the last cut."

"Yes, you did."

"No, I didn't. I ruined the little chance I had with those photos—or hadn't you heard?" Bitterness left a sour taste in her mouth, but she took a deep breath and did her best to sound like she couldn't care less. About the pictures or about what Ford thought of them. Or her. "Gives me more time for other stuff, so it's all good. That's why I'm calling actually. Think you could get me into the press box on Saturday?"

"I could, but I don't see why you don't just ask your dad." Amusement lightened Ford's tone. "Let me guess. Daddy wasn't too happy about seeing his baby girl getting banged on the balcony. By Carter of all people. You really that desperate, kid?"

"Fuck you, Ford. Who I let bang me is none of your business." Her grip tightened on her phone as she resisted the urge to hang up on him. "So will you get me in the box or not?"

"What happened to Sebastian? Was he too nice for you?"

"Ugh. Forget it." She jammed her thumb on the "End" button and tossed her phone on her bed. "What a dick."

The phone rang. She ignored it until it stopped.

I should ask Silver.

It rang again.

Or Oriana. She won't say anything to Dad.

And again. She snatched it up and snapped as she answered. "What?"

"Relax, Jami. I'll get you in," Ford said dryly. "Under one condition."

"Naturally." She dropped her head onto her pillows and stared at the ceiling. "What do you want?"

"There's another practice tomorrow morning. Be there."

"What aren't you getting? I. Am. Not. On. The. Team." *Idiot.*

"Actually, you are on the team." He used the slick, arrogant tone she'd always hated. His every word made her wish they were talking face-to-face so she could slap him. "Say 'Thank you, Ford.'"

She bit back a string of insults, recalling how much it used to turn him on when she got "all feisty." Her tone came out tight, but level. "I don't need you pulling strings for me."

"You're right. You don't." He paused and sighed. "Seriously, Jami, I've been following the whole judging process and they were going to take you—you impressed them. The photos messed things up a bit, but I fixed it. I'm kidding about the 'thank you.' You did this on your own."

And there he was again. The man she'd fallen for before things had gone bad. A decent human being when he wanted to be. She still wasn't sure if she could accept his help though. Not if he still wanted her back—which she should have considered before calling him.

"I'm with Sebastian, Ford. If you're doing this hoping—"

"I'm hoping we can be friends." He laughed. "And I've never wanted that with one of my ex-girlfriends, so count yourself lucky."

"You're such an ass." She shook her head and smiled. "Okay. Friends. And I'll be there tomorrow. Anything else?"

"Would you consider upgrading to friends with benefits?"

"Don't push it."

He chuckled. "Couldn't help it. All right, we've got a deal. And,

Jami?"

Tonguing her bottom lip, Jami sat up and spoke quietly. "Yeah?"

"Sebastian's a lucky guy."

After ending the call, Jami returned to the living room, watching Akira with Peanut for a bit without saying a word. She knew her friend would be excited to hear that she was back on the team, but she couldn't quite believe it herself. Or even understand why it mattered at all. All she'd wanted to do was show her dad she supported him. Because Mom never had.

It wasn't about him anymore though. Now it was about being part of something. Part of something she cared about more than she'd been willing to admit, even to herself.

A smile broke out on her lips, so wide her cheeks hurt. She approached Akira. "Hey, guess what!"

Akira murmured soothingly to Peanut, who shrieked, startled. "What?"

"We're going to the game *and* . . ." Jami held her breath, then let it out with a laugh. "I'm on the team!"

Muffling a scream with her hand, Akira slowly moved away from the sofa and put Peanut back in his cage. Then she spun around and threw her arms in the air. "Oh my God! Are you serious? How—wait, never mind. I don't care how!" She lunged forward and hugged Jami. "This is awesome!"

"I know!"

"We should celebrate!"

"We should." Jami grinned. "Strawberry daiquiris?"

"Works for me." Akira danced toward the door. "You have no idea how much I missed you at practice today. Amy was nasty to everyone, but no one sees it. All they see is how perfect she is. They split the finalists into five groups of ten and, just my luck, I'm with her. And she's the team leader."

"Ugh, that sucks." Hell, she didn't like taking advantage of who she knew, but in this case . . . "Maybe I can do something about that—get you moved to whatever group I'm in."

"I hope so. I won't argue that Amy is talented, but I swear she's trying to ruin the chances for anyone who doesn't worship her." Akira ducked her head as if saying anything bad about Amy made her uncomfortable. "Maybe I'm making too much of it, it's just... she put me and two other smaller girls in the back. We had a hard time seeing the choreographer, and Amy made sure to point out every mistake. We get cut to thirty after the playoffs. Only thirty get to go to the mansion and take part in the reality show. I need this."

"I know you do." Jami put her hand on Akira's shoulder as they left the apartment and went out to her car. "And don't worry, I'll—"

Her breath lodged in her throat. Across her windshield the words "No more whore" were painted in big, red letters. Pulse pounding in her skull, she spit in her hand and scrubbed at the paint until the words were gone, ignoring Akira when she took the keys from her pocket and went back inside. The windshield looked like it was smeared with fresh blood. She held her hands up and leaned against the hood of the car, trembling.

Just another stupid prank. Chill out.

Akira came back. With some paper towels and Windex. She silently cleaned Jami's hands, then went to work on the windshield.

Jami shook her head to clear it and laughed as she grabbed some paper towels. "Guess Amy knows I'm back in."

"I don't think this was Amy." Akira passed Jami the spray bottle and folded her arms over her stomach. "Can you think of anyone else who might do something like this?"

"No."

"Maybe we should call the police."

"Because someone painted on my car? Look how easy it came off." Jami pointed at the now shining windshield. "We would have had to take a picture, and even then I bet the cops wouldn't do anything. For all we know it's one of the team's bunnies, pissed off about seeing me with Sebastian and Luke."

"Crazy puck bunnies?" Akira's brow raised. "Now that's scary."

"Hey, them chicks can be rabid." Jami stuffed the paper towels in a nearby trash bin and unlocked the car. She started the engine as Akira climbed in. "Let's forget about it and enjoy our night. I really need that drink now."

"Me too." Akira wrinkled her nose as the stereo came on, playing *Every Breath You Take by The Police.* "Hey, mind if I change the station?"

"Go for it, I hate this song. It's fucking creepy."

Akira turned the dial. It came off in her hand.

"Shit. Sorry about that." Akira tried to put it back on. "I'll pay for it."

"It's not a big deal." Jami looked over at the stereo and frowned. "That's odd. Is the CD player on?"

"Looks like." Akira leaned over and pressed the "Skip" button. The song started over. Again and again. Every time she pressed the button. "What the—"

"Just turn it off."

"I can't. The power button . . . it's stuck."

Jami killed the engine to stop the music and bent down to get a better look. With only the streetlight to see by, it was hard to make out what was wrong with the stupid thing.

She wasn't sure she wanted to know. The confined space in the car became stifling and she suddenly wanted out.

"I got a better idea." Jami opened her door, forcing a smile as Akira met her on the sidewalk. "Let's take the bus."

* * * *

Ford polished the bar, chuckling as his bouncer and best friend, Cort, went over the books for the bar, mumbling under his breath about getting "fancy shit for a dive." A cute brunette sitting a few seats away from the big man waved to Ford for a refill. Her flirty little I'm-having-naughty-thoughts-about-you smile got him to abandon the bar to fetch her, and himself, a drink. The sweat from the beer bottles slicked his palms as he brought them around the bar and took a seat next to her. He hadn't gotten any play in days and her blatant, seductive lip licking told him he was pretty much guaranteed a good, uncomplicated fuck.

Before he could even get past the "my name is" preliminaries, the front door of the bar swung open and the regular patrons went silent. Cort stood, his hand inching toward the small of his back where he kept his gun. He let his hand fall to his side and eased onto his stool as soon as he caught sight of who had come in. Out of place in a no-nonsense black business suit, steely grey eyes a few shades darker than his receding hair, the man had quite the build for a guy in his late fifties. But that wasn't what made him dangerous. The shit he was capable of made him a scary motherfucker.

"Hey, Dad." Ford grabbed the rag from the bar and quickly dried his hands as his father, Roy Kingsley, held out his to shake. He clenched his jaw so he wouldn't react to the intentionally painful grip, then went behind the bar to get a glass of his father's favorite whiskey. "What did I do now?"

"You've done nothing, Ford. And that's the problem." His father sat and didn't speak again until he'd taken a sip of the golden liquor. "I'm beginning to question your loyalty. Perhaps the benefits of being a Delgado outweigh those of being my son?"

Lee stood just a few feet behind his father, his heavy jowls jiggling as he restrained a laugh. They all knew the Delgado "fortune" was almost nonexistent at this point. Without the Kingsley money—and whatever Silver managed to contribute, Ford admitted grudgingly—the Dartmouth Cobras would go bankrupt. The team was starting to bring in enough revenue to stay afloat, but it would be years before they turned more than a negligible profit.

The team didn't matter. The Delgado's didn't matter. But damn it, he wasn't a kid to cringe whenever his father's shadow fell over him. He leaned on elbow on the bar and shrugged. "Don't see how being a Delgado changes anything, but whatever."

"*Whatever?*" The muscle in his father's jaw ticked. "I suggest you take a more respectful tone when you speak to me."

"Sure, but tell me one thing. What exactly do you expect me to do? The league is watching our every move. I can't do anything that'll come back on us." Ford scowled at Lee. "Guess your little ass-licker didn't tell you I found a way to mess with two important players? If I'm right, I can—"

"Mr. Lee has kept me very well informed. You seem much more interested in that little tramp you were seeing than in using whatever you've learned about the players."

"What little tramp?"

"Don't play at ignorance with me, Ford. Threatening men with gossip won't decide games." His father lowered his voice and leaned close. "I've warned you to stay away from that girl, but in a way, I'm glad you haven't. She may prove useful."

Ford's eyes narrowed. There was a very short list of the ways his father considered women useful. "How do you figure? We'd already agreed using her against her father wouldn't work. He'd cave if she was threatened, yeah, but he starts telling players to throw games, and we'll be in the same mess we were in with the coach."

"I have no intention to use her against her father." Brushing invisible dust from the lapels of his black suit jacket, his father gave him a razor slit smile. "I plan to use her against you. And as an added bonus, the other men she's involved with. They'll likely be off their game once they discover she's in danger."

The calm exterior he always managed around his father snapped. He slapped the glass from his father's hand and snarled. "Leave her the fuck alone!"

Pain exploded in his jaw. Blood spilled down his chin. He stared at his father as he picked up the rag to dab his knuckles. The man hadn't hit him in years—he usually had one of his thugs do it. He only did his own dirty work when he was really pissed.

"I didn't raise you to be this pathetic, but bad blood and all... not that it matters. You're costing me money, Ford, and you know that's never a good idea." Shoving the rag at Ford, he sighed, changing his tone to the slow, condescending one he used to make Ford feel stupid. "The girl will be fine—so long as you don't irritate me any further. She may be a little frightened, but that will only help our cause. Forget her. Actually, I see no need for you to involve yourself further in this. Continue as you have been. Control the money. Distract your sisters so they don't get in my way. I've learned something recently—which you failed to tell me, which will almost guarantee a loss tomorrow night."

"That's good." Ford circled the bar, spat into the sink, and observed his father from a safe distance. He swiped the blood from his chin and tried to make it look to his patrons—who were smart enough to pretend not to be watching—like everything was cool now. "Don't know what you've got, but the Cobras look like a sure bet next game."

"Yes, they do." His father smirked. "Show your support for the team tomorrow—free beer on tap if they win. Buffalo wings and whatever else the fans like. You're not good for much, but you make an excellent bartender."

Ford plastered a stiff smile on his lips. "Thanks."

His father left and seconds, only seconds later, his sister walked in. His blood ran cold as he thought of what would have happened if she'd come in just a bit sooner. So far she'd managed to stay under his father's radar. Which would change if she got too close to Ford.

Yeah, well I ain't gonna let that happen. He pulled another beer out of the fridge beneath the bar and popped the cap. After a long swing, he arched a brow at his sister. "Can I help you?"

Folding her arms over her breasts, Oriana looked him over and frowned. "What happened?"

"Ah, this?" Ford pointed at his busted lip. "This guy came in, all upset because he found out I was fucking his mother. What can I say? I was in the mood for MILF."

"You're lying."

"Yeah, I do that." Ford's lips curved into a smirk. "So what do you want? As you can see, I'm very busy."

"Don't be like that, Ford. We're family—"

"Like I give a fuck? Sorry, *sis*, but the Delgado clan is only useful to me as a way to screw around with the team. You do know I'm still doing that, right? You and Silver make it so easy, since you're both . . ." His jaw seemed to lock and his stomach turned. Damn it, why couldn't Silver have come instead? He couldn't look Oriana in the eye while being an asshole to her. "Well, you get what I'm saying."

"No, I don't think I do." She gave him a hard look, her eyes, so like his, flashing with rage. "Say it. Since we're both the team whores."

He turned his head to hide his wince and distractedly picked up the bloody rag to toss it in the trash. "Yeah, pretty much."

"You're better than this. I came to you for help, but now I'm starting to think you're the one who needs it." She put her hand over his on the bar and stared at him until he met her eyes. "Is it your dad? Maybe there's something I can—"

He jerked his hand out from under hers and grabbed her wrist. His voice was harsh, but low. "Promise me you'll stay out of anything involving my father. Promise me, and I'll help you in any way I can."

She bit her bottom lip and nodded.

Smart. He relaxed his grip and backed up a step. *At least she's smart.*

"Sloan's playing hurt. I tried to talk him out of it, but he insisted the team needs him and he's right. But it's gotten worse, and if he keeps going the way he is, he'll end his career. As long as the trainers tell the coach he's good to go, he'll let him play. I know you've got a couple under your thumb."

Ford brought the beer bottle to his lips, grip tightening to stop his hand from shaking. She knew way more than she should. "What makes you think that?"

"It doesn't matter. Just do it. Please?"

"I'll see what I can do. Just get out of here." He glanced over at the few people seated at tables circling the bar. They were too quiet. Any one of them could be working for his father. Maybe he was paranoid, but he had plenty of reasons to be. "Next time, call me."

"Sure, but you do the same, all right?" She gave him a grim smile. "Even if I can't do anything, I need you to know I'm here for you."

Fuck. He hated it when she was . . . nice. People weren't nice to him. He didn't let them because it made him weak. If she'd grown up with his father, she'd know better. Hell, even growing up with Anthony Delgado, she should know better. But somehow, she'd turned out decent. She shouldn't be wasting her time with him. It would be a lot safer if she didn't, even though he kinda wished . . .

"I can't replace Antoine, Oriana. I can't be your brother, not the way you want me to be."

"I don't expect you to replace Antoine." She reached out and patted his cheek in that big sisterly way she had which let him know he was family, whether he accepted it or not. "But you *are* my brother. Get used to it."

A few minutes after she walked out, he closed the bar, scrapping tabs to make up for making people leave without finishing their drinks. Ford had a few shots to loosen up the ache in his chest, Oriana's words coming back to him. "We're family."

Yeah, well, family just means blood. And that shit's messy.

Cort, the only person left in the bar, helped himself to a bottle of vodka, pouring them both a shot before resting his huge, tattooed forearms on the bar beside Ford. "You giving the little girl a heads up?"

Ford shook his head. "No. It'll just make things worse if my dad finds out I warned her. She'll talk to the guys she's with, and they can look out for her. If it messes with their game, it might be enough for him to back off her."

"They won't be back for a few days." Cort took his shot, then refilled his glass. His dull green eyes, his rough, almost ugly face, made most people see him as nothing but a hired gun, but he was damn smart. Nothing got past him. Those who knew him, respected him.

He was the closest thing to a brother Ford would ever have.

Staring at his glass, Ford nodded slowly. "Yeah. You mind—I mean, until they get back? You'll have to be careful—"

"Not a problem. Won't be the first time." Cort grinned and slapped his hands on the bar as he stood. "You pay in cash and ass. I don't mind a bit of overtime."

Ford shook his head and laughed. With Cort watching over her, Jami would be safe. He followed Cort to the door, locked up, then pulled out his cell. Held it in his fist as he made his way to his car. Oriana had come to him for help with Sloan. Worse thing was, Sloan's injury was probably what his father planned to exploit. If he hadn't done so already. Ford had heard some things from the trainers—things that would make his sister more than just a little worried.

He could fix this. But did he want to? It would mean folding his last hand—the one he'd held on to because he actually felt a little guilty. Because of Oriana.

Fuck. This was easier when I could say I didn't give a shit and mean it.

Rubbing his lips with his fist, he shook his head. And dialed.

"Yeah. Clear Mason. No. Today. I want him on the next plane. He's playing tomorrow."

Chapter Sixteen

Soaked with sweat, refreshed from the early morning skate, Luke strolled into the locker room, whistling as he made his way around the noisy crowd of players to his stall. He quickly stripped off his equipment and tossed it inside, wrinkling his nose at the stench—worse than the insides of his rank old running shoes.

Mischlue braced his hands behind him on the bench in front of his stall, fine lines forming around his curved lips as he glanced over to Bower, who slouched beside him, shirtless, but still wearing his goalie pads. He said something in French and Bower laughed.

Luke rolled his shoulders and cocked his head. "What's so funny?"

"He said you should get laid more often." Bower grinned. "And he's right. Nice to see you're not moping around anymore."

His face heated slightly, but he shrugged. "Some of us can't go months without. When's Silver gonna pop anyway?"

"August 5th." Bower's whole face lit up—like it always did when he got to thinking about his kid. He started unstrapping his goalie pads as a blotchy red blush spread out over his darkly stubbled cheeks. "But if you're under the impression that I ain't getting any, you couldn't be more wrong."

"Really?" Demyan's brow shot up. He leaned forward to see around Pearce, who was pulling on his leather jacket. "I always wondered what it would be like to fuck a pregnant chick."

Bower narrowed his eyes at Demyan, but Perron stepped between them and distracted him. Demyan rolled his eyes, then shouted "Hey!" when Pearce *accidentally* cracked him in the head with his motorcycle helmet.

Chuckling, Luke went to grab a towel and moved toward the showers, lost in thought. He'd thought waking up in bed with Seb would be weird, but it wasn't much different than waking up with Bower sleeping in the next bed. Except . . . well, Bower didn't hold him down and kiss him until his brain went numb and his morning hard-on throbbed before letting him up. He felt a stupid grin steal across his lips as he recalled the look Seb had given him when he grumbled about having his clothes picked out for him. His neck was still a little sore from Seb tightening the tie to the point that it almost cut off his air.

Seb had cupped his balls through his pants and pressed the heel of his palm against his dick. "Tell me you don't enjoy me taking control of you, even in this, and I'll stop."

"Damn it, Seb, I can't breathe."

"Tell me."

"No! I fucking love it, okay? You keep it up and I'm gonna come in the pants you just ironed so nice for me." Luke gasped and dropped onto the bed when Seb released him. "I need to—"

"You need to learn to restrain yourself." Seb turned away from him, tidying up the room as if nothing had happened, though his accent had thickened slightly. "Work on winning the face-off today with the trainer. You're sloppy."

"Like I can think about that now?" He groaned and heaved himself off the bed. "I'm going to take a shower. Gotta relieve some pressure."

Seb looked up from where he was clearing the plates from breakfast. "No."

"No?" Luke scratched his scruffy jaw. "Look, buddy. If I don't, I won't be able to focus."

"The appropriate answer is 'Yes, Sir.'"

"But—"

"You promised to show me you can focus on the ice despite what we do when we are alone. You will prove it."

"And what if I do?"

"Sucking your dick is nothing compared to what I plan to do to you, niño." The edge of Seb's lips curved slightly. "But if you'd prefer to use your own hand . . ."

Luke swallowed and shook his head. He didn't know what Seb was gonna do to him. But he couldn't wait to find out.

"Hey, braindead. You going in or what?"

Demyan's shove knocked Luke back into the present. He shook his head and backed up. "Naw, I'm gonna head to the training room. Wanna spot me?"

"Sure." Demyan stepped up to his side as he headed down the hall. His brow creased as he shoved the door to the training room open. "You all right, man? You seem distracted."

I do? Luke frowned. He thought he'd done pretty well on the ice.

Coach and the trainers seemed happy with him. Seb hadn't said anything, but he was busy doing his own thing. "Just stoked about tomorrow night. Aren't you?"

"Yeah, but I don't got some sweet young thing on the brain. If I did, I'd have her on webcam every time I was alone—or maybe that's what you're doing already. You and Ramos sharing a room so you can watch her put on a show together?" Demyan blocked the door before he could pass and spoke quietly. "You taping that shit, pal? I've kinda hit a dry spell. Since you don't mind sharing—"

"You're too fucking much, Demyan." Luke rolled his eyes. "You really think she's that kinda girl?"

"*Hell*, yeah! But it's not a bad thing!" Demyan laughed. "I've heard she's all kinds of freaky. Doesn't hurt to let me look."

"And what would we get if we let you look." Seb's voice came loud and clear from inside the room. As Demyan pushed the door open wide, he rose from the weight bench and rubbed his hands on his tight black shorts. His black tank top stretched over his wide chest, snug enough that his muscles seemed carved in matte black stone. "Whether or not Luke and I share, I don't see why we would share with you."

Demyan stepped into the room and propped himself against the wall by the door. "What do you want?"

Seb gave Demyan a slow, appraising look. "I haven't decided yet. But I will let you know."

What the fuck? Luke scowled as he strode up to the free weights, kicking the blue mat as he squared his feet. He hefted up the twenty pounds so quickly he almost cracked himself in the face.

"Your form is lacking, *hombrecito*." Seb came to his side and pried both weights from his hands. He glanced over at Demyan—who had stripped and climbed into the hot tub—and spoke low. "Nothing we do with Jami will be done without your consent."

"Sure. Whatever." Luke took a step away from Seb, ready to walk out and not quite sure why. The weights thunked on the thick mat behind him. He had to lock his arms to his sides when Seb latched onto his wrist to keep from cracking him a good one. "What the fuck do you want, man?"

"Speak to me, *semental*." Seb's brow furrowed. "What I said to

Demyan—does it bother you?"

"Why should it?" Luke twisted his wrist from Seb's loose grip. He gritted his teeth and did his best not to shout. "Not like me and you are in a relationship or anything."

"I see. This isn't about Jami, is it?" Seb nodded slowly, as if answering his own stupid question. "Perhaps you do not see this as a relationship, but I do. And I apologize for upsetting you. Your expectations weren't clear, but I believe they are now."

"I'm not upset."

Seb didn't comment. Instead he turned away and picked up one of the weights. Sat on a bench and braced his elbow on his knee for some bicep curls. His muscles bulged, displaying strength that made Luke think of how easily the man overpowered him. And damn it, his blood instantly rushed down, causing his dick to swell. His shorts were too tight to hide it. He had to get the fuck out of there before Demyan noticed.

"I changed my mind. I'm gonna take a shower." He gulped when Seb gave him a hard look. "A quick one. I'll see you back at the hotel, S—Ramos." He glanced over his shoulder at Demyan. "Maybe we can hang out later, or tomorrow."

Demyan grunted his response as he sank deeper into the tub.

Luke got to the shower in record time, thanked God that no one else was in there, and stood under the cold spray, grateful for the temporary relief.

You're feeling this way because of a dude, man.

Rubbing a muscle in his thigh which stiffened in response to the cold, Luke laughed.

Yeah, I am. But I'm cool with it.

* * * *

"I got it."

Sebastian drained the last of his second beer and smiled when the text came in. Per his instructions, Jami had gone to an adult shop to purchase her first toy. The first time they'd spoken, she'd begged him not to "make her go," but he could tell by her tone the idea of being forced to do something she perceived as naughty thrilled her.

So he calmly persuaded her to go through with it. After hanging up, he'd come to the bar to wait. Rather than call him, she'd sent texts, several while she was in the store which included pictures. Someone in the shop had finally come to offer assistance, which only embarrassed her more.

She had no idea how much more humiliating he could—and would—make this for her. He'd read her well. Not many women would enjoy being put in such a position, but she did. He could picture her, clenching her thighs as she stood in the center of an aisle, cheeks hot and pink, bottom lip between her teeth as she struggled against the arousal which had her moist, eager for the night he'd planned.

He hated being away from her, but he had ways to make her forget the distance between them.

Shortly after, Sebastian stood in the room he now shared with Luke, eyes on the younger man as he hung the "Do not disturb" sign, then closed and locked the door. Teammates had a habit of strolling in and out of one another's rooms. He wanted Luke to feel comfortable in the fact that no one would bother them tonight.

"Have you set up the webcam, *niño?*" His tone took on an edge as Luke's lips parted and not a sound came out. "A simple 'Yes' or 'No' will suffice. Adding 'Sir' would please me."

Wetting his lips with his tongue, Luke nodded. "Yeah—I mean, yes, Sir. It's just . . ."

The edge of Sebastian's lip twitched. His *niño* wasn't often at a loss for words. "You mustn't be afraid to speak to me, Luke. I have not asked for your silence. Yet."

Luke scowled. "I'm not afraid—quit saying that, it pisses me off."

"Does it?" Sebastian closed the distance between them in one long stride and trapped Luke between the bed and the wall. "So noted. But in the future, if you have anything to say to me during a scene, you will do so respectfully."

Luke's throat worked as he swallowed. "Are we in a scene?"

"Oh yes, *semental.*" Sebastian framed Luke's jaw with his hand, his grip firm as he spoke against his lips. "Voice any concerns you have now. You have my full attention."

Beads of sweat broke out under Luke's bottom lip, making the short stubble glisten. Sebastian could stop himself from tasting it with the tip of his tongue. Loosening Luke's tie, Sebastian lowered to taste his throat. To tease the racing pulse along the length with his teeth.

"Jami." Luke gasped. His words came out gruff and breathless. "You sure she's okay with this?"

"I am sure she is as eager as you are." Sebastian brushed his lips up to Luke's earlobe. Sucked it gently. "Are you ready?"

Again, words seemed to escape him, because Luke simply inhaled and nodded. When Sebastian stepped back and put his hand out, Luke laid his wrist in his palm. He drew him to the bathroom. Luke's laptop was set up on the wide, marble counter by the sink. The bathroom fan made a soft, whirring sound and would hopefully be enough to keep the steam from building up. The webcam was attached to the top of the screen and could be rotated to follow the action. Sebastian had left his supplies in the drawer under the counter earlier that day. He left Luke standing by the closed door and pulled out the wrist cuffs.

Luke's eyes widened as Sebastian wet the suction cups attached to the cuffs under the tap, then stuck them to the tiled wall above the foot of the bath. His lips parted once Sebastian had them secure enough that they wouldn't come loose with a sharp tug.

Sebastian smiled and gestured to the laptop. "Please connect us to Jami, *niño*."

Gulping hard, Luke nodded and clicked on the mouse several times. Jami appeared on screen, sitting on the edge of her bed, positioned almost exactly as he'd instructed, legs spread wide, eyes lowered. But one hand drifted down from where it should be resting above her knee, palm up.

"You had not planned to start without us, had you, *mi cielo*?"

Jami sat up straight, snapped her legs shut, and let out a little squeak. She shook her head and bit back a smile. "You're late."

He chuckled. "And you are cheeky. Back into position, *gatita*."

With slow, provocative grace, Jami let her legs part, tossed her head to sweep her hair away from her breasts, and lay her hands, palm up, on her thighs. The black lace, crotchless panties he'd asked her to purchase, framed her pinks folds nicely. The matching chemise barely covered her breasts, with the V neckline reaching all the way down to her navel. Her sweet young face was all innocence, but she was displayed in a deliciously shameless way. He could tell from the flush of her cheeks, from the moisture between her plump pussy lips shining in her well-lit bedroom, that she knew exactly what they saw when they looked at her. And she relished it.

By his side, Luke tugged at his tie, a wolfish grin on his lips as he savored every inch of Jami with his eyes. "You have no idea what I want to do to you."

Sebastian took hold of the end of Luke's tie and wrapped it around his fist. He jerked on it to bring Luke against him. "Tonight is about what I will do to you."

* * * *

Jami panted as she watched Sebastian undo Luke's tie, then undo the buttons of his shirt, one by one with a flick of his thumb, while he claimed Luke's lips in a fierce kiss. Her hips wiggled as she fought the urge to touch herself. Seeing her men together like this, sharing the same wild passion she'd shared with them both, lit a fuse deep within. Her whole body had become a stick of unstable dynamite, ready to go off even without the flames licking at her from her hard nipples, to her incredibly wet pussy. She'd never been this turned on in her life.

Sebastian turned Luke to face her as he pulled off Luke's shirt. His eyes locked onto hers as he pulled down Luke's pants and boxers. Then he straightened and pressed against Luke from behind, fisting his hand around Luke's dick.

"Remove the chemise, *mi cielo*." He pumped Luke's cock at a languorous pace and smiled at her as he gripped Luke's shoulder with his free hand to hold him in place. "Take your time."

Easing off the bed, Jami slid her hands over her breasts, down to the bottom of her chemise, loving the way the soft lace felt as she caressed herself. She trembled as she looked into Luke's eyes and saw the hunger there. Even though Sebastian was touching him, she was part of his arousal, which made her more than a voyeur to the scene. It made her an important part of it.

She drew the chemise up, over her head, then tossed it aside. She needed to please Sebastian, needed to feel he controlled her as much as he did Luke, but she couldn't prolong the teasing.

Take him. Her lips moved with the silent words, and her teeth dented her bottom lip as she looked to Sebastian to see if she'd disappointed him by going too fast.

She found no disappointment in his dark brown eyes. There was only heat, and it spilled over her, through her, so intense that moisture slicked her inner thighs.

"On the bed as you were before. Use your fingers and play with your clit as you watch us." Sebastian moved away from Luke and went to turn on the shower. He tested the temperature, then inclined his head to Luke. "Get in."

Luke nodded, but stayed where he was, staring at her. His hand dropped down to his cock.

"No." Sebastian raked his fingers into Luke's hair and forced him up to the bath. He pushed him down so Luke had to brace his hands on the ledge. Then he pulled off his belt. "Who does your pleasure belong to, Luke?"

"You." Luke growled. "Sir."

"Yes." Sebastian folded the belt in half. "How many strikes would you give a sub so willful?"

"Five." Head bowed, Luke's voice became muffled, but she could still make out his every word. "If it was Jami, no more than five. Hard and fast so she wouldn't enjoy it."

"Because she enjoys pain."

"Yeah."

"And so do you." Sebastian placed his hand between Luke's shoulder blades. "Do not make a sound unless you need to say red."

Luke glanced over his shoulder and gave her what she was pretty sure was supposed to be a reassuring look. "Yes, Sir."

Sebastian hauled back and the belt came down with a ripping *Crack!* A wide red welt spread instantly over both tense butt cheeks. Jami squirmed, then winced at the next *Crack!* She was torn between admiring Luke's firm ass, and being a little jealous because she'd love nothing more than to be in his place right now. Somehow, she knew

Sebastian would never hit her that hard. Not using his full strength.

Not unless she proved she could take it.

She rubbed her clit until the tiny nub at the tip swelled, and bit back a moan.

Crack! Crack! Crack!

Holding Luke up as his legs gave out, Sebastian murmured something and kissed his temple. "In the shower, *semental*. Unless you can't stand on your own?"

Luke shook his head and laughed. "I can stand, but—fuck, that hurt more than I thought it would. It's not the same without warm-up."

Since they weren't looking at her, Jami dipped her finger into her throbbing cunt and stifled another moan. She was . . . So. Damn. Close! Her lips parted as she reached the pinnacle.

"Jami." The sharp way Sebastian said her name made her go still. His lips were fixed in a firm line as she met his eyes. He shook his head. "I have few options to punish you at the moment. But I can shut the laptop and deny you this night, which will ruin what I hoped to share with you. It displeases me that you would attempt to be sneaky."

"I won't do it again." She placed her hands by her hips and blinked fast. The way his disapproval affected her was almost physical. Like the way she'd felt after taking her first drag of a cigarette, then her first joint—knowing it was wrong, and bad for her, but doing it anyway. The way the acrid smoke made it hard to breath. "I-I'm sorry. I really am."

"*Mi cielo*, do not take it so hard. You are testing your limits. I do understand." He approached the camera and lifted his hand, as if he wished he could touch her. "I need you to know the limits are there. We will work on it together."

She took a deep breath and nodded. She had a feeling she had been missing something before, missing how this was more than just sex. As far as she knew, sex had one goal, and the kinky games revved up the heat. But the way Sebastian handled her—handled them both—made it seem less like a game. Not only this time, but every time they were together. He was trying to show them something.

And she was finally ready to see it.

Sebastian's smiled at her as if she'd told him so out loud. "Move to the center of the bed, *gatita*, knees bent and parted as much as possible. Tease yourself with the toy, but do not push it inside you until I tell you to."

The glass dildo she'd bought earlier that day sat on the bed behind her, disinfected and ready to use. She picked it up and ran her fingers over the wide head, then down the pale blue winding ridges. Sebastian had told her to pick one that matched him in size, but she must have overcompensated. If Sebastian was this big, he never would have fit inside her.

"I showed it to you, right?" She tongued her bottom lip. "It's pretty big."

"I can see that." The edge of Sebastian's lip twitched. He reached into the shower where Luke stood under the spray and ran his hand from the nape of Luke's neck to the small of his back. "But it will be the only thing to fill you until I am with you again. Try it, Jami. If it hurts too much then I will buy you another."

"Yes, *mi Rey*." She scooted backward on the bed and opened her legs. Then she stroked the cool, smooth glass head of the dildo between her folds. Her eyes fluttered shut as arousal flared deep in her core. She forced them open and moaned at the sight of Sebastian stripping, of him stepping into the shower to pull Luke, dripping wet, into his arms. They kissed, slower than before, with Sebastian easing off several times and speaking quietly to Luke when it looked like he was trying to rush things.

Jami had a hard time paying any attention to the glass dildo, growing warm with her body heat. She stared as Luke clasped his hands behind his neck and closed his eyes. He swallowed, nodded, and let Sebastian guide him down to his knees.

Her lips parted as Luke's did. Her mouth went dry as Sebastian took hold of his dick with one hand, put the other hand on the back of Luke's head, and eased him forward.

"That's it, *semental*. Very good." The muscles in Sebastian's forearms and stomach hardened, as if it took all his strength not to thrust it. "Circle the top with your tongue. And breathe. Yes. Now open wider."

Inch by inch, Sebastian's dick disappeared into Luke's mouth. He stopped with about half his length inside and drew out.

"More this time. Use your lips with the same pressure you enjoy Jami or I using on you."

A rough sound came from Luke as his lips glided over and over the slick flesh, and he accepted more and more. Sebastian groaned and began to fuck Luke's face at a faster pace. His balls bumped Luke's chin, and he rasped in a harsh breath. Held Luke in place with his cock stuffed in his mouth.

"I love the way you look like this, *niño*. On your knees, sucking my dick. I could fuck your hot mouth all night." Sebastian slid out and pulled Luke to his feet. "But I'd rather fuck you."

"Oh God!" Luke shook as Sebastian turned him to face the wall which had the cuffs on suction cups stuck to it. "God, I'm gonna come!"

"Not yet." Sebastian reached around and fisted his hand around the base of Luke's cock and squeezed. "I won't help you next time. Calm yourself. You may come when I am inside you."

Luke's jaw hardened. He nodded and positioned his hands so Sebastian could attach the cuffs.

Once Luke was restrained, Sebastian stepped out of the bath to retrieve something from the counter. He glanced over at Jami as he held up the lube and squirted some into his palm. "We will be watching you now Jami. Stretch yourself open with that glass dildo as I stretch him. Match my pace."

"Okay." Jami held the glass dildo against her slit as Sebastian stepped behind Luke. She was so wet that half the head slid easily inside her as she watched Sebastian push one lubed finger into Luke's ass. She worked the tip in and out, panting as Sebastian's thick finger sank in all the way.

"Push back against me, *niño*," Sebastian said as he added a second finger. "Yes. Yes, just like that."

"Fuck that feels . . . almost too good. Ah!" Luke bowed his head and gasped as Sebastian pumped his fingers in and out. "Please! Please . . ."

Sebastian combed his fingers into Luke's hair and jerked his head back. His tone was rough with passion. "Tell me what you want me to do."

"Fuck me, Sir!" Luke rasped out. He twisted his head slightly and looked at Jami. "I need you to fuck me now!"

Jami whimpered as she pushed the dildo in deeper. It felt uncomfortably big. And she was so desperate to be full.

But then Sebastian latched onto Luke's hip with one hand and used the other to aim his dick to where his fingers had been. He rocked his hips forward and she shoved the dildo, crying out as it impaled her and her core rippled around it with a violent orgasm. She had to hold the end to keep her body from pushing it out. Her thighs quivered with the sensation, like an electric bolt striking the same spot, over and over. Red spots filled her vision, but she could still make Sebastian out, on the screen, watching her.

He held still for a moment. Then made Luke bend over a little more.

She held her breath as he thrust in.

****

Luke nearly bit through his tongue to keep from shouting as the shock of burning pain spread. He rested his forehead against the tiled wall and clenched his fist above the cuffs, tempted to fight them until he freed himself. Until he escaped the pain.

A gentle stroke down his side startled him, and he locked his knees to stop himself from jerking away. But he moved just enough to feel Seb shift inside him. To trigger a strange pleasure unlike anything he'd ever—no. No, he'd felt something almost like this once. With that damn butt plug Chicklet's sub had used.

No way would he embarrass himself and come that fast again. Not in front of Jami.

He looked over his arm at her and grinned as she twitched with that huge dildo stuffed in her cunt. Fuck, he wished he could be with her now. He would lift her legs over his shoulder and ram his dick into *her* ass. Make it so she'd feel him and the dildo slamming into her together. It would be pretty hot if Seb fucked her mouth at the same time. Scenes like that were always hot.

Scenes like that were what he was used to. Not this.

Everything else, having Seb suck his dick, even getting on his knees to suck Seb's, wasn't so bad. But this—this seemed like he'd crossed a line and he wasn't sure he should have.

"Look at me, *semental*." Seb caught hold of his jaw and forced his head back and to the side to face him. "Do not close yourself off from me now. Feel me, feel what I am doing to you. You wanted this."

"I don't think—"

"You shouldn't be thinking. You will convince yourself this is wrong." Seb kissed him and rotated his hips, grinding in deeper. He smiled against Luke's lips as Luke panted into his mouth. "It's not wrong."

"I'm. Not. Gay." Luke heard a dry laugh in his head and pressed his eyes closed to shut it out. *I'm not!* But he wasn't so sure anymore. And the way Seb moved, gliding in and out, sparking all his nerves to life, made it harder and harder to care. "Shit, don't stop."

"I won't." Seb barred one arm across his chest. Dug his fingers into his hip. "Move with me."

As Seb slammed in, Luke thrust back. The impact created a loud, wet slapping sound. The water spraying down on them had lost its heat, but Luke's body became feverish as he turned off his brain and did as Seb said. He felt what was being done to him without worrying about what it meant. Before long, his balls tightened and his muscles tensed as he clenched around Seb's dick.

"Go ahead, *niño*. Come for me."

Luke fell forward, held up only by his wrist and Sebastian's arm across his chest. Pleasure tore through his body and he shouted as he came. Cum hit the tiled wall. A deep thrust into his ass had more spilling out of his twitching dick. Seb wrapped his hand around him and stroked fast and hard to draw out the last few spasms.

When Seb pulled out, Luke winced and tugged at his wrists. He suddenly felt dirty. Used. He needed to get out of here.

"Shh." Seb undid the cuffs and drew him under the shower, hugging him tight. "You are a strong man, Luke. Do not forget that. You have accepted something many fight their whole lives. Something you needed."

"But I didn't need it." Luke scowled, but kept his face pressed against Seb's chest. He didn't feel strong. If he was strong, Seb wouldn't need to tell him he was. But he didn't feel quite so weak with Seb to lean on. So he said what he needed to say. "I didn't need it before you. But now I do."

Seb kissed his forehead. "I have no words for what that means to me, *semental*."

"That's okay. Neither do I." Luke twisted his lips and eyed Seb's slack dick. *Jeezum, how'd he fit?* A throb of pain as he clenched his ass had him talking fast, and being way too honest. "I like you, though. A lot. I guess that's all that matters."

"It is, Luke." Seb curved his hand under Luke's jaw and smiled as he stroked his bottom lip. "And I feel the same for you. But we have neglected our sweet *gatita*. I believe she's fallen asleep on us."

Luke glanced at the screen.

Jami lifted her head from her pillow and gave them a sleepy smile. "I'm still awake. It's just been a long few days. Haven't slept much. Miss you guys."

"We miss you as well, *mi cielo*." Seb turned off the shower, then stepped onto the bath mat and grabbed a towel. "If you will stay with us a little longer, we will move the laptop to the bedroom. I cannot rest until I see you close your eyes."

"I'd like that." Jami pulled the blanket up to her chin. Her lip quivered as she hugged her knees to her chest. "I miss you."

"And I you." Seb hesitated by Luke's side as he picked up the laptop. "Is there something more, Jami? You would tell me if something was wrong?"

Jami looked away, then nodded. "I would tell you."

Seb frowned, but even after an hour of gentle probing, Jami didn't tell him more. She whispered "I love you" as she fell asleep and Seb sat in the darkness, shadows deepening the lines in his face.

"Hey." Luke put his hand on Seb's thigh and squeezed. "She's probably just lonely. This whole scene was a good idea, but . . ." He frowned. "She wasn't really with us, right? So she probably just needs to be held and shit. Told she isn't being replaced. Because . . . well, what if she thinks you're really only into men?"

"She knows better." Seb lay with his back to Luke, not sounding too sure of his own words. "And if she doesn't . . ."

Yeah, I got it. Seb would show her that Luke meant nothing to him. And Luke didn't care. He would back up whatever Seb said. Wouldn't be hard. Not like *he* would miss Sebastian or Jami when they realized having him around was putting a rift between them.

But early that morning, he woke to a hard, passionate kiss. Still half asleep, he let Seb roll him to his side and writhed as Seb massaged his ass with lube-slicked hands. He grunted as Seb prodded his asshole with two fingers and hissed as they dipped inside.

"I need to take you. Alone. Gently this time. I should have . . ." Seb withdrew his fingers and pressed his dick against Luke's tight, sore hole. "You must know I am not using you. You are more, *semental.*"

More? His heart skipped like a badly scratched record. "More than what?" Luke reached behind him and latched on to Seb's thigh as his dick smoothly penetrated. A brief pain followed by exquisite fullness and a surge of pleasure stole his breath. He had to force himself to keep talking before he lost himself to the sensation. "Ah! Wait. Slow down and tell me. More than what?"

"More than the others. So much more." Seb thrust in and held him tight, one arm angled across Luke's chest, hand curved around the side of his throat, the other across his stomach. Kissing his shoulder, then his throat, Seb whispered. "No man has ever meant as much to me as you do."

"Sebastian." Luke pulled Seb's thigh over his hip, then stroked it as Sebastian's confession opened a floodgate within. "I told you; I never needed this. Until you. I need you. Just you."

"How can we do this? I will do nothing to hurt Jami. Or you. But I am hurting you both."

"No, you're not." Luke pushed Seb's thigh off his and wrapped his ankles behind Sebastian's calves, pulling him in deeper. "Maybe I'm not really a Dom. Or not just a Dom. But I've learned enough to know you won't have all the answers. You give what you've got. Which you have. That and more."

"Yes, I have. I will always give you all I can." Seb kissed his throat as he moved, sliding in and out, not fucking him, but . . . making love to him with such tenderness that erased all the pain, all the uncertainty, and left only pleasure. And a connection which went beyond any Luke had allowed before.

"I love you, man." Why had he said that? He tried to laugh it off even as he smothered a moan with his forearm. "Friend love, you know? With extras?"

"I understand." Seb gently curved his hand around Luke's dick. "And I love you. Take that as you will. But come for me. I want to feel you lose control one last time before I must let you go."

Luke pressed his eyes shut as he pushed back, urging Seb to quicken his pace. A growl of frustration escaped him when Seb trapped him snug against his body, torturing him with shallow thrusts and light strokes, but Seb's chuckle made him smile. The man would never let him take over.

But even going slow, Seb's hands, his body, set Luke off like bottle rocket, shooting up . . .

"Brace yourself." Seb hissed in his ear. He drew out and slammed in, over and over, covering Luke's mouth with his hand to muffle his roar as pleasure exploded. Rough sounds broke out from deep in his chest, scoring his throat. One last thrust, followed by spilling warmth within, had Luke shuddering, gasping.

He didn't move when Seb eased out and left the bed. Arm draped over his face, he decided that today was as good a day as any to play dead. Maybe he'd get up later to play that game he got paid shitloads to play—what was it again?

"You look well sated," Seb said. The mattress shifted and a warm cloth covered Luke's softened dick and sore balls. As it slid between his ass cheeks, Luke clenched and tried to roll over, but Seb clucked his tongue and held him still. "Let me tend to you, *semental*. Then you may have an hour or so to laze about before we meet with the team."

Peeking out from under his arm, Luke mumbled. "What about you? You gonna 'laze about' too?"

"I had planned to go for a run."

"Don't run." Luke shifted over and slapped the bed beside him. "Stay."

Seb didn't say anything for a long time. Luke had almost drifted off to sleep when Seb finally lay down beside him. He grunted as Seb pulled him over, easing him up so Luke could rest his head on his shoulder.

"You are comfortable with me now, Luke?"

Eyes closed, Luke turned his head to kiss Seb's chest. "Yeah, 'cause it feels right, you know?"

He felt Seb's nod as he pressed a light kiss on his brow. "I know."

Chapter Seventeen

Sloan leaned on the table in the training room, gritting his teeth as the trainer stuck the needle into the center of his hand. The needle itself didn't hurt, but having his hand, which had frozen into a claw overnight, spread open, shot agony up his arm. His skin broke out in a cold sweat. His stomach lurched. The painkillers he'd popped this morning hadn't helped much, and when they wore off, he found it hard to even eat. The pain had been pretty bad before he'd caught that puck. Now it was almost unbearable.

Almost.

But as the drug did its work, he was able to move his hand again. It wouldn't fully clench, but he'd be able to hold on to his stick. The trainer handed him another bottle of Oxycodone and told him he was good to go.

"You've got to be fucking kidding. You're not letting him play like that, are you?"

The trainer's eyes widened.

Sloan sat up and forced a smile. "What the hell are you doing here, Dominik? I thought you were still doing therapy for your knee."

Dominik ignored him and stepped up to the trainer. "Say goodbye to your job, asshole."

"He wanted to keep playing!" The trainer shuffled backward, holding his hands up. "I'm not a doctor. I'm just following orders."

"You're full of shit." Dominik shook his head. "And if you're not, we've got a bigger problem."

"Hey, man, relax." Sloan put his good hand on Dominik's forearm and leaned in close. "He's right. I asked for this. And I'm okay. I promised Oriana I'd have it looked at this summer. I can tough it out until then."

Fisting his hand into Sloan's tight, black t-shirt, Dominik snarled. "You're an idiot. You call this okay?" He wrapped his hand around Sloan's wrist and held his hand up to the light.

The black and purple blotches spreading out from the heel of Sloan's palm up to the center of his middle fingers made the injury look pretty bad, but it was just a bruise. He wrenched his hand free and scowled. "You're a fucking hypocrite. You got a shot after you fucked up your knee so you could finish the game. And it wasn't even the playoffs."

"Took me two months longer to get back on the ice after that stunt, Sloan. I'm not a hypocrite. I made a mistake, and I won't let you make the same one."

"Try and stop me."

"I plan to."

And with that, Dominik swivelled around and strode out of the room.

Sloan followed, rage tempting him to physically stop the man, reason urging him to try to talk him down. But it was too late. Tim waited in the hall, arms folded over his chest, one of the team doctors at his side.

"Let me see it," the coach said.

The doctor he had with him wasn't the one who'd let Sloan continue playing. He was the one who'd dealt with Dominik. With Tyler. He had the final fucking say, which was why Sloan had avoided him so far.

There was no point to lying about his injury any longer, but he couldn't help but try to play it off as if it was nothing serious. He should have asked the trainer to tape his damn hand. Instead he was stuck here, holding it out of sight like a little kid hiding something valuable that he'd broken behind his back.

"My game is good and I was fine at practice. Let it go. I've already been cleared."

"Not by me." The doctor's grey eyebrows shot up to sit on the edge of his receding hairline. "You're not playing, Callahan. Once I check out your hand, I'll have a better idea of how long you'll be out. The drugs you're taking may be another issue—they're highly addictive."

Sloan laughed and shoved the bottle of Oxycodone at the doctor. "You think so? Take them. I don't need the goddamn pills. But I am playing tonight. Check my hand tomorrow if you want."

"It's not up for negotiation, Callahan." Tim reached out and patted his shoulder. "You're already out of the lineup. I've spoken to both Mason and Oriana. You've covered this up long enough. It's over."

Sloan gave the doctor a curt not and held his hand out. He glared at Dominik as the doctor gently poked and prodded. *Fucking traitor.*

"I'll need to take some X-rays, but I'm fairly certain there's at least a hairline fracture—possibly a ruptured tendon. I'm sorry to say you'll be lucky if you can start the next season with the team. I'll call in and see if I can get everything started tomorrow when we get back home. For now, get it wrapped by one of the trainers—one of the *other* trainers." The doctor's eyes narrowed as he looked past Sloan to the trainer who'd given him the shot. "Try not to use the hand. You've done more than enough damage to it already."

The coach and the doctor turned away, dismissing him. Dominik rubbed his jaw and opened his mouth.

"I don't want to hear it." Sloan moved to step past him.

Dominik grabbed his arm. "Sloan—"

Sloan hauled back and punched Dominik in the face, catching him just under the eye. His bad hand hung by his side, leaving him open to a swift uppercut under the chin that had his head ringing.

He laughed and licked the blood from his bitten lip. "Come on, Dominik. Don't hold back. I know you've been wanting to do this for a while."

"You're damn right I have." Dominik's teeth glistened like wet pearls in a bed of coal as his lips curled away from them. "Somebody's got to beat some sense into you, and I'm just the person to do it."

"Hey!" Max ran up to them, not even flinching as he pushed between them and almost got clocked in the head by a punch Sloan checked just in time. "Dominik, take a walk." He shoved Dominik when the man simply glared at him. "Go. Show some of the goddamn control that makes you such a good Master."

Clenching his fist at his sides, Dominik inclined his head and strode down the hall. The locker room door slammed behind him.

Max closed his eyes and let out a heavy sigh. "This has to stop, Sloan—"

"I'm not listening to any more of this shit." Sloan sidestepped, then sucked his teeth when Max cut him off. "Get out of my way."

"No." Max shoved him back into the wall and pinned Sloan there with his hands on his shoulders. "I get it, okay? You're pissed at the whole world right now, and I get it. But you're my best friend, man, and you're scaring me."

"Fuck off, Max." Sloan tried to laugh off Max's concern, but didn't try to push him away. "How am I scaring you? Just 'cause I'm playing with a busted hand?"

"Because you're popping pills like fucking Tic Tacs. You'd get up in my face if I pulled something like this, wouldn't you?"

The bastard was right. But fuck, the team needed their captain. Needed him to . . . Sloan's anger deflated as he finally faced how incredibly stupid he'd been. The whole playoff craze had swept him up and numbed his brain. He'd do more than get in Max's face if he risked his career, and his health, for a game, no matter how much it meant to them both.

He nodded slowly and met his best friend's eyes. "Yeah, damn you, I would."

Max grinned. "All right, you ornery fucker, give me a hug and head upstairs to the press box. You're gonna watch us play, right?"

That's all I'll be able to do for a while. Sloan rolled his eyes and pulled Max in for a rough hug. "I'll watch you. But I'm heading home early so our woman can fuss over me. And you don't get to watch."

"Asshole." Max chuckled and thumped him on the shoulder. "You know—"

Bright white flashing blinded Sloan, and shouting cut off whatever Max was about to say. Sloan squinted at the cameramen and reporters swarming into the hall.

"Callahan! Are you ready to come out?"

"Sloan, can we get a statement about your feelings on men hiding homosexuality in the league?"

"Is Oriana Delgado just a front? Does she know?"

Shoving Max in the direction of the training room, Sloan snapped under his breath. "Stay in there. I'll get Tim to clear out the vermin."

Eyes wide, Max shook his head. "No way. We'll just tell them—"

"No talking to the press during playoffs, Max. Team policy. Get in there."

Once the door shut and the lock clicked, Sloan made his way through the crush. Microphones were held in his face. Questions were shouted at him. But he just kept going, repeating over and over, "No comment."

By the time he got to the locker room, Tim was already herding reporters away from the door, promising an interview after the game. He waved Sloan inside and manned the door until the team's PR showed up.

Dropping to a bench beside Carter, Sloan massaged his temples and groaned.

What a fucking mess. He wanted to smash something, like maybe a few cameras—or skulls—but the men didn't need to see him lose it. Not again. Not right before the game. Then again, they didn't need the drama with the press either.

Kinda unavoidable now.

He could deny being gay all he wanted, but the press wouldn't believe a fucking word he said. And even if they did, if he didn't say just the right thing, they'd crucify him as some kind of bigot or something. He had a feeling the PR would be scripting a response for him. He hoped it included something along the lines of "It's nobody's goddamn business who I fuck."

Very unlikely.

"What's going on?" Carter stuck the end of his mouthpiece in the space where he'd lost a couple of teeth, grinning like a fool, but pale as a death mask. "Did I just hear one of those reporters call you a fag?"

Sloan shrugged. "They saw me hugging Perron. Like straight men can't hug. But whatever, they'll find something else to salivate over by tomorrow. They got bored of going on about the whole 'ménage' thing. They'll get even less from this."

"You think?" Carter chewed irritably on his mouthpiece. "I mean, if you were gay, they wouldn't let up right? They'd make a big deal about it?"

"Probably. But I'm not worried about it. Sucks for the guys that *are* gay—hell, sucks for a lot of us. You might have noticed me and

Oriana don't go out in public? She's married. Kinda looks bad, and getting called a whore and a cheater was getting to her." Sloan recalled the pictures of Carter and Jami Richter. The kid had probably already had a taste of what he was going through. Maybe that was why he looked so freaked out. "Jami never talked to the press, and you did pretty good with the little 'I'm sorry if I showed disrespect to my team and my parents with my actions' speech. They move on when you don't tell 'em nothing. You'll be fine."

"Hey, I'm not worried either. Not like they could show those pics in anything but the tabloids." Carter let out a strained laugh. "But . . . I mean, what would you say? Like, to any guy that does want to come out? You know they're gonna ask."

"They'll ask." Sloan slapped Carter's shoulder and stood as he caught sight of Tim gesturing to him. "But I'm got only one thing to say to them unless the PR tells me otherwise."

"What's that?"

"No comment."

"'No comment.'" Carter nodded and hunched over to tie his skates. "Guess that covers it."

Standing with Tim and the PR lady, Sloan did his best to pay attention as they told him what he'd said had been perfect, that he'd handled the press well. And maybe he had.

But he couldn't help but feel giving Carter the same answer had been very, very wrong.

* * * *

Final minutes of the third period and neither team had scored, but anyone who knew the game could see the Sabres set the pace. They had played solid defensively the entire game, avoided fights, and made opportunities whenever the Cobras let down their guard.

Which happened far too often for Sebastian's liking. The absence of their captain seemed to have shaken the younger men. Mason's presence helped some, but he was restricted to limited ice time since he hadn't spent much time practicing with the team. Which meant the energy he brought to the ice came in short bursts and died down just as quickly.

"Wake up, guys!" Bower shouted as the third line dragged their feet and eyed the clock. "Let's finish this!"

The coach shouted for a line change and the Sabres used their brief power advantage to launch another attack. Sebastian quickly covered the shooting lane and sent the puck flying to the other end of the ice. Demyan snapped it up and chipped it to Luke. Luke raced behind the Sabres net and angled a pass to Pearce who let it rebound off his stick toward the net.

A metallic *clink* drove the crowd to their feet. The Sabres goalie gloved the puck and kissed the post with enough enthusiasm that even his own team laughed.

Forty-five seconds left. The Sabres coach called for a time-out. The Cobras gathered by the bench, half listening to Tim's last minute instructions, the other half looking like they had somewhere else to be.

Tim made a sound of disgust and picked up a large bottle of Gatorade. He took a sip, his eyes in slits as he looked them over. Then he spat on the floor and threw the bottle. It slammed into the inner board near the center bench with a *thunk* and burst open. The players started and stared at him.

Sebastian rested his hands on the top of his stick, using them to hide his smile. Tim was known as one of the most level-headed coaches in the league. Seeing him lose his cool wasn't something the men could shrug off.

"The second fucking game in the playoffs, just the second game, and less than a handful of you showed up to play." He shook his head and laughed, raking his fingers through his hair. "*Pathetic*. All right, Pearce, I want you to stay on with Carter and Demyan. The three have you have shown some grit and I'm impressed. Ramos, if you're hurting, let me know now. Otherwise, you're on with Mischlue. Nothing gets through, hear me?"

Time-out ended.

"I am well enough." Sebastian inclined his head to Tim when the man nodded, then skated into position.

The ref tossed Demyan out of the face-off. Luke took his place.

A quick slap off Luke's stick blade skirted the puck between Sebastian's skates. He angled his skate to redirect the puck and carried it out to center ice. Demyan received his pass cleanly, but a solid check knocked him off his feet. He scrambled up and followed Luke and Pearce into the defensive zone to cover his man.

Luke dove to block a shot, then moved swiftly out of Bower's line of sight as the Sabre's retrieved the puck. Sebastian read the play and covered Bower's left flank. Hot pain flashed through his side as the puck cracked into his ribs. He hissed in a breath through his teeth and tightened his grip on his stick as his muscles seized.

Mischlue knocked the puck away from the attacking forward and caught an elbow in the jaw. Bower dove to make a save and lost the rebound. Luke covered and kicked the puck toward Bower's glove. Three Sabres crashed the net, knocking it loose and falling into a pile of bodies.

The buzzer sounded, but there were still a few seconds left for one last face-off. Bower helped Luke to his feet, putting his hand over the one Luke had pressed to his cheek.

"Shit, man." Bower winced. "Get that looked at."

Blood trickled down to Luke's chin and Sebastian forgot the game. He spun around, ready to follow Luke to the bench, but a hand on his shoulder stopped him short.

"Bad idea, Ramos." Bower glanced around quickly and lowered his voice. "You don't want the press making something out of nothing. He's okay; he just got nicked by a skate. Give it three seconds and you can fuss over him in private, *tu sais*?"

"Yes, I understand." Sebastian's jaw hardened as he slid over to the point.

Pischlar took over for Luke. No one bothered setting up a play when the puck hit the ice. The regular periods were done. They were moving into overtime.

Once Sebastian reached the bench, the men let him pass, patting his shoulder and speaking quiet words he couldn't quite make out. They seemed to be offering their support, but he couldn't be sure. Until he saw for himself that Luke was all right, he couldn't find it in him to care for anything else.

****

Luke's stomach did a dead-fish-flop as the thread tugged at the skin on his cheek. His eyes stung, but he managed to man up and take the pain. Wasn't so bad, really. He'd had worse.

Seeing the skate flash right near his eye had scared him more than anything.

"There you go. Only twelve stitches." The doctor sat back and pulled off his gloves. "Might leave a small scar, but you're good to play if you're feeling up to it. You didn't hit your head, did you?"

"Nope." Luke grinned at the doc and grabbed his gloves from the table. As the doc checked on Mischlue, who was icing his jaw, Luke went over to his stall and slumped onto the short wooden bench. He nudged Demyan and gestured to the mirror he stared at cross-eyed to check a small bruise between his eyebrows. "Mind if I borrow that?"

"Sure." Demyan handed him the mirror, then leaned over to inspect Luke's stitches. "Came close, didn't it? You're lucky. Another inch and—"

"I'm sure Luke knows how lucky he is, Demyan, *mon Dieu*!" Bower scowled at Demyan as he ambled up to them. He handed his gloves to a trainer and gave Demyan a pointed look. "How about you make yourself scarce? Ramos wants to check on the kid."

"Ah." Demyan's crooked smile as he glanced past Bower to Seb set Luke's teeth on edge. "Got it. I'll give you two some privacy."

For fuck's sake, like we need it? Luke glared at his skates as Demyan let Seb take his spot. The guys were acting like they knew something. And the whole press thing with Callahan and Perron made it clear that even suspicions were bad. Not that he was ashamed or anything, but did Seb really need to fucking advertize their . . .

Call it what it is. Relationship. Luke pressed his tongue against the inside of his cheek until the cut stretched and throbbed. He held up the mirror and bit back a groan. If this kept up, he was going to look like Frankenstein.

"It is not so bad."

Luke inhaled and faced Seb, with his deep natural tan, skin smooth above thick dark stubble, no scars except for a small one at the bridge of his nose. If he looked close enough, he could tell Seb's nose had been broken once or twice—it wasn't *perfectly* straight—but he could dress up nice and have people see him as more than a jock. He could pass as a clean cut businessman easy. When his career was over, he could do anything he wanted with his life.

"Hey, I'm not looking to model for any girly magazines." Luke laughed and nodded his thanks when the trainer handed him a fresh pair of gloves. "Good thing we've got you and Demyan to do that, right? I'm fine getting called Scar Face."

One eyebrow raised, Seb observed him with a small, amused smile. "I do believe our captain already holds that title."

"Yeah, but he's got all his teeth."

"Actually . . ." Perron grinned as he leaned on the shelf of the stall above Luke and shrugged. "Sorry to butt in, but just thought I might check on our favorite smart ass. And thought I should let you know Sloan had to have a busted molar pulled when his face was torn open. I ain't gonna pretend I didn't hear why your girlfriend dumped you, Carter. But you've got Jami and I've gotta say, you traded up. She's a good girl."

Seb chuckled and Luke couldn't help but grin. *Right, our girl's an angel.*

"All righty then, don't know how well behaved she is, but I do know she won't ditch you because of a few scars." Perron shook his head. "Anyway, I don't want to know, got it? I still look at her as that awkwardly cute fourteen-year-old girl who used to follow her daddy around the forum, blushing whenever one of the guys talked to her. Leave me with my illusions, okay?"

Luke nodded and watched Perron join the coach at the other end of the room, able to relax a bit because Perron was treating both him and Seb normal-like. But he froze when Seb latched onto the back of his neck and pressed their foreheads together.

"I see nothing wrong with your mouth, *semental*." Seb's husky tone caused goose bumps to rise all over his flesh. "And my opinion should be the only one that matters."

"Not here, man. The press—"

"Tell me you understand and I will leave you." Seb gave him a hooded look. "Until we return to our hotel room."

Anticipation blazed through his veins. Luke swallowed and nodded. As they headed back out to the rink, all Luke could think was he couldn't wait for the game to end.

Three minutes into overtime, Pearce scored the winning goal with a sick dangle that stunned both teams. Luke howled as the Sabres goalie looked into the net behind him like he couldn't believe it was over. Pearce's lips curved slightly as he skated a wide circle toward his team. Any other player on the team would be celebrating, hot dogging, something, but Pearce seemed to be quietly soaking it in.

"Hell, Pearce, would it kill you to crack a smile?" Demyan whooped and barreled into Pearce, pushing him into the crush of his teammates. "That was fucking sweet!"

Luke crowded the man with the rest of the team, pumped about the win and impressed by the goal, but everything passed in a blur as Seb brushed against his side, congratulating Pearce, his voice rough from shouting. Seb's tone brushed over his flesh like a million fine bristles. His nerves tingled, the hairs at the nape of his neck rose, and his entire focus locked on Seb, on his big body, so close. And what the man would do to him when they were alone. He decided to wait for his shower, not sure he could play his hard-on off as excitement from the win if he saw Seb naked. He went to his locker and dressed in his rumpled suit, grinning to himself as he considered how Seb would react to him not using the hangers to keep it nice and neat. The man was a little OCD about his wardrobe.

"Sloan, give me a statement and I can fix this. I'll write something about the manly camaraderie between players and how it can be misunderstood."

Fisting his tie in his hands, Luke cast a hooded glance toward Bower's sister, Becky, as she trailed after Callahan.

Callahan stopped short and tipped his sunglasses down as he met Becky's bright, inquisitive grey eyes. "What if I don't want to fix it? Let people believe what they want."

"But you're not—"

"So what? I don't feel the need to defend what I do behind closed doors."

Fuckin' right, man. Luke wanted to high-five his captain, but making himself as inconspicuous as possible seemed a lot smarter.

"Then make a statement saying as much. You're in a position to help those who are afraid of public scrutiny."

"I get why people may think that, Rebecca, but I'm sorry, I feel no need to draw any more attention to myself than I already have."

Becky bit her bottom lip and nodded slowly. "Can I quote you?"

"I'd rather you didn't." Callahan sidled past her. "Tim, if I've got a script, let's get to it. I want to get out of here."

"Sloan, give me *something*!" Becky crumpled her tiny notepad in her fist. "The other reporters won't care how this looks—"

A cold chill slithered down Luke's spine. She was right.

"*I* don't care how this looks." Callahan's lips drew into a thin line as Demyan and Bower joined them in the hall outside the player's lounge. "You're lucky your brother is our goalie. Otherwise, I'd tell you where to go."

"Callahan . . ." Bower stepped forward, looking ready to defend his sister. "She's just doing her job."

"So am I," Callahan said.

"Yeah, but you're doing it with respect for the team." Demyan opened his locker, letting the metal door slam into the one next to it. "Bower, get her out of here. Seriously, I'm fucking sick of her using that she's your sister as an excuse to get an inside scoop."

"Fuck off, Demyan." Bower approached Becky, speaking low. "I'm sorry sis, but we're not supposed to talk to the press during playoffs—not unless the PR—"

"Scott, you're not still sour about the article I did on you and that girl, are you?" Becky pushed past her brother and squared her shoulders. "She *was* underage."

"Yeah, and she fooled both me and the bartender. But whatever, I'm sure you got a nice bonus. Good for you." Demyan ran his tongue over his teeth and laughed. "Not much you can do to make me look worse, but how 'bout you leave the rest of the guys alone."

"I'm just trying to help."

All the men grumbled, but as Mason stepped into the room, they went silent. He folded his arms over his chest and cleared his throat. "I'm sorry, Rebecca, but you'll have to wait outside for your brother. You are welcome to attend the press conference in the morning, but until then, we have nothing to say to you."

"But—"

"Now, pet."

Becky paled and retreated a few steps. She cast one last pleading glance at her brother, but he stared at the floor, refusing to meet her eyes.

Seb met Luke by the lockers just as Becky left, brushing his hands aside to fix his tie. "You are a mess."

"Yeah." Luke pressed his eyes shut, forcing himself not to move closer for support, or push away before someone saw them. He opened his eyes when he couldn't feel Seb touching him anymore. "Yeah, I am. Let's go home, man. I can't deal with this shit."

"I know." Seb bowed his head and sighed. "But thank you for telling me. I respect honesty."

Luke nodded, but he couldn't help but feel he hadn't been completely honest. It wasn't just that he couldn't deal with this now.

He wasn't sure he could deal with it at all. Ever.

Chapter Eighteen

The scent of leather, mixed with the subtle, spicy note of her Hypnotic Poison perfume, rose with the crisp breeze as Jami stepped up to Sebastian's door and knocked softly. Holding her worn jacket closed above where the zipper stuck midway down her chest, she shivered and glanced around at the quiet street and all the houses with their darkened windows, feeling like someone was watching her. Her mouth went dry at a rustle in the bushes surrounding the neighbor's yard. She squinted and spotted a pair of glowing eyes. A scream lodged in her throat as a puffy ball of grey fur sprang out.

Just a cat, chickenshit.

"Come in, *mi cielo*."

At the sound of Sebastian's voice coming from inside, all the tension that had been building up over the past few days evaporated. Jami slipped into the house, shut the door, and leaned against it. She wet her bottom lip with her tongue as her gaze drifted to where Sebastian slouched on the sofa in a crisp, black suit. Her focus slipped from his broad, welcoming smile, down to Luke who wore nothing but a pair of pants. On his knees, hands clasped behind his back, his head moved up and down at a steady rhythm as he sucked Sebastian's cock.

"Remove the jacket, *gatita*. Come to me." Sebastian stroked Luke's hair, his eyes never leaving Jami as she let her jacket fall, revealing the costume she'd chosen from her second trip to the sex shop. "Lovely." The approval in his tone as he took in her slutty French maid's outfit had her glowing from the inside out. "Was the experience less embarrassing this time?"

Heat spread from the exposed swell of her breast right up to her cheeks as she approached him. "A little. Getting the outfit wasn't so bad. Wearing it while I picked out a dozen different vibrators was horrible. That was mean, Sebastian."

"Was it?" Sebastian chuckled. "Then I suppose your next trip will be unbearable."

Oh boy. She tugged at her bottom lip with her teeth as trepidation and arousal swirled into a pool of liquid heat deep in her core. "I should have kept my mouth shut."

"I disagree." Sebastian's hooded look turned her legs to Jell-O. He tugged Luke's hair lightly, then gestured for him to move aside as he drew Jami down for a soul-searing kiss. She lost her balance and fell onto the sofa beside him. His breath, hot and cold all at once with a hint of mint, caressed her lips as he whispered. "You know I can do so much worse. And you complain because you hope I will."

"Mmm." Jami tipped her head to the side as he pressed soft kisses down the length of her throat. His beard tickled her, and the sweet sensation feathered down to her nipples. They drew up and hardened, throbbing with her pulse, aching to be touched. "I need . . ."

"Yes, *mi cielo*, I know." Sebastian patted Luke's head. "Take Luke's place, pet. I need to feel my little *puta's* mouth on me. Though it will take quite an effort to please me more than he has. Do you think you can?"

A challenge. Jami grinned and slipped off the sofa. She licked and bit along Sebastian's inner thigh as she knelt beside Luke, then dipped her head down to suck Sebastian's balls into her mouth. The scruff on Luke's chin lightly scratched her cheek as he moved closer and kissed the edge of her lips. She moaned as he used her bun as a handle to pull her up, tasting her mouth with deep thrusts of his tongue before forcing her over the thick, swollen cock, still slick with his saliva.

"Say 'Thank you for preparing *mi Rey* for me, Sir.'" Sebastian's knuckles grazed her cheek.

Jami gulped as Luke let her come up for air. *Sir?* She'd assumed that since Luke was on his knees, Sebastian would dominate them both.

"Say it, boo." Luke bit her throat and tightened his grip on her hair. "I'm looking forward you being a slut for me again. You're such a fun little toy to play with."

The heartbeat of pain erased her reservations. Power licked at her from all around, and she melted into it, surrendering.

"Thank you for preparing *mi Rey* for me, Sir," she whispered. A spark of mischief lit a smirk across her lips. "Now let me show you how it's done."

Luke laughed and pushed up to stand over her. "I won't argue that. You've got a mouth made for sucking cock."

Batting her eyelashes, she rose up on her knees so her face was level with his crotch and nuzzled against the erection straining his zipper. "Too bad you have to wait."

Hissing in a breath through his teeth, Luke stared down at her, eyes glazed with lust. She blew him a kiss, then turned her focus to Sebastian, easing her lips over his cock. Gliding all the way down until he hit the back of her throat, she kept her lips slack, her jaw muscles relaxed just holding him deep inside for as long as possible. Swallowing, she looked at him as she slid up and stroked her hand along the wet path.

The heat in his eyes, fierce passion mingled with tenderness, stole her breath. "*Mi corina.*"

For a moment it was only the two of them, and that moment was enough to remind her how much he meant to her, to assure her that she meant just as much to him. Nothing he did to her would change that. If anything, it would solidify what she already knew. He accepted her exactly as she was, freakiness and all.

"Hands behind your back, *gatita.*" Sebastian trailed his fingers down her cheek. "And do not stop."

Her heart beat like the wings of a hummingbird caught in a net, frantic and fast as she sensed Luke behind her. His hands moved around her, binding her with a thick red rope, over and under her breasts, so snug it pulled the material down past her nipples. She bobbed her head, simply keeping her mouth open to glide along Sebastian's pulsing length as her arms were pinned to her sides and her wrists bound together. The metallic rip of a zipper brought her head up, and she stared at Luke as he fisted his hand around his cock.

"I don't feel like waiting anymore." He gave her a crooked smile as he latched onto what was left of her bun, forcing her to move sideways on her knees until she faced him. "I told Seb how your ex's friends used you, one after another. He liked the idea. So while you're here, we are going to use you just like that." He pressed her down until the head of his dick touched her lips, his grip on her hair the only thing keeping her from falling forward. "Your mouth, your cunt, your ass. Whenever, and however, we want."

Sebastian sat up and rolled her skirt over her hips, then patted her ass as Luke thrust into her mouth. "Spread your thighs, *coño sucio.*"

Dirty cunt. She had told him how she'd played with herself after looking up a bunch of Spanish curses, how she'd imagined him calling her all those nasty words. Something about hearing them from him—and Luke, which surprised her a little—made her feel free to act slutty, to have things done to her that she would never consider otherwise. She became a hot, wild thing, not held down by the chains of what was right or wrong. And she fucking loved it.

Spreading her thighs as much as she could, Jami pressed her eyes shut as Sebastian's thick finger pushed against her wet slit. She whimpered as Luke slammed in hard and harder. Nothing could be better than having Sebastian fuck her pussy while Luke fucked her mouth. Two fingers, then three, filled her, ramming in hard. Violent torrents of pleasure ripped through her and she tensed, ready to lose herself to the climax.

And suddenly she was empty. Luke withdrew from her mouth. Sebastian's fingers left her.

"No! Ugh!" Something cold and hard pushed into her pussy, stretching her so abruptly pain edged her away from the quick orgasm and tossed her to another level of sensations. She made a low, keening sound in her throat as Sebastian pulled her to her feet. "Oh pleasepleaseplease."

"Not yet, we plan to play with you first, *puta.*" Sebastian curved his hands around the back of her neck. "Do not let it slip out. If you do, you will serve our pleasure and have none of your own."

The thing inside her was so big, clenching on it as Sebastian walked her around the sofa was almost impossible. She took quick little steps to keep up. Sweat trickled between her bound, throbbing breasts and beaded on her face. Her clit swelled past her pussy lips, and she almost came apart as Sebastian pushed her face down over the back of the sofa and cool leather pressed against the tiny nub.

Luke knelt on the sofa in front of her and held her face tight between his hands. "If you bite me, I'll slap you."

Yes! For some crazy reason, the threat made her want to use her teeth on him, just to see if he'd do it. She opened her mouth.

Sebastian tone snapped through the air like a whip. "Will you slap her, *niño?*"

"What?" Luke gentled his hold and went perfectly still. "I—"

"I happen to know slapping is a hard limit for you, Luke." Sebastian stroked her bottom, his gentle touch separating her from his displeasure. But she saw the impact it had on Luke as Sebastian's voice became harsh and cold. "Do not suggest it again."

Luke's cheeks reddened as he dropped his gaze to her face, then away. "I won't."

"Look at me," Sebastian said.

Frowning, Luke looked at him.

"Do not think on it anymore. I trust you to keep your word." Sebastian sounded like he was smiling that deliciously wicked smile he had. "Let us see how well you can trust Jami not to hurt you while I am hurting her."

Hurting me? Jami's eyes widened. She tried to look over her shoulder at Sebastian, but Luke chose that moment to fill her mouth in one long, deep thrust. Sebastian rubbed and massaged her ass, warming her flesh. Then his hands left her.

Smack!

A wide, fiery pain flared over her butt cheek. The huge thing inside her slipped as moisture spilled around it. She clenched to hold it in and wiggled her butt as the stinging faded.

Smack! Smack! Smack!

Groaning, she tried to suck in the saliva dripping past her lips as Luke pistoned in and out of her mouth. Her jaw went slack, so her teeth weren't a problem. Every time Sebastian's rough hand connected with her flesh, the feeling of pain intensified, evaporated, and became pure, raw pleasure. She wanted more. She wanted the sharp edge of that first strike that spread hard and fast.

She jutted her hips up, but Sebastian's hand didn't come down. A low whine sounded in her throat as Luke pulled out.

He curved his hand under her chin and grinned as he ran his thumb over her wet bottom lip. "I want to hear you scream."

Soft strands, like suede, caressed her feverishly hot flesh, trailing the crease of her ass. They swept down from side to side, picking up speed until the ends bit and stung with each impact. As they nipped the edges of her parted pussy lips, stretched around the dildo, an orgasm rolled over her, pounding at her core like a bass drum. Her body pushed at the solid thing inside her, and she cried out as it slid from her and hit the floor with a loud *thunk*.

"Bad *gatita*." Sebastian pressed his lips to the fiery skin that felt stretched thin over her butt. "I would punish you, but I need to see what it will take to make you scream. Come here, Luke. I have heard Chicklet is quite experienced with the tawse. Show me how much you learned from her."

Luke flashed her an evil grin. "My pleasure."

Tears filled her eyes as Luke moved away from her and Sebastian took his place. She was empty. Pain slipped under a dull throb, and her orgasm felt like it had been cut short, leaving her desperate to have what she'd been denied.

Sebastian used his thumbs to dry the tears spilling down her cheeks and kissed her lips. "Do not be ashamed to use your safeword if you need to, *mi cielo*."

"I don't need to yet." She sniffed, hoping her nose wasn't all red and wet. "Unless you're planning to stop."

Brow furrowed, Sebastian nodded slowly. "We will not stop. But I must be honest—giving pain is something I do to heighten a subs pleasure. I do not enjoy it as some do."

"I do," Luke said from behind her. He laid something slick and cool across her ass. "Tell me now if you have a problem with me leaving marks, boo. The ones Seb left will fade in a day or two. I'd love to leave marks that will last for a week."

She sucked in a breath and nodded. "Yes. Yes please, Sir."

Her lips parted as Sebastian rose up on his knees to slip his dick into her mouth. A vicious, stinging snap slashed across her ass, searing almost as hot as an iron grazing flesh. She gasped, jerking away from Sebastian.

"Wait." Sebastian gave Luke a hard look, then bent down to look into her eyes. "Don't try to be brave, Jami."

"It's not . . ." She shuddered as her body tried to assimilate the strange, severe sensation, torn between wanting to get away and never wanting it to end. It was almost impossible to voice her concerns through the foggy haze. "Bite . . . I don't want to bite you. There must be a way—"

"There is." Sebastian framed her face with his hands and spoke against her lips. "Are you sure? This may overwhelm you."

She shook her head, frustrated that her brain didn't want to work right. "I need it all, *mi Rey*. I won't . . . I can't . . . if I'm worried about . . ."

"All right." Sebastian stood. "Keep her in this place, Luke."

"Will do," Luke said.

Luke's bare chest brushed the back of her thighs, as though he'd knelt behind her. He kissed the base of her spine, and his finger traced the ropes around her wrists. Then he sank his teeth into her ass so hard her whole body jerked. The deep, bruising sensation dropped her deeper into the haze. She blinked as a white fog warped her vision, whispering, damp threads of smoke caressed her skin and she drifted into herself, lost in clouds rimmed in tiny electric bolts.

Before she noticed Sebastian had gone, he had returned. He cupped her cheek and spoke softly. "Open your mouth, *mi cielo*."

A wide metal ring slipped between her lips, behind her teeth. Straps pressed snug against her cheeks. Her mouth wouldn't close.

She hauled in a panicked inhale and tossed her head.

"There you go. Tossing your head, pulling away, will take the place of your safeword." Sebastian ran his finger underneath the strap close to her lips. "The scene need not end because it becomes too much. We can do other things that will not frighten you."

I'm not . . . But he couldn't read her mind. And wouldn't assume she was okay. She did her best to tell him with her eyes that she wanted this. Needed it. She let her lips relax around the wide open gag and tongued the metal. It felt . . . odd. But safe. She wouldn't hurt him with this in her mouth.

All she could do was hold still and pray he understood.

Sebastian's lips curled up slightly. "You have no idea how beautiful you look right now."

If only she could smile. Instead, she flicked out her tongue and eyed his dick, wet only at the tip with shiny pre-cum. As he tipped the head into her mouth, she tasted it and made a raspy sound in her throat. Slick and salty, the head passed over her tongue and dipped further, brushing her palate before surging into her throat.

Sebastian groaned. "Now, Luke."

Crack! Red, then white-hot pain drove in, vibrating inside her in a beautiful chorus of agony. Again and again, one strike lapped over the other until shimmering flames replaced all that held her together. The pressure in her throat matched a sudden pressure filling her cunt. She broke into a million shards, each one glowing, shattering with tiny exquisite bursts of ecstasy. She tore herself away from the high and somehow found her way back to reality. To feeling Luke ramming into her pussy. To tasting Sebastian's cum thick on her tongue before he thrust into her throat. His pulsing cock blocked her air. Almost choked her as she swallowed. Her head spun as her heart slammed into her ribcage.

Fingers dug into her hips, and Luke shouted as he came inside her. The quick jerks of his cock triggered endless spasms within. Sebastian drew out, knelt on the sofa, holding her against his chest, smearing tears and saliva as screams scored her throat. Sebastian undid the straps of the gag and pulled it out. She threw her head back, and a ragged sound crossed her lips as she quivered and twisted in the throes of a merciless orgasm.

The twisting tightened the ropes holding her until it felt like they would break through her skin and crush her ribs. She couldn't get enough air. Sobbing, thrashing, desperate to get free, she cried out. "Let me go. Red! Red!"

"Shh, it's over, *mi cielo*." Sebastian pulled her up and over the sofa, into his lap. "Cut the ropes, Luke. Check the table, yes, there. Quickly."

A sharp *snip* and she was free. Loose and tumbling into a deep, dark pit.

Hard muscles wrapped around her, making her solid. Grounding her. She sniffed and the scent was familiar. Mint and soap. And something more. Musk and sex and sweat. No. More. Her brain had checked out, but it knew what that scent meant.

"Sebastian."

I'm safe. I'm okay.

"I am here, Jami. No, *semental*. Stay with us." Sebastian's chest vibrated with the deep resonance of his voice as he cradled her in his strong arms. "You are part of this. She will need to see you when her head clears."

Luke? Jami blinked and tried to see him. He was far away. Too far. Her face crumbled and she sobbed. "Don't leave again! Please! Please pretend—"

"Pretend?" Luke moved toward her in a blur. "There's no fucking pretending with me, boo. I'd love nothing more than to hold you until you can tell me I didn't hurt you too bad. Until you tell me I didn't completely fuck up by hitting you too hard."

"But you didn't." Jami shook her head, confused. "What you did was . . . was . . ."

"Luke, she doesn't know. We will discuss it in the morning." Sebastian brought her close to Luke, trapping her between them as he kissed him. "It is nothing. A small mark. I would have stopped you if I thought you had done real damage."

"I should have been more careful," Luke said, kissing her forehead. "Jami, I'm sorry."

"Sorry?" *What is he talking about?* Exhaustion made her brain even fuzzier than it had already been. She blacked out and found herself in Sebastian's bed, disoriented, only aware that Luke needed her. Needed to know he'd done nothing wrong. She crawled over Sebastian and found him, curled up on the edge of the bed.

His eyes were closed, but she knew he wasn't sleeping. She kissed his scruffy cheek and snuggled against his side, not happy until Sebastian turned and spooned her from behind, throwing one arm around her and Luke's waists. Her butt throbbed a little with the pressure of his bare thighs pressing against it, reminding her of the unbelievable sensations she'd experienced. That she wanted again.

"Don't be sorry, Luke." She blindly traced his face, over his cheeks, down to his lips. "Don't regret what we did."

"I cut you, Jami. I let the leather cut you."

"I don't care."

"But I do. I don't know what happened. I slipped up."

"So what?" Jami couldn't keep her eyes open. She felt drained, which had been good until she realized that Luke was still beating himself up over whatever had happened while she'd been out of it.

"What we did . . . I don't regret it. Do you?"

"No, but that scares me. It's so easy to lose control when I'm with you and Seb." Luke flopped onto his back and groaned. "I've done things I never thought I would."

"You haven't answered my question." Jami pushed up on one shaky arm and looked down at him. "Do you regret it?"

"You want the truth?" Luke pressed his eyes shut and covered his face with his hand. "I don't know."

Jami didn't know what to say. She stretched out on the bed and found herself clinging to Sebastian when she woke, hours later. As she opened her eyes, she found him smiling down at her, and everything seemed all right.

But then the door creaked open. For a second she thought Luke was trying to sneak out.

Then he sat straight up beside her.

A man with dark hair and skin that looked like bleached leather stretched over sharp bones stood in the doorway. He laughed and shook his head. "You found another one, Sebastian?"

Sebastian pushed off the bed and stood, spine straight, naked as he stepped between the bed and the man. "Why are you here, Agustín?"

"You told me I was welcome. The door wasn't locked."

"Wait for me downstairs."

"Sure, but I just have to ask one thing first." Agustín jutted his chin toward Luke. "Does he know this isn't the first time you've used a pretty girl to get a man in your bed?"

"That is not the truth." Sebastian fisted his hands by his sides and turned to face Luke. His accent thickened and he seemed to struggle to find the right words. "Do not hear him."

"I hear him, Seb." Luke scowled and pulled the blanket off the bed to cover himself as he stood, leaving Jami with only the sheet. "And I've got to say, I'd really like to know what he means by 'it's not the first time.'"

Jami jerked the sheets up to her neck, but they couldn't shield her from the cold dread that hovered around her as the men left the room. Agustín must be Sebastian's cousin, the one who refused to stay here once he found out about Sebastian and Luke. She wanted to believe that nothing he could say would change things.

But she knew it would. She knew it already had.

* * * *

"I don't want any fucking coffee, Seb." Luke resisted the urge to smash the coffee cup Seb offered out of his hand. Seeing it break into pieces on the floor, seeing the black liquid spread, might give him a second of shallow satisfaction, but it wouldn't make things any better. And it would make him look even more pathetic. "If what he said isn't true, tell me what is."

Seb nodded and pulled out a chair at the head of the kitchen table. He gestured to the chair at his right. "Very well. Have a seat, Luke."

"Thanks, I'll stand."

"You will sit and give me the respect of hearing me out calmly."

Luke shook his head and laughed. "Give you respect? You're kidding me, right? You didn't say Agustín was lying." He jutted his chin to where Seb's cousin sat at the other end of the table. He had no idea why the man was still here, but he was kinda glad he hadn't left. Seb wouldn't be able to sugarcoat anything. "You said, 'That is not the truth.' You meant not the *whole* truth, didn't you?"

Flattening his hands on the table, Seb leaned forward and spoke in a measured tone, his dark eyes fixed on Luke. "You are in my home. You *will* show me respect, or you will leave. And if you leave, you will not have your answers."

"Fine." Luke gritted his teeth and sat. "I'm listening."

The soft padding of bare feet came from the hall, and Luke glanced over his shoulder as Jami crept into the room. She was wearing one of Seb's black dress shirts, long enough that the hem reached her knees and the sleeves covered her hands. Her gaze flitted from him to Seb as she chewed on her bottom lip.

"Please join us, *mi cielo*," Seb said.

Jami fidgeted with the buttons at the collar of the shirt and eyed Agustín. "I'd rather not, *mi Rey*. Tell me whatever you think I need to hear—"

"This isn't a goddamn scene! You knew about this, Jami. You

can pretend he's your Lord and Master all you want, but you fucking knew. I suspected when all this started, but I was stupid enough to believe that you got into this because you were interested in me." Luke shook his head and let out a bitter laugh. "Be straight with me, boo. You knew I wouldn't get involved with him without you."

Pulling out a chair, wincing at the harsh scraping sound it made against the tiles, then wincing again as she sat, Jami shook her head. "Not exactly. When this all started I was . . ." She pressed her lips together and glared at Agustín. "Do you really need to be here? This is between the three of us. You've created enough problems."

"I asked him to stay, Jami." Sebastian took a sip of coffee from his big, white mug, then sighed. "It is obvious Luke has no faith in me. Perhaps Agustín can confirm some of what I say."

"I guess." Jami sat and hugged herself, staring at the table. "I was worried you'd take my place, Luke. I figured if I showed Sebastian I was okay with him fooling around with you—"

"You do know that's pretty fucking sad, right, Jami?" Luke almost felt sorry for her. She might be just a few years younger than him, but in a lot of ways, she was still a kid. "If he cares about you, you shouldn't have to worry about competition."

Jami frowned at him and shook her head. "It's not like that and you know it."

"Bullshit," Luke said. "You let Ford use you. Now you're letting Seb do the exact same thing. Maybe you need therapy or something. All those drugs messed with your head and—"

"Enough!" Seb stood and slammed his fist on the table. Coffee sloshed over the edge of his mug. "Take your anger out on me, not her. The whole truth is yes, I have been attracted to straight men and I have used women to seduce them. There is more to it, but that is irrelevant. I did not use Jami to seduce you."

Liar. Luke stood and sucked his teeth. "The first time you fucked me, you used her. That's why you had her on webcam."

"I did that to include her. And to make things easier for you."

"Fuck that. You did it to make things easier for *you*." His guts twisted in acidic sludge, everything he'd let happen making him just as disgusted with himself as he was with Seb. "I'm a fucking idiot. I was falling in love with her, and you played on that. You made it clear every time we were together that I couldn't have her without you."

Seb blinked and pushed away from the table. Big and tough as he was, he looked almost vulnerable standing there in nothing but a pair of snug, grey boxer-briefs, color draining from his swarthy skin. "You did not want me."

"I thought I did. You're good, I'll give you that." Luke tipped his head back and pressed his eyes shut. "Damn it, I should have listened when Silver said you could convince anyone to do anything. She was right."

"Silver warned you away from me?" Seb seemed confused, as if he couldn't picture Silver doing that. "Why would she—"

"No, she didn't, but I heard her joking about it with Bower once." Luke remembered how Bower had rolled his eyes. "It sounded funny then, but not anymore."

"Luke, listen to yourself!" Jami reached for him, then let her hand fall to her side as he jerked away. "Sebastian didn't make you do anything. And neither did I. There's nothing wrong with being—"

"Being what? Gay?" Luke pressed his lips together and nodded. "You're right. There's nothing wrong with it. But I'm not gay."

"Neither am I." Sebastian dropped into his chair and bowed his head to his hand as he braced his elbow on the table. "Though I do not expect you to believe me. You clearly do not trust me."

"Why should he?" Agustín spoke up for the first time, shaking his head as he gave his cousin a look full of sympathy. At first it had seemed like he wanted to make trouble, as Jami had implied, but his next words told Luke otherwise. "You've lied to him, and you're lying to yourself. If there's nothing wrong with being gay, why won't you admit you are? You've never been happy with a woman."

Seb lifted his head. His lips were drawn into a stiff smile. The hurt in his eyes hit Luke hard enough that he almost wished he could take it all back. His words came out lifeless. Empty. "I was happy with them."

"If you thought that would last, you are a fool," Agustín said.

"I am a fool. I believed you accepted me, cousin." Seb rolled his neck and took a deep breath. "Please go. All of you. I am done with this conversation. It is getting us nowhere."

Luke swallowed and glanced over at Agustín as he passed on his way out, nodding when the man patted his shoulder. He retreated a few steps, but couldn't make himself go any further when he saw Jami kneel at Seb's feet and whisper something to him.

The truth had pissed Luke off. He couldn't forgive Seb for playing him, but part of him still felt broken, as if his core had been cut open with a blunt, rusty knife. Only pride kept him from kneeling next to Jami and telling Seb none of it mattered.

But it did matter, and he refused to pretend otherwise. His only regret was how right he'd been. He couldn't have Jami without Seb.

And forcing himself to walk away from her was one of the hardest things he'd ever done.

* * * *

The light pressure of Jami's fingers digging into Sebastian's thigh was the only thing that grounded him. He wasn't the kind of man to turn to drink, but he could see the appeal. Even this early—it couldn't be past nine a.m.—the bottles of hard liquor in his library beckoned. He'd never thought his family would have the power to hurt him again, not after all his grandfather had done to his mother. But he'd been so very wrong. His cousin had managed to drive a stake right into the heart of his relationship, and Sebastian could still feel the piercing agony, deep in his chest, leaving splinters behind as he struggled to pull himself together.

He rubbed his lips with his knuckles and brushed his hand over Jami's loose, rumpled hair. "You should go, *mi cielo*." He managed to keep his tone light. Devoid of emotion. "I am not fit company."

"Yeah, because your freaking out is scaring me." Jami grinned up at him, but she was blinking fast. "Actually, I take that back. I'd be less freaked out if you let yourself lose it a bit. Throw something. It will make you feel better."

Ay dios mio. Sebastian shook his head and let out a rough laugh. *Mi cielo, you are too precious for words.* "Do you break things when you are angry, *niñita?*"

"Damn right, I do." She stood and picked up his empty mug.

Then she smashed it on the floor. "Fuck! Ah! See?" Her giggle was cut off by a sob. "It's therapeutic. And I swear, I will so buy you a new cup."

Sebastian shook his head and rose from his seat. He stepped carefully around the porcelain shards scattered across the floor, then picked Jami up and held her against him. "Do you feel better?"

"No." She hid her face against his neck, clinging to him as he carried her to the kitchen counter, not letting go until he sat her on the ledge. She hissed in a breath, readjusted to take some pressure off the left side of her bottom, then pressed her fingers to his lips as he moved to take her down. "Don't fuss over me. It's only a little sore." Shaking her head, she sighed. "I just didn't know Luke could be such an asshole. How could he listen to your cousin?"

How could he not? He studied her face, touched by her faith in him. She hadn't even considered that there may be some truth in Agustín's words.

"He is very confused, Jami." Sebastian inhaled and pressed his lips to her forehead. "I should have spoken to him more about my past, but I never considered it would be an issue. What concerns me now is what you said. Did you believe that I would choose him over you?"

"I was scared that you would. And then . . ." Jami's brow furrowed. "I didn't think you should have to. You weren't making me choose."

"I never would have."

"I know that." Her bottom lip trembled. "But it's over, isn't it? I just proved all that your jerk of a cousin accused you of."

"No." Sebastian refused to let her take this on herself. His own misjudgment had left plenty of room for doubt. He should have seen this coming. Luke would have reacted badly no matter how Sebastian's torrid past was revealed, but he may have been willing to listen if it hadn't come from another. He wouldn't make the same mistake with Jami. "Agustín was not being cruel. I think seeing you between Luke and myself prompted him to speak up."

"Why?"

"Because you are young. When one looks at you, all they see is innocence." Sebastian looked away from her, disgusted with himself because he hadn't considered any of that when he'd taken her. Lust and love didn't excuse ignorance. "I believe Agustín was trying to protect you."

Jami snorted and hooked her fingers to the front of his boxers. "He doesn't know me."

"And you do not know me, *mi cielo*." He gathered her face in his hands and laced his fingers through her hair. Aware that he could lose her any moment. Needing to hold her before he did. He tensed as he felt himself trembling, desperate to hide his weakness from her. "My first time with a man was after I met his wife. Sarita." Saying her name brought the image of her to his mind, painted with surreal perfection. Long, black hair, luscious curves, big brown eyes simmering with heat every time she looked at him. "I was sixteen and even though I was obsessed with him, I couldn't deny her allure. She told me both she and her husband were looking for ways to 'spice up their sex life.' She was a friend of my mother's."

"That's a little twisted, you know."

"Not to an inexperienced teenage boy, but yes, I eventually accepted she had manipulated me. Used me." But at the time, Sarita had been such a magnificent creature, so powerful and beautiful, he would have done anything for her. She took him home with her one day after his grandfather had said horrible things about his father, about how worthless the man had been. Sebastian hadn't wanted his mother to see how much his grandfather's words upset him, so he had gone to her friend, hoping since Sarita had known his mother all her life, that she might be able to help him protect her. A few drinks was all it had taken for Sarita to make him forget why he'd come. He couldn't hide his shame as he told Jami, with blunt honesty, how foolish he'd been. Her eyes were wide as he admitted that he had been completely submissive to Sarita. That his first taste of dominance had been with her husband. "I learned from her. I wasn't the first to join them, but I was the first man. I lost my virginity to them both. After they moved on, it took a long time for me to be with any other woman. None compared to her. But men . . . men were easier. I didn't know then it was because dominance came naturally. Once I explored that part of myself, I felt drawn to women, which was difficult for a long time. Many believe you cannot be attracted to both."

"Wait." Jami took his hand and brought it to her lips. She kissed his knuckles while looking into his eyes. "You're leaving something out. 'When they moved on'? You were okay with it?"

"I was young. Of course I hoped they would keep me, but they did not. You are avoiding the issue, Jami."

"And what's the issue, Sebastian?"

"Women have been involved in my seductions. I considered straight men a challenge." He stroked the curve of her cheek with his knuckles and gave her the smile that had filled his bed for over a decade, urging her to see what he was capable of. "You have no idea the lengths a man will go to, the things he will do, to make love to a beautiful woman beyond his reach. Such tempting bait. And I am well aware of my allure. I've used any means necessary to get what I want."

"But you didn't do that with me." She released his hand and glared at him, as though daring him to argue with her. "Or Luke."

Her trust humbled him. He did not deserve it. Part of him wanted her to doubt him so she could save herself. He turned on the taps to the kitchen sink and began washing dishes, using the mundane chore as a way to make everything else seem normal. "Are you so sure, *mi cielo*?"

"You're damn right I am." Jami grabbed his arm and jerked so hard the plate he was washing slipped from his hands and splashed into the half-full sink of water. "You're not getting rid of me that easy, mister."

He shut off the water and dried his hands on a cloth. Shifting over, he tugged on Jami's knees until she wrapped her ankles at the base of his spine. "I will do anything in my power to keep you. But I will use the truth."

"Good. Then tell me this." She wiggled her hips and settled against him. "When we met, were you thinking of anyone else?"

"No."

"When you were holding Luke with a knife against his throat, were you thinking about me?"

Sebastian dropped his gaze to his hands on her knees. "No."

"Then the truth is you were honest with your feelings. We're both special to you, and if Luke doesn't see that, he's brain dead."

"I don't believe he is 'brain dead', *gatita*," Sebastian said. "He is angry and hurt. And he has every right to be."

"Are you gonna try to talk to him again?"

"Perhaps, but first I will give him some space." Knowing Luke would want space from him—no, *need* it, made it so hard to breathe it felt like the ropes Luke handled so skillfully had been wrapped around his neck. He cleared his throat and hauled in air past the choking sensation. "He will want answers. I will tell him all I have told you when he is ready to ask."

"What is he's never ready? What if he just avoids you?"

Sebastian smiled and shook his head. "That is very unlikely. But if it happens, I have a promise to keep to you both. I swore I wouldn't give up on him."

Jami wrinkled her nose. "This could get messy."

"Yes, it could." Sebastian lifted Jami up off the counter and let her slide down his body as he kissed her. "But it is my mess, *mi cielo*. Let me worry about it."

"Are you telling me not to meddle?" Jami wrapped her arms around his waist and laid her cheek against his bare chest. "Because I can't promise I won't."

"I am asking you, Jami." He suddenly felt exhausted, the late flight and lack of sleep after the night he'd spent with Luke and Jami finally catching up to him. Too tired to filter his words. "I'm not sure if I could handle him lashing out at you. Do not give him a reason to."

"Fine." Jami sighed and rolled her eyes. "I'll try to be nice. Which will be much easier if I avoid *him*."

"This need not ruin things between you. He does love you."

"Right. I could tell." Her teeth scraped over her bottom lip hard enough to make it redden and swell. "Not that it matters. I loved you first."

Por amor de Dios! She was so young. Young enough to give her loyalty to him blindly, without compromise. He had some confidence he could mend things between himself and Luke, given time, but the damage done to the very fragile relationship Luke and Jami had developed was a different matter. His own loyalties were somewhat torn between them, but they ended where they'd begun.

If he had to choose between them, he would choose Jami. But he would avoid that in every way possible. And the only option he could see was keeping them apart.

"Do not be bitter, or cruel, if you do see him, *mi cielo*." Sebastian pressed his face to her hair and inhaled. The faint spice of her perfume, the fresh aroma that was hers alone, soothed him. He had to trust that things would turn out well in the end. "But you are right. It may be best if you avoid him for now."

At her next words, he closed his eyes and stifled a sigh.

"That won't be a problem, *mi Rey*. He's right about one thing." Her tone became cold. "He *can't* have me without you."

Chapter Nineteen

Luke fiddled with his tie as the team meeting finished, keeping his hand over it as Seb walked by. And then felt damn ridiculous for doing so. Who cared if Seb noticed he was wearing a clip-on? Not like his opinion mattered anymore.

He bit the inside of his cheek, forcing himself to stay put as Seb stopped by the door to chat with Mason. Both men had the beginning of thick beards covering their jaws, cheeks, and upper lip. Even in expensive suits, they both looked rugged, dangerous. Fit and well rested for the game tonight.

For some reason, seeing Seb like that pissed him off. Luke hadn't been able to sleep right since he'd left Seb's place the day before. His daily nap consisted of staring at the ceiling. He'd tossed and turned all night. His bed seemed too big. Too empty.

Staying mad made it a bit easier not to think about Seb, even though he'd almost rolled off the bed in the middle of the night, seeking his solid body. His heart had stuttered when he'd come in for the meeting and Seb's pain filled eyes met his. He'd almost knocked Mischlue over in his rush to find a seat at the back of the room. He'd sat stiffly through the video lecture and did his best to pay attention to Tim pointing out all the ways they could improve their game against the Sabres.

But his gaze kept slipping over the wide set of Seb's shoulders, trailing over the dark length of hair bound low. His fingers twitched as he recalled the soft texture. His blood burned in his cheeks and his lips as he remembered how it felt to have that huge body pressed against him, those firm lips touching him everywhere. That voice, commanding, then tender, always reaching deep inside, lending him strength even when he was on his knees.

Luke never thought he'd fall in love with a man. But he'd fallen in love with Seb.

Yeah, too bad he's a fucking liar.

"Hey, you okay, pal?" Demyan put his hand on Luke's shoulder. "You look like shit. Need to get it off your chest or something?"

"Naw, I'm good." Luke stood and walked with Demyan out to

the hall, ducking his head as he passed Seb. Out of spite, he nudged Demyan in the ribs and spoke loud enough for Seb to hear. "Wanna go grab a couple of drinks before the game?"

He smirked as he caught Seb's frown from the corner of his eye.

"I would, but a bunch of the guys are meeting up for an early dinner, and I was kinda hoping to hook myself up with a date." Demyan laughed and hunched his shoulders as he shoved his hands in his pockets. "I'll be straight with you—the Delgado sisters are gonna be there. And Richter. They only signed me for a year, and that year's over in a few months. I figured a bit of sucking up wouldn't hurt."

"They'd be stupid to let you go, man."

"Yeah, well they might get a good draft pick for me. I'd rather not take any chances."

"I hear you." Luke cast Demyan a sideways glance. "Need some moral support?"

"That would be cool. You gonna bring Jami?"

"If she'll come." Luke hadn't told either of his roommates about what had happened. Too weird to try to explain—impossible without telling them about him and Seb. "So where are you hunting for a date?"

Demyan chuckled. "Ice Girls, buddy. Figure I've got my pick since they're all obsessed with the team. There are two groups skating right now, so I'm heading to the rink. Kinda like picking a bunny out of a crateful, you know?"

"Sounds good." *Jami might be there.* Luke tongued his bottom lip. He'd tried calling her once and wasn't all that surprised that she hadn't answered. Actually, he'd been a little relieved. It would be better if they could talk face-to-face. "Why don't we get our skates on and join them on the ice? The press will get a kick out of it."

"You sure we're allowed, man?"

"Who's gonna stop us?"

* * * *

Racing across the rink, Jami closed her eyes and sank into the sensation of gliding across the ice, utterly free. The damp chill rising up from the ice caressed her bare skin and filled her lungs. Loud pop

288

music echoed around her, drowning out the laughter of the other girls, isolating her as she let it pump into her skull and move her. She ignored the flashing cameras, the people in the stands, completely focused on the burn in her muscles as she circled the rink, going faster and faster, for a moment leaving all her troubles in the snow kicked up by her skates as she abruptly changed direction and sped to the other end.

Colors whirled around her as someone caught her by the waist and spun her in a wide circle. Her hands flattened on a solid chest. She locked her eyes on a spot in the stands to center herself and stop her head from spinning. She laughed as she realized that fixed point was Sebastian, watching her from just beyond the glass, and she blew him a kiss as she stopped spinning. It was too perfect that he was the one to steady her. But then he stood and frowned and the ice under her feet swayed.

She latched onto steel-corded forearms, and her eyes went wide as she stared up at Luke.

"Hey, boo."

"What do *you* want?" She pushed away from him, skating backward. "You shouldn't be here."

"I just wanted to . . . shit, Jami, this is messed up, and we both know it." Luke raked his fingers through his hair, then shrugged. "It doesn't have to be. Let's start over, okay? Just me and you. We both know *he* won't mind."

"Wait. *What?*" Tension coiled up at the front of her skull as she dug her toe picks into the ice and smacked her hands against his chest to stop him from getting closer. "What are you saying? And be very clear, Luke. I'm not in the mood for games."

"I want to take you out. On a normal date."

"*Normal?*" Damn it, she'd promised Sebastian she'd be nice, but it was very hard with Luke acting like a delusional dick. "So what am I, your token girlfriend so you can pretend to be straight?"

"I *am* straight." Luke scowled at her. "You've experimented and regretted it. Is it that hard to believe that I did the same?"

"Are you going to pretend that Sebastian means nothing to you?"

"I'm not pretending."

"Funny, for someone who demands the truth, you're awfully full of shit." She shoved him back, speaking quietly even though she was tempted to scream. As much as she wanted to expose him, if only to force him to face reality, it wasn't her place. She'd keep his little secret because she knew Sebastian would want her to. "You seem to be avoiding the fact that *I* set you up. Sebastian had nothing to do with it. You're going to hold it against him, but forgive me? How stupid are you?"

"I thought we had something." Luke slid away from her and scowled. "Maybe I was wrong."

"We *did* have something. You screwed it up." Her eyes burned as she glanced toward the stands. She couldn't find Sebastian. She needed him. How the hell was she supposed to handle Luke without him around? Since Luke had left them, she'd clung to Sebastian and done her best to ignore the hollow space inside. Refused to admit she missed Luke. That she wanted things to be like they had before. "If you want to fix this, do it right."

"And what's right?"

"Admit that it's not just me and you."

"It's just me and you, boo." Luke slid forward and cupped her cheek. "Or it's nothing."

She pulled away and stared at the ice. "Then it's nothing."

"Got it." He let his hand fall to his side and turned away from her. His voice carried across the rink. "Sucks because I really need a date tonight."

Good luck with that, asshole.

Snow sprayed up Jami's legs as Amy skidded to a stop beside Luke. "I'm putting on a show tonight, but if it's early enough, I'm free. Make me an offer."

Luke smiled and whispered something in Amy's ear. The bite of the tawse, which Luke had regretted so much, was nothing compared to this. Jami hadn't felt the leather cut her flesh. But Luke hitting on Amy—of all people—sliced straight to the bone.

Amy bit her bottom lip, gazing up at Luke with pure worship. "Oh, you're bad. I don't know. You could totally ruin my reputation."

"I plan to." Luke gave Amy a heavy-lidded look. "Is that a yes?"

"Yes." Amy pressed her breasts against his chest and gasped. "I just hope you won't take advantage of me. I have to admit, I'm a big fan. I cried when I saw Bower holding your bloody face after that skate cut you."

"Why, because you knew my face would be even more messed up?"

"No. I find scars hot." Amy simpered. "I just didn't like seeing you hurt."

"I'm fine, sweetheart," Luke said. "But it's nice to know you cared."

Jami blinked and circled away from them blindly. Someone grabbed her and through a blur of tears she made out Akira's face. She gulped back a sob as Akira led her off the ice. Akira knew everything. She didn't have to hide how she felt. But she tried because there were so many people around. People who would make something of her falling apart.

"*Mi cielo*, look at me."

Akira had handed her off to someone, and Jami could tell by scent alone that it was Sebastian. This was why he'd disappeared from the stands. He'd come for her.

"We don't need him, Sebastian." Jami rubbed her face against his shirt to dry her stupid tears. Luke wasn't worth getting upset over. He could be replaced. Her throat locked as she pictured someone else coming between them. Someone else who would want to tear them apart. They didn't need that. Why not find someone easier to handle? Someone fun and uncomplicated? She knew Sebastian would be happy with her, but she also knew he enjoyed having a man in his bed. And she would find a way to give him one.

"Jami . . ." Sebastian tried to hold her, but she was already looking, looking to find someone to replace Luke.

Scott Demyan hesitated by Sebastian's side, his lips pressed together as he drew in a harsh inhale. One of Amy's friends waited for him a few feet away, looking annoyed, but Scott ignored her. "I know about you and Luke, Ramos. I think a few guys do, and we've been trying to support him, but—"

Jami pulled away from Sebastian. Slid her hands behind Scott's neck. "You know? Then let me give you something to think about."

She pressed her lips against Scott's, tugging his bottom lip with her teeth. He wasn't Luke, and there was something missing in the kiss, but she didn't need it. Not having some big, strong connection would make things so much simpler. As he groaned, she whispered against his lips. "Sebastian is having a party after the game. I hope you'll be there."

"I will." Scott stroked her side and swallowed hard, wincing as Luke passed and glared at him. "Shit. This is gonna get fucked up, but I'll be there."

"I'm a package deal, stud." Jami ignored Luke, with Amy trailing behind him, and drew her finger down Scott's chest. "You okay with that?"

Sebastian did *not* look pleased, but he didn't say a word. He moved in close enough to trap Scott between them.

"Fuck." Scott pressed his eyes shut and nodded. "Yeah, I'm okay with it. But don't tell anyone, okay? I'm on thin ice already. This party will be private-like, right?" He opened his eyes and looked to Sebastian. "Nothing that will make me look bad? I can't afford to give the press anything more than I already have."

"She has chosen you, and for her, I will protect you." Sebastian gave Scott a cold smile, as if he was testing the man. "Only those I trust will be at the party. You have nothing to fear."

"Yeah, the way you just said that doesn't make me so sure."

"Let me amend my words." Sebastian's lips curled. "Do as I say, and you have nothing to fear."

"You're a scary bastard, you know that?" Scott cringed as the locker room door slammed down the hall. "He's going to be pissed if I agree to this. I can't . . . if he's still involved, leave me out of it."

"He's not." Jami batted her eyelashes and ducked her head. "But I get it if you're scared."

Scott frowned. "I'm not."

"Good. Then I'll leave it for you two to discuss the details. I'll be watching from the press box. Hope you can still play, even while you're thinking about what my Master will make me do to you."

"Damn it, seriously?" Scott swallowed again, hard, looking to Sebastian as he slid his hands down her sides. "You'll do whatever he says?"

"Yes." Jami smiled. "Will you?"

"Yeah." Scott leaned close and whispered. "But I've got a dinner date, business stuff, just so you know it doesn't mean anything."

"Whatever happens between us won't mean anything either, Scott."

"It will. But I trust you. If you were able to deal with Carter and Ramos . . ." Scott's breath was hot against her neck, and she suddenly realized he wasn't attracted to her alone. He was trusting her not to judge him. And his next words proved it. "I don't have to pretend with you, do I?"

"No." His flesh felt feverish on her lips as she kissed his throat. It scared her a little that he might be using her to get to Sebastian, but she didn't plan to get emotionally involved, so it didn't really matter. "You don't."

"Good." He bowed his head and closed his eyes. "Because I'm fucking tired of it."

"And I'm tired of people being fake. At least I know what you want."

As Scott moved away, she met Sebastian's eyes. Uncertainty painted harsh lines across his forehead as he leaned down to her.

"Are you sure, *mi cielo*?"

Everything inside hurt so bad it felt like some had broken her ribs apart and exposed her heart. She needed to show him she'd be okay without Luke. She *would* show him.

"I am sure as long as you are, *mi Rey*."

"I am trying, *gatita*, but I do miss him."

"Forget him. Let me give you someone else."

"I've no interest in anyone else." Sebastian drew away from her, and the distance between them became more than physical, became a solid brick wall that made it impossible to reach him. "Give him time."

"Time's up. I can't handle how much he hurt you. He's easy to replace."

"You don't truly believe that."

"I do. Trust me, okay?" Jami wanted to grab Sebastian and shake him. He was giving Luke the power to hurt him, and she wouldn't allow it. "I have to go back to that shop, don't I? Before the party?"

"Yes."

"Don't make it easy on me." Hell, the tension was working up to a full-fledged migraine. Nausea made it impossible to think straight. "I'm okay. With whoever you choose. At least Scott is safe."

"Safe?" Sebastian shook his head and kissed her. "Safe isn't enough. You are all I need."

"Be honest. You're tempted. Please tell me I'm not the only one being shallow. The only one thinking we can have some fun and leave all the drama behind."

"That is not how I do things, Jami." Sebastian sighed. "But it is tempting."

"That's enough for me. Don't dig too deep. This doesn't need to be complicated."

"Jami..." Sliding his hands up to her shoulder, gently massaging the taut muscles, Sebastian nodded slowly. "Very well. Go home and have yourself a drink. Only. One. Then go to the store."

"What am I getting this time?" Jami plopped down on the floor in the hall and undid her skates. She giggled when Sebastian took a knee to pull them off, and a few Ice Girls shot her glares stained ugly green as they passed. "If it's something really bad, I might need a few hard shots to go through with it."

"One." Sebastian chuckled when she pouted at him. "And someone will meet you with my instructions. I expect you to show her the same respect you would show me."

"*Her?*" Jami winced as she took her skates back and the blades pinched her palm. She stood and peered up at Sebastian, not sure how she felt about this new twist. He was leaving her to the mercy of a *Domme?* "I'd be more comfortable with a man, Sebastian."

"This is not for your comfort, *gatita*. This is for my pleasure." He tapped her chin lightly with a fingertip and smiled. "Be a good girl for me—make me proud by how well you behave."

"But I *never* behave!"

"I suggest you do in her presence. She is quite creative with punishments."

"Ugh. She's allowed to punish me?" Jami wrinkled her nose. "I'm not crazy about this idea."

Moving close so she was pinned against the wall by his big,

muscular body, the surprisingly soft material of his suit jacket brushing the top of her breasts, Sebastian leaned down and whispered in her ear. "That may be. But it has distracted you enough that you have relaxed. You've forgotten your hurt. Which makes me thinks 'this idea' is a good one. We both need to forget for a little while."

The dull ache inside had faded. And he'd smiled and laughed for the first time in way too long. She took a deep breath and hooked her fingers to his crisp, white collar. "Are you going to play better if you know I'm being a 'good girl'?"

"I will."

"All right." She let the reason for hitting on Scott, for insisting that Sebastian not cancel the party, blank out everything else. She wanted to see the Cobras win. And more importantly, she needed to see Sebastian happy again. "Then it's a *great* idea."

* * * *

The weather had hiked up to smoldering by midday, so Jami had gone home to change. The black lace and fishnet stockings she wore under her cutoff jean shorts, along with a black sleeveless shirt, laced loosely up the deep v-neck, made her feel sexy, but comfortable. She planned to throw Sebastian's jersey over the outfit for the game, but this would be what she wore to the party.

Not that she'd be wearing much for long. She chewed on her bottom lip as she slipped into the sex shop, Naughty Pleasures, and blushed at a smirk from the cashier. At least the multi-pierced Goth recognized her from the last two times. There would be no questions about her age—which had embarrassed the hell out of her after she'd gotten up the nerve to step inside on her first visit—but Devon, the cashier, would probably ask her some intimate questions about her purchases. Or give her a lecture, like she had about the glass dildo not being a good choice for an anal virgin.

How much you want to bet this is gonna be ten times worse?

"Don't you look nice and terrified?"

Jami started and gaped up at Chicklet. Her short, spiky hairdo, paired with faded jeans and a white tank top, gave her a young, approachable appeal, but Jami knew the woman from a few brief encounters. And reputation. She pretty much lived in Dartmouth now to be close to her sub, Tyler, but she made trips back to her hometown to play goalie for the local team. Kept fit by joining Sloan and some of the other guys at the gym a few times a week. And attended BDSM events in Montréal several times a year to come up with evil new ways to torture her female sub.

The last Jami had overheard her father telling Landon and Silver when she was supposed to be helping her grandmother with supper during one of their visits. Silver had laughed nervously when Dad had hinted at some new ideas Chicklet had given him.

And if Silver was intimidated by the woman, Jami knew she should be too.

"You're adorable." Chicklet laughed and draped her arm over Jami's shoulders. "Blushing already and I haven't done anything yet."

A short, curvy woman lingered behind Chicklet, head down, lips curved in amusement. She winked at Jami, then straightened her long, knee length skirt and spoke softly. "May I speak, Mistress?"

"Yeah, sure. Sorry, I'm being rude, but it's been awhile since I've been allowed to play with someone else's sub." Chicklet grinned. "Sloan and them all are so possessive! You, however, have a nice, open-minded Dom. You two get to know each other while I let Devon know what's going on."

As Chicklet strode away, shouting to Devon, her sub drew Jami aside. Even though she looked to be in her mid-thirties, she didn't give off that motherly vibe most older women did whenever Jami was around. It was like they were on the same level.

"If you're being punished, give me a heads up. I'll distract my Mistress so she's not too hard on you."

Jami wasn't in trouble—*yet*—but she was touched that the woman had her back even though they didn't know each other. "Why would you do that?"

"We subs have to look out for each other. I'm Laura, by the way." Laura glanced over at Chicklet, then leaned close. "And you're Jami Richter. I have to say, I'm surprised that Chicklet agreed to this. She really respects your dad."

"Which makes it weird."

"Not really. Chicklet's cool. She sees him like her boss in a way since she's a DM at his club. I don't think she'd let you in there, but since none of this will be happening at the club, she's looking at you as another toy she gets to play with." Laura licked her bottom lip and drew in a sharp inhale. "Are you okay with that?"

"I think so." Jami swallowed and turned in a slow circle, taking in the mannequins on platforms dressed in latex and leather, the racks displaying more kinky toys than she had names for. The wall dedicated to whips and floggers and crops. The place was brightly lit, immaculate, no different, really, than any other store. But the low drone of pulsing, erotic music, the atmosphere, made it impossible to forget why she was here.

There weren't a lot of people around, but those who were seemed comfortable in their surroundings. An older couple, mid-sixties at her best guess, huddled over a glass display case which she knew held fancy nipple clamps and funky body jewelry. Two men were inspecting cock cages. The bigger one flushed as the other held a small steel and leather cage close to his crotch as sizing it.

Jami's eyes widened when he cupped his lover's package right there, massaging him through his pants as he whispered and changed the cage for a slightly bigger one.

"If either of them was interested in women, I'd have you go over and offer to help." Chicklet's warm breath teased the hairs at the nape of Jami's neck, making her shiver. She laughed and lightly chewed on her gum. Her lips brushed Jami's earlobe. "It's your lucky day, slut. Your Master's decided you need some attention. And I'm going to make sure you get it."

Oh, fuck. Jami laced her fingers together in front of her and tried to figure out how Sebastian would want her to react. Would it bother him that her blood was already surging low, that she was more turned on than embarrassed at Chicklet's words?

No. This is why you're here. Her face heated as she peeked up at Chicklet. "He told me to show you the same respect I'd show him."

"That's a very good idea, little girl." Chicklet shot dismissively over her shoulder as she went over to a rack full of long dresses, all different colors and lengths. She waved Jami over and thrust one at her. "Go try this on."

In the changing room, Jami hung the dress on a hook and leaned against the wall. The reflection in huge mirror at the back of the stall was all bright eyes and blotchy cheeks. Her heart thumped hard and fast against her ribcage. Her hands shook as she held them up.

Get a grip. You're just putting on a dress.

But the black dress was all sheer mesh, with only two narrow strips for modesty. Walking around the store in the maid costume had been bad enough.

"No bra. No panties—not like I should have to point that out," Chicklet said, sounding bored.

Jami pressed her eyes shut as moisture gathered on her lashes and between her thighs. *Damn it!*

Her reactions scared her. She needed to be brave and make Sebastian proud. But she wanted to run home and hide.

A buzz in her pocket made her jump. She fished her phone out and her knees went weak, dropping her onto the short shelf-like bench. Answering, she hiccupped, then laughed. "Hey, you! Checking up on me?"

"I am, *mi cielo*," Sebastian said. "Chicklet sent me a text. She does not seem confident that you will use your safeword if you need it."

"Why would I need a safeword for shopping?"

"I would be very surprised if your 'shopping' has not already overwhelmed you a little, Jami. You are learning your limits—feel free to speak up if you are uncertain about anything. Chicklet will push you; I have asked her too. But only you will know if it has gone too far. I'd rather avoid her guessing."

"I guess . . . I guess I'm a little worried about how far it will go."

"My limits have been outlined clearly. Nothing physically sexual other than by your own hands."

"My own—"

"Does that bother you, *gatita?*" Sebastian's voice came low through the phone, almost a purr, closer to a growl. "As I rest before the game, I will be touching myself, thinking of you, picturing how you will tease yourself to the brink. How tears of frustration will fill your eyes because you must stop before you climax. That edge will linger, sharpen, all night long."

Jami held the phone to her ear with both hands. "I think you are going to drive me completely insane."

Sebastian chuckled. "Perhaps. But we will share the insanity. It will be pure torture to see others play with you while I ache to have you. It will be a challenge to focus on the game with my dick hard and my mind on your sweet, wet cunt."

She melted a little more with each word. The phone slipped in her damp palm. "So you won't . . ." She licked her lips. "But you're the Dom. You can do whatever you want."

"This is true," Sebastian said, his tone turning husky. "And what I want is to wait for you."

After hanging up, Jami moved as though in a dream, but no dream had every made her so aware of her own skin. She slipped out of her clothes and into the dress. Her fingers hesitated over the changing room lock, but then her lips curved. Sebastian was making her do this to get her all worked up. She wouldn't deny either of them the experience. When she told him what had happened, she wanted it to be more than anything he could have imagined.

"Very nice, girl." Chicklet circled her, adjusting the straps of the dress, smoothing her hands down Jami's side. "Kneel."

Jami dropped to her knees and winced as they struck the grey tiled floor.

Chicklet shook her head. "Laura, show her how it's done."

Laura lowered gracefully, kneeling with her thighs spread. She didn't seem to notice the old couple who'd stopped at the end of the changing rooms to watch.

"That's my pretty kitten." Chicklet's tone changed as she stood over Laura, admiring her with a tenderness in her eyes that made Jami's chest ache for some of the same. She needed Sebastian to look at her just like that. Chicklet caught her sigh and smiled. "Laura and I have been together for years. She needs to please me, and I've taught her how. Tyler is more like you. He tries, he wants to do it right, quick, and he's hard on himself when he makes mistakes. But the most important lesson he has to learn is the effort is what counts. As long as I know he's trying to please me, I'm happy."

"I'm trying." Jami scowled at the floor. Maybe she wasn't trying hard enough.

"I know you are, sweetie. Otherwise Seb wouldn't bother with you, and neither would I." Chicklet patted her cheek. "Copy Laura. Think of it as using your poise to show your Dom exactly how much he means to you. Every gesture, every word, is a display of your submission. His entire focus is on you, is on fulfilling your every need. Yours should be on fulfilling his."

Jami's muscles relaxed, and the bottom of the dress hiked up to her hips as she parted her thighs. She rested her hands, palm up, above her knees, mimicking Laura.

"Lovely." Chicklet's approval covered Jami with a warm glow, like the springtime sun chasing away the last winter chill. "Now stand, slowly. Be conscious of every movement. The more aware you are, the more you feel. And that's the point."

Jami rose to her feet with all the elegance she'd show following a dance routine. Not perfect, but decent. She knew she could improve—*would* improve—by the time she did this for Sebastian.

"The dress is damn sexy, Sebastian will want it for you, but let's try a few more."

In and out of the changing room, a different outfit every time, Jami sank deeper and deeper into the mentality of not being just a girl trying on clothes, but a woman who had a man who would do anything for her, and this display was nothing but an effort to give him a little of that in return. Chicklet joined her in the changing room to lock a chastity belt. Jami stood still and held her breath as each lock snicked shut.

"Five locks. Perfect." Chicklet touched her cheek and smiled. "I'll be working hard to win the keys to them all tonight. You're too precious."

The belt was unlocked and set aside. Chicklet called both Jami and Laura out to the changing room hall to kneel in front of her. They both wore dull grey slave dresses and nothing else. Jami couldn't stop fidgeting with the ragged hem that barely covered the top of her thighs even standing. Her jaw nearly hit the floor when she turned her focus from her dress to Chicklet.

In her hands were two vibrating eggs with strings on the end and . . . remote controls?

"I'll be controlling these neat little toys—they've got more of a kick than any we've tried before, don't they, kitten?" Chicklet grinned when Laura nodded and blushed. "We're all going to the game to support our men." She turned to address Jami's curious gaze. "Tyler wants to go, and Sloan is like a brother to me. I think they'll both need support since they've got to sit out one of the most important games this season. And maybe some prayers that the goddamn team doesn't prove they can't make it without them."

Sloan was like a brother to Jami too. And she wanted to support him.

"The team will miss them, but with Sebastian and L—" Jami bit her tongue and scowled. "They've got plenty of awesome players. We'll all be cheering them on. But what's the point of chastity belts and . . . *those*."

"My job is to get you warmed up for the party." Chicklet pushed the button on one remote. It vibrated softly, much like a cell phone. A few more presses had it sounding more like the blender Jami used to make her strawberry daiquiris. There was an evil, knowing glint in Chicklet's eyes as she shut it off. "And keep you simmering."

Murder by humiliation. Jami gulped, stared, and shook her head. "But Sloan—"

"Will appreciate your support. Don't let the moody bastard intimidate you."

Might be hard if I can't look him in the eye because of all that buzzing. "How about we get started?"

Chicklet pressed a pink egg into Jami's palm, and a purple one into Laura's. Laura didn't hesitate. She stayed in position, with one hand between her thighs holding the egg against her clit. Her hips trembled slightly as she rocked them forward.

Her lips parted as the vibrations revved up. "M-mistress."

"A little more, Laura, you can do it, baby."

Laura nodded, panted, and seemed to regain control of her body.

"How wet are you, kitten?" Chicklet whispered as she petted Laura's hair. "Wet enough to slide it in easy?"

"Yes, Mistress."

"Good. Go ahead and I'll lock you up tight."

Jami watched them for a bit, entranced by how they could be so blatantly sexual and tender all at once. Even when Chicklet was being wicked, there was something more behind it. Laura worshiped her. And she treasured Laura.

I want to wait for you.

Damn it, Sebastian's words meant so much more suddenly. He would have waited, even from the beginning. She had rushed things, but it hadn't changed his opinion of her. Rather than judge her weird ways, he was doing everything he could to explore them with her.

Which made this about the two of them, even though he wasn't here.

"All right, cutie, your turn." Chicklet looked up as she finished locking Laura up tight. "And I suggest you don't forget 'red' and 'yellow' are vital parts of your vocabulary."

"I won't." Jami held her breath as she brought the egg close to her slick folds. The lowest setting made her gasp as it touched her clit. Delicate tendrils of pleasure unfurled and she shifted slightly, adding more pressure. The vibrations intensified and she jumped at the sound. A breathless moan escaped her lips.

"I didn't know you'd added a peepshow, Devon." One of the gay lovers grinned at her as he drew the other man along with him into the short hall. "Will you be adding some variety? They're sweet, but not really my thing."

"As if you don't play with your boy here, Pat," Devon said, joining them. "There are perks to knowing the owner's sister." She gave Jami a lustful look, then glanced over at Chicklet. "Is she yours? I didn't think Laura was cool with you taking on another muffin."

"No, she's not mine." Chicklet frowned at Jami and mouthed something.

"Red?"

Jami shook her head and pressed her eyes shut to block out all the people watching. Her cheek blazed, but moisture slicked her fingers as she stroked the egg up and down, spreading the vibrations so they travelled deep, deep inside. She pictured Sebastian as she let the egg slip past her entrance, imagined telling him, as dramatically as possible, about this little scene. And she saw him smiling as he kissed her, as he demanded even more details. As he pulled her under his body and filled her as the egg was, only so much more.

Her core rippled around the egg. The vibrations stopped.

"I'm going to have to take it easy on you, kid." Chicklet helped her stand, then backed her into the stall to put on the chastity belt. "You took off for a bit, didn't you?"

"Yeah, I was with *mi Rey*." Jami smiled at Chicklet, feeling nice and fuzzy and not the least worried about the egg or anything else. "He's going to be proud of me."

"Yes, he certainly will." Chicklet eased her onto the bench and shook her head. "He knows just what makes you tick, doesn't he? You in a good place, hon?"

"Mmmhmm." Jami's eyes drifted shut. She could feel Sebastian's presence all around her. And someone else. Someone who belonged. "I'll stay here a bit, if you don't mind."

"Jami, me and Laura will get you dressed in your own clothes. Then I'm going to see if you can see Sebastian before the game, okay?"

"Yes." Jami sighed and shook her head, letting out a breathy laugh as the other presence became clear in her mind. "And Luke."

"Oh, sweetie . . ." Chicklet looked upset.

"It's all right. He belongs." Jami whispered as Chicklet called Laura in and the two women fussed over her. She was in her jeans shorts and t-shirt again. Then no longer in the store. Then in a car. Everything around her moved like a film, skipping forward, but in her head things moved nice and slow. So perfect because everything was . . . right. "He belongs."

Chapter Twenty

Luke stopped short in the hall outside the player's lounge. Retreated a few steps and swallowed back the name that almost spilled past his lips.

Seb sat on one of the big leather sofas, holding Jami. He spoke quietly over her head to Chicklet who shook her head and fiddled with a half-full bottle of water. A few feet away from them, Perron stood by the refreshments table, looking like he wanted to say something, but wasn't sure what.

I know what to say. Luke scowled and stepped forward. Seb had pushed Jami too far with some kinky shit or something. He didn't fucking deserve h—

"Don't." A heavy hand fell on his shoulder and jerked him back into the locker room. Mason stared down at him. "I don't know what's going on between the three of you, and frankly, I don't care. He just got her calmed down, so give her some time to pull herself together. She was crying because of you."

"What the fuck did I do? You don't care what's going on, but you're blaming me?"

"Relax, kid." Bower moved up to his side, close enough to force Mason back. "She just had a bad drop. You don't need to explain yourself to anyone."

"Yes. I do." Luke sidled past both men. He winced at the hard look Chicklet gave him as he inched closer to Jami. But, much as he respected Chicklet, her opinion of him didn't matter right now. "Hey, boo. Can we talk?"

Jami sniffed and wiped under her eyes quickly before lifting her head from Seb's chest. "Why? Bored of Amy already?"

Fuck this. His jaw hardened. "I don't know, you bored of Demyan?"

Perron cleared his throat. "Might could be a good idea to have this little chat somewhere else."

Seb stood, pulling Jami up with him. "That's an excellent idea, Perron. Luke, I think we should—"

"We?" Luke's eyes narrowed. "I didn't say I wanted to talk to *you.*"

Pain washed over Seb's face so fast Luke blinked and was sure he'd imagined it. Seb's eyes had gone cold. His lips drew into a tight line. "Very well. The training room is empty."

"Jami?" Luke already knew she wouldn't come. Actually, from the look of her, he'd be lucky if she didn't come over and kick his ass.

"You can't be serious."

"Should I take that as a no?"

"Fuck you, Luke." She turned her back on him and rose up on her tiptoes to give Seb a quick kiss. "Sorry for falling apart like that."

"There's no need to be. Please stay with Chicklet during the game." Seb's brow furrowed slightly. "And consider the scene over."

Luke sucked his teeth. *Good call, Ramos.*

Jami shook her head. "But—"

"It. Is. Over." Seb cupped her cheek and kissed her forehead. "Go, *mi cielo.*"

Chicklet managed to drag Jami out without too much fuss, but as the door closed behind them, the tension in the room rose like a thick, rancid smog. Seb walked by Luke without even sparing him a glance, but the other men were watching him with a mixture of pity, confusion, and disgust. Mischlue muttered something in French to Bower as Luke entered the locker room.

Bower glared at him. "*Tu n'en sais rien.* He didn't start the fucking drama. I get that Jami is the team's sweetheart, but she's not innocent in all this."

Seb halted in front of his stall, his back stiff.

Before he could say anything, Tim stormed into the room. A row of sticks clattered to the floor as he kicked the wooden stand. "What the fuck is going on in here?"

Every man in the room went silent.

"I'm sorry, did getting ready for the playoffs interfere with your soap opera?" Tim kicked Pearce's helmet across the room. Then grabbed one of Bower's pads and slammed it into the goalie's chest. "I don't care who's fucking who; it stays out of this goddamn room! Now get your asses on the fucking ice!" His jaw ticked as Pearce stood. "Is that too complicated for you, Pearce?"

"No," Pearce said, straight-faced. "Just getting my helmet, Coach."

Luke bit the inside of his cheek so he wouldn't laugh. The tension broke as Tim looked over at the helmet on the floor between Demyan's feet. A few guys snickered.

Tim rolled his eyes. "That's hilarious." He sighed. "Seriously, guys, you need to pull it together out there. We haven't sold out like this in months. No one expected us to be real Cup contenders for years. Bring it home, and you'll all have a team to play for, years from now."

"Wait." Velcro ripped as Mason pulled a strap to tighten his knee brace. He looked up and frowned. "I thought the team was stable."

"I'm not saying it isn't." Tim rubbed the back of his neck and shrugged. "But I've always been straight with you guys, and I'm telling you, how far you go in the playoffs will have a big impact on what the league decides to do with us over the next few seasons."

Bower was concentrating really hard on doing up his pads. He obviously knew something. Luke studied the other men. They all looked worried. Except for Seb. He caught Luke's eye as he rose from the bench and fisted his hand around his stick.

"One game at a time." Seb spoke quietly, but their teammates, their coach, had gone silent. All eyes were on him. "Tonight, we win this one."

The men broke out in wild victory shouts, but Luke didn't join them. He couldn't look away from Seb. Not until the man inclined his head, which Luke took as some kind of truce. Whatever happened off the ice didn't matter. Somehow, Seb knew Luke needed his strength. And he was letting Luke know, without words, that he'd be there.

I could hate you, man. Luke picked up his stick and nodded at Seb. *Fuck, it would be easier if I did.*

But he didn't. And right now, he'd accept any help he could get. Even if he hated *himself* for accepting it once the game ended.

* * * *

Over twenty thousand fans stared at them, spilling down expectations built over years. They'd been led to believe that this team which should never have been was worth their support. Worth their hard-earned money, worth their passion. If the Cobras hadn't made the playoff many would have hopes for "maybe next year," but since they had, hopes were high. Anything less than the Cup would be a disappointment, but at very least, the Sabres, the team that had earned the hatred of every man, woman, and child in the forum, must be buried.

So serious. So important. They had all forgotten that this was a game. That it was supposed to be fun.

Sebastian slid onto the ice, and the cheers crashing from above humbled him. He'd never been this important to a team, but for some reason the fans saw him as vital in their road to victory. If he played well, they would raise him high on a precarious platform. If he didn't, they would come down on him with a vengeance. And he wasn't the only player who would feel their wrath. It seemed the louder they screamed your name, the louder they would condemn you if you failed them.

Bower's presence on the ice brought the crowd to their feet.

The man singing the anthem was a Maritime celebrity, which didn't mean much on a grand scale, but local talent endeared the fans. Ray Parris had made it to Broadway, so it wasn't all that surprising that Silver Delgado had chosen him to sing tonight.

But Sebastian imagined she regretted the choice as the man butchered the American anthem. The off-key notes made Sebastian wince, but he tried to keep his face blank. From the corner of his eye, he saw other players trying to do the same. And then the Canadian anthem began.

Most often the Canadian anthem was sung in both French and English. The English part was as bad as the American anthem had been, but the French . . .

Likely nervous, the man stumbled over several words, skipped a few, then carried on with renewed confidence. He seemed to think volume made up for the errors. Sebastian heard a rasping cough behind him and furtively glanced over to Bower.

Bower had his gloved hands fisted over the top of his stick and pressed against his mouth. His shoulders shook and his eyes shone. He made the mistake of looking at Mischlue, who hid his face in his glove, laughing so hard he appeared to be choking.

Standing by Mischlue, Luke reached out and patted his back, singing along as he often did, loud enough to be heard across the ice. His face showed on the screen above, and the crowd laughed and cheered. Ray Parris stopped to let the crowd sing, and for a split second, all that could be heard was Luke.

Luke sounded even worse than Ray, and it clearly wasn't done in mocking, but that wasn't what made Sebastian's chest swell with pride. It was the passion, candid and raw, that changed the atmosphere from amused to eager. The crowd joined him, continuing with Ray, almost drowning him out. After he took his bow, Ray paused and sought out Luke. He smiled at him as though to say "Thank you."

Giving him a thumbs up, Luke shouted. "*Fiddler on the Roof* rocked! I'm a big fan, man!"

Mason nudged Sebastian as he passed, bringing his focus back to where it belonged. Before Jami and Luke, nothing could distract him from the game, but now they had to be forced from his mind before he could ease into the flow. Even now, his attention split between Luke, taking the face-off against Nelson, and Jami, high above in the press box.

The rasp of blades on ice jerked him back into his own body, into play. He cupped a soft pass and lunged forward with long strides. A large body plowed toward him, but he evaded the check with a smooth spin and then clipped the puck back to Demyan.

Shot. Rebound. The Sabres goalie trapped the puck under his body. Another face-off. Play went from end to end, through one shift after another, nothing getting past either netminder. Long spans without a whistle exhausted each line, and changes were quick for both teams to keep the players fresh. Cheers from the fans died down, and an edge of expectancy filled the crisp, ice-bitten air. The pace of the game became repetitive, dragging with both teams carefully guarding their zones.

Leading by two games, the Cobras lacked urgency, but the Sabres grew desperate as they reached the last seconds of the first period. They needed this game. They needed a way to prove to themselves they wouldn't be swept from the playoffs, shamed by a newer team who had yet to prove they belonged. Back on the ice, Sebastian found himself scrambling after reckless, unexpected plays. A slash dropped him to his knees.

No penalty was called, but he didn't bother to look at the ref. Pain tore through his side as he pushed up to his feet and thick bile rose in his throat. His gaze locked on the puck, he dove forward to block a shot. Black and red spotted his vision. Stick blades jabbed into his ribs, stabbing the spot the puck had struck. The sharp whistle pierced his skull as he pushed up to fists and knees. The sound chimed off bruised bones. But he refused to stay down.

A hand jutted out in front of his face. "Can you stand?"

"Yes." Sebastian forced a smile to his lips and let Luke help him up. He tightened his grip on Luke's hand, holding on longer than necessary because it was allowed, out here, on the ice. Because Luke had no reason to pull away. His pain dulled to a throb as he searched Luke's eyes and found nothing but concern. "Thank you."

"Seb . . ." Luke's teeth dented his bottom lip as he stared at their clasped gloves. He jerked free and skidded backward as the ref approached. "Nothing's changed here." His throat worked as he swallowed. "But only here."

"Of course." Sebastian inclined his head and squared his shoulders. He should have expected this. Luke was a professional. Life beyond the ice was only a brief pause, a distraction. For one as young as Luke, the game was all that mattered. And he believed what they'd had was too complicated to be worth the many risks.

Now was not the time to try to convince him otherwise. But that time would come.

* * * *

"I'm sorry, Akira!" Jami hugged Akira tight, still feeling horrible about forgetting to meet her before the game. She'd tried to tell her a few times after she'd come into the press box, but Akira had shushed her. And hadn't taken her eyes off the game until the first period ended.

"It's okay, but..." Akira pulled her away from where Chicklet stood between Laura and Tyler. She ducked her head when Sloan glanced her way, pulled the sleeves of her huge jersey—with Sloan's name and number on the back—over her hands and inched closer to Jami. "What's going on? Ford said you were crying."

Sneaky son of a bitch. So that's how he'd gotten Akira to come with him. Jami scowled at Ford as he lifted his head as though he'd heard her thoughts. He stood on the other side of the room, looking more like security than one of the team owners in his faded, torn black jeans and white tank top. She knew he usually wore suits to the forum, which meant he probably hadn't planned to attend the game.

"I wasn't crying, I just..." Jami rolled her eyes and shook her head. "I'll tell you about it later. Thanks for checking on Peanut for me."

"No problem. I was just a little worried when you didn't come home." Akira frowned. "And then none of the girls had seen you, and the guy stopped me at the elevator and didn't know I was allowed up here—"

"I'm a really crappy friend."

"Oh, shut up." Akira planted her hands on her hips. "You are not. Just call me next time something's up."

"I will. I promise." Jami hugged her again, holding her close to whisper in her ear. "So Ford was okay? He didn't make you uncomfortable or anything, did he?"

Akira glanced over at Ford, then lowered her voice. "No, actually he was very polite."

"Polite?" *Ford?*

"Yeah. He got the security guy to back off, then told me he recognized me from tryouts. When he asked me to follow him, I..." Akira dropped her gaze to her feet. Her slick black hair fell over her cheeks. "I almost got right back on the elevator. He must have noticed I was ready to run, but he acted like he didn't. Then he mentioned you crying, and I forgot to be scared."

Jami grinned, looked over at Ford again, mouthing "Thank you." He shrugged like it was nothing, glanced over at Akira, then shoved his hands in his jean pockets and moved closer to the glass to stare down at the Zamboni as it cleaned the ice. She turned to Akira.

"Well, as you can see, I'm fine. Are you enjoying the game?"

"Oh God, yes! This is ten times better than I ever dreamed! So different than watching it on TV! I—" Akira blushed as Chicklet chuckled and Sloan smiled at her. She covered her cheeks with her hands. "Way too fangirly."

"No. It's the playoffs." Jami sighed. "I wish I had half your enthusiasm. I almost did for a bit, but . . ." She wasn't sure how to explain it. When things had been good between her, Sebastian, and Luke, watching games had turned into a way to be close to them. But she couldn't help but resent the fact that the game was now the only way Sebastian could be close to Luke. She knew it had to bother him, but all he said was Luke needed time and space.

Not a problem. I'll give him plenty of that. A lifetime's worth.

"Right. We can talk about that later too." Akira stepped back and sat on one of the large leather chairs, leaning forward as Jami took the one beside her. "Are you ready for the show on Tuesday? Amy looked really good with her team out there."

"We'll look better." Jami put her hand over Akira's. "We've got the better team leader."

"I can't believe they picked me after Claire twisted her ankle."

"I can! Who else would they have chosen? You're the best skater, the best dancer—"

"That's not true. And besides, I get so nervous counting out the moves. The trainer had to tell me to speak up so often at practice, and I know all the girls were wondering why the hell they picked me."

Truthfully, Jami had wondered too. There was no question about Akira making the final cut, but she was obviously more comfortable following instructions than giving them.

"You might want to get used to leading a group, Akira." Ford kept his eyes on the ice as he spoke. "You did mention in your application that you plan to teach figure skating."

"Yeah, but . . ." Akira's eyes went wide. She whispered to Jami. "You don't think he—"

"No way. He's got nothing to do with the Ice Girls." Jami bit the tip of her tongue. She hated lying to Akira, but she knew what it was like to have someone pulling strings hanging over her head. She was just grateful Ford hadn't decided to make her a team leader. And hoped his helping out Akira was just a gesture of friendship. Her life was complicated enough without dealing with another man.

What about Scott?

She shoved the thought aside. With Scott, it would be nothing but hot sex at a kinky party. More for Sebastian than her. He needed the distraction.

"Oh, before I forget, I picked up your mail." Akira dug into her purse and pulled out three envelopes. Her lips pressed together, and for a moment, it seemed like she was debating her next words. Then she nodded toward the top envelope. "If you're having money trouble, I can help you out."

Jami wrinkled her nose and shook her head as she tore open the envelope from the credit bureau. "I saved up a lot of money when I was living with my grandmother. She made sure I worked and I never spent much. I just . . ." She stared at the amount owed, then crumpled the letter in her fist. "I put it off. I'll take care of it on Monday."

"Would it help if I reminded you?"

"Sure." Jami took a deep breath, and let it out in a sigh. She caught Ford's steady gaze from the corner of her eye. When they'd been together, he'd taken care of stuff like her cell phone bill. And she'd let him because she couldn't be bothered. But now she was determined to make it on her own. And paying her bills was part of that.

She'd figure out how to manage her budget, even though the thought of working out all those jumbled numbers made her physically ill.

The next letter was a bill. She set it aside to deal with later. The last was blank. No address. She frowned as she pulled out the folded paper and almost dropped it as she scanned over the words.

"Jami?" Akira touched the back of her hand.

Jami jumped, then laughed as she stood and ripped the letter in half. "It's junk. Just someone trying to sell me something."

Over the trash at the back of the room, Jami continued ripping the letter until nothing was left but tiny pieces. Her empty hands shook hard. The hairs on the back of her necks rose, and she glanced over her shoulder. It felt like someone was watching her. It always did lately.

She went to the refreshment table for a bottle of water. Drained it in long gulps. And tried to regain her composure, but for the longest time, all she could do was stare at the wall. And see the words sprawled across both sides of the page.

"Stay away from him. No more, whore. I'll be watching you. I'll be watching you. I'll be . . ."

Over and over. Like the song in her car. The CD player had been glued shut. It was fixed now, but sometimes at night, she could still hear it.

Whoever had broken into her car had left this letter. It didn't seem like a prank anymore. They were trying to send her a message.

She knew she should tell someone. Sebastian. Or maybe even her father. But then she'd have to admit she was scared, and the freak doing this to her would win. Because that's what they wanted. To scare her.

Digging her nails into her palms, she spun around and lifted her brow at Ford's intent look. Then she joined Akira in front of the glass as the second period started and immersed herself in the game.

Only once did she let the stupid letter and the other weird crap slip back into her head, and then it was just so she could dismiss the loser who thought he—or she—could get to her with such lame shit.

It's Amy. It has to be. "Leave him"? How much more obvious can you get?

The slight tremble of her hands stopped as logic crept into her brain. She almost felt sorry for Luke until she thought of how much he'd hurt Sebastian.

You can have him, you crazy bitch.

Her stomach twisted. She clenched her jaw.

But only because I don't want him anymore. I'm not afraid of you.

But she was a little afraid that she might be wrong.

****

Luke shifted his weight from leg to leg, lining his stick up with Nelson's for the center ice face-off. He'd used the break to get his head back on straight. Seeing Seb go down had shaken him, and he'd reacted without thinking, but Seb was fine. No one had brought up any weird vibes he and Seb might have let off. Anything beyond putting the Cobras on the scoreboard could be dealt with later.

The ref dropped the puck. Nelson let Luke scoop it up, then crashed into him, tangling their sticks together. Luke struggled to knock the puck loose, over to Pearce. But Nelson stopped it with his skate, trapping them in a stalemate.

"He watches you out here, you know." Nelson smirked as he spoke, his helmet pressed against Luke's. "It's kinda sweet, how protective he is. He stop me from kicking your ass so it's in good shape for him?"

Pulse faltering, Luke clenched his fists in his gloves. *Cool it. Don't give him what he wants, Carter.*

"You might wanna be careful, Nelson." Luke bared his teeth as he shoved his shoulder into Nelson's chest. "Ref hears any gay comments, and he'll throw you out of the game."

"Hey, I've got no problem with fags, Carter." Nelson freed his stick and glided backward, gesturing Luke forward. "But I've heard you and your boyfriend are having problems. You sure you're good to play?"

Rolling his eyes, Luke followed Nelson across the neutral zone. "I've heard you're getting a divorce. But I've got too much class to chirp about it. Just try and keep up."

He swiped the puck off Nelson's stick and shot forward, eyes on the goalie as he weaved around the Sabres' defense, never slowing his pace. Pearce and Demyan followed him over the blue line. The goalie poke checked, and his stick struck Luke in the gut. Luke absorbed the impact and twisted to the side. He grinned as the goalie's stick skidded across the ice. Took a shot. And collided with the post as the goalie blocked with his glove and clipped Luke's shin with a knee.

Three Sabres pinned Luke, throwing punches so fast all he could do was cover his head and wait for his team to step up. One man was wrenched away. Luke glanced over to see Seb raining down punches. Demyan threw his weight into a man, knocking him off Luke. Mason plowed into a third and Pearce beckoned to another. Fights broke out across the ice, but the Sabres' goalie and one defenseman held onto Luke, using his body to knock the net loose. The metal stuck his thigh like a baseball bat swung at full force.

"Son of a bitch!" Luke tried to twist free, but the defenseman held on to his jersey, shaking him like a rag doll. He took a swing, but his twisted sleeve cut it short. His face heated up as the men restraining him laughed.

The crowd screamed as Bower crossed the ice to call out the Sabres' goalie. A fist to the temple dropped Luke to his knees. The ref pulled the man away, and Luke nodded to let the official know he was okay. He hefted up to his feet, shaking his head to clear it. Grabbed a man skirting by him to protect his goalie. And held him, not paying much attention to the violently twisting body in his arms as Bower latched on to the Sabres' goalie's jersey and drew his fist back, waiting for an opening.

Bower was a head taller than the Sabres' goalie and had a longer reach. He grinned as he shook the man, spinning him as he moved. The Sabres' goalie swung his fist and lost his balance. Bower held him down, shouting something Luke couldn't hear as he checked a punch.

Most of the fighters had been dragged to the penalty box. The linemen and the refs hovered around Bower and the other goalie, looking relieved when they released each other without landing a punch.

After releasing his man, Bower glanced over at Luke, concern carving deep lines on his face. Luke licked his bloody bottom lip and touched his cheek, sticky and warm where his stitches had come out. He probably looked like shit, but he felt good.

He grinned at Bower. "I'm a pro—" His eyes widened as the Sabres' goalie took a swing. "Look out!"

The punch cracked Landon as he spun around. A line of blood spilled down his face from a cut along his cheekbone. Bower nailed the goalie between the eyes.

Fucking KO. Luke fist pumped and followed Bower to the bench as the refs worked out the penalties for both teams. The Sabres' goalie had been tossed. There were so many men in both boxes, the lineman had a hard time closing the doors. It would be four on four for a while.

"Bower, that was fucking awesome! *Pow!*" Luke did a nice, slow replay of the punch, then dropped against the board, laughing so hard his gut ached. "Did you see him drop? Fuck, he's gonna be seeing tweety birds dancing around his head all night!"

"It was pretty sweet." Bower took a bottle from the trainer and sprayed water into his mouth and over his face. He leaned over to let another trainer dab at the cut on his cheek. "I planned to let the guy go, but he's one dirty bastard. Should have figured that by the way he went after you."

"Thanks for having my back, man. I mean, I could've handled it—" Luke rubbed his knuckles on his chest. "But I don't like showing off."

Bower laughed. "You're so full of shit. The way you covered your head and rolled into a little ball, I'm surprised you didn't grow a shell."

"Hey, I don't turtle! I was going for a sneak attack!"

"*Suuure.*"

As Luke slid onto the bench, tipping his head back so the trainer could patch him up, Demyan plunked down beside him and gave him a toothy smile. "The rest of us don't get a thank you?"

All the adrenaline, all the excitement, drained away like someone had pulled a plug in the center of Luke's chest. He gritted his teeth as the trainer swabbed a cut with alcohol. He pictured Demyan kissing Jami and clenched his fists against the bench. "You're getting my girl, pal. What else you want from me? You want a fucking rim job, you know where to go."

"Why are you being a dick about this, Carter? If you wanted Jami, why were you all over that cunt at dinner?"

"Boys, let's keep our heads in the game," Tim said, sounding fed up.

Luke ignored him and turned to Demyan, rolling his eyes as the trainer tightened his grip on his chin. "What do you want, Demyan, my fucking blessing? Fine. You can have her tonight, but after that, back the fuck off."

Skate blades cutting into the floor halted steps away. Seb cleared his throat, his eyes narrowing as Luke straightened. "She is not yours to give."

"Yeah? We'll see about that." Luke jutted his chin toward the hall leading to the locker room. "You get thrown out?"

"Yes." Seb pulled off his gloves, then swiped his thumb over an oozing nick on his lip. "You are welcome to the party tonight, Luke. As I've told you, you have a say in what happens."

"How fucking generous of you." Luke pulled away from the trainer and spat a mouthful of blood on the floor between his skates. "The way I see it, she needs to get you both out of her system. I'll wait."

Seb pressed his eyes shut and seemed to mutter some kind of prayer. He continued down the hall without another word.

Demyan stared at Luke like he'd just caught him shaving his balls with a rusty blade. He opened and closed his mouth twice, then shook his head. "You're a moron."

"Says the guy who fucks anything that moves."

"No." Demyan sat back and held an ice pack to his jaw as play resumed. "Says the guy who's never had it half as good as you. All I'm getting is a taste, and I've got the brains to appreciate it. Too bad you don't."

* * * *

Dean cursed under his breath and turned his back on the game, pacing to the bar at the other side of the box. The last thing they needed was their goalie getting in a fight. If they lost Landon out there... he stiffened as fingers curved around his forearm, then sighed and pulled Silver into a firm embrace. "Are you okay?"

"Yeah." Silver sniffled and rubbed her tiny, red nose. "Being pregnant really sucks, you know? I get all emotional over nothing."

"You're always like this when Landon gets hurt."

"I am not." Silver's gaze slipped back toward the ice, smudges of dark makeup under her eyes making her look even more pale and tired than usual. Suddenly her eyes went wide, and she giggled as she rubbed her swollen stomach. "This kid is going to be a handful. I swear there's a target on my bladder, and he never misses."

Nodding, Dean's thoughts drifted to another kid who was a handful. Only, she was an adult now and he had no idea how to handle her. For days he'd tried calling Jami, but she wouldn't take his calls. And to be honest, he couldn't blame her. It had taken him a while to accept it, but between Silver and his mother, he'd been forced to face the fact that he'd gone too far. With what he'd heard about the situation between Ramos, Carter, and his daughter, she could probably have used his guidance. His support. But he'd been too quick to judge, and she wouldn't accept his help anymore.

But she'll accept Ford's?

Right now she was in one of the press boxes, watching the game with him. Probably listening to all his lies because he could be oh so sympathetic about having a father who tried to control him.

Shit. If I can be compared to either Delgado or Kingsley, I really fucked up.

But he couldn't discuss any of this with Silver. All Silver saw when she visited her father was a man too sick to remember who she was. A man who broke her heart by calling her by her mother's name, or asking to see his son. Not Ford. He wanted Antoine, who had been dead for thirteen years.

He seemed to find peace when Ford visited though. Ford humored him and answered to the name of the brother he'd never known. Dean could almost feel sorry for the young man. But he knew Ford was just in it to gain control of the team. Not for the money, because there was nothing left.

Silver sighed and tugged on his tie, loosening it. "I think I should be the one asking if *you're* okay. Is it Jami, the team, or next year's budget stressing you out? Or should I just assume all of the above."

"You shouldn't worry about any of it, my little dragonfly." He tapped her nose and smiled. "The doctor said no stress."

"Not knowing what's going on is stressing me out." Silver frowned and peered down at the ice. "We've got a good team. I may not like Ford, but his—the Kingsley money has bailed us out a few times this year. There are new investors interested in the team. Fine, it will be a pain in the ass to have a committee wanting to make all the decisions, but even if my family sells half their shares, you'll still have controlling interest from what my dad sold you. Nothing will change."

"You're probably right." He kissed her forehead, relieved for once that she didn't pay much attention to the numbers. The

Kingsley's had spent the last year buying out the other investors. By next season, Ford would be the one calling the shots. Unless the Delgados didn't sell, and that was looking more unlikely every day. But he and Landon had agreed not to break the news to Silver until after she had the baby. He rested his hand on top of Silver's belly, chuckling as a foot or a fist bumped against it. "She's an active little one. I still think it would be a good idea to stay with my mother over the summer—just to make sure you can get some rest."

"Dean, I love your mom, but really, no thanks." She relaxed against his side. "I want our baby at home. I want to see him in that crib you and Landon built. I want to cuddle him at night with you both in our great big bed. I want to show everyone I can be a great mommy."

Our baby. Dean's chest tightened as he lowered his face into Silver's hair. There was a time when he'd been concerned that Landon and Silver sharing a child would force him to the outskirts of their relationship, but not anymore. They both included him as a part of their family without a second's hesitation. Landon referred to the baby as "our daughter" and teased Dean about being a father again in his old age. Silver would say "our son" was lucky to have two amazing daddies to teach him how to be a man. Not to say things were perfect, but no matter how often they disagreed, no matter how many times tempers flared, he never felt for a moment that this child would be anything other than his own.

"You will be a great mommy."

She smirked and laid her hand over his on her stomach. "I'm glad you agree."

A comfortable silence settled around them as the third period started, and they both turned their focus to the game. The Cobras played well, but the young defense, scrambling to keep up since both Ramos and Mason had been ejected, left Landon exposed more often than not. He seemed to thrive under the pressure, frustrating the Sabres' best scorers with impossible saves.

Demyan and Carter played double shifts for the first half of the period, but for some reason, they didn't click as they had all season. As the clock wound down, Dean cursed under his breath, watching easy plays fumbled because neither man would fucking pass. He didn't know if there was some kind of rivalry between them, or if each simply wanted the glory. Either way, he was relieved when Tim benched them and sent out Perron, Pearce, and Hjalmar, a big Swedish forward who might not be exceptional, but played with grit and heart, never afraid to crash the net or fight his way into the corners.

Perron led the last charge, with Hjalmar and Pearce on his heel. Right down center ice, passing over the line, and driving forward to receive a long pass. He tucked the puck back to Hjalmar, then hovered close to the crease, stick on the ice. The Sabres' backup goalie shoved at him, sliding out a little too far, then skirting back as though reading the play and deciding he'd made the wrong move. Hjalmar and Pearce passed back and forth on the line. Pearce took a shot and surged forward as Perron trapped the rebound. Perron feinted another shot, let the puck skid back to Pearce, then stepped aside as Pearce let it fly.

Silver screamed and hopped up and down as the red light flared. Below, Pearce brought his glove to the edge of his helmet as though tipping a cowboy hat. He grinned as his teammates plowed into him, but didn't look overly excited.

Dean had to admit, he liked the man. He was steady. Serious. And had the attitude that the game wasn't over until his team was skating off the ice with a win.

With a one point lead, and two minutes to go, not a man out there had a right to believe otherwise.

Center ice face-off, then a brutal play that had two Cobras skating slow and stiff, and the rest of the team chasing the Sabres around the defensive zone. Landon stood tall and alert, not watching the puck, but the plays, like a chess player always three moves ahead. He made a save. The rebound trickled away. Bodies crashed the net and he dropped to cover, stretching his pads out to the posts. The ref blew the whistle just as the buzzer sounded.

The pile covering Landon moved slowly. Every eye in the forum was on Landon, half in the net, twisted awkwardly with his arm tucked under his curved body.

Landon rose up to one knee and held up his glove.

No goal.

Screaming fans flowed up from their seats in a wave. Energy exploded from the stands, blasting on the ice as the team converged into one wild, hollering crush. Lights and music flashed and boomed from all around.

Holding his breath, Dean moved closer to the glass. He watched Landon laugh. Accept shoulder slaps from his teammates. Landon hid it decently, but Dean knew him well enough to see he was hurt. And he still hadn't tried to stand.

Carter clasped his hand to Landon's and tried to pull him up. Landon's leg gave out. He hunched over on hands and knees.

"No." Silver covered her mouth with her hands.

Trainers rushed onto the ice. The cheers from the crowd died down.

Face white and strained with pain, Landon let Carter and a trainer lift him up. Arms over their shoulders, he leaned heavily on them, only one skate on the ice. The crowd clapped in uncertain spurts, clearly happy that he hadn't needed a stretcher, but aware that he'd been injured.

Which changed everything.

"I have to go see him." Silver turned toward the door. All the color left her face. She gasped, then pressed a hand against the bottom of her stomach. "Dean . . . Dean something's wrong!"

Dean's heart stopped. His hands shook as he came up to Silver's side to support her. "The baby?"

"Fuck it hurts, Dean!" Sweat beaded up on Silver's forehead as she bent over. "It's too early!"

Way too early. Dread wrapped talons around his throat. He took slow, measured breaths and did his best to sound calm. "Shh. You'll be okay, sweetheart. You'll both be okay." Dean lifted Silver up and cradled her in his arms. He carried her out to the hall and spotted a security guard. The man stuttered and tripped toward them, but calmed at Dean's hard look. "Can you please call an ambulance for Miss Delgado?"

"Yes, sir!" The man pulled out his phone and spoke as he ushered Dean toward the elevator. "There's going to be a crowd. I'll have my guys clear out the hall on the bottom floor . . ." He paused as he listened to whoever was on the phone. "There's already an ambulance coming in for Bower. Maybe they should take her first?"

"No!" Silver pressed her eyes shut. Her teeth raked at her bottom lip, drawing blood. "Dean, tell him no!"

"I can't, Silver. Landon will never forgive me if I don't take care of you and the baby."

"What about him? He's hurt!"

"He probably just pulled something in his leg." Dean arched a brow when Silver shook her head. "You need to relax. Freaking out won't be any good for either of you."

Silver nodded and inhaled, then winced and dug her nails into the side of his neck. "Oh God! If anything happens to the baby . . ."

"Stop. Silver, listen to me. The baby is strong and healthy." Dean stepped off the elevator and glanced over to where two guards held the door open to the parking lot. "Now it's up to you to be strong. When Landon sees you, you need to convince him everything will be okay. Because it will be."

"I'm making things worse, aren't I?"

"You're allowed to be scared, dragonfly. But be brave for him." Dean stepped past the door and plastered on a calm mask as he caught sight of Landon. The man had gone from white to green. He tried to push away from Carter and the trainer. Dean shook his head. "Stay put, Landon."

"Silver!" Landon elbowed Carter and lunged forward. He snarled when Carter and the doctor hauled him back. "Dean, you take care of her! Don't you leave her!"

Dean lowered Silver to the stretcher, then straightened. He smoothed Silver's damp hair away from her face, eyes locked on Landon. "I won't. Fuck, you know me better than that."

"I know." Landon pressed his lips together, his whole body shaking as he slumped into Carter and bowed his head. "Tell her it's gonna be fine. Tell her I'll be with her as soon as I can."

Silver jerked away from the medics, tossing her head back in pain, rasping in air over a whimper. She was in pain but doing her best not to scream. Dean swallowed and took her hand, so fucking proud of her because he knew she was holding back for Landon.

Her words came out hoarse, but with enough strength to tell Landon, to tell them all, that she'd get through this. "Landon, your son might be with us tonight. You get yourself fixed so you can hold him."

"I will." Landon pressed his eyes shut and didn't struggle as Carter latched onto the back of his head and whispered something that seemed to calm him down. He didn't seem to notice the cameras flashing from the parasites that had made it into the lot. "I'll see you soon, *mon amour*. And Dean is with you. You won't be alone."

"Neither will you." Silver hissed in a breath through her teeth, then looked at Carter. "Stay with him."

"I've got nowhere else to be." Carter grinned, then used a fist to rub his eyes. "Shit, you two are killing me. If you make anyone else that kid's godfather, I'll never forgive you."

Landon let out a choked laugh. "You've got the job. If—"

"Don't start with that shit, man." Carter blinked fast. "He's tough. He's got to be." He inhaled sharply. "He's yours."

Dean climbed into the ambulance with Silver, head bowed as the EMTs checked on Silver, lips moving soundlessly. *Hang in there, little one. We need you to be strong.*

He never released Silver's hand. The way she gripped and wrenched at his fingers, he wouldn't be all that surprised to find out every bone was broken, but he didn't care. He needed to know Silver would be okay.

And then he needed a moment to be with Landon. To erase the fear he'd seen in his eyes. Months ago, he'd gone to the grave of Landon's son with him. He accepted that a few times a year they would all make the trip.

But he refused to believe that they'd have to make two trips. Fate couldn't be that cruel.

Chapter Twenty One

Jami's vision swam with tears and more wet her cheeks. She held her phone to her ear, hardly breathing as her father spoke. In the player's lounge, men huddled around where she sat curled up in Sebastian's lap, all waiting to hear if the baby was okay.

She lifted her head to look around the room. "The baby's okay."

Sebastian's big arms wrapped around her, and the men shouted out their relief. Her father went silent. She held up a finger.

"Dad?"

"They gave Silver a shot to hold off labor. Which is good." Her father paused. "I heard the men—you might as well tell them since they're with you. Landon tore muscles in his thigh. He won't be finishing the playoffs."

Who cares about the playoffs? Yeah, she hated that Landon was hurt, but the baby was alive. Even though she knew the kid wasn't her dad's, it was still her little brother or sister in every way that counted. What happened with the next game, with the season, didn't matter. Not much mattered besides that little baby.

After letting everyone know what was going on with Landon, Jami cupped her hand around the phone, speaking quietly. "Do you want me to come down? I want to, but I've been such a bitch—"

"Jami Richter, not another word. Silver is always on me about letting you live your life. And frankly, I don't want to know what you'll be doing tonight. But do something that will make you happy."

"But Silver—"

"Is resting. And Oriana's not letting anyone but Landon and me in that room, and only for minutes at a time. I'll call you if there's anything."

"All right." She sighed. "I'll find something to keep me busy."

"May I suggest bowling?"

Jami laughed and rolled her eyes. "*Dad.*"

"Mini-putt?"

"Goodbye, Dad."

"Goodbye, sweetheart. I love you."

"I love you too." Jami hung up, biting her lip as she nuzzled against the side of Sebastian's throat. Pretty messed up that it had taken something like this to get her and her dad talking again. At least she knew her dad wouldn't tell her to carry on with her night if Silver wasn't okay. Still, part of her felt guilty for even considering it, no matter what she'd said.

"Your father does not want you to go to the hospital." Sebastian's lips whispered against her ear as he spoke. Tiny goose bumps prickled all over her arms under the jersey.

She nodded. Then muttered, "He wants me to do something tonight, but—"

"But your conscience is making it difficult."

"Yes."

"Perhaps your overactive mind needs a rest." Sebastian stood her up, caging her between his thighs to study her face. "Once you return home, I'd like you to shower, then curl up in bed with a book. Dress again in what you are wearing under my jersey. I will join you shortly."

Spending the night with Sebastian would definitely distract her. But she couldn't help but feel a twinge of disappointment. She'd been damn curious about the party, eager to see what Sebastian had planned for her with Scott and Chicklet and . . .

You're such a . . . puta. Jami squeezed her thighs together as heat pooled up from her core. The word didn't have the negativity often attached to "slut"—not for her, anyway. She could almost hear Sebastian saying it in the heat of the moment. See him hovering over her as he forced her to do deliciously naughty things with another man. Or woman.

But not tonight. She had to fight not to sigh. "So I guess we'll have to reschedule the party for some other time . . . ?"

"No, *mi cielo*, I did not say that." Sebastian's dark eyes took on an evil glint. "But certain things will have to be . . . improvised."

The team had dispersed, some heading for the showers, others leaving in groups, making their own plans. No one was paying any attention to them, but she whispered because it felt weird talking about . . . "certain things" here. "Improvised like our game of make-believe?"

"Yes, Jami. Exactly like that." He stood, brushed a kiss over the scared-rabbit fast pulse at her throat, and chuckled. "You inspire me to be *very* creative."

* * * *

Luke hung around the hospital for a bit, just in case Bower needed him, not leaving until Richter came out to tell him the man had fallen asleep in a chair-turned bed at Silver's side. He got Richter to promise to call if anything came up, then wandered out of the hospital, walking aimlessly in the general direction of the forum, where he'd left his car.

A warm breeze ruffled his hair, and his stomach rumbled as he caught the scent of steak on a barbeque. The food had been pretty good at the small restaurant he'd gone to with Demyan and the Delgado sisters before the game, but he'd lost his appetite after spending about five minutes getting to know his date.

Amy was an A-class bitch.

The worst thing was, he'd gone out with her just to piss off Jami. Instead, he'd hurt her. And that bothered him more than knowing what she and Seb had done to lure him in.

His sneakers kicked up dirt as he headed off the road and toward a grassy area near the piers. Angry grey clouds rolled over the horizon, smothering the moonlight. A fresh hint of coming rain dampened the air, and the sweat still coating his skin made him uncomfortably sticky. He probably smelled rank.

I should go take a shower if I'm gonna . . .

Gonna what?

Hell, why bother lying to himself? He wanted to talk to Seb. He wanted Seb to tell him he'd been different from all the other guys he'd been with. He needed to believe he hadn't been played. Again.

But it was easier to stay pissed off. Safer even. He already found himself kinda jealous of Bower. He could picture him in that wheelchair, holding Silver's hand, Richter rubbing his shoulder.

Only, Richter and Bower weren't . . . involved.

Not as far as he knew anyway.

Not that it made a difference.

Pressing his eyes shut as he leaned over the metal railing just off the walkway, Luke recalled the whole mess with Callahan and Perron. The media was all over them over a fucking hug. Worse rumors were going around about Luke and Seb. Nelson's comments proved it.

Not that he gave a shit what Nelson thought.

Or what anyone thought.

Bullshit.

All right, so he wasn't ready to come out or whatever, but he couldn't keep going like this. On the ice, it had been damn easy to pretend like he and Seb could be nothing more than teammates. But that wasn't gonna happen. He couldn't go a day without thinking about the man. He couldn't stop thinking about him now.

So fix it.

No. It wasn't up to him to fix it. He'd give Seb a chance though. Hear what he had to say.

The only problem was Jami. They had to make up. The relationship would be the three of them, or nothing. And he didn't want it any other way.

But he had an idea. Jami was a chick after all. If he got her something nice, she'd hear what *he* had to say.

Seb got her a bird. How you gonna beat that, Carter?

Luke shook his head and pulled out his phone.

"Hey, Mom. Can you help me out? I kinda got myself in a jam. No, I'm fine. Just . . . remember that girl? Well, I'm gonna lose her if I don't do something. I don't think flowers will cut it. And . . . and there's something else I need to tell you." He took a deep breath. His mother didn't say a word. "Are you sitting down?"

* * * *

Jami dressed quickly and wrapped her hair in a towel, glancing toward the door every now and then, hoping Sebastian would walk in. They'd exchanged keys before his last road trip, but he hadn't used his yet.

Peanut twittered, fluffing up his feathers in that irritated way he had. Poor thing. Over the last few days, he'd spent more time with Akira than her. And he'd gotten pretty attached to his owner, just like Sebastian said he would. She smiled as she went to open the cage and let him out. He flew over her hand, landing on her shoulder. After nipping her earlobe hard enough to make her yelp, he buried his face into her hair and cooed.

"I deserved that." Jami stroked his back with a finger. "I swear, I'm gonna be around more. It's just been a hectic week." She stepped up to the sofa, careful not to disturb him. "I . . . I lost someone. Someone I cared about a lot."

A little tug at her hair was Peanut's only reply.

"He's such a jerk, though! I mean, fine, I get what Sebastian's cousin said sounded bad, but he should have trusted us more. I trust—trusted him." She rolled her eyes at the sting of tears. "Ugh, I swear, I'm about to start my period. I'm getting way too worked up about this."

Another tug. Peanut chirped, then bumped his head against her cheek.

"Sebastian's right. My brain's in overdrive. You know I'm supposed to be reading? But you're such a good listener. We should chat more often."

She placed Peanut on the sofa and went to fix him up some fresh fruit. For the next hour, they worked on a few tricks, but Peanut seemed more interested in singing to her sweetly to earn treats than playing dead.

After placing him back on his perch and covering his cage so he could sleep, Jami went to her room and stretched out over her rumpled bed to read the book Akira had lent her a few days ago. Only a few pages in, her cheeks got so hot it felt like she'd stuck her head in an oven. The Doms in the exclusive club reminded her of Sebastian. She imagined him cuffing her to the X-shaped cross, naked and exposed to a roomful of people, pressing against her as he told her all the naughty things he would do to her.

The lock to the front door clicked. Jami held her breath and went perfectly still. Two sets of footsteps sounded in the hall, coming toward her room. Anxiety and excitement swirled together, rushing through her veins. Her hands shook as she held the book and tried to pretend that she didn't hear them. Part of her wanted to look, to see who had come with Sebastian.

Luke?

No. Sebastian wouldn't bring that asshole. He knew she didn't want anything to do with him.

But for a split second, as the end of the bed bowed and someone not big enough to be Sebastian crawled over her, she felt a tiny spark of hope.

A hot, raspy breath, close to her ear. "Don't. Move."

Scott. She moved to turn her head, but a large hand curved under her chin. Sebastian took a knee by the bed, his eyes hard as he leaned toward her. "You do not listen well. Bind her wrists, Scott. I have a feeling she will not cooperate."

"Which means we'll have to hurt her." Scott's tone was rough, but the hint of anticipation in it told her he liked the idea. He pulled her hands behind her back. His grip slipped as she wrenched at her wrists. "She's not going to make this easy."

"I would be disappointed if she did." Sebastian raked his fingers into her hair and jerked her head back. His lips brushed over hers. His hand slid from her hair, down her throat. He bit her bottom lip when she moved in for a kiss. "*Coño sucio.* You are not afraid, are you? You would let two strange men fuck you with only a token resistance."

She shivered, shaking her head, mouthing "No" even as her body screamed "Yes!" Her panties were already damp, but she wanted the game to play out. She wanted to ride the edge of fear, like bungee jumping off a cliff, free-falling, forgetting about the cord until it snapped her to safety.

"If you don't let me go, I'll scream." She whispered the words against Sebastian's lips, then tossed her head back. She bumped Scott's chin a little too hard and winced at his grunt. "Shit. Sorry."

Scott wrapped her wrist with some kind of tape that didn't seem the least bit sticky. Then he rolled her over and straddled her hips. His leather pants were cool on the bare flesh along her sides where her shirt had ridden up. She stared up at him, her gaze sliding down from his mussed up light blond hair, to his chest. A snug white T-shirt outlined his muscles, not bulky like Sebastian or Luke—*damn it, get him out of your head!*—but nicely chiseled. He was still much bigger than her. And strong enough to hold her down without too much effort.

But he used none of that strength on her. He was a little too gentle. Gentle enough that she felt bad being rough with *him*.

"How sorry?" Scott ran his tongue over a small cut on his bottom lip. "Sorry enough to stop fighting?"

She bit back a smirk. *You asked for it, buddy.* Batting her eyelashes, she nodded. "If you don't hurt me, I'll do anything you want."

Rubbing his hand over his lips, Scott looked over at Sebastian like an actor who'd forgotten his script.

"You offer what we can take." Sebastian stood, his leathers rasping against her comforter as he bent forward and dragged her out from under Scott. He latched onto her bound wrists as he turned her to face the wall by her bed. His hand pressed between her shoulder blades as he licked up the length of her throat. "Scream. Bring the neighbors. The police. They will enjoy the show."

"No," she whimpered, squirming as he reached around to unbutton her shorts. "No, I don't want them to know what a whore I am."

Sebastian chuckled. "I imagine you do not. Are you wet, *puta?*"

Fuck. The question made her cunt throb. She nodded.

"I do not believe you." Sebastian barred an arm across her chest, spinning around so she faced Scott. "Remove her shorts and panties. If she lied, we will tie her to the bed and let the men in this place have her. I've no taste for dry pussy tonight."

Jami whimpered as Scott knelt and jerked her shorts and panties down to her ankles. He ran a hand up the inside of her thigh, hissing in a breath as his fingertips grazed the crease of her pussy.

He held his fingers up. They glistened in the lamplight. "She's dripping. And she smells fucking hot. I want a taste."

"Do you want him to taste you?" Sebastian cupped her breast, massaging it through her shirt. "Do you want his tongue on your cunt?"

"No." Jami gulped in air, digging her heels into the floor as her heart took arms against desire. She wanted Scott. Then she didn't. As soon as her brain got involved, she was confused. *I shouldn't be letting this happen. It's . . . it's wrong. So, so wrong.*

"What if you have no choice?"

She moaned and leaned her head back against Sebastian's chest. "I don't know."

"Jami." Scott straightened and cupped her cheek. "This whole scene aside, I know I'm not any kind of Dom. I'm not sure if I want to be. But this is kinky and fun. I won't deny I want you . . . still, if I've learned anything, I know you can end this with a word. The only one I know of is red. Say it if you want this to stop. No hard feelings."

Her fear was all fake, but looking at Scott, she saw his was real. Being torn out of the scene and offered a choice was all that was stopping her. She trusted Sebastian, and since he'd brought Scott, she trusted him too. Her uncertainty came because of Luke. Because he had a place in her heart whether she'd admit it or not. If he hadn't left them, the three of them would have negotiated what was allowed.

He did leave. He gave up having a say.

So the only opinion that counted was Sebastian's. If she focused on him, she had no doubts. But this would all end if she didn't make that very, very clear.

"Scott, you're making me think. I don't want to think. I want to feel." She tongued her bottom lip, swollen from Sebastian's teeth. "I like this game. Can we keep playing?"

"Yes, *mi cielo*. But first, I believe Scott needs some assurance that you are willing, despite your protests." Sebastian spoke in a low, hypnotic tone, causing lust to pulse through her veins. The same lust filled Scott's eyes as Sebastian whispered, "Show him you want him."

Jami tipped her chin up, lips parting slightly as Scott kissed her. He tasted her with a tentative dip of his tongue, groaning as she pressed against him, inviting him deeper. His mouth slanted and his tongue swept in. The kiss became hungry, almost feral as he used his teeth and tongue to explore her. He nipped her chin, trapping her gaze with blue eyes sharpened with desire. He lowered, pressing light kisses down the length of her throat. His teeth grazed her collarbone.

Sebastian slid his hand into her shirt, cupped her breast, lifting it over the low neckline to offer it to Scott. Scott's hot breath rushed out over her hardened nipple. He flicked it with his tongue, then let out a rough sound as Sebastian pushed his fingers into his mouth.

"I will not use you tonight, Scott." Sebastian pulled his fingers out, using the wet tips to draw a circle around Jami's nipple. He chuckled at Scott's shocked look. "But if you please her, I may consider it soon."

Jami frowned. *Why not tonight?*

"Shit, man. As long as someone uses me . . ." Scott's eyes drifted shut. He sucked at her nipple, rolling it against the roof of his mouth until she gasped at the zing of pleasure stretching in a taut cord down to her clit. His hands curved around her hips as he dropped to his knee. "As long as someone does, I don't care."

There was something sad about Scott's resigned tone, but he didn't give her time to dwell on it. His lips closed around her clit. He sucked hard. She cried out as sparks burst in the tiny bundle of nerves. Her legs quivered as he thrust two fingers into her wet slit, fucking her with them hard and fast. He seemed determined to make her come as quickly as possible.

"Slowly, *hombre*. Tease her." Sebastian wrapped her hair around his fist, tugging her head back so she could see his ominous smile. "We want her hot for our friends. If she is wet enough, fill her cunt and lock her up. I am eager to bring her to a place where her screams will not be heard."

Scott's fingers curved inside her, reaching a spot that sent her spiraling closer to climax. She panted, pleading with her eyes for Sebastian to either stop him or let him finish.

"In case you are confused, *gatita*—" Sebastian kissed her cheek "—you do not have permission to come."

A moan of frustration escaped her lips. She was so, so close! Scott's tongue circled her clit, avoiding the tip, as if he knew one touch would set her off. His fingers made as soft, wet sound as he slowed his thrusts.

Her brain shut off. Her entire being narrowed down to the rippling within. Liquid heat spilled as Scott eased his fingers out. She arched her back, spread her thighs shamelessly. "Don't stop. Please don't stop."

Something hard and round pressed against her entrance. Stretched her slightly before settling inside. She whimpered as her pussy clenched around it, but found no relief because it wasn't moving. Cool metal cover burning flesh. A lock clicked, then another and another.

The chastity belt.

"No!" She slumped back against Sebastian's chest as Scott rose up in front of her. She scowled as Scott kissed her. "You two are fucking evil."

Scott grinned. "Are kidnappers supposed to be nice?"

"Yes." She pouted, then jumped as the thing inside her—probably the stupid egg Chicklet had bought for her—began to vibrate. Her core simmered, reached a boiling point that had her holding her breath in anticipation.

The vibrations cut off so abruptly her legs almost gave out. She pushed Scott away so she could turn to glare at Sebastian.

His dark brows rose slightly. He held up the remote as though to remind her he could make things much *much* worse. "Patience and self-control will serve you well, *gatita*. You will be punished for demands."

"And if I behave? If I let you take me and don't fight?"

"You will be rewarded." He bent down to pull her shorts and panties over the chastity belt. "Scott will remove your restraints now. I would rather not risk your neighbors seeing you bound."

"That's a good idea." But as Scott undid the tape, she trembled, feeling off-balance. She suddenly couldn't face the man. What would he think of her? She'd let him do intimate things to her, even though she didn't know him well. Fooling around with random guys had been much easier when she was drunk or stoned. She lowered her gaze when she caught him frowning at her. "I guess we should go."

"Wait." Sebastian put a hand on Scott's shoulder before he could move toward the door. His eyes darkened as he studied her face. "Speak to me, *mi cielo*."

She wrinkled her nose. "I don't know what to say."

"Are you uncomfortable with this?"

"Not exactly." She knew he wouldn't let it go, so she did her best to put her thoughts into words. "It's just . . . Scott's not a stranger. When this is all over, I'll have to see him around, and I'll always wonder what he thinks of me."

"He is my teammate, Jami. I understand your concerns, but I

would not have allowed this if I thought things would become awkward on or off the ice."

"They won't." Scott rubbed her arms. "I promise."

"That's easy to say, for both of you. You're just sharing a chick. A lot of the guys do it."

"There are some things the 'guys' do not do, *mi corina*." Sebastian jerked Scott toward him, one hand gripped firmly to his jaw as he kissed him.

Scott fisted his hand into the front of Sebastian's shirt, holding on when it looked like Sebastian would pull away. Jami stared, more shocked at seeing these two men kiss than she'd ever been when it was Sebastian and Luke. For some reason, the connection Sebastian had with Luke made it seem natural. Right.

This was hot. Sexy as hell. But just as random as her letting Scott kiss her. Almost more.

And Scott looked as miserable as she'd felt when it ended.

"To some, pleasure needs no strings attached. No commitment," Sebastian said, not releasing Scott until he could clearly stand on his own. "Scott is one of those people. This is why you chose him, is it not?"

"Yes." But suddenly, that seemed selfish. Shallow. Almost as bad as what Luke had accused them of. But she waited until they got to Sebastian's car before she voiced her concerns, quietly so Scott, who was sitting in the backseat, staring out the window, wouldn't hear her. "I'm not sure I'm okay with this. I don't want him to feel used like—"

"Nor do I." Sebastian's jaw hardened as he stared ahead at the dark road. "But he expects nothing from us. Or anyone. We cannot change that." He paused and glanced over at her with a tight smile. "But I may know someone who can."

Good. She relaxed into her seat, feeling a bit better. She didn't know who'd come to the party, but if Sebastian said Scott would be taken care of, he would be.

If only . . .

No. She wouldn't think about Luke again. She wouldn't!

But he kept slipping back into her head, like the cravings for the countless addictions she'd broken in the past. Only worse. Because things could have been so much different if he'd been willing to listen. Sebastian was a good man. Better than either of them deserved.

She pictured Sebastian kissing Scott and pressed her eyes shut. He'd done it for her. So she wouldn't feel weird about what had happened. Or what *would* happen.

He hadn't wanted to though. Because he still thought Luke would come back.

Tonight, she'd do everything in her power to make him forget the idiot. And if that didn't work . . .

Then what?

Then I find Luke and knock some sense into him.

Sure. Beat the pigheaded jerk into submission. That would go over well.

I'll tell him Sebastian needs him.

And he'd figure she was playing bait again.

Then I'll tell him . . . I'll tell him I need him.

Every ounce of pride she had rebelled against admitting that to Luke. Even though it was true. She could forgive him for lashing out right after Sebastian's cousin had said all the crap—she probably would have been hurt and confused too. But going out with Amy, of all people?

He was probably with her now. Probably . . .

Stop it. How are you going to get Sebastian to forget him if you can't?

The egg inside her buzzed to life, vibrating fast, then slow, reawakening her body and fogging her brain. She gasped as Sebastian's fingers stroked lightly above her knee, finding a sensitive spot that sent a sizzling current straight up to her covered clit.

"Your mind seems very busy, *mi cielo*." Sebastian watched her from the corner of his eye, shaking his head slowly when she opened her mouth to speak. "Are you considering how much the bad people I'm bringing you to will hurt you? How they will use you? Because nothing else should occupy your thoughts right now."

"I'm trying, *mi Rey*." Jami pressed her eyes shut, doing her best to lock her thoughts on the carnal night that lay ahead. But she slipped the second the vibrations within ceased.

The car stopped. Before she could open her eyes, Sebastian hand covered them, cutting out the dim lights from the street with had filtered red through her eyelids. Her world became nothing but darkness. And the sound of his voice.

"There's no need to try any longer." His tone dropped, low and feral. His teeth grazed her neck. The moist heat, the pressure right over her pulse, had her instincts kicking up in a wash of cold, even as lust blazed through her. He chuckled as she pressed her hand against his chest, holding him back even as she offered up her throat. "You are afraid, but your body betrays you. Do you know I can smell how wet you are? I can practically taste it. Can you Scott?"

Cold air hit her as the passenger side door beside her opened. A warm hand, damp with sweat, stroked up her thigh as Scott whispered, "Yes."

"She is eager to be fucked. To be used like the little toy she is." Sebastian's accent thickened, and tenderness seeped into the crude words, softening the blow so she reached the headspace she needed to act like a whore, but still feel cherished. "You will let us do anything we want to you, won't you, Jami?"

No. The response came automatically, because it was the right one for the game they played. But she didn't need to play. She just needed to let go. "Yes, Sebastian. I'll let you do anything. Always."

His hand moved. Slid down to cup her cheek. She didn't open her eyes, but she could hear his smile in his voice. "Very good, *mi corina*. Because your pleasure is mine. You will not forget?"

"No," she whispered, hoping he knew she felt the same. "I'll never forget."

Chapter Twenty Two

Cigar smoke filled the basement room in a light grey haze, sweet and pungent, drifting over light musky arousal from the women and soap and sweat from the men. Sebastian studied Pearce over his cards—his only real competition. In black jeans and a snug black tank top, not quite slouched into the high-backed leather chair but relaxed into it with his ankle on his knee, lazily puffing on his cigar, he waited for Scott to make his move. Beside Pearce, Chicklet licked a droplet of whiskey from her bottom lip as she watched Scott, still playing in a way even though she'd folded her hand. She was a savvy player, but losing two red keys—those to Laura's chastity belt—to Sebastian, she had begun to take fewer risks and added a mental edge to her game. Which could be dangerous, but Sebastian wasn't overly concerned. Nothing she could say or do would distract him from his goal.

It had taken one hand for Sebastian to get a feel for four of the five players he'd invited to his home for a scene which revolved around a poker game and two pretty, trussed up victims. Two offered no challenge at all. Wayne tended to scowl for a split second when the deal didn't go his way, then played on as if backing down insulted his manhood. Scott started off strong, confident, but as the stakes went up, his hands began to shake. As they were now. He considered the other players, hunched his shoulders, and eyed his cards once again. He had likely thrown in too much on a pocket pair and had only one key left.

Pearce however... Sebastian couldn't read him. His expression never changed. He'd won three of Jami's blue keys and one of Laura's red ones by bluffing. None of the players besides Sebastian would chance calling him as he raised the stakes because too often he turned over a hand that proved either luck or skill was on his side.

Sebastian would bet his last three keys it was skill.

His jaw ticked as Pearce's gaze flicked over to Jami, lying on her side on a padded bench to the right of the folding table where they played, blindfolded, gagged with a strip of black silk, restrained with bondage tape around her wrists and ankles. Laura lay in a mirror to her to the left. Both women moaned softly as the vibrating eggs inside them pulsed randomly, keeping them on the brink of a climax, but allowing them no relief. Pearce's focus on winning Jami's keys either meant he planned to win her for himself—or . . .

He thinks to distract me. He doesn't want her for himself.

He had a feeling he knew why Pearce wanted her. And perhaps he could use that against him.

After laying his cards down on the table, Sebastian pulled out Jami's remote and pushed a button to a higher setting. She thrashed and let out a muffled cry.

Scott groaned and pushed his remaining chips to the center of the table. "I'm cashing in."

Chicklet smirked. She stopped the timer at the end of the table, then sat back. "About time someone did!" She laughed. "Our poor little jackpots have been waiting four hands for some action."

Clicking the button on the remote to cut off the vibrations, Sebastian nodded to Scott. "You have skin, wax, and two items of clothing. I will buy them from you for a key."

Pearce sat up, his lips turning down slightly. "I'll buy them for two. And I'll share."

The game was a strange one, but one Sebastian had enjoyed a time or two in private Los Angeles clubs. Like in a friendly game of poker where each player paid twenty or fifty dollars to play, everyone started with an equal number of chips. Only no money was involved. The colors of the chips counted for different things. In this game, it was clothes, skin, wax, and impact, the value mounting with each. They could be cashed in once between the blinds being raised, at any time, but cashing in without a certain combination was pointless. Keys were worth the most, but were not cashed in because what good was unlocking one lock out of five? However playing with a sub in any way, especially when one wasn't likely to win, was tempting. Scott would trade in his last key for more chips, but as the stakes rose, he would have to offer something of himself to win a key from another.

Few Doms would gamble themselves, but Sebastian seriously doubted Scott had the makings of a Dom. He'd actually counted on Scott offering himself, planned to push Pearce into throwing in a key or two in the hopes of winning him. Unless he'd read the man wrong, Scott was the one he really wanted.

So why not let him use up all his chips?

You've used women to lure men. Sebastian's stomach clenched as he pictured Luke, hurt and angry, believing he'd done just that with Jami. *Pearce will use Jami that way if he can.*

He refused to allow that. If Peace wanted Scott, he would lay all his cards on the table now.

"Think carefully, Scott." Sebastian palmed his stack of black impact chips, shuffling them in his hand. "If you offer yourself, I will accept nothing less than you on your knees with my dick in your mouth."

Chicklet let out a hum of approval. "I'd offer up a key to have your face between my thighs, hon. I think any of us would. Go for it."

Wayne laughed. "That's easy, Chicklet. Pretty boy's probably used to nomming pussy. But I want to know if he'd make it worth my while. You ever sucked cock, boy?"

"Don't call me, 'boy'." Scott fisted his hands on the table, his gaze shifting from Sebastian to Pearce. "You want to know what I have to offer? Yeah, I've sucked cock. And eaten plenty of pussy. I'm good at both. I'm not out of this game yet, but luck ain't on my side, I'll be damned if I don't get something before you all bury me." His chin jutted up as he fixed Pearce with a hard look. "I've cashed in. You want to win me? Pray to the poker gods for a good hand."

"I will," Pearce said quietly. "Make it worth her while. She deserves a reward for bringing you here."

"Yeah, she does." Scott licked his bottom lip as he turned to Sebastian. "I've never done wax play. Help me make it good for her?"

Sebastian inclined his head and stood. "She's drifting with the lingering pleasure. Bring her back to you. I will guide you through it and make it good for you both."

He smiled as Scott bent down to Jami, whispering in her ear as he undid the laces of her shirt. He kissed her reverently before using scissors to cut her bindings. After pulling off her shirt, he undid her bra, then set both aside.

"Sebastian is here, Jami. He'll make sure it only hurts in a good way," Scott said.

Jami smiled, her arms hanging limp over her head where Scott had placed them. "I know."

Scott kissed her again, then moved down, laying soft kisses along her throat, between her breasts. He curved his hand under one and lifted it to his mouth to suck on the nipple. He groaned as she arched up, his lips leaving her breast with a load smack. He buried his face into the other, rising up slightly to flick the rosy nub at the tip with his tongue.

He was breathing hard as he turned to Sebastian. "Can you light a candle for me? A red one. I want to cover her breasts—want to see how she reacts to the hot wax spilling over them."

After pulling a red candle from a bag of toys under the table, Sebastian lit it, tested a few drops on his arm, then nodded his approval as Scott did the same. He turned his focus from Scott to Jami as the wax spilled, watching her lips part and her body thrash. Every person in the room went still as she rasped in a breath. Scott drew circles around one breast with the wax, leaving her nipple bare. He did the same to the other breast. Paused, then let a hot drop on a hard, peaked nipple, quickly moving to the other as Jami cried out.

"Ah!" Her screams were echoed by Laura. A faint buzzing told Sebastian that Chicklet had decided to use the other remote to give her sub some relief. Sebastian hardened as he looked from one woman to the other. Both were tossing and turning as though coming apart from the inside out. He pressed a button on the remote in his hand so Jami's pleasure would linger. So she would be satisfied until he won the game. Because he had to win. He had to know, before the night ended, that he had given her everything she needed.

Some petty, jealous part of him wanted to own her pleasure, but this whole scene went beyond what he wanted. Even if the night ended with one—or more—of the other players making her come until she was too exhausted for him to do more than hold her, he would be satisfied. Because in the morning, she would be in his arms. And every morning after, as long as she would allow it.

Besides, they could only have so much of her. He'd set his limits, though he hadn't discussed them with her yet. They could touch and taste and play with her. But only he would make love to her. All his talk of fucking was shallow, because he would never allow anyone to do that to her who didn't care for her as deeply as he did.

He refused to put a name to who that person should be. He had immersed Jami into the scene so keep her from dwelling on things he was powerless to change. It would be best if he led by example.

The game resumed. Shortly after losing his last key, Wayne eliminated himself by cashing in his skin and impact tokens on Laura. As the *whoosh* and *snap* of a flogger filled the room, followed by Laura's muffled cries, Sebastian tended to Jami, checking the pulse at her throat, the restraints still around her ankles, the circulation in her feet with a light touch that made her giggle.

He moved up to the other end of the bench, kissing her cheek and whispering to her how lovely she looked. She didn't need demeaning words now, not when she'd been made the object of a game. This fulfilled her in a way he was much more comfortable with. She was a prize, treasured and valued by the few he trusted not to give her regrets the next time they met. Even Wayne, crass and rough as he could be, had spoken of her as though she was an acquisition to be admired. Rare art.

Sebastian smiled, smoothing sweat-slicked strands of dark blue hair from Jami's temples. She craved objectification, loved being called a slut and worse, but still needed to know he didn't see her that way. And hopefully he had proved that he never would.

You are priceless, mi cielo.

A few hands later, Chicklet called all in and won all of Laura's keys. She let out a sigh of relief and cashed in. "I would have enjoyed playing with Jami, Sebastian, but I have to admit, I need to get my hands on my pretty girl. And since I'm so generous, you can play with us, Wayne—if you don't mind a woman's lips around your dick?"

Wayne grinned. "Not at all. I've seen your girl's skills. You've got her well trained."

Chicklet inclined her head at the compliment. "That I do."

The pair went to Laura, Wayne cutting her restraints while Chicklet unlocked the chastity belt and pulled out the egg. They spread her out on the bench with her head hanging over the end, her wrists taped to the legs and a spreader bar Sebastian provided attached to her ankles. Chicklet pressed her face against her sub's pussy, groaning as she lapped up the slick juices. Wayne covered himself with a condom and fed his dick into Laura's eager mouth.

"Jesus." Scott swallowed, shifting in his seat. "I don't know how much longer I can play."

Pearce gave him an amused half-smile. "Not much longer unless you have a good hand and something to offer." His expression turned serious as he looked to Sebastian. "I have three of Jami's keys. You have two. I say we call it a draw after this hand and share her. The winner will enjoy Scott as a bonus."

"Agreed." Sebastian tossed two cards, nodding his thanks as Pearce dealt him two new ones. "But you assume Scott will not fold."

"He won't fold," Pearce said, eyes on Scott, as though issuing a challenge.

Scott nodded slowly. And kept all his cards. "You're right. I won't. But what do I get if I win this hand?"

"If Sebastian agrees, you can play with Jami as well." Pearce thumbed the edge of his cards, took a deep drag on his cigar, his lips pulling provocatively on the thick end. He replaced three cards. "And I'll suck *your* dick."

With nothing more to bet, they all laid their cards on the table. Scott beat both Sebastian and Pearce with a straight.

Then shook his head and laughed. "You don't have to do it, man. Seriously, it's just a fucking game."

Pearce smirked. "I would have made you do it. Besides, I want to."

"You do?" Scott stood quickly as Pearce rose and moved toward him. "But—"

With his hand around the nape of Scott's neck, Pearce pressed Scott's hand against his crotch. "Did you miss the fact that *you* were the prize I was playing for? I consider this a win."

Sebastian pulled off Jami's shorts, then unlocked her chastity belt, a small smile of satisfaction playing at his lips. He took off Jami's blindfold, removing her gag when her brow lifted in question.

"You knew Zach wanted Scott?"

"Yes."

"So they won't be playing with me?" Jami didn't sound disappointed, which pleased him.

Even though she was wrong. He chuckled. "They will play with you, *gatita*. I do not imagine either will pass up on the opportunity. It will not be offered again for quite a while. I did mention I am greedy after I share?"

"Scott wants to taste her." Pearce stroked Scott's bottom lip with his thumb as he trapped Jami with a hungry look. "And so do I."

"Do you hear that, *putina*?" Sebastian used his thumb and finger to hold her plump, outer labia open as he tugged the egg out. He wet his fingertip in the moisture spilling from her, then used it to slick her lips. She stared at him as he slid two fingers into her mouth. "They will taste you. Together. Their tongues will tangle as they lick your hot cunt. Your body will bring them together."

Jami's eyes glistened, but she seemed to like the idea. Not only of the pleasure—of something good coming of it. She sucked his fingers suggestively, pouting when he pulled them away. "And what will you be doing?"

"Not what you expect." Sebastian reached under his suit jacket and pulled out the knife sheathed to his belt, hidden there throughout the game because using it was an option for him alone. "I really must remove the wax. Your breasts will be tender. They are too often neglected, but tonight, I will toy with them. Abuse them with a flogger, then my mouth. And once you feel you cannot take any more, I will decorate your nipples with clamps. The metal teeth will bite into them. And when they are removed, you will feel pain like nothing you have ever experienced."

"Fuck, Sebastian." Jami gasped and pressed her eyes shut. Tears streaked down her cheeks. She whimpered as Pearce pushed her thighs apart. "Do it. Please do it. You're driving me insane."

"And how do we experience insanity, *gatita*?" Sebastian pressed the flat of the knife to her cheek as he kissed her.

Her breath caught. Her eyes went wide, unfocused. But she managed to answer before she floated into the sensations of three men torturing her with pleasure.

"Together."

* * * *

Rain thrashed Luke from all sides as he ran from his car to Seb's front door, soaking through his white T-shirt and ripped blue jeans. Four familiar cars had taken up all the parking spots in front of Sebastian's house, forcing Luke to park a block away. The temperature had dropped drastically at some point during the drive here, and Luke shivered as he pressed his thumb to the doorbell.

Combing his fingers through his hair, Luke frowned at the stuffed puppy he'd bought for Jami, all the fluffy white fur of the pillow-sized husky now lumpy and wet, despite his efforts to shield it with his body. His mom had told him to get "his girl" something cuddly, had said her heart always melted when a man brought her something she could snuggle with.

His mother had a pile of stuffed animals in the attic. Most from his father, who'd often needed a way back in after lashing out. Luke had almost ditched the suggestion when he recalled his father's contrite expression as he offered flowers and chocolates and something snuggly with shallow apologies. But his mother had ended the call with a few last words of wisdom.

"Don't let it get to the point where she has a dozen gifts because 'you're sorry'. Make this one special. An offer for a fresh start." She'd laughed then. *"If Sebastian is half the man I think he is from all you've told me, he won't put up with you hurting her this bad again. See that you don't. I'm looking forward to meeting them both."*

He grinned, weirdly happy even though he was freezing and working things out with Jami and Seb wasn't gonna be pleasant. Besides the two of them, and Bower—because he loved the man like a brother—his mother's opinion was the only one that mattered. And she'd been really cool about him being gay.

No. Bi. He laughed as he recalled how his mother had corrected him. He could still give her grandbabies. Not that she'd mind if he was gay, so long as he adopted before she died . . .

His heart lodged in his throat. He hugged the wet, stuffed dog. Her surgery was getting closer, and he could tell she was scared. All the things that had seemed so important—like staying mad—seemed stupid now. Life was too fucking short.

As he lifted his hand to ring the doorbell again, the door swung open. He braced himself for the impact seeing Seb again would have on him, but his carefully detached "Hey" drifted off as he met Chicklet's narrowed eyes.

"You shouldn't be here," Chicklet said, almost slamming the door in his face.

He slapped his hand against the door and frowned at her. "What the fuck, Chicklet? I thought we were friends?"

"Luke, I'm so fucking disappointed in you, I don't know what to say." She shook her head. "I never thought you'd be this ignorant. I didn't get details, but I do know you reacted because of all the press, and that just makes me sick."

"It wasn't the press."

"Don't lie to me." Chicklet folded her arms over her chest, her jaw ticking as she glanced down at the pitiful gift. "Maybe something else triggered it, but it wouldn't have if you hadn't already been so insecure about someone finding out you weren't a straight little player."

Okay, he kinda got Chicklet being angry if she believed he'd lashed out at Jami and Seb because he was afraid of being exposed, but did she really think that little of him? "Did you know Seb used women to seduce straight men?"

Chicklet's eyes widened. Her lips moved. She took a deep breath. "Who told you that?"

So she'd known. He tried not to let it bother him. "Sebastian's cousin. A warning would have been nice."

"If I'd thought Sebastian was doing that with you—"

"Why didn't you? What made me different? Is it so horrible that I was fucking shocked? That was dropped on me after I'd already fallen . . ." He ground his teeth in frustration. Everyone besides Bower assumed he was in the wrong. "You know what brought me here? I looked back at all the things I've done with Seb and realized I wouldn't have let it happen if I didn't trust him. You taught me that. You made sure I knew how important trust was, and I should have trusted him enough to hear him out. I fucked up. I know that. But so

347

did he."

Chicklet nodded slowly. "Are you going to tell him that?"

"Yeah. Soon as you let me in."

"All right." Chicklet stepped aside to let him pass. "But no matter what you see, don't you dare judge them. Whatever your reasons, you left. You don't get a say."

"I know." But still, Luke winced as he followed Chicklet down to the basement, the moans and a sharp crack of leather striking his heart and his dick all at once. He couldn't tell Chicklet, but if he saw Demyan fucking Jami—or Seb fucking Demyan—he'd lose it. Anything else he would take in stride.

Nothing prepared him for what he saw when he reached the bottom step.

Demyan had his face between Jami's thighs, his mouth covering her pussy as he groaned. Pearce knelt in front of him, taking Demyan's dick into his mouth as he massaged his balls. Luke had to drag his jaw off the floor as he watched. He didn't know Pearce well, but it had never occurred to him that the man could be into guys. Actually, he'd assumed every man on the team was straight. Except him and Seb. But obviously they weren't the only ones keeping secrets.

He avoided looking at Seb for a bit, turning his attention instead to Wayne who was fucking Laura so hard the bench she was bound to moved across the floor with a harsh, scraping sound accentuating pounding flesh. And Wayne was supposed to be strictly into men.

Or maybe Luke had been looking for clear lines where there were none.

Luke's heart stuttered as he finally allowed himself to look at Seb. In a white shirt, with his sleeves rolled up over massive forearms, he flicked a flogger over Jami's breasts, magnificent in all his restrained strength. Luke's muscles tensed as he recalled the feeling of Seb's hand, and belt, on his flesh. The feeling of Seb's mouth, of his body pressed against him.

He let out a soft sound, wishing he could just let it all go and throw himself into the scene with Jami and Seb. Wishing he could belong with them again.

Seb went still. His shoulders stiffened. He glanced over, and the longing in his eyes tore Luke to shreds.

"Luke." The flogger hit the floor. He took a step away from Jami, then stopped and took her hand. "Jami . . . he is here."

Jami cried out as she jutted her hips up against Demyan's face. "He can't . . . can't see me . . . not like—"

"Shh . . ." Seb pressed a finger to Jami's lips. "He sees us, *mi cielo*. More clearly than he ever has. And I believe, this time, he has no intention of looking away."

Tears clung to Jami's lashes, glistening as she blinked fast, emotions as naked as her body, her passion, beautiful and raw, leaving her more vulnerable than ever. "He'll hurt us again."

Cold droplets trailed down Luke's back as he shook his head. He'd never wanted to hurt her. Or hurt either of them. But what could he say with so many people around? A small smile tugged at his lips. "I come in peace, boo."

Her startled laugh made her breasts jiggle. Then her lips parted and her back bowed. Luke's gaze drifted down, and his mouth watered as he watched Demyan devour her with renewed vigor, as if he knew she'd be taken from him soon and wanted to enjoy her to the very last drop.

"*Mi Rey* . . ." Jami tossed her head, probably struggling to find words through her pleasure-induced haze. "Will you make things right? Please tell me you will? I can't . . ."

"I will, *mi cielo*." Seb nodded to Pearce who stood and took Jami's hand.

Pearce kissed Jami's throat, speaking quietly. "Will you let Scott and me play with you, pet? I will steal him away from you soon."

"Not too soon." Jami whimpered. "He's . . . he's going to make me . . ."

"Wait." Pearce hissed in a breath as he fisted his hand in Demyan's hair. "I need my mouth on you this time, with his. Don't come until you feel both our tongues inside you."

"Oh God!" Jami's back bowed as Pearce bent over her, his mouth close to Demyan's. "Oh, please!"

Luke sucked in a breath through his teeth, floored by how much seeing those two men on a woman he considered his affected him. When Seb offered his hand, he clung to it, his legs suddenly boneless, nothing holding him up besides that firm grip.

"I cannot leave her, not now." Seb pulled Luke close, running his fingers through his wet hair, over his eyes, and down his cheek as though memorizing his face through touch. He framed Luke's jaw with his hand, lips close enough for a kiss. "But we will speak later?"

"Yes, but . . . can I touch her?" Luke needed to feel them both, but he was afraid to say the wrong thing. Afraid Seb would think he was taking advantage of Jami being too spaced out to slap him and tell him to fuck off. "I just need her to know I'm not going anywhere."

"Yes, *semental*." Seb brushed a soft, chaste kiss over his lips, pulling away before Luke could move in for more. "I think she needs it as much as you do."

Steadying himself, Luke stepped up to Jami's side. He cupped her face between his hands, leaning down so he filled her vision, so that no matter what she was feeling, she saw only him. He touched his forehead to hers and said the only thing he could think of. "I missed you, boo."

She moaned and pressed her eyes shut. "I want you, Luke. Please . . ."

Luke shook his head. "Ask me again in the morning—if you haven't decided you hate me again."

Jami mumbled something incoherent, twisted her hips, then gasped. Seb gestured Luke to the top of the bench, took his place beside Jami, and tugged hard on the clamps attached to her nipples.

His lips slanted as he prepared to remove them. "Brace yourself, *gatita*."

As the clamps came off, Jami held her breath. Then screamed. Demyan and Pearce latched onto her thighs, holding them apart as they licked and sucked until she bucked and screamed again. Her whole body trembled with the throes of a violent orgasm which seemed to go on and on. Sweat beaded on her forehead, tears covered her flushed cheeks in a light sheen.

When she finally opened her eyes, Luke could tell she had drifted again—to somewhere nice by the look of it. While he was breathing like he'd sprinted twenty times across the long forum rink from just watching, Jami's breaths came slow and even as they did when she slept. He kissed her forehead, then helped Seb sit her up to free her wrists.

Seb lifted her up into his arms, murmuring to her as he carried her up the stairs. Once he reached the top step, he called back. "Wait for me in the library, Luke."

Dismissed, just like that. Luke made a face as he glanced over at the action still going on in the room. Demyan and Pearce, roughly tearing at each other's clothes. Chicklet on a chair with her thighs spread wide, her hand fisted in Laura's hair, her head thrown back as her sub worshiped her cunt with her tongue. On hands and knees, Laura whimpered as Wayne worked his thick cock into her ass.

Holy shit, that man looks like he can go all night.

Rubbing his dick through his jeans, his own ass clenching, Luke sighed and turned toward the stairs. Nothing like showing up late for an orgy that he couldn't take part in. But as he left the scene behind and entered the quiet of the library, his whole reason for being here came back to him.

He could get fucked anytime, by pretty much anyone. He'd done that for years and it never meant a damn thing. Losing Teresa had hurt a bit, but mostly because she'd confirmed all the worst things he'd thought of himself.

Absently tracing the jagged line of the ugly scar that ruined his bottom lip, Luke paced slowly around the room. He couldn't find the book he'd started reading last time on any of the shelves with the Dean Koontz books. Then he found it on the leather armchair in the center of the room. Right where he'd left it. Only there was a bookmark stuck between the pages, in the middle of the book.

Seb had been reading it.

Thinking of their last time in the library, Luke settled into the chair. Seb's words came back to him. *"I know you care what I think, Luke. And I know you are fighting, very hard, not to. When you're done fighting it, let me know."*

Luke had reached the same point in the book where Seb had left off when the library door creaked open, hours later. He set the book aside as Seb approached him. Took a deep breath. And looked Seb straight in the eye as he spoke. "I'm done fighting it."

Seb nodded slowly. "Fighting what exactly?"

"Everything. I'm still scared of what will happen if people find out. I wasn't interested in starting a relationship with anyone, and I still can't believe I'm in love with a man, but—"

"In love, *semental?*" Seb quietly shut the door. "Then you are ready to admit it?"

"Yes, you son of a bitch!" Luke shot out of the chair and closed the distance between them, stabbing his finger into the center of Seb's chest. "I *was* ready, which is what pissed me off so much. Do you know how stupid I felt—how stupid I *still* feel—learning about how you manipulated people? Even Chicklet knew!"

"I used those who used me, Luke. You've fucked bunnies who only wanted you for what you represent and not who you are. What I did was no different. But it was never like that with you or Jami."

It was hard to picture anyone using Seb, but if they had, Luke could kinda get him not feeling bad about it. But if he wasn't ashamed of what he'd done, why hide it? "Why didn't you say something?"

"Because it never seemed important. I had not planned to fall in love with a young woman whose own desires disturb her, or a man, a teammate, who loved the game more than he ever loved anyone. Including himself."

Got me fucking pegged, don't you? "That might have been true once, but it's not anymore."

"I know that." Seb held out his arms in surrender. "Luke, you forced me away from the mind-numbing order I'd created; you make me feel truly alive. You are cocky and arrogant and sometimes you drive me mad, but there is such passion in you. Such fierce loyalty... and intelligence. You are much smarter than anyone, including yourself, gives you credit for."

"Okay, I'm flattered, but if I'm so smart, didn't you think maybe I'd understand why you did what you did with all those other guys?"

Seb took a step closer. "It is no excuse, only, when we are together, you both keep me in the moment. I forget the game, forget my past. I should have given more of myself, asked more of you. I was not even aware that your mother was ill until Tim mentioned it. These are things we should share."

Yeah, we should. There was no excuse for him keeping shit to himself either, but with the playoffs, it had been hard to think about anything else. Hard to put as much into the relationship as he should have. And Seb was just as dedicated as he was. He'd tried to stay away from Luke once because this thing between them was messing with his game.

I asked him not to give up on me. Guilt snagged inside Luke's chest, tearing at the last threads of anger. *And then I gave up on him.*

"From now on then, okay?" Luke scuffed the sole of his sneaker against the wood floor and shrugged. "All I want is you to trust me as much as you ask me to trust you. You don't have to be perfect, but you've got to be honest." He picked up the book he'd left on the chair and grinned. "Open fucking book, got it?"

"Yes."

"I should stay mad at you a bit longer. See what I can get out of it."

Seb smiled. "Shall I get you a puppy?"

"Hey, stuffed animals are for chicks."

"Not a stuffed animal. A real one." Seb took the book, tossed it to the chair, and slid his hand up the side of Luke's throat. His thumb stroked lightly over Luke's hammering pulse. "I have every intention of asking you to stay."

"Stay?" Luke stared at Seb, not sure he was hearing him right. "You want me to move in with you? You sure? I'm a slob and your place is so nice."

"I believe you can be trained."

Fuck. For some reason, his dick liked that idea. "I snore."

"Yes." Seb chuckled. "I know."

"My mom wants to meet you," Luke said in a rush, mind racing, heart swelling, part of him sure this was too good to be true. "I usually have her stay in a nice hotel when she visits, but your place is big so—"

"She is more than welcome to stay here."

Luke nodded, his gaze slipping to Seb's lips. He really didn't want to talk about his mom right now. He swallowed. "You can't get me a puppy tonight."

"Then what would you like me to give you, *niño?*"

"Shit, man. You gonna make me say it?" Luke groaned as Seb

backed him into a wall of books while sliding his hand under his jeans and boxers to grab his ass.

Seb ground his pelvis against Luke's so their dicks rubbed together through their clothes. "There is only one thing I need you to say, Luke."

Balls tightening, blood pumping into the head of his dick, Luke threw his head back so hard it cracked against a shelf. He didn't feel any pain. His brain wasn't working right. He barely managed a "What?"

"Please."

* * * *

Sebastian pulled Luke down to the floor with him, clucking his tongue as he checked his head for a bump. He found a tiny one, but nothing to be concerned about. He peeled Luke's still damp shirt off, tossed it aside, then went to work on his jeans, which seemed to have molded themselves to his body.

"Please, Seb. Fuck, please!"

Luke trembled under him, but he didn't seem cold. Or overly hot, which would have ended everything so Sebastian could tend to him. He was angry with himself for leaving Luke in his wet clothes this long, but the scene with Jami had demanded his full attention. He had to train himself to be better able to handle them both. But not now. Now, Jami was tucked away in his bed, sleeping peacefully. His guests were gone.

There was only Luke.

And as much as he wished he could be slow, gentle, desperation drove him on at a furious pace. He had Luke naked, tearing at his shirt, tugging at his belt. He needed to be inside him, to feel the man he loved completely lose control, to prove to his heart and his body that this was real.

Holding Luke's wrists in one hand, Sebastian pulled his leg over his shoulder, then spit on his palm to slick his dick. He took a moment to spread Luke open with two fingers, but a rasped plea soon had him shoving the head of his cock against that tight hole, grunting as he slid halfway in and Luke's muscles clenched around him like a vise.

"Breathe through the pain, *semental*." Sebastian checked his urge to slam in as he felt Luke tense even more. "I should not take you like this. Tell me if it is too much."

"It's not. Just . . . oh fuck. This is so much better than with the lube." Luke dug his heel into Sebastian's back. "I can feel all of you. Don't stop."

Sebastian pressed his weight down on Luke, forcing his way in inch by inch, the grip around his dick, the friction, such a carnal, burning pleasure that he knew he wouldn't last if he let himself go. But he lifted Luke's hips off the floor so he could take him deeper. He angled his cock until Luke moaned and struggled to free his wrists. Then paced his long strokes to hit the same spot again and again.

"Fuck! Seb!" Luke cried out, panting into Sebastian's mouth. "I'm gonna come!"

"Come, *niño*." Sebastian reached down to squeeze Luke's balls. "This time, there is no need to hold back."

Warmth hit Sebastian's stomach, spreading as he leaned down to swallow Luke's hoarse cry. Only when Luke stopped shuddering did he find his own release with one, hard thrust. Pleasure erupted from his balls and shook him to the core. A roar scored his throat as he dropped his head to Luke's chest, his body sated, but his heart bruised and battered. He found himself wondering if Luke would pull away. Be disgusted with himself for letting the man he'd believed used him fuck him in such a rough, careless manner.

"Seb?"

"Yes, Luke?" Sebastian kept his head bowed. He could almost hear Luke telling him to "Get the fuck off me."

"I'm crashing here tonight. Right here. Mind getting me a pillow?"

Sebastian lifted his head and laughed. He kissed Luke, whispering, "You will stay?"

"I need to see you in the morning," Luke said, as though it should be obvious. After Sebastian eased out, he rolled to his side, resting his head on his arm with a contented sigh. "I might even make you breakfast."

Chapter Twenty Three

A trilling ring woke Jami, and she reached blindly for her phone, which she usually left right by her bed on her night table. Then she remembered she wasn't at home. She was at Sebastian's house.

Her phone was on his dresser.

Stumbling naked from the bed, wrinkling her nose at the slight tugging pain in her breasts, she went to the dresser and picked up her phone.

The number was vaguely familiar. She eyed the clock on the night table at the other side of the bed. 5:00 a.m. Who the hell would call her so early?

"Hello?"

"Miss Richter, it's Greg Hasher—the superintendent? The police are at your apartment." He paused and cleared his throat. "One of your neighbors called after they heard noises. It seems your apartment has been broken into."

She felt behind her and sat hard on the bed. "What?"

"I think you should come see if anything's missing. File a report."

"Yes, yes of course. But . . ." She shook her head, her lips trembling as she considered the only thing she had that meant anything. "Greg . . . I know we're not supposed to have pets, but I have a bird . . . is he okay?"

Greg didn't answer for a very long time. Then he took a deep breath and sighed. "I'm sorry this happened, Jami. Come to the apartment. The police will be able to tell you more."

Jami numbly told him she'd be right there, then rifled through Sebastian's drawers for some clothes she could borrow. She found a pair of Luke's shorts and almost dropped them before she could pull them on under Sebastian's big shirt. Had he really come back? She wasn't sure how she felt about that. The night was a blur. It had been good. Awesome actually. But she couldn't think about that now.

Her sweet little bird, Peanut . . . he had to be okay. Whoever had broken into her house had their pick of valuable electronics to steal.

Her TV. Her stereo. Why bother with her harmless little baby bird? He couldn't have made that much noise with his blanket covering his cage. Unless... unless he'd thought she'd come home and was excited to see her. He chirped a little when she came in to get her attention.

Oh please... please let him be okay.

She was halfway out the door before she considered telling Sebastian what had happened. Light shone under the door in the library. Had he stayed up late again, reading?

Easing the door open quietly, she peeked in, then shut the door, careful not to make a sound. Luke *was* back. She pressed her forehead against the closed door, blinking back tears. If she'd seen Sebastian and Luke cuddled together on the floor before finding out about her apartment, she would have been nothing but happy for them. Mostly for Sebastian because she knew how much he'd missed Luke. She might have gone in there and snuggled up with them— then pounced on Luke with some choice words first thing in the morning.

But as it was, the best she could do was not disturb them. Sebastian would be pissed about her not telling him right away, but she couldn't pull him away from Luke, not yet. It just didn't feel right.

Not like there's anything he can do anyway except get all worried and tell me to stay while he makes sure it's safe.

The cops were there. So he didn't need to worry. But she knew he would.

She shut and locked his front door behind her. Called a cab from the corner. And went home, praying for the best.

And expecting the worst.

She wasn't prepared for what she saw when Greg led her past the police crowding her living room. He made her sit in the kitchen and got her a glass of water.

"You look like hell, kid." Greg crouched in front of her. "You didn't drive here, did you?"

Jami took a sip of water and shook her head. "I took a cab. I was at my boyfriend's—"

"Why isn't he with you?"

"I didn't want to wake him up."

"If he's any kind of man, he won't be happy when he finds out." Greg frowned at her. "Is there anyone else I can call? Maybe your father?"

She shook her head quickly. "He's got enough to deal with." Her eyes narrowed as Greg glanced toward the hall. "What aren't you telling me, Greg? You brought my bird out so all the cops would scare him, right? That was really nice of you. I—"

"Jami . . ."

"Tell me he's okay!"

"He's not here."

Shoving her chair back so hard it cracked against the tiles, Jami stood, moving around Greg to check the living room where Peanut's cage should be. She shouldn't have missed it, but she was an idiot sometimes. Spacey.

Or maybe she'd moved him to her room and forgotten. She scowled as Laura appeared in front of her, blocking her path. How fucking typical. The whole scene had fucked up her brain so bad she was seeing things.

"You don't want to go in there, sweetie." Laura shook her. She glanced around and lowered her voice. "Hey. Look at me. Where is your Master?"

Jami stared at her, taking in the uniform, still convinced she was tripping out. "You're a cop?"

"Yes. A friend asked me to cover her shift. Chicklet wasn't thrilled, but I'm glad I did. You're in no shape to deal with this alone. Let me call Sebastian—"

"No! This is my home! I'm a big girl, I don't need a man holding my hand to deal with this shit!" Jami covered her mouth as a sob wrenched out of her chest. "Greg said Peanut isn't here. Where is he?"

"Peanut?"

"My lovebird. He's just a baby. Sebastian gave him to me. I have to make sure he's all right. He must be so scared with all these strangers around."

"He's *not* here, Jami." Laura took a firm grip on her arm. "Come with me. I'm calling Sebastian right now."

"Don't you fucking dare." Jami jerked free. "He's with Luke. He's finally happy. I won't spoil this for him."

"But—"

"Why won't you let me in my room? This is my fucking house! It's not bad enough that someone broke in? Violated my home? Took something from me?" Jami hugged herself. "If you don't let me see, I'll assume the worst. Tell me Peanut isn't—"

"Let her see, Tallent." Another officer stood in the doorway of Jami's room, gesturing her forward. "Maybe she can give us some idea of who would do something like this."

Laura let Jami go, following her into the room. Jami gasped and tripped backward as the red words smeared on the wall above her bed burned into her skull like a fiery brand.

"No more, whore. Leave him. This is your last warning."

"Blood." She covered her mouth with her hand. "No. Please no."

"It's not blood." Laura put her hand on Jami's shoulder. "That's what I thought when I got here. I thought it was yours until my partner, Cruise, let me know your superintendent had gotten ahold of you. It took a while to get someone to come in and check it. Seems like it's some kind of paint."

"But Peanut isn't here." Jami paced around her room, her gut clenching as she stepped over her emptied panty drawer. Something white was smeared over her dresser mirror. All her makeup, perfumes, and pictures had been swept off the top of the dresser and laid in a pile in the corner. A picture she'd never seen took their place.

She was being helped out of Sebastian's car. Sebastian held his hand out to her, but if she hadn't recalled that moment, she wouldn't have known it was him. His face was covered in the same blood red of the words on her wall.

This wasn't Amy messing with her because of Luke. This was someone who didn't want her with Sebastian.

"Last warning"

Whoever it was probably knew Sebastian had given her Peanut. And as much as she loved the little bird, as much as she was afraid something bad had happened to him, Sebastian's face blotched out scared her so much more.

"Fuck." Laura came up behind her, taking the picture and holding it up to the light. "Jami, this isn't random. And it's not the first time someone's sent you a message, is it? You weren't that surprised by the words. You've seen them before."

"Yes." Jami groaned as she leaned her elbows on the dresser, staring at her own pale face in the dirty mirror. "I thought it was a girl on my team trying to get to me. I thought if I ignored her, she would give up."

"But you don't think it's her anymore?"

"No. She wants Luke. This is about Sebastian. I don't know who—"

"Do you have a jealous ex who might feel like Sebastian is taking what belongs to him?"

Ford? No. Ford wouldn't do this. He'd always been straightforward with her. He cared about her. Even if he was an asshole sometimes, she knew he was looking out for her. That he wanted to see her happy. He wouldn't play games if he had a problem with her and Sebastian. If anything, he was brutally honest about his opinion. He'd never stoop to mind games and intimidation.

"I don't know who's doing this, but this proves I made the right choice in not bringing Sebastian. Fuck!" Jami massaged her forehead with her fingertips. "I should have reported all the other shit. The letter, what this freak did to my car... I was hoping it would go away."

"Did you keep anything? Take any pictures?" Laura groaned when Jami shook her head. "If you had, I could report this as a stalking, maybe have someone tailing you, try to catch the bastard. I don't know if I can with what little we have. You should go back to Sebastian's place. Or come stay with me if you're afraid someone will go after him. I get it. If I thought someone would go after Chicklet, I'd keep my distance."

"Good. Then you understand why Sebastian can't hear about any of this." Jami pushed away from the dresser. "Thank you for the offer, but I need to get away for a bit. If I'm out of town, this person won't have the press pushing him—or her—to do anything stupid. I'll check into a motel for a few hours. See if they follow me. If nothing happens, I'll go stay with my grandmother. Out of sight, right?"

"It doesn't work like that, Jami. But I might be able to get someone to keep an eye on the motel. Kinda like using you as bait... which I don't like—" Laura her pursed her lips. "File a report. Don't leave anything out." She pulled out a pad and pen and jotted down a number. "Call me if there's *anything*. If you see something even the least bit suspicious. And promise me you'll call Sebastian and let him know what's going on once you get to your grandmother's place."

"I will." Jami grabbed a knapsack from her closet, then shoved some random clothes into it. "He'll probably assume I went to see Silver in the hospital. I'll tell my dad I'm going to visit my grandmother. That should buy us some time."

"Don't try to handle this on your own." Laura called after her as she headed out the front door. "This person is obviously dangerous."

As if I couldn't figure that one out. Jami ground her teeth as she tossed her bag to the passenger seat of her car and climbed in behind the wheel. She wasn't gonna try anything brave—or stupid—but she was going to do whatever she could to keep this freak as far away from Sebastian as possible.

After checking into a motel just out of Dartmouth, Jami went to her room, locked the door, and shut all the blinds. She turned on the TV for some background noise, then called her father. Voice mail came on right away. He was probably still at the hospital with his phone off. She left a quick message, doing her best to sound normal.

For what seemed like hours, she paced around the room, peeking through the curtains for some sign of the . . . stalker. Strange scenarios played through her mind as she studied each person strolling down the street at a jarringly slow pace. The younger ones made her wonder if maybe one of her "friends" from her time with Ford was having some weird LSD-induced fantasy about her. The older ones made her wonder if some associate of her dad's was trying to use her against him. Ford had planned to do that. And he probably wasn't the only one who'd thought of it.

The best scenario she came up with was that someone had

stolen Peanut for some kind of ransom. She considered her savings, hoping she could offer them enough to get him back. But then dismissed the idea because it didn't fit with all that had happened. This person wasn't after money.

They want me.

Her stomach pitched and she made it to the bathroom just in time to dry heave over the toilet. A soft tap at the front door made her blood run cold. She scrambled into the main room, dialed Laura's number, and hid behind the bed as it rang.

"Jami?" Laura sounded as scared as she felt.

"Someone's at the door."

"One sec . . ." Laura let out a tense laugh. "Okay, sorry about that. Seems they sent someone without telling me. Go ahead and answer."

Holding her cell to her ear with her shoulder, Jami answered the door. A young officer with bright red hair and freckles gave her a sheepish grin and held out a coffee. "Hey, I'm Officer Jenkins. Thought you'd feel better knowing I was here. I picked this up for you."

"Thanks." Jami took the coffee, then glanced past the officer to the parking lot. His squad car was parked right next to her Beetle. "Umm . . . I do feel safer knowing you're here, but how likely is it that the stalker will show up with a cop in plain sight?"

"Not very." Officer Jenkins shrugged. "Just let us do our job, Miss. I'm keeping an eye on you while your place is being checked out—in case someone followed you. Tallent mentioned you'd be going to stay with your grandmother in Halifax. I'll let you know if you're good to go."

"Great. I appreciate that," Jami said before retreating back into the room. She wasn't sure whether or not she should be relieved. What would have happened if it hadn't been the cop at the door? What if it had been whoever was after her? Not like she'd suddenly master her inner ninja and kick the psycho's ass.

All she could do was run and hide like a coward and hope the cops caught him before he found her. She curled up on her bed and hugged her knees to her chest.

The phone rang. She let it. Only once it stopped did she force herself to sit up and check the message. In case it was her dad.

It was Akira. Jami's chest seized as she listened to the message. Akira was going to her place to "Get her ass out of bed" because she was going to miss practice.

Fuck! "Don't go to my place," Jami said as soon as Akira picked up. "I'm not there."

"Oh... well, where are you then? We're doing a show at Tuesday's game, you know. I want to go over the routine—"

"I don't care about the routine. I'm going to be staying with my grandmother for a bit." Jami bit her tongue. The idea of Akira anywhere near the apartment—her hands shook. She hadn't even considered her best friend could be in danger too, if only because she'd witnessed most of what the stalker had done. If she put it together... "I'm sorry, Akira, but I just need to get away for a bit."

"Did something happen with Sebastian?" Akira's tone was soft, would have been comforting in any other situation. She really was a better friend than Jami deserved. "Come to my place, Jami. We can go over the routine tonight, and you can tell me what an asshole he is. I promise to agree until you two make up and you tell me how much you love him again."

"I do love him." Jami's voice cracked. She swallowed to smooth it out. "I swear, I'll explain everything when I come back. I can't right now. Just please don't go to my place. And don't say anything to Sebastian."

She hung up before Akira could talk her into saying more. Tried to kill some time with sleep, but the slightest sound from outside jolted her awake. For a while she just stared at the ceiling, tears spilling down her cheeks as she thought of Sebastian, Luke, Akira... and whoever else might be in danger just for knowing her.

Her stomach twisted and she half crawled to the bathroom, sobbing as she weakly puked out the coffee which seemed to have turned sour on the way up. She curled up on the bathroom floor, back against the closed door, and finally found a brief escape in darkness.

****

Ford stepped onto the elevator, scowling as he went over the team's finances. His father was being cheap lately, and Delgado was fucking broke. If he didn't get a new investor interested in the team soon, Delgado would have to sell his shares in the team to Kingsley Enterprises. Which would be a mess in court since he'd already sold some to Dean Richter and given the rest to both Ford and Silver. As much as Ford loved pushing Silver's buttons, he knew she was the only reason the team hadn't been forced to claim bankruptcy yet. But she was almost as bad as her father at throwing money into extravagant ventures that had little to no payoff. Sure, the charities and the Ice Girls got the team much needed exposure, but didn't bring in much revenue. It would take years for most of Silver's "projects" to make a difference, and they didn't have years.

Whether his sisters liked it or not, he'd have to look into cutting some fat off the roster. If they held on to a few key players, and met the minimum salary cap, they might manage to make it through another season. But they just couldn't afford to pay some of the men what they were worth.

The playoffs might have helped, if they could have made it to the second round, but with Bower out, he didn't have much hope of that. The farm team had a promising young goalie he knew Richter would bring up as a backup, but there was no way to know if he'd perform well during the playoffs. That was the problem with using the same goalie for over ninety percent of the game, they couldn't just—he cursed under his breath as he stepped off the elevator and crashed into something tiny. His papers flew across the hall.

"I'm sorry!" Jami's friend, Akira, bent down to gather the papers at her feet. She flinched when he crouched and his hand brushed hers. "*Don't.*"

"Don't what?" Ford snatched the papers from her and arched a brow as she gaped at him. "Listen, shorty. I'm an asshole. Not a very nice person—ask anyone. But I don't bother with women unless they throw themselves at me. Do you plan to do that?"

Akira shook her head and burst into tears.

Good job, Ford. He dropped the papers in a pile between his feet and pulled the white handkerchief from his jacket pocket. He handed it to her, careful not to touch her. "Shit. I'm sorry, Akira. I just meant that you don't have to worry about me. You're beautiful, and sweet, and any man would be lucky to have you."

She hiccupped. Shook her head. "It's not that. But thank you. It's just been a rough morning. Amy came in to watch me lead my team with a few of her friends. I messed up some moves, and she laughed at me. I could have ignored her if Jami had been there—"

"Wait." Ford frowned. "Why wasn't Jami there?"

"I don't know." Akira dabbed under her eyes with his handkerchief. "She said she had to get away for a bit. And she wouldn't tell me why."

"Maybe she got in a fight with Sebastian . . ." Ford straightened as Akira stood, all his papers forgotten. He seriously doubted Jami would ditch her best friend and her team because of an argument with a guy. It just wasn't like her. She used to drive him nuts by how easily she could bounce back from an all-out screaming match between them. Her sweet smile always had him forgetting why he'd been mad.

Even when he'd been right.

"I don't think it has anything to do with Sebastian. She told me she loves him. And not to go to her place. And not to say anything to him."

"Not to go to her place?" Ford rubbed his lips with his forefinger, brow furrowed. "Do you two hang out there a lot?"

"All the time. I go there on my own sometimes to check on her little bird. Peanut." Akira's lips curved up slightly. "Not that I mind. He's a sweetie."

"Yeah." Ford's shoe bumped his papers. He bent down to pick them up. "It's weird that she suddenly doesn't want you to go there."

"I know, but I was thinking . . ." Akira ducked her head. "Never mind."

"Oh no, you don't." He gave her a hard look. "Jami's my friend too. If you think she's in trouble, you better tell me."

"I guess." Akira's chin jutted up. "Actually, she told me not to talk to Sebastian. She didn't say anything about you. Some weird things have happened to her lately. Someone put pictures in her locker—I'm sure you heard about that?"

Ford nodded.

"And then there was a message on her car. And this CD playing the same song over and over. She thought it was a girl on our team, but... I'm worried. And I'm sure she hasn't told me everything." She took a deep breath. "You've known her longer. Maybe she'll tell you."

"Maybe." Ford reached out to touch Akira's cheek. For some reason, he couldn't help himself. This time, she didn't flinch away. Her soft, flushed skin felt hot against his palm. He smiled at her. "Hey, thanks for telling me all this. I'm worried too. I don't think she'll tell me anything she won't tell you, but there might be something I can do."

"Good." Akira shivered, wrapped her fingers around his wrist, and slowly drew his hand down from her face. She held his wrist for a few beats, nibbling at her bottom lip. "Call me if you hear anything?"

"Sure." He chuckled when she released his wrist and moved toward the elevator. "You'll have to give me your number. Mind reading isn't one of my many talents."

"'Many talents'?" Akira gave him a cheeky grin. "Jami told me your ego wasn't lacking."

"Really?" Ford arched a brow. "What else did she tell you about me?"

Akira blushed, her hand drifting up to the deep V neckline of her Ice Girl uniform. "Nothing."

"You're a horrible liar, shorty." Ford cuffed her chin. "Either give me your number, or keep your eye out for smoke signals."

"Smoke signals? Wow. Maybe you do have a few worthy skills."

His lips curled. "More than a few."

Her throat worked. She backed up a step, holding out her hand. He passed her his phone, watched her type in her digits, then took it back. He waited in silence with her for the elevator, well aware that the harmless flirting had made her uncomfortable. Part of him wished the playfulness of before could have continued, but he didn't want to push it. For some reason, she couldn't seem to relax when men were around. But for a moment, she had with him. Which made him feel kinda good.

The elevator opened. Akira whispered, "See you around," then stepped on. Before the door could close, she blocked it with her hand. "Whoever is doing this wrote 'No more, whore' in every message. Does that mean anything to you? I guess it could be because she's with two guys, but . . . I don't know. I was thinking it could be more."

Ford blinked. Forgot how to breathe. Stared at her. "In every message?"

"Yes."

"Okay. That helps." Ford inhaled and forced a smile. "Thanks."

Akira's eyes narrowed with suspicion. "You know something."

"I do." Ford gently moved her hand away from the elevator door so it could close. "And you can either thank me—or hate me—for it later."

Metal doors cut between them. Ford turned toward the garage, deciding to reschedule his meeting with the coach. Right now, he had to have a chat with his father.

Only one person had been around when he and Jami had the big blowout about his friends calling her a whore. Ford had said those very words.

"No more, 'whore.' You don't get it, do you? That's what my father used to call my mother when he got mad at her. He'd call her a whore. If slut or fucktoy gets you off, fine. But not that."

Jami hadn't understood, but at the time, she hadn't understood much. And it wasn't until he found out how often she was stoned out of her mind that he'd gotten it. Hell, even then, he hadn't really understood why she'd want people to treat her like a dirty slut. Maybe he'd made things worse by trying to "fix" her. By telling her she needed fixing. Sebastian had obviously found a way to deal with her . . . kink. Without making her feel guilty about it.

He was a good man. Ford was happy Jami had hooked up with him. But whatever trouble she was in, she didn't want Sebastian to know about it.

And Ford had a feeling he knew why.

****

The French doors hit the walls outside the dining room. Glass cracked. Ford ignored his mother's gasp and glared at his father. "What have you done?"

His father set down his napkin, glancing apologetically at his two business associates before turning to Ford with hard, cold eyes. "If you have a problem, Ford, we will speak privately. After brunch. As you can see—"

"No," Ford said. "We're talking now."

"Please excuse me." His father's jaw hardened as he strode across the room, gesturing Ford out impatiently.

In the grand room, a short, dark skinned man in a crisp, grey suit approached his father. "Shall I entertain your guests while you deal with your son, sir?"

"Yes, I'd appreciate that, Patrick." His father waited until the man disappeared into the dining room. Then grabbed Ford's arm and shoved him against the wall. "You have some fucking nerve."

Ford wrenched free, fisting his hands by his sides so he wouldn't shove his father back. "What happened to your other assistant? Or should I even bother asking?"

"He became . . . obsessed with a small job I gave him. It was affecting his work, so I let him go." His father arched a brow. "You never liked Lee. I don't see why you'd care."

Skin crawling, Ford recalled the way Lee used to look at Jami. He used to think it was pathetic and disgusting because the man was old enough to be her father. But now it was fucking scary. "The other job was Jami, wasn't it? You told him to mess with her."

"A few pictures. Perhaps following her from time to time, scare her a little. You'll be pleased to know I've lost interest in her. There are far more effective ways to influence future games."

"I don't give a shit about the games. Jami's in trouble. Call Lee. Get him back here before he—"

His father laughed. "Now why would I do that?"

"Because I'm asking you to. Please." Ford swallowed his pride, the same way he always did when he asked his father for anything. The man seemed to enjoy seeing him reduced to begging. His eyes burned with tears of rage, of humiliation, as he spoke. "Don't take it out on her because I've failed you. I'll do anything. Just tell me what you want."

"I want a son I can be proud of. But you'll never be that." His father smirked. "I supposed it doesn't matter, since you aren't really my son."

A fucking punch in the face would have hurt less. *You're no fucking prize either, old man.*

"Roy!" His mother stood in the open doorway of the dining room, her hand over her mouth. "You don't mean that. You raised him. He's your son in every way that counts."

"Of course, my love." His father gave his mother a brisk, condescending look. "But that does not mean I must waste my time dealing with *his* little whore. Let's not neglect our guests. Ford is a big boy. He can take care of his own problems."

Straightening his dark blue suit jacket, his father returned to the dining room, dismissing them both. His mother came to Ford's side, her lips pressed together in a tight line as she fussed with his rumpled jacket.

"Lee still has one of your father's cars. Cort has a way to track it. Call him, he'll help you." She gave him a shaky smile. "She'll be okay, Ford. Lee is a weak, pathetic man. I never liked him either."

"No, you asked Dad to keep him away from you because he gave you the creeps. We have no idea what he's capable of."

"Oh, sweetie. You don't think he would . . ." His mother paled. She'd never dealt well with unpleasantness. Both he and his father tried to shield her from it as much as possible, but maybe they shouldn't have. Or, at least, *he* shouldn't have. Maybe being forced to face reality would have made her stronger. He could already tell she'd be popping meds and spending all day in bed because she couldn't deal with even the *thought* of something horrible happening.

But old habits were hard to change. "You're right about Cort, mom. I'm glad you reminded me. I'd forgotten. We'll find her before Lee does anything."

"Good. Please let me know when you do. This whole ordeal has my nerves shot." She clasped her hands over her chest. "Maybe I should see my doctor again. I don't think the medication is working. You have no idea how difficult it's been lately with your father so stressed about that team! I'm sure that's why he was so cruel."

"Yeah. I'm sure." Ford kissed her cheek. "I have to go, Mom.

But I promise, I'll call."

"Yes, yes you should go." Her hand fluttered up to her throat. "This is dreadful. She's such a sweet girl."

On the way to his car, Ford called Cort, who quickly tracked down Lee's car. He waited on the line while Cort drove to the spot where Lee was parked.

Cort laughed, the wind around him making the sound staticky as he got out of his car. "What a moron. The cops are watching the motel where your girl's staying. He's a block over, sitting in his car, puffing away and jerking off. Sick freak."

"The cops haven't noticed?" Ford frowned as he leaned against the open door of his car, feeling a bit better knowing Jami was okay, but uneasy knowing Lee was so close. "How many are there?"

"Just one. But he's on the ball. He watched me pull over across the street. I'm going into a café so I don't look suspicious."

"Good idea." Ford got into his car and started it up. "Where are you? I'm on my way."

After getting directions, Ford hung up. He put in his Bluetooth and called Jami, figuring if he told her he was coming, she could tell the cop to let him in. As much as he trusted Cort to watch out for her, he wouldn't feel comfortable until he saw for himself that she was okay. But she didn't pick up.

His phone rang. Cort. He answered. "What?"

"She just got into her car after talking to the cop. She went one way, the cop went the other."

"And Lee?"

"He's following her. But so am I. We're on the Macdonald Bridge, heading toward Halifax."

"Don't let her out of your sight."

"I won't . . . fuck! Where the hell is she going? Hold on, she's speeding up . . . I think she spotted him."

"What's going on, Cort?" Ford pressed his foot hard on the gas, hoping he could cut the ten minute drive into five. "Talk to me, man!"

"She changed directions at the last second, turned onto the 103! I think she's trying to lose him!"

From what Akira had said, Jami planned to go to her

grandmother's. But Ford knew she wouldn't lead Lee to her grandmother's place. She probably wasn't even thinking of herself now. She probably wanted to keep Lee away from the people she loved, which is why she hadn't told Sebastian about any of this. The threat to him might have been more direct, but she was probably assuming the worst.

He couldn't blame her. He was too.

"I just crossed the bridge," Ford said. "Try to catch up with her. She'll feel safer if she sees you. She always liked you."

"Yeah, I liked her too. Just not as much as Lee apparently. What the fuck were you doing sharing that girl, kid?"

"Ruining her life, apparently." Ford pulled onto the 103, speeding up even more as he hit a long stretch relatively free of cars. "Fuck, I can't see you guys. How fast is she going?"

"Way too fast. He's catching up with her. There's no way she can get away from him in that crappy car of hers. I'm gonna try to cut him off."

"Don't! Cort, what if he—"

Screeching tires. Crunching metal.

The phone went dead.

His warning, like everything else he'd done, was too late.

Chapter Twenty Four

Sunlight pierced through the shattered windshield. A jarring pain tore at Jami's side, throbbed in her cheek, her nose. Warmth oozed down the side of her face as she lifted her head away from the cracked driver's side window. She felt around for the door handle, hissing in a breath as her hand spasmed. Something was wrong with her arm.

Worry about that later. Just get out.

She used her other hand to open the door, stepped onto the road, and took a few deep breaths of muggy air to clear her head. She'd swerved into the guardrail as the two cars behind had collided, trying to avoid being hit as well. The sun blinded her as she tried to make out the other drivers.

One had climbed out of his car. Was coming toward her.

Lee.

Choking out a strangled scream, she lurched past the guardrail, stumbling into the ditch as the soles of her boots slipped on loose earth. Small, jagged rocks grated her hands as she half crawled up the other side of the ditch. The long stretch of grass looked peaceful. Empty. There was no sign of a house, just a gravel road a few yards away that seemed to go on forever.

An engine roared in the distance, coming closer. She straightened, screamed, waved her arms. A sleek sports car sped by. If the driver hadn't noticed the wreck, they wouldn't see her out here. Maybe she could flag down help from the street—no, that would make it easier for Lee to get to her.

So she ran, hoping to at least reach the trees so she could hide. Use her phone. *Something.*

Everything hurt as she pushed herself to go faster. A jarring pain in one calf forced her to limp. She couldn't keep up this pace for long. And the sound of Lee's harsh panting was getting closer.

He mumbled something as he chased her. Her guts twisted as she made out the words.

"My whore."

He was too close. Each breath tore through her side. She

couldn't outrun him.

Stopping short, she spun fast, dodging to the left as he lunged at her. Keeping just out of reach, she grabbed a palm-sized rock and whipped it at him.

The rock bounced off his shoulder. He didn't even blink. His pudgy face, slick with sweat, glowing red from the run, changed into a mask of hunger and rage. He'd always been a pig, disgusting, but harmless. He wasn't anymore. Something had shifted, making him wild, more like a boar who'd charge until he gored her.

"Stay away from me, Lee! Ford will kill you if he finds out!"

"My turn. It's my turn, you little whore." Lee licked his thick lips and made a grab for her. "He let everyone else have you, but not me. It doesn't matter. You're mine now."

"Fuck you!" She jerked away. "Ford didn't 'let' anyone have me! It was my choice! I never wanted you!"

"I know who you're with—what he does. You don't want choices." Lee circled her, smacking away the next rock she threw like a bug. "I'm not giving you any."

Jami screamed as he barreled toward her. She reached down, clawing at a bigger rock, jarring it loose just as he knocked her to the ground. She swung hard. The rock hit his face with a meaty *thunk*. He dropped on top of her, his weight pinning her legs, his blood dripping onto her face as he lifted his head. She fought to drag herself out from under him as his hand slid over her stomach, under her shirt. His lip pressed against her cheek, slimy and wet.

She stared into his wild eyes. At his face, a mask of blood spilling from where the rock had smashed into his temple. He fumbled with the button of her jeans. She went perfectly still.

He leered at her, saliva dripping over his bottom lip. "That's right. Don't fight. I'll make it good for you."

As he shifted his weight to tug down her jeans, she twisted and jammed her fingers into his eyes.

He let out a hoarse scream. Rose up on his knees, covered his face with his hands.

Crack!

Lee toppled over sideways. Cort stood over him, a blood-smeared bat in his hand. He tossed it aside and hauled Lee off of

Jami, nodding toward the road as a car pulled up. "Ford's here. Let him take care of you while I deal with this fucker."

Jami scrambled backward as Cort pulled out a gun and pressed the barrel to the back of Lee's head. Tremors ran through her as his finger touched the trigger.

"Cort, don't!" Ford shouted, running toward them. "I'm not letting you go to jail for this piece of shit."

"Too late," Cord said, his tone sickeningly calm as he nudged Lee with his foot, then bent down to check his pulse. "He's dead."

A wash of cold went over Jami. She whimpered as a hand closed around her arm, her vision flicking in and out of darkness as the grip tightened. *He's not dead! He's not! You can't stop him!*

"Jami, look at me," Ford said, cupping her cheeks in his hands, his hold, solid and familiar, dragging her back to reality. "You're okay. Come on, I'll get you out of here."

"I want Sebastian." Jami leaned against Ford and sobbed. "But . . . don't let Lee . . . don't let Lee hurt him! Please!"

"I won't. I swear it, baby."

"Give me a head start before you let her report this, all right?" Cort grunted. "Not too long, obviously. She needs a hospital."

"So do you. Fuck, Cort, you were helping her. If you'd shot him, then there'd be a problem, but—"

"I'm not taking any chances."

"Fine. Do you need me to drive you somewhere?"

"No. I'll get my brother to come pick me up. I'll be long gone before anyone finds the body."

He's not dead. Jami dug in her heels as Ford led her to his car. Before she could look back to make sure Lee hadn't gotten back up, Ford turned her to face him.

"You don't need to see him, Jami. I swear to you, he's dead. He can't hurt you anymore."

"You don't know. You can't be sure . . ." Jami swallowed, wanting to trust Ford. He'd come for her. And Cort . . . "Cort, I need to thank him. He saved me. I don't know why—"

"Because you're worth saving, Jami."

Her high-pitched laugh pierced her skull. "No. I did this. You know I did. We need to call the police. I need to tell them—"

"We'll call them." Ford sighed as he opened the passenger side door for her. "After we get you to the hospital. They should . . ." His throat worked as he looked down at her still undone jeans. "He didn't . . ."

Jami blinked at the open zipper. The missing button. Her skin crawled and she could almost feel Lee, touching her. Wanting to . . . *But he didn't.* She shook her head. "No. Cort stopped him. I'm just a little roughed up. I don't need to go to the hospital. I need a shower. Can I go to your place and—"

"The cops might want evidence."

Pulling on her seat belt, Jami shook her head. "What evidence? He didn't *do* anything. Cort made sure of that. He needs a head start, right? He'll have plenty if I take a shower."

"Jami—"

"No! You don't get to tell me what to do, Ford. You knew something was going on, didn't you?" He must have. Her brow furrowed as she though over how convenient it was that he and Cort had gotten here, just in time. "That's why Cort showed up—why you came so fast. If you'd said something, none of this would have happened. But you didn't." She rubbed her arm. It had gone completely numb. The rest of her quickly followed. "Not that it matters. I made him like that. With all the things he watched me do . . ."

Ford shook his head. "Stop talking like that. You know it's not true."

"I don't care what's true. I just want a shower. Please let me take a shower. That's all I want."

"All right. If it will make you feel better, you can take a shower." Ford's knuckles went white as he tightened his grip on the steering wheel. "You let me know how you want to handle this."

A lifeless laugh left her as she leaned her head back on the headrest. "I don't."

* * * *

Sebastian ground his teeth as he ran to his car, parked in front of Jami's apartment. His blood pumped hard and fast in his veins, urging him to keep moving, to find something, someone, to fight. But who? What? He'd been given nothing. The day had begun better than any over the past week, but after finding Jami gone from his bed...

He slammed the door to the car and started the engine. "Did you hear anything?"

Luke threw his phone onto the dashboard. "Bower said she went to her grandmother's. She should be there by now, but her dad called and she isn't. He's pretty worried."

"Someone broke into her apartment." Icy claws sliced down Sebastian's spine. "Likely the same person who took those pictures. There were other things as well, things she told no one."

"Maybe she just didn't want to talk about it."

Sebastian let out a bitter laugh. "*That* does not surprise me. We talk very little in this relationship. I have already regretted it more than once."

Luke winced. "Yeah... well, that's gonna change."

"Yes. It is." Sebastian's phone rang. He pushed the speaker button. "Hello?"

Ford's voice sounded worn, as though he'd been shouting. "Sebastian, I have Jami. You need to come here right away. Some shit went down, and I know she didn't tell you anything—she was scared for you." He paused. "She needs you. She locked herself in the bathroom. I think she's hurt. She won't—"

"Give me your address."

After getting directions, Sebastian dropped the phone aside without ending the call. The tires squealed as he jammed his foot down on the gas. He pulled up in front of Ford's moments later and left the car without bothering to shut it off or lock the door. Luke caught up with Sebastian as he pounded his fist on the door, holding out the car keys, then stuffing them in his own pocket when Sebastian didn't take them. As soon as Ford opened the door, Sebastian pushed past him.

"He didn't do much to her—Cort got to her in time. But she wrecked her car," Ford said, a step behind him. "I was gonna take her to the hospital, but she didn't want to go."

'Wrecked her car'. Sebastian's steps faltered. A jagged blade of fear sliced deep into his guts. "How badly is she hurt?"

"I. Don't. Know." Ford scowled. "I'm not a fucking doctor."

"Then why didn't you make her see one?" Luke asked, enunciating each word as though speaking to someone mentally challenged.

"I've never been able to make Jami do anything. I'd figure you two would be able to control her. Isn't she your goddamn sub?"

Sebastian turned quickly and grabbed Luke before he could go after Ford.

"You fucking asshole!" Luke went wild, struggling to free himself, looking like he wanted to beat Ford to a bloody pulp. "You think we knew this would happen?"

"Maybe you would have, if you'd done more than fuck her!"

"I love her! More than you ever did! It's your fault she was on drugs! Was it one of your sick friends that went after her?"

Ford moved close to Luke, as though daring him to take a swing. He lowered his voice, but practically spat out every word. "I wouldn't exactly call him a friend. I probably should have given her a heads up, though. I knew my father had sicced someone on her."

Sebastian released Luke. Grabbed Ford by the throat and lifted him up to slam him against the wall. He swung his fist, redirecting at the last second to hit the wall by Ford's head. "Where. Is. She?"

"In there." Ford rasped, struggling to nod toward the door at the end of the hall.

After dropping Ford, Sebastian crossed the hall in long strides, forcing himself to calm with each one. He tapped on the door and spoke softly. "Let me in, *mi cielo*."

The door creaked open. Jami threw herself into his arms and sobbed. Blood matted her hair, crusted on her cheek. Her eyes were glassy as she tipped her head back. "You're here. You're okay. I thought he'd gotten to you. I tried to keep him away."

He kissed her forehead. Her skin was cold. "I'm here."

"I need to take a shower. I'm so dirty. He wanted me because I'm dirty." She tore at her shirt with one hand, the other hanging limp at her side. "Help me get this off. I can't. I need to be clean, but I can't take this off!"

"Shh." Sebastian stroked her hair, carefully pressing her head against his chest. "You are not dirty."

"I am! I am, and you shouldn't touch me!"

"Come then. Come and we will clean you." He picked her up and sank to the floor, holding her as he glanced up at Luke. "Call an ambulance."

"No! I don't want to go to the hospital!" Jami trembled in his arms. "They'll see! They'll know how disgusting I am!"

"No, *mi cielo*. The will only see my beautiful *gatita*. But he hurt you . . ." Sebastian's voice caught. *What did he do to you?* Luke held his cell phone to his ear with his shoulder as he found a face cloth in a drawer by the sink and wet it with warm water.

"He didn't hurt me. He . . . he kissed me. Touched me."

The air around them became thick. Sebastian tried to keep his hand steady as he took the cloth from Luke and gently cleaned the blood from Jami's cheek. "He never will again."

"No. No, he won't. He's dead." Jami sobbed. "They said he's dead! I don't believe them!"

"Jami . . ." Sebastian dabbed at her lips with the cloth, wiped it down her throat, wishing he knew where the *cabron* had touched her so he could wash away any traced of him for her. But he didn't know if she was more traumatized by whatever had been done to her, or because she was afraid it wasn't over. "He's gone. And you were so very brave. You stopped him from taking you away from me."

"I won't let him, Sebastian." She latched onto his wrist. Her eyes turned fierce. "And I won't let him take you away from me. Not like he took . . . oh god, Sebastian! He took Peanut! You trusted me to take care of him!"

"You did all you could, Jami." Sebastian couldn't think of the bird. He would feel the loss in time, but at the moment, all he could think of was doing his best to hold Jami together as she fell apart in front of him. He swallowed hard as he held her tight against his chest, as he should have the night before. If he had, none of this would have happened. "I will stay with you, but promise me you will tell the doctors everything. I hope you will tell me—"

"I wanted to tell you, but I couldn't ruin things for you. You were finally happy." Her face crumpled. Tears wet her lashes and spilled down her cheeks. "But I did anyway, didn't I?"

"No." He took her good hand as he heard Ford letting the EMTs in. "Nothing is ruined, Jami. Luke is with us. You are safe. We will work on everything else together."

Jami nodded, but as soon as the EMTs approached her, she shrank away, refusing to let the women touch her.

"Be still, *mi cielo.*" Sebastian held her gaze as he slid his hand around the back of her neck, using just enough pressure to hold her attention. "You will let them take care of you."

"Yes, *mi Rey*. But . . . where's Luke?" Jami whispered, and for a moment, Sebastian wasn't sure he should have mentioned Luke at all. But then she looked past him, reaching out with her good arm as the medic checked the other. A laugh broke through a sob as Luke brought her fingers to his lips. "You dickhead. If I wasn't so happy to see you, I'd hit you."

"I said you could if you needed to." Luke pressed so close to Sebastian's side that he could feel the young man shaking. But his tone was steady and Sebastian felt his chest swell with pride. "You might need to be pieced back together first though, boo. Does it hurt?"

"Does what hurt?" Jami smiled at Luke, and Sebastian did his best not to look down at her arm. By the lump pressing against her flesh, he knew it was broken, but he didn't want to draw any attention to it if she was too far gone to feel the pain.

I don't want him to be dead. Sebastian stared at the wall, blinking as tears of rage blinded him. *However he died, it was too quick. Too easy. I would have made him suffer.*

"She's in shock," the EMT said quietly. "The man who called mentioned an accident. How long ago was this?"

Sebastian turned to Ford, who stood just outside the door.

Ford cleared his throat. "About forty-five minutes ago."

To Sebastian, it seemed much too long. But the EMT simply nodded. "Okay. She should be fine until we get her to a doctor. Sweetie, we're going to put you on the stretcher now. Try to relax. Take deep breaths. We need to get your pulse down."

"I can walk," Jami said, tightly.

"I'd rather you not." The EMT frowned. "You shouldn't have been moved after the crash. Any internal damage could have been made worse."

"I feel fine. I—"

"Jami." Sebastian lips drew into a firm line as she peered up at him with big eyes that begged him not to make her go. He shook his head and helped the EMT ease her onto the stretcher. He held her hand as a blanket was spread over her. She let them check her blood pressure, put in an IV, all without a whisper of protest. He managed a smile as she looked away from the needle in her wrist. "That's my girl. You do not need to fight anymore. I will stay with you."

"Luke, too?"

"I'm afraid only one of them can come with you," the EMT said.

Luke grinned and whispered something in Jami's ear that made her smile. After she nodded, he walked away, twirling Sebastian's car keys around his finger. He had put on a decent show of taking things in stride, but once Jami was strapped down and brought outside to the ambulance, Sebastian caught sight of Luke in his car, head bowed, shoulders hunched, shuddering as if it had all suddenly become too much.

Sebastian almost went to him, to take his keys back, to force Luke to call a taxi rather than risk the roads. But then Luke tipped his head back and rubbed his face. Took hold of the steering wheel. He met Sebastian's eyes. Inclined his head as though to say "Go on."

The ambulance doors closed. Sebastian clasped Jami's cold hand in his, stroking circles in her palm with his thumb as he watched her press her eyes shut and focus on breathing as the EMT had instructed. Only once the ambulance pulled to a stop did she open her eyes, whimpering as Sebastian moved away to let the EMTs pass with the stretcher. "Don't go."

"I will be here, *mi cielo*." Sebastian nodded his thanks to the EMT who stepped aside to let him take her small hand in his once again. "It will be a long time before I let you out of my sight."

Chapter Twenty Five

"Ingerslov will probably be in nets on Tuesday."

"You can't be serious! They're not going to let you play? Idiots!" Luke bent over laughing as Bower rolled his eyes. He sobered up at Silver's dirty look and cleared his throat. Okay, so maybe it wasn't that funny. But if he didn't laugh, he was going to fucking scream. And while he was in Silver's room, he had to pretend he was okay. He cocked his head and glanced over at Bower. "You'll be good for next season, though, right?"

"Depending on how the surgery goes . . ." Bower shrugged, his eyes never leaving Silver's basketball-sized belly as they sat by her hospital bed, trying to use talk about the game to distract them all. And failing. "The doctor said best-case scenario, six months. Then rehabilitation. Dean's bringing someone up from the minors."

"We're gonna suck without you."

"You'll manage."

Luke nodded slowly. He had a feeling the whole thing with Silver and the baby had changed Bower's priorities. Which he understood way more than he would have a month ago. The game on Tuesday—the biggest one in Luke's career so far—just didn't seem all that important. Normally, he'd be getting plenty of rest, working out like crazy, watching past games every chance he got to find ways to fix his own fuckups and take advantage of the other team's . . .

I should still be doing that.

But it had been nearly impossible to leave Jami's hospital room. He'd still be there now if Seb hadn't told him to get out and stretch his legs. This late at night, Jami technically shouldn't have more than one visitor, but her doctor had allowed them both to stay since it kept her calm.

When Richter had passed him in the hall on the way to Jami's room and told him Bower and Silver were still awake, Luke had decided to stop in for a visit. He got to feel the baby kick, which gave him something good to tell Jami when he went back to her. Maybe she'd stop thinking about what that sick freak, Lee, had almost done to her. Maybe she'd stop finding ways to blame herself.

"You really need to get some sleep, Carter," Bower said, grinning when Luke arched a brow at him pointedly. "Yeah, yeah, so do I. I just hate hospitals. Dean's already threatened to have the doctor give me something to knock me out. You better watch it or he'll do the same to you."

"No need. I'll crash in Jami's room for a bit. Maybe I can convince Seb to get some sleep too."

"That's a good idea. You guys need each other right now."

"This whole thing... it doesn't weird you out?"

"What, you and Ramos? Fuck, no! He's a great guy. I didn't see it when I thought he was playing Jami, but it's obviously not like that."

"But he's a *guy*." Luke wasn't sure why he felt the need to point that out. Did he want Bower to have a problem with it?

Bower's brow furrowed as he studied Luke's face. "It took you a while to accept how you feel about him, kid, I get that. But that doesn't mean everyone's going to have a hard time with it. Not the people who matter."

"I'm moving in with him."

"Damn. Give Ramos my condolences."

Luke laughed, gave Bower the finger, then bent down to hug Silver. *Very* carefully. "Keep an eye on this dumb lug for me, 'kay, sweetie?"

"I will." Silver patted his cheek. "And you take care of Jami. And Sebastian. You have no idea how lucky you are to have them."

"Believe me." Luke straightened, giving Bower a one-armed hug before heading for the door. "I know *exactly* how lucky I am. And I don't plan to ever forget it again."

The hall was quiet as Luke made his way back to Jami's room. The nurse at the desk glanced up from her papers as he passed, nodded, and moved on to the next clipboard. An orderly pushed an old man in a wheelchair into the private room across from Jami's. Another man came out of the room with a mop and bucket. The scent of disinfectant filled the air.

As quietly as possible, Luke slipped into Jami's room, lips curving a little when he saw Sebastian, on the chair transformed to a very small bed, by the large window, fast asleep. His body was way too big for the bed, but lying on his side, his head pillowed on his arm, he seemed comfortable enough.

Strands of loose, dark hair spread across Seb's face, reaching the edge of the bed, as though Jami had been stroking it before he passed out. There was some tension in the big man's jaw, shadows under his closed eyes. A lot of people looked vulnerable while sleeping, but not Seb. Tonight he looked physically and emotionally beaten.

Luke had done that to him. Not alone, but it wouldn't happen again.

A soft, panicked sound from the bed snapped Luke's gaze to Jami. She sat up straight, pressing her fist to her lips. Her broken arm in its blue cast slipped off the pile of pillows propping it up. She winced, then glanced over at Seb.

"Hey." Luke stepped silently up to the other side of the bed, adjusting the pillows and sweeping Seb's hair aside so Jami wouldn't pull it and wake him up. He had a feeling she was doing her best not to bother him. He gently positioned her arm, then cupped her cheek in his hand. "You okay, boo?"

"Shh." Jami touched her finger to his lips. She smiled shakily as she looked him over. "I might have to kill you if you wake him up."

Luke grinned. "You're such a flirt."

"Luke, please. I'm serious. I've never seen him this stressed out. Not that you'd noticed."

"I noticed. But he was trying to hide it, so I let him."

"Oh, *that's* helpful."

"Jami, what would be helpful is neither of us giving him more stress." Luke sighed, lifting himself up to sit beside her on the bed. "If he finds out you were awake, having another meltdown, and didn't wake him up, he's going to be mad. He'll be less mad if he knows I made you feel all better."

"There's no way he'll sleep through you making me 'feel better.'" Jami sniffed and pulled the stuffed puppy he'd swung by Seb's to pick up for her from under the sheets. She used an ear to dry her cheeks. "And I can honestly say I'm not in the mood."

"Good. Neither am I." He snorted at her doubtful look. "It

happens. 'Specially when my girl won't tell me how she's doing. So not sexy."

"I'm doing fine." Jami hugged the stuffy. "The doctor only had to sedate me once."

"I know. I was here." He ran her fingers through her hair, tugging lightly when she avoided his gaze. "But that doesn't explain why you were crying."

"I wasn't—"

"Boo, your ass ain't broken. Lie to me again. I swear you won't enjoy being pulled over my knee." He added as she wet her lips with her tongue. "Try the truth. I swear, it won't hurt."

"That's rich, coming from you." She buried her face in fake fur. "You gonna tell me you've finally embraced the truth?"

"About what? About the fact that I love you? That I love Seb? Yeah, I've embraced it. So how 'bout you stop changing the subject?"

"I had a nightmare. Lee wasn't really dead. He came back." She shivered, biting her bottom lip hard enough to draw blood. "Ford and Cort were there, but they were too busy talking about how to kill him to notice he was . . . and you and Sebastian were running toward me, but you were too far away." She pressed her eyes shut. Swallowed hard. Swiped impatiently at the few tears that spilled down her cheeks. "I almost woke Sebastian up when I realized it was a dream, but he needs his sleep."

"Why did you want to wake him up, Jami?" Luke didn't wait for her to answer. He already knew. "You need to feel that he's real. That he's really here."

She let out an empty laugh. "Yeah. Selfish, right?"

"I don't think so." He curved his arm behind her back, easing her down to lie with her head on his shoulder. "But I'm awake. I'm here. Think I can stand in until he's gotten some rest?"

Sighing, she snuggled close as she could without shifting her broken arm. "You're not a stand-in for him, stud. But I need to feel you're real too. Can you just talk to me? Maybe I'll hear your voice instead of . . ."

Fresh tears dampened his T-shirt. Luke clenched his jaw, wishing Cort had left something of Lee for him. He took a deep breath, speaking softly, even though, looking past Jami, he could see Seb's eyes were open. "It's a good thing you hate hockey. Without Bower, I don't see us making it to the next round. I was thinking before that it doesn't bug me as much as it should—"

"Why?"

"Because I've finally got more than the game." He smiled. "I'm not saying getting my hands on the Cup wouldn't be sweet, but for the first time, summer ain't gonna be time to kill before the next season. We'll do stuff. Like visit my mom. Maybe take a trip somewhere. I was thinking of talking Seb into bringing us to Spain."

"I'd like that, but . . . don't give up, Luke. I don't hate the game when you're playing." She tipped her head back, wrinkling her nose. "You've at least gotta take out the Sabres."

"We don't have a goalie."

"Fuck off." She scowled at him. "Ingerslov isn't *that* bad. And the guy my dad is bringing up from the minors seems solid. Promise me you'll win on Tuesday."

"It means that much to you?" He inhaled as she nodded, not sure he should make a promise he probably couldn't keep. But then he thought about it. It wasn't impossible. They were one game away from sweeping the Sabres. Maybe he could do it. For her. "All right. I promise."

For the next hour or so, the girl who hated hockey had him talking strategy, challenging him with keen observations even as she drifted into dreamland. Her last words mumbled words had him grinning at Seb.

"Nelson's jealous, huh?" He lowered his voice. "Maybe you should invite him to your next party."

Seb pushed up, his hair falling sleekly over half his face as he leaned over to kiss the back of Jami's pale hand, right below the blue fiberglass cast. "It will be a long time before I host another party."

Luke chewed on the inside of his cheek and decided not to comment on that. Besides, he was stuck on the promise. "You really think we can pull it off—winning on Tuesday?"

"Yes." Seb fixed Luke with a hard look. "Jami does not ask much of us. Losing is not an option."

"When is losing ever an option?"

Chuckling softly, Seb took Luke's hand and squeezed hard. "That is a very good question, *semental*."

Nodding quickly, Luke looked down at his hand in Seb's. The air in the room was hot, making it hard to breathe. Making his eyes sting. He forced a laugh. "I promised her. I'm gonna make it happen. I won't lose . . ." He stared up at the ceiling, swallowing past the lump in his throat. Jami was sleeping. There was no one else around. Just Seb. And he would understand. "We almost lost her. I can't— I—"

Moving quietly, Seb came around the bed. He pulled Luke up and into his arms, tightening his grip when Luke stiffened. "It's all right."

"I know. She's tough." Luke's clenched jaw was the only thing that kept a sob from following the words. She shouldn't have had to be tough. She shouldn't have been out there alone.

One of the guys on the team had swung by the wreck and sent pictures of Jami's car. Luke didn't think he'd ever get that image out of his head. Every time he closed his eyes, he saw her climbing out of the car, hurt. Afraid. And that man chasing her, wanting to . . .

"Let go, Luke." Seb whispered in his ear, still holding him close. "You were strong when she needed you to be, but now you need to let go."

A rough sound tore out of Luke's chest. Then another sob. He pressed his face against Seb's chest, accepting his strength, his support, the way he wished Jami had done with them.

And he let go.

* * * *

The cool draft in the hospital corridor wisped around Jami's bare legs as she left her first meeting with the therapist she would be seeing for the next few weeks, if not longer. Goose bumps covered every inch of her, and she couldn't help tensing up every time a man passed. None of them looked like Lee, but for some reason, they all had his eyes. An elderly man smiled at her, and her blood ran cold. She quickened her pace. She'd asked Sebastian, Luke, and her father to meet her back at her room, but now she kinda wished she'd asked them to stay.

Off to the left, two nurses in green scrubs pushed through swinging doors, chatting and laughing. Jami ducked her head as they passed. Rehashing everything made her feel raw, exposed, as if any stranger could look at her and know exactly what had happened to her. And why.

"It is not your fault that man stalked you, Jami," The therapist had said in a firm, no-nonsense tone at the end of the meeting. *"He may have made you feel that way, but it is not your fault."*

Right. Easy to say it wasn't Jami's fault when she didn't know all the details. When she didn't know the things Jami had done with Lee right there, watching . . .

Get a grip, Jami.

But it was too late. She could already hear the song, playing over and over in her head, the lyrics like tiny maggots, crawling all over her skin.

I'll be watching you. I'll be watching you. I'll be—

Jami reached out to press the button for the elevator. Her hand was shaking so hard, she pulled it back and stuffed it in her pocket before someone noticed and asked her what was wrong. She couldn't tell just anyone. Her fingertips brushed over her cell phone, and she pulled it out without thinking. Found Sebastian's number and sent him a text.

"I need you."

Her throat locked as she leaned against the wall. How freakin' pathetic. All she had to do was get on the elevator and go up to her room. But she couldn't seem to make herself move. Thinking of Sebastian was the only thing that kept that song out of her head.

The phone vibrated in her hand.

Seb: "Where are you?"

Before she had a chance to change her mind, she replied. *Right outside the office.*

Moments later he was stepping off the elevator, pulling her into his arms as she shook her head, opening and closing her mouth, not sure what she wanted to say. Part of her wanted to explain that he shouldn't be touching her. Because . . .

"I am a whore, and I should have told her, but I couldn't." She fisted her hands into the front of his white shirt even while trying to twist out of his arms. "I have to tell you though. It's not just words. The things I did—"

"*Mi cielo*, stop." Sebastian gently pried her fingers from his shirt, then slid a hand up to the nape of her neck. The slight pressure steadied her, but she gasped in air as though she'd been running. Away from him. Toward him. She wasn't sure which. He inhaled slowly, his eyes locked with hers. "Breathe with me. Slowly."

She matched his breaths, feeling calm flow over her like a cool, silk sheet. Tears clung to her lashes, and she tried to blink them away.

"Very good." Sebastian kissed her forehead. "Now, tell me what you could not tell her."

A tear ran down her cheek. She quickly wiped it away. "I'm a whore. A dirty, disgusting whore."

"No. And I do not appreciate you saying such things about my *gatita*." He gave her a hard look, then caught another teardrop on his finger, shaking his head when she tried to turn away from him to hide her tears. "You have every right to cry, Jami. Don't try to hide it." His throat worked as he swallowed. "I've cried for what was done to you. Because I couldn't protect you."

"I wouldn't have needed protecting if I hadn't been such a whore!" She covered her trembling lips with her hand, glancing up and down the hall to make sure no one had heard her. Speaking quietly, she brought her hand to his chest. "I know you love me, but I don't think you understand what I did. He watched different men fuck me. He had every reason to believe he'd get his turn."

"So you're of the mind that every women dressed provocatively in a bar is asking for it?"

"It's not the same. Those women aren't letting different men use them."

"Listen to what you just said, Jami. 'Letting.' It was your choice to be with those men. Just as it is your choice to be with Luke and me." He brushed his hand over her hair. "Two men who respect you, who understand your needs, and don't think any less of you for them."

"I don't know . . ." She leaned against him, sighing as more tears spilled. "I don't know what I need anymore."

"You said you needed me, *mi cielo*." He hugged her tight, then bent down to kiss her. "I'm here."

"But what about the other stuff? Like the party and—"

"The party is over, and the only thing I regret from that is not joining you in bed that night." His finger covered her lips before she could object. "As for 'the other stuff,' our relationship is more than ropes and whips and games. I would love you without any of it."

"Why? I'm a wreck, Sebastian. I have no plans anymore—I obviously can't be an Ice Girl." Moving away from him, she held up her broken arm. The cast wasn't all that heavy, but all the things she couldn't do because of it made it feel huge. She couldn't even wash with anything other than a cloth because of the stupid thing. And she was so dirty . . . "You deserve someone decent. Clean—"

Sebastian's jaw ticked. He drew her closer to the elevator and pressed the button to call it. "There are many reasons why I love you, *gatita*, and I will list them all, from your kindness, to your playfulness, while I do something very important."

She blinked up at him as he guided her into the elevator. "What?"

"Find a way to make you feel clean, even if only physically for now. And perhaps if I tell you often enough that. You." He framed his hand under her jaw and she closed her eyes as he leaned in. He kissed her eyelids. "Are." He kissed the tip of her nose. "Not." His lips brushed softly over hers as he whispered, "Dirty." His lips slanted over hers and she moaned as he ravished her mouth, stealing her breath. He smiled against her lips when the elevator stopped. "You'll eventually believe me."

"But . . ." Tonguing her swollen bottom lip, she moved with him onto the floor of her hospital room, loving the idea of him helping her but not sure how he could. A long, hot shower, with his hands all over her, soaping her up, might do the trick. Her cheeks heated as her father came out of the room down the hall. "My dad's here. And I can't shower yet."

"Your father really should go spend time with Silver." Sebastian's hot breath on the back of her neck made all the tiny hairs rise. "And I do believe a sponge bath would be safe."

Chapter Twenty Six

Dean held the passenger side door open for Jami, struggling not to help her more than necessary as she eased into the seat. She sighed when he did up her seat belt, but didn't complain. Her friend, Akira, climbed into the backseat, then leaned between the seats to continue the argument they'd had going since Jami was released.

"You are not taking the futon. Not until you're out of that cast."

Jami groaned. "Akira, I'm not kicking you out of your own bed."

"It's not up for discussion." Akira smirked. "You said you'd do *anything* to make up for scaring me so much."

"I can't believe you're going to use that against me for our sleeping arrangements!"

"Sweetie, I'm just getting started. Just wait until you *dare* try to clean or cook. You might as well get used to it." Akira sat back, clicked her seat belt in place, then grinned at Dean through the rearview mirror. "Don't worry, sir. I'll take good care of your daughter."

Chuckling, Dean inclined his head. "I believe you will."

At first, Dean hadn't been crazy about the idea. He wanted Jami home with him, where he could watch over her every minute of every day. Every cut and bruise on her face, every haunted look in her eyes, every wince, had his heart so battered it felt like someone had bludgeoned his chest with a steel pipe. But Jami turned him down with the same stubborn determination she showed when Ramos had made the same offer. Ramos would have been Dean's second choice, at least he had the strength and motivation to keep her safe, but Jami had pointed out that she didn't need protection anymore. And she refused to let what had happened change her life so drastically.

But she couldn't return to her apartment. Not even to pack. Ramos and Carter were there now with a truck, moving most of her things into storage. They would meet her at Akira's with clothes and whatever she couldn't live without. The list she'd given them had been short. Dean had a feeling she would have replaced it all, but she had her pride, and refused to use his money. Her savings were dwindling, but she already had a plan in motion. And had done the one thing he'd never thought she'd do.

She'd applied for a job at the Delgado Forum. After emailing her resume, she'd made it perfectly clear, before either he or Silver could offer a well-paying position in one of their offices, that she'd be working her way from the bottom up. And trying out again for the Ice Girls next season.

"Without anyone pulling strings for me this time," Jami had said, hugging Silver. *"I appreciate everything you've done for me, but I think I can do this on my own."*

Dean's lips curved as he drove them to Akira's place.

That's my girl.

Ramos and Carter were waiting for them outside the apartment when they arrived. Dean could see the effort it took for Ramos not to go to her when she waved everyone away and got out of the car by herself.

Carter hefted up a large box to his shoulder from the trunk of Ramos' car. "You sure you don't want to stay with us for a bit, boo?"

Jami sighed. "I'm sure."

"Akira's place is tiny."

"It's about the same size as my old place."

"Seb's got a bigger bed." Carter wiggled his eyebrows, then jumped when Akira strode up to him and punched him in the shoulder. "Hey! What was that for?"

"In front of her father?" Akira folded her arms over her chest. "Behave yourself."

"Or what?" Carter's eyes went wide as Ramos stepped up behind him and spoke quietly in his ear. "Damn, you guys are no fun. Richter knows his daughter—"

"*Niño*, be silent." Ramos glanced over as a car pulled up behind his. His eyes narrowed. "*Hijo de puta.*"

Son of a bitch. Dean didn't know much Spanish, but he knew that one. And couldn't agree more. He stepped in front of Jami as Ford emerged. "You've got some nerve showing your face here, Ford."

"What I'd like to know is how you found the place." Carter cracked his knuckles. Stepped forward. Then groaned as Ramos blocked him with an arm. "Come on. Just one? He wants it so fucking bad."

Ford raked his fingers through his hair. "Akira's address was on file. I figured Jami would come here."

"What gave you the idea that *you* should?" Ramos asked.

"I just wanted to bring Jami something." Ford opened the back door of his car and pulled out a cage covered with a black blanket. "I owe her something good after everything I've done."

Jami screeched, sobbed, and ran toward Ford. "Peanut?"

"Yeah, I found him at Lee's place. Along with—" Ford winced at Ramos' sharp look. "Never mind. I'm just happy I was able to bring him back to you."

"Thank you." Jami knelt and set the birdcage on the sidewalk. She flipped the blanket off, whispering, crying as the bird chirped at her. "Oh God, Ford." Her voice cracked. "Thank you so much."

Akira crouched down beside Jami, sticking her finger between the bars even as she peered up at Ford. She opened her mouth a few times, shook her head, then put her arm over Jami's shoulders. "I appreciate you bringing Peanut." She took a deep breath and dropped her gaze. "But please . . . don't come here again."

Ford took a step back, shoulders squared. He nodded slowly. "Got it. Want me to erase your number too?"

Keeping her eyes down, Akira cleared her throat and said softly, "Would you?"

"Consider it done." Ford glanced over at Dean. "I'd like to arrange a meeting after the next game. I have a few ideas I'd like to run by you."

"Do you?" Dean arched a brow. "Such as?"

"We're not selling to the Kingsleys."

Dean laughed. "I don't see how that changes anything. You *are* a Kingsley."

"Not anymore."

With that, Ford returned to his car. Sped away without looking back. Dean wished he'd seen the last of him, but unfortunately, besides being a partial owner in the team, he was family. Silver may have no interest in her brother now, but that could change. Oriana had been working hard on bringing her siblings together. She seemed desperate to see something good in Ford.

But maybe not after this. Dean could only hope.

Doesn't matter, either way. Dean smiled as he watched Ramos pull Jami to her feet while Carter picked up the cage. He may have had reservations about the relationship, but not anymore. *Ford's in her past. And it looks like he's going to stay there.*

* * * *

Jami sat at Akira's kitchen table, feeding Peanut apple pieces. She petted his soft blue feathers, cooing softly, happy tears sheening her eyes as she looked him over.

He's okay. She bit her bottom lip as he bumped his head against her hand. She'd been afraid that he'd be skittish after his ordeal. What if Lee had shaken his cage? Or yelled at him? But he sang softly, vying for attention like he always did. Like nothing had happened.

Across the kitchen, he father stood with Luke and Sebastian, gesturing with his beer as he argued with them on the best strategy to win the next game. Then he shocked her, setting down his beer and shifting the topic to her.

"The Spatz Theater in Halifax is putting on *Cats* next week," he said. "You should bring Jami."

"That is an excellent idea." Sebastian tipped his bottle to his lips, then paused. "There is a restaurant she rather enjoys. I plan to bring her again soon. Perhaps you and Bower would like to join us with Silver before the show?" He inclined his head to Akira. "You are welcome to come."

Akira grinned. "Sure. That way I can make sure you don't keep her out too late."

Frowning, Jami held her hand out so Peanut could hop onto Akira's palm, then went to stand beside Luke who was staring at Sebastian like he'd just sprouted another head. She snatched Luke's beer bottle and took a long swig before handing it back. "Umm . . . no offense, Dad, but we are so not going on a double date. That's just weird."

"Why?" Her father chuckled as he finished his beer. "Don't you think I should get to know the men who are with my daughter a little better?"

"Sure. We'll get together for the holidays or something," Jami said. "But we need some time alone."

"We will have that, *mi cielo*." Sebastian placed his beer on the counter. "Perhaps we can have coffee before then. Or lunch."

"Lunch?" Jami shook her head. "Okay, how about we talk about this after my dad leaves. I think you're getting at something, but I'm not sure what."

"My cue." Her father kissed her forehead, then headed for the door. "I'll see you boys at the rink tomorrow. And Ramos?" He grinned as Sebastian met his steady gaze. "You have my blessing."

"Thank you, sir." Sebastian shook her father's hand. Once her father was gone, he pulled out another beer. He offered it to her, his lips quirking as she continued to frown at him. "You were saying?"

"After the game tomorrow . . . can I spend the night?"

"No."

"Can you tell me why?"

"Certainly. You need time to heal." He uncapped the bottle. "And we need time to get to know one another better."

"You're punishing me." She grabbed the bottle from him, gulped down a few mouthfuls, then scowled. "Is it because I'm not staying with you?"

That's so not fair. She gave Luke a dirty look. *Lucky bastard.*

"Not at all. If you were, you, like Luke, would have your own room." He met Luke's startled look with a calm smile. "And you would be sleeping in your own bed. Every night."

"Huh?" Luke choked on his beer. Akira slapped his back, amusement lighting her eyes. He ignored her. "I'm with Jami. What are you getting at?"

Akira giggled as she carried Peanut back to his cage. "I'm going to set Peanut up in the bedroom."

Sebastian moved to the table. Pulled out a chair. Waited until both Luke and Jami joined him before he spoke. "Things have progressed much too quickly between us. We have been given the opportunity to start over. And we shall."

"So . . ." Jami took a deep breath. "Nothing?"

"Nothing." Sebastian put his hand over hers. His lips hardened as she jerked away from him. "I will not make love to you until you feel comfortable speaking to me. About anything. It may take some time, but I am willing to wait."

"That's a bit drastic, don't you think?" Luke chewed his bottom lip, his gaze slipping down to her cast resting on her lap. "Okay, I can kinda see why, but—"

"No buts. I will not risk something like this happening again." Sebastian's chair scraped across the tiles as he stood. "I expect the two of you to show some restraint as well, but I cannot dictate what you do. I simply hope you understand why I am doing this."

"What happened to me shouldn't change anything!" Jami turned to Luke, expecting him to support her. But he looked away. "I didn't tell you because I was afraid for you! Not because I can't talk to you!"

"*Mi cielo*, you kept things from me long before you thought I may be in danger. With what we do . . ." Sebastian shook his head. "That is not acceptable. Luke, you said things would change."

"I know, but—" Luke sat back in his chair.

"Now they have."

Sebastian bent down to kiss her. She stiffened, almost turned away, then stopped herself. She refused to be sulky and childish about this. If Sebastian needed her to prove that she could talk to him, that they had more than hot, passionate, mind-blowing sex between them . . .

This is gonna suck. She curved her hand around the side of his throat, stroking the rough hair covering his jaw, letting her lips touch his as she whispered. "I love you, *mi Rey*. I swear, I'll never keep anything from you again. It could be worse. If all I have to do is earn your trust back, I'm getting off easy."

He chuckled as he kissed her, sucking on her bottom lip, claiming her mouth. His eyes were hooded as he drew away. "You are assuming you won't be punished?" He smiled at her hesitant nod. "Don't."

She shivered and glanced over at Luke. He came over, brushed a soft kiss over her lips, then whispered in her ear as Sebastian moved toward the door. "Being cut off indefinitely trumps anything else he can come up with."

"Are you sure about that, *niño*?" Sebastian gave them an amused look. "If you are, then I have been much too lenient on you."

Luke swallowed. "Fuck."

Jami squeezed Luke's hand, rising to follow him to the door. After closing and locking the door, she leaned against it, heart racing.

We're in trouble.

Chapter Twenty Seven

The dark blue silk tie slipped from Luke's hands as he tried to copy the neat, Windsor knot Seb had shown him over and over. Groaning at the tangled mess, he slapped his hands on the dresser in his spacious basement bedroom. He had no problem tying intricate knots during a scene, but this stupid tie wasn't a nice sturdy rope. And he never tried to please anyone but the sub when he worked the ropes.

Pleasing Seb was . . . important. He knew Seb would expect him to look his best, and he wanted that look he got from the man when he'd done something right. Dressing nice shouldn't be too fucking difficult.

But it was.

"Is there a problem, Luke?"

Luke took a deep breath, turning to face Seb who stood in the open doorway. "No. I'm good."

Seb gave him a curt nod. "I see."

"Wait." Luke ground his teeth and let his hands fall to his sides. "This is going to sound stupid, but I can't do this. My hands are shaking, and the knots always look like shit."

"Would you like me to do it for you?"

"I should be able to do it myself." Luke scowled. "It's pretty pathetic that you need to dress me."

"I enjoy doing it, *semental*." Seb crossed the room, eyeing the three other ties on Luke's dresser, all hopelessly wrinkled from previous efforts. "All you need do is ask."

"Please?" Luke held still as Seb deftly fixed his tie and smoothed it down. His pulse quickened as his flesh heated under his crisp, pale grey shirt. He really wished Seb was stripping off his clothes, rather than dressing him, but this was nothing compared to last night.

After leaving Akira's, Luke and Seb had gone to pick up some stuff from Luke's house. Tyler was there, with Chicklet and Laura. Laura's face had gone red as she glanced up from where she was scrubbing the kitchen floor. Naked. A sharp word from Chicklet had her looking down and scrubbing harder.

"Nothing's worse than a sub that decides there's things you don't need to

know." Chicklet winced, then smiled at Tyler as he knelt beside her and rested his head on her thigh. She stroked his hair, then finally lifted her gaze to Seb. "I'm sorry. You know I would have told you, right?"

"I do." Seb had observed Laura silently, then shook his head. "I hope you are not being too harsh with her. Jami asked her not to say anything."

Laura had gone still. She lifted her head. "May I speak, Mistress?"

Chiclet's brow furrowed. She leaned over to kiss Tyler's cheek. "Go ahead."

"My Mistress respects loyalty, so she's taken it easy on me, but I know what I did was wrong." Laura bit her bottom lip. "It's hard when it comes to my job—it's never been an issue before. But I should have known better. Jami needed you."

"She did not know that, pet." Seb sighed. "But I do hope this helps you with whatever guilt you feel."

"It does." Laura ducked her head. "But it's not enough."

Seb's brow shot up. "It is enough for me. And for your Mistress. I would not push if I were you."

For some reason, Luke couldn't stop thinking about the exchange, all the way to his new home. After dropping his stuff off in his room, he met Seb in the kitchen.

"Am I being punished?"

"Do you need to be?" Seb stood over the stove, making popcorn the old fashioned way. He poured the popped kernels into a big bowl, then added melted butter and salt. "I cannot think of any reason why."

"I should have talked to you after what your cousin said."

"You were upset. Understandably so."

"But . . ." Luke shook his head, confused. "You're punishing Jami—you won't . . . do anything with her. Or me."

"That is not a punishment, Luke." Seb picked up the bowl, then went to the fridge for two cans of Coke. "I was hoping we could enjoy a movie together. Your choice."

"Sure. Cool." Luke picked Stepmom. Halfway through the movie, he shifted from the armchair to the sofa, snuggling with Seb as his throat locked. Since sex was off the table, he found himself opening up to Seb, telling him all about his mother's condition. Admitting that he was fucking scared.

Having another man hold him would have been weird in any other situation, but with Seb, it felt right. They'd reached another level where Luke wasn't ashamed of his tears. Wasn't afraid to look weak.

But once Seb kissed him goodnight, and Luke headed down to the basement, visions of the party, of Jami with Demyan and Pearce, of Seb watching over them, got him rock hard. He jerked off, taking longer to come than he ever had because he couldn't help wishing it was Seb's hand on him, rather than his own.

But he got it. Their relationship had been all about sex. And things had gotten pretty messed up because of it. He'd needed to know the three of them had more. Seb needed to know it too.

Seb was watching him, patiently letting sort out his thoughts.

Luke made a face. "This whole thing is driving me nuts. You have no idea how many times I've wanted to get on my knees and beg you to fuck me."

"But you haven't."

"No. And I won't. I need you to know you mean more to me than a way to get off." Luke tongued his bottom lip as Seb buttoned up his suit jacket. "Because you do. But it gets harder every time you touch me."

"Does it?" Seb tugged on the lapels of Luke's suit jacket until their bodies pressed together. Until he could feel Seb's hard length against his stomach. His tone roughened as he spoke close to Luke's lips. "Because you have that effect without laying a hand on me."

Reaching between them, Luke stroked Seb through his pants. "Let me help you."

Seb pressed his eyes shut and shook his head. "No."

"It's not sex, Sir, just me sucking your dick."

"*Madre de dios*, Luke." Seb let out a strained laugh, raking his fingers through his sleek, bound hair as he retreated a step. "We have a game to play."

Baring his teeth in a broad smile, Luke shrugged, slipping by Seb to head up the stairs. "My apologies, Sir. I thought we were already playing one."

* * * *

In the hallway by the locker room, moments before the team was to head onto the ice for warm-up, Sebastian leaned against the wall, caressing Jami's cheeks with his fingertips, amazed at how well she looked after a good night's sleep. Many of her bruises were concealed with makeup, but the difference went beyond the superficial. The shadows below her eyes had faded. Her eyes were bright with youth and energy. There would be nightmares, memories to haunt her for months, but she had found the strength not to let them drag her under.

But how long will that last?

"You have to stop worrying about me." Jami took his hand and kissed his fingertips. "At least tonight. I came to watch you win. To watch Akira's show. If not for that, I wouldn't have left the house."

"Why didn't you mention fear of going out over lunch?" Sebastian's jaw tensed. Her promises meant nothing if she was already avoiding sharing her feelings.

"Because I wasn't scared then." She wrinkled her tiny nose. "It comes and goes. I woke up like it was any other day—except I overslept and got your message just in time to get dressed and meet you. I was happy to see you. Then I went back to Akira's place and it hit me. I still haven't taken a shower." Her lips thinned as she fingered the sling holding her arm close to her chest. "I've never broken anything before, so I'm paranoid about getting this stupid thing wet."

"Was it the shower that made you think of . . ."

"Yeah. I felt gross and my hair was all greasy. And then I couldn't stop thinking about how this happened." She rolled her eyes. "I had a complete meltdown. But Akira went out and bought some dry shampoo. She fixed me up and I felt human again."

"I am happy you have Akira." Sebastian ran his hand over her loose hair, trailing over her shoulders like midnight woven into silk. At least she hadn't gone through it alone. "I would still have liked it if you had called me."

"*Mi Rey*, I didn't feel like talking to anyone." Her fingers traced the gold collar of his jersey. "But I told you. That counts, right?"

"Yes." Sebastian's breath hitched as her fingers dipped down, teasing the short hair of his chest. His nerves were hypersensitive, sparking at the slightest touch. Arousal flared so abruptly he had to pull her hand away from him. Erections on the ice were to be avoided at all costs. "I enjoyed having lunch with you. We should do that again soon."

Her lips curved slightly. "I agree. But, before you go out there... can I give you a good luck kiss?"

"Can I have one too?" Luke asked from behind them. He moved in while Sebastian was still trying to decide how wise it would be to taste her sweet lips while his control waned. Luke latched onto Jami, holding her in a firm embrace as he took her mouth. He was breathing hard as he released her. "Mmm, bad girl. You're not supposed to be drinking with your meds."

"I only had a sip!" Jami planted one hand on her hip, wincing as she automatically tried to do the same with the other. But her cheeks were flushed and her eyes glazed with lust. Her pain was the least of their problems. "And you don't get to lecture me, mister. You taste like beer, and I *know* you're not supposed to drink before games."

"You little liar!" Luke chuckled, shaking his head as he shifted closer to Sebastian. He took off one glove, dropped it, then slid his hand around the back of Sebastian's neck. "I can prove it."

Sebastian groaned as Luke's tongue thrust into his mouth, all wet heat, the sweet tang of Gatorade, and the desperate pressure of longing and lust. Luke made Sebastian forget where they were. Who might see them.

A throat clearing off to the side made Jami yelp, and Luke stumbled back like he'd been gut checked.

Tim held the door open, looking more amused than shocked. "How about we save the celebrations until after the game, boys?"

Cheeks glowing red, Luke nodded and ducked into the locker room. Tim gave Sebastian a pointed look, tapped his wristwatch, then followed him.

"You did lie. Are you trying to rack up punishments?" Sebastian snorted a laugh as Jami's eyes widened. "I will be bringing both you and Luke to Spain once the postseason is finished. I would rather not spend the entire trip disciplining you."

Jami blinked. Bit back a smile. Then shrugged. "Discipline's better than nothing." She rose up on tiptoes to kiss him. "Good luck, *mi Rey*."

She spun away from him, strolling down the hall, hips swaying provocatively. Her tight jeans—which she couldn't have put on alone—had his hands itching to pull them off. He'd know abstaining would not be easy.

Apparently his lovers were determined to make it nearly impossible.

* * * *

Red lights flashed across the darkened ice. A lion's roar ripped out as "Animal" by Kristina Maria exploded from the speakers. The Ice Girls weren't wearing their uniforms. Their flesh gleamed in the spotlight as they pulled away from a provocative tangle of bodies. Tan loincloths and matching tube tops revealed most of their bodies. Akira rose from her crouch in the center of the dancers, whipping her hair over her shoulder as she began moving like a sleek, wild cat, unleashed.

Ford's mouth went dry. He'd seen some of the routine, broken down as Akira perfected each move with her team, but he never could have imagined the impact of the whole performance. The crowd buzzed with the energy the girls threw into the stands with each hard thrust of their hips. He pressed his fist against the glass, tearing at his tie with his free hand as he watched Akira's body undulate to the wild rhythm.

"Fuck, they're good." Sahara, one of the Islander Ice Girls who would be doing a televised dance-off against the Cobra finalists in a few weeks, leaned against the glass beside him. "I bet, by next year, half your ratings will be from people just wanting to see these girls."

"I'd be a fool to take that bet." He pushed back and forced a smile as he met Oriana's questioning gaze. Not like he could tell her he wanted to go down there and drag Akira off the ice. He didn't want anyone else to see her like that. Anyone but him. And the girl wanted nothing to do with him. So he turned to a subject he knew would distract his sister. "I hate to admit it, but Silver might have saved the team by making it more about sex than the game."

"Don't be bitter, Ford. You're better than that." Oriana folded her arms over her chest. She looked so small in Callahan's Winter Classics Jersey, so much smaller than Ford, but somehow her size didn't make her any less imposing. "Besides, we both know the team needs money now." She glanced over at Sahara, then seemed to decide it didn't matter if the girl knew what was becoming a well-known fact. "Unless we bring in a new investor, we don't have it."

"We do now." Ford avoided Richter's hard look from across the room and lowered his voice. "I sold the forum. And half of my shares."

"What?" Oriana put her hand over her mouth. "To who?"

"Someone with the money to pull this team out of the black. With my shares, and the ones my father bought out from the other investors, the new guy holds the majority. I know Silver won't like it, but I had to act fast." He rubbed his temples. "Before my dad figured out what I was doing."

"You don't need your dad anymore. Selling your shares should have made you financially stable."

"Yeah . . . except I didn't keep the money." He laughed. "I put some into buying myself a new bar so my dad couldn't use his influence to shut me down. And I put the rest in an account for Silver. I know she'll use it for the team—once she gets over it coming from me."

"I'll talk to her accountant. She doesn't need to know right now." Oriana put her hand on his arm. "She's on bed rest. No stress. You said you wanted a meeting later this week. Let Dean figure it out."

"I gave up having a say." Ford scowled at his gleaming black shoes. Not that he'd ever really *had* a say. His father had always called the shots. "Hell, at least I won't have to wear suits anymore. And I'll have nothing to do with the team. Silver will be happy."

"Shut up, Ford. You kept me around after my father cut me out. I'm doing the same for you."

"Please don't." Ford's lips curled away from his teeth as the Ice Girls left the ice and the large dance mat was rolled up and carted away. The game was about to get started. He turned his back on the rink. He had no interest in seeing the team their family had sunk all their money into lose. "I'm not like your men, sis. I don't give a fuck about the game. I was always in it for the money. So the *Kingsleys* could milk the team for all it was worth. Now that's ov—"

"Yes!" Sahara jumped up and down, then ducked her head,

giggling as a camera flashed in her direction. "Oh my God, I so shouldn't be cheering you guys!"

Ford shook his head at her, stepping up to his sister's side to watch the replay. Straight off the face-off, Scott Demyan had snatched up the puck, moving in a blur, weaving around players like they were practice pylons. He let the puck go without a second's hesitation, raising his arms in celebration before the ref even called the goal.

"Nice," Ford said with grudging admiration. Hell, he was Canadian. He knew a good goal when he saw one.

Oriana elbowed him in the ribs. "What were you saying about not giving a fuck, bro?"

His lips quirked. He elbowed her back. "All right, so I'm full of shit." He schooled his features as he caught Richter studying him from across the room. "Just don't tell no one, okay? I've got a bad reputation to live up to."

"I won't have to tell anyone." Oriana smiled serenely at Ford as she settled into a chair to enjoy the rest of the game. Brow arched, she patted the seat beside her. After Ford plunked down, her lips slanted into a smirk. "Keep it up. They'll see for themselves."

* * * *

Sloan entered the owner's box in the third period, having watched most of the game from the press box where he'd given several interviews during commercial breaks and between periods. He avoided any mention of his relationship with Oriana, Max, and Dominik. Spoke openly about his expectations for the second round of the playoffs, as if a win was guaranteed. Even though, by the second period, it didn't look likely.

Ingerslov had let in three goals in five minutes. And another two at the beginning of the second period. Tim had finally been forced to pull him and put in Dave Hunt, all of twenty with negligible experience above the minors. He'd probably be exceptional in a few years, but now?

"Yeah!" Over to one side of the room, Ford leapt to his feet beside Oriana, hugging her tightly as she squealed. Sloan blinked and shook his head. He knew Oriana had embraced Ford as her brother, but the young man usually showed her nothing but cool detachment—something that had made Sloan want to nail him to a wall more than once.

Give him time. He'll do something to upset her, then all bets are off.

As Oriana glanced over at Sloan, her eyes, sparkling with laughter, warmed him like a shot of good, strong whiskey. He smiled at her, then inclined his head to Ford. Max insisted they had to be nice to the kid. As far as Sloan was concerned, leaving the punk with all his teeth this long was pretty decent of him.

"Callahan, I was hoping you'd stop by." Richter waved him over, then gestured toward the ice. "What do you think of the kid? You know I like Ingerslov, but he's not a playoff goalie. Hunt just might be."

Running his tongue over his teeth, Sloan observed the young goalie slamming his stick against the post and screaming at the ref over what he apparently thought was a missed call. "He's got a temper."

"So do you."

"True."

"He's also been to the club. Wayne told me he's too hotheaded to be a Dom, not until he grows up a bit—he got mouthy with a few members. But . . ." Richter rubbed his jaw. "He showed a lot of interest in the impact play. Didn't flinch from the hard-core stuff."

"What are you getting at, Richter?"

"Talk to him. You might have a few things in common."

"Wayne thinks he's a sadist." Sloan took a deep breath, letting it out slow at Richter's nod. "Fine, I'll see what I can do."

Nearing the end of the game, Sloan found himself slightly more motivated to take the kid under his wing. He was cocky. Undisciplined. Too quick to anger and too slow to recover from a bad play. All the things Sloan couldn't stand in a player. But he had potential.

And maybe, just maybe, learning how to use a whip the way all the best Doms did—from the other end—would smarten him up. Sloan's lips curved into the edgy smile that had most subs quivering when it was turned on them.

I think I'm gonna enjoy this.

A minute left. The score tied. Several miraculous saves by Hunt, and impressive goals by Max, Pearce, and Demyan had turned the tide of the game. Carter had been strangely quiet, uncharacteristically calm and focused. He'd racked up assists on almost every goal, but seemed to be biding his time. He even passed back to the defenseman on the point rather than drive forward into a clear path for the net.

Nelson bolted for the defenseman. A solid hip check sent him flying. Carter picked up the loose puck, firing from center ice as the clock counted down the last seconds.

The fans went berserk as the sirens screamed. Carter dropped to his knees, threw aside his gloves, and clasped his hands as though in a prayer of thanks. Ramos reached him first, dragging him up to hug him even as the rest of the team crashed into them. A close up on the Jumbotron showed Ramos knocking off Carter's helmet to kiss the top of his head.

No big deal really, not with what Carter had just pulled off. But the press would use it.

Richter glanced over at Sloan.

Sloan nodded. "I'm on it. Send PR to the locker room. We can't keep the press out now."

Insanity reigned in the locker room. Blue droplets of Gatorade trailed down Carter's cheeks as he accepted congratulatory abuse from his teammates. His hair was ruffled. He was punched in the arms and given bear hugs. Sloan made it in the room just in time to watch his smile fade as the reporters swarmed around him.

"Did the recent incident with your captain make you feel more comfortable being open about your relationship?"

Carter's lips moved. He paled. "What?"

"How long have you been with Ramos?"

"I . . ." Carter gave Ramos a helpless look. Mouthed something like, "I can't do this."

"Hey, this isn't an interview for *Cosmo*! We just fucking won!" Demyan elbowed his way to Carter's side, leaning his arm on the younger man's shoulder. "Ask him how he did it, because that was fucking beautiful!"

Ramos tried to pull Carter out of the horde. They pressed in closer.

Several of the reporters shifted their questions back to the win, but the rag vermin were still hanging on to questions about Carter's sexuality, coming at him again and again as though pushing for him to snap and say something they could use.

Sloan moved with the other players until they surrounded Carter, forcing the reporters to aim their rapid-fire questions at them. But Carter still seemed overwhelmed. He glanced toward the door, as though hoping a path would clear so he could escape.

Only one player remained apart, stripping out of his uniform like nothing that was happening affected him at all. Pearce chuckled softly as a few reporters took notice. "If you're looking for a story, I can give you one. You're wasting your time with the kid."

Slowly, the room quieted, everyone waiting to hear what Pearce would say.

"I've only ever been with one woman. And it's been years." He slouched against the side of his stall. Seemed bored. "I prefer men."

Hours later, in a bar the team had chosen to celebrate—Ford's new bar, actually—Sloan brought Carter a beer and slid into a chair at the corner table where he sat alone with Ramos.

"Shit, kid. I'm sorry about that. They might not have come down on you so hard if I'd—"

"Hey, it's okay." Carter took a swig from his fresh beer, looking a little tipsy as he leaned back in his chair. "I'm just glad it's over. And I kept my promise."

"Your promise?" Sloan raised a brow at Ramos when Carter simply smiled and shrugged.

Ramos dropped his arm over the back of Carter's chair, squeezing his shoulder. "He told Jami he would win."

"Well, I owe her a beer too then!" Sloan grinned and lifted his beer. "To Jami!"

"To Jami!" The rest of the players echoed, clearly paying way more attention to the private conversation than they should.

By the bar, Richter shook his head and lifted his bottle.

"Carter—Luke." Sloan placed his beer on the table, holding it between his good hand and his damaged one. "I get you not wanting to come out in front of the press, but you know you don't have to hide or anything, right? The whole team has your back."

"I saw that." Carter hunched his shoulders. "It's not that I'm trying to hide it. I'm just not ready to . . ."

Ramos slid his hand to the back of Carter's neck, massaging corded muscles gently. "You kept another promise tonight, *semental*. You were honest with me. That matters more than you declaring anything to the world."

Sloan stood, sensing that Carter and Ramos needed time alone. And happier for them than he could say without things becoming awkward. He understood their position, probably better than anyone. While Silver flaunted her relationship and couldn't care less what anyone thought, Oriana preferred to keep things private. Not because she was ashamed of what they had, but because her feelings were for her men alone.

"Enjoy the rest of your night, boys." Sloan lowered his voice, tipping his beer for one last cheers. "To the game. And to teammates who know how to deal with the press."

Bottles clinked with his. Both Carter and Ramos glanced over at Pearce, who sat with a few men who weren't part of the team, letting them buy him drinks while turning down their advances. His eyes sought the door often, but Sloan doubted anyone besides him had noticed. A brief exchange between Pearce and Demyan when the team had first converged on the bar told Sloan everything he needed to know.

For the first time ever, Demyan didn't want the attention. Unlike the rest of the team, he wasn't showing his support. He'd taken off with two puck bunnies, smiling for the cameras as he draped an arm around each of their shoulders.

Carter wasn't hiding anything. Sloan truly believed that.

But Demyan was.

Finding Oriana in a heated conversation with Hunt, who seemed to be humoring her, Sloan hugged her waist and kissed her throat. Dominik eyed them from the other side of the table.

"Time to go home, pet. I want to celebrate." He chuckled as she rested back against him. "And it's going to hurt."

"Mmm. That sounds good." Oriana licked her lips as she tipped her head back. "Just the two of us?"

"I won't celebrate with the whole team; I'm too greedy for that." He nipped her earlobe. "But I suppose you could bring a man or two, if you'd like." His tone turned husky. "Choose wisely."

She immediately reached out for Dominik. "Sorry, Hunt. Maybe we'll see you around the club?"

"I'd like that." Hunt stood, running his fingers through his tight black curls before offering his hand to Sloan. "I've heard a lot about you. I look forward to working with you. On and off the ice."

Hunt's gaze lingered just a little too long on Oriana. Sloan tightened his grip on the man's hand, jerking him forward. "Good. Then you know the only way I'll let you leave marks on her is if you let me leave marks on you." He bared his teeth as Hunt gaped at him. "Don't answer now. Take your time. Consider *very* carefully."

Oriana ditched them to find Max. Dominik followed Sloan out to Max's car, since Max had agreed to be the designated driver.

Predictably, Dominik stepped up to Sloan the second they were alone. "I don't like him. We will discuss this before he goes anywhere near Oriana."

Sloan smirked and rested his hip against the passenger side door. "Of course. As long as we're sharing, we make all decisions together."

"What aren't you saying, Sloan?"

"I've been offered a coaching position in Calgary—they know this injury has probably ended my career. The Flames are also making a bid for Max." Sloan cocked his head as Dominik drew away from him. "So, yeah, we have a lot to 'discuss.'"

Dominik's jaw ticked. "You're not taking her away from me."

"Not tonight, no." Sloan saw Oriana and Max approaching from the corner of his eye. "Do you really want to get into this now?"

"No." Dominik forced a smile, muttering under his breath. "But this isn't over."

"Not by a long shot," Sloan said pleasantly as he held the back door open for Oriana. "We've only won the first round. We shouldn't be overconfident."

"Yeah," Dominik said. "That's the smartest thing you've said all night."

Hand on the door, Sloan hesitated before climbing into the car beside Oriana. Beer made her sleepy, so he wasn't all that surprised when her head on his chest slid down to his lap. He knew it would upset her if she knew what had passed between him and Dominik, but thankfully, Dominik cared about her enough to mask his anger.

What surprised Sloan the most was how long he'd waited to confront the man. Because he did care about him. As a teammate. As a friend.

But the restrictions Dominik imposed on his relationship with Oriana were more than he could take.

After tonight, that would end.

Chapter Twenty Eight

Luke knew his scruffy, pathetic playoff beard looked like shit. And that there was no reason to keep growing it. But he couldn't bring himself to scrape away his only reminder of how close they'd come to the Cup.

If we'd hung on, just a little longer, we could have been in the same building with it. He shook his head at his pitiful reflection. A week after the Kings had swept them from the semifinals and he was still in mourning. Beating the Sabres gave him such a rush his expectations had soared. He'd never admit it to the other guys, but he hadn't limited his hopes to making it to the finals. Again and again, in his dreams, he felt the weight of the Cup as he hefted it up, tears in his eyes which he didn't try to hide because a win like that was one of the only times it was okay for a man to cry.

His mother had even told him she would be there. She didn't know much about hockey, so when he told her this was the year the Cobras would go all the way, she believed him.

Get over it, Carter. Squaring his shoulders, Luke used a facecloth to clean away the gunk in his eyes, rub away the weariness of not enough sleep and too much beer. *There's always next year.*

If the team survived that long.

"You really need to shave." Jami came into the bathroom, hugging him from behind with her good arm around his waist. "I hate seeing you like this, stud."

Luke gave her a half-smile as he rubbed her arm. "And the rug burns on your neck probably suck, right?"

Jami giggled as he pulled her in front of him to nuzzle her neck, already red from the night before. With her hair short, it was much easier to access her sweet spots. One of the few perks to the loss of the long, silky strands.

"Not at all. But I miss you looking all pretty."

Growling softly, Luke nipped her earlobe. "It will take more than a shave to make me pretty, boo."

"Perhaps, but if you cleaned up and stopped sulking..." Seb slipped into the room with a small black bag, the skin around his eyes and lips creasing slightly as he looked Luke over. "You would certainly be more appealing."

"I've told you before. I'm not sulking." Luke kissed Jami's forehead, then turned to Seb with his arms folded over his chest. "I'm—"

"In mourning," Jami and Seb said together.

"Yeah." Luke raked his fingers through his hair and nodded slowly. "All right, I get it."

"Good." Seb unzipped the black bag, pulled out a leather pouch. Inside was a straight blade, which he flipped open with a flick of his wrist. "Then you will not object to me seeing it done properly."

Eyeing the blade, Luke swallowed. Shook his head. Blood surged into his balls, making them hot and heavy. For some reason, a knife in Seb's hands turned him on. Then again, it had been over a week since he'd gotten any. Maybe he was just *that* desperate. "No, Sir."

Seb took a hand towel out from the bathroom cupboard, dropped it into the sink, and turned on the hot water. He laid out the rest of the supplies from his bag. An old-fashioned, stiff-bristled shaving brush, cleanser, and a bar of shaving soap. He had Luke sit on a small, ornate stool across from the sink, wrung out the towel, then used it to cover Luke's face.

Steam seeped into his pores and his pulse raced as arousal flashed silver in the darkness, slicing low. Seb wouldn't cut him, but the risk in letting someone else hold something sharp against his flesh was heady. Seb removed the cloth, smoothed on the cleanser, and Luke trembled with anticipation. He shifted impatiently as Seb began applying the lathered soap with the brush.

"Be. Still." Seb's dark eyes were hooded as he lightly scraped the blade over Luke's throat. His knees pressed between Luke's parted thighs. "I wouldn't want to cut you."

Hissing in a breath, Luke closed his eyes, fixated on the blade gliding over his skin. On the slight pull of Seb's fingers on his cheek. On the repetitive motion, which lulled him into a passive haze, where he moved only when Seb guided him to one side of the other. He didn't feel spacey, just . . . extremely relaxed.

But the last scrape on his cheek left him aching for more. Water ran in the sink. He groaned as Seb pushed two damp fingers into his mouth.

Seb's hot lips pressed against his clean-shaven cheek. "So smooth. I will do the same to other parts of you during the trip." His voice dropped, low and husky, close to Luke's ear. "And you will let me."

"Fuck, yes." Luke groaned as the next scrape, up the length of his throat, reverberated into the base of his cock. He shook as he fought to keep still. The idea of a blade on his balls shouldn't have him so close to losing control. But it did. Moisture seeped from the head of his dick, and he cursed under his breath. "Do it, Seb. I want you to do it now."

"I know you do, *niño*." Seb finished shaving him with one last slow graze up the other side of his neck. "Be patient."

After applying a stinging aftershave, Seb patted his cheek and left to finish packing for their trip to Spain. Luke inhaled roughly, tossing a shaky grin over at Jami, who hadn't moved from where he'd placed her in front of the sink. "Learned your lesson yet?"

"Hell, yes. And I know *exactly* how you feel right now. When he helped me take a bath the other day . . ." Jami lifted her hand to her shoulder, as though to play with hair that no longer reached that far. She shook her head and fiddled with the collar of her snug, white lace shirt instead. "I have to admit, though, it's getting easier. I wasn't thinking about sex when we went to the charity ball. Or when we visited your mom. She's . . . amazing. I can see how you ended up the way you are."

Luke wasn't sure what to make of that. So he asked, "Is that a compliment?"

"Definitely." Jami's fingers inched up to the close-cut hair at the nape of her neck. "You're strong. And smart. And so fucking dedicated. I wish . . ." She shook her head and backed out of the bathroom. "I should go get ready."

While visiting with his mother, Jami had broken down once and told him and Seb that she wished she had a mother like his. One who cared. After a good cry, sitting in Seb's lap with her head on Luke's shoulder, she'd pulled herself together and told them they were forbidden to bring up her mother ever again. Luke didn't have the heart to argue with her, but was surprised Seb had agreed.

We can talk about my mom though. My mom loves her.

Hands braced on his knees, Luke bit his trembling bottom lip. He couldn't look at Jami without seeing the grateful tears in his mother's eyes. But he hadn't told her what it had meant to him, not really. His choked "thank you" hadn't been enough.

He found her in the guest bedroom, trying on some hats—which Seb had told her she'd need for Spain to prevent sunstroke. He watched her open the suitcase she'd brought over from her place days before, pulling out several styling brushes to place on the bed.

"Can I tell you something?" He winced as she jumped, tripping over the side of the bed, her face tense with pain as her cast hit the footboard. "Aw, boo, I'm sorry. I wasn't thinking."

"It's okay." Jami took a deep breath and glanced up at him. "What's up?"

Luke stepped up to her side, pulling her into his arms, holding her tightly against him as he breathed in the sweet scent of her fruity shampoo. Absorbed her warmth. "What you did for my mom—"

"It was nothing."

"It was everything." He stroked his hand over her cute pixie cut. "You're one hell of a woman, you know that?"

"Not like her. She's so strong—the kind of woman I want to be. The entire time she was there, all she talked about was how proud she is of you. How she never doubted you'd make it. I can't imagine . . ." Jami smiled. "No, actually, I can. My dad's like that. And I never really saw it before. All I thought about was how my mother wasn't there for me. But it was stupid to hang on to that when I have so much." She shrugged, picking up a thick comb, which she stuffed into her suitcase before zipping it shut. "The only thing your mother would admit was that losing her hair for the surgery bothered her. The way she welcomed me into her home, the way she told me I was everything she'd always wanted for you—I had to give her something in return."

"You didn't have to." Luke's hand shook as he cupped Jami's face in his hands. "But I'm glad you did. I'm kinda shocked that Seb let you though."

"Are you? Really?" Jami arched a brow. "He wouldn't take credit for it, but if he hadn't paid extra, they wouldn't have been able to make the wig so fast. I think he got to the technician, telling her about your mom. She cried when we told her we loved what she'd done with my hair. Seb called her before we left to tell her your mom loved it."

"She does. But . . ." Luke flicked a strand over Jami's ear. "Are you okay with it?"

"Sure." Jami shrugged, moving away from him to study herself in the mirror. She narrowed her eyes at a small red cut on her forehead. The bruises around it had faded, but it would likely leave a small scar. "It's nothing compared to . . . ugh, I don't know. I wish there was a way I could get clean." She held up her hand before Luke could protest. "I know, I know, 'I'm not dirty.' But I still feel like I am. Like if I'd been . . . normal, Lee wouldn't have been interested in me."

"What's normal?" Luke reached up to press his hand gently against her cheek. "I don't think a 'normal' girl would have cut off all her hair for a woman she hardly knows. A normal girl wouldn't be able to love two men the way you do." He grinned to lighten things up a bit. "And a normal girl wouldn't be able to call me on my shit."

"True." Jami gave him a crooked smile and smacked his chest. "Speaking of which, you're breaking all the rules. No sex. If Seb had caught you in my bed last night—"

"We didn't have sex!" Luke winked at her doubtful look. "Ask Clinton."

"Still . . . you're going to get punished."

"I certainly hope so." Luke moved closer to her, making a low sound in his throat as her soft breast flattened against his chest. "Do you think he'll spank me?"

Jami snorted. "I think he knows you like it as much as I do." She reached between them, unzipped his jeans, and slipped her hand right into his boxers to cup his balls. An evil little smile slid across her lips. "He might not let you come for a month."

Luke curved his hand around the back of Jami's neck, breathing hard as she teased him. "He's already doing that."

She frowned. "He never said a month. The trip—"

"Is another way to get close. With all the activities he's planned, I doubt we'll have time for . . ." He groaned as Jami withdrew her hand. "I want you so much it hurts."

"Then maybe we should do something about it." Jami kissed her fingertips, then touched them to his lips. "I'll meet you out at the car."

"Sure." Luke shook his head when she reached for her luggage. "I've got it, boo. Go before Seb starts thinking something's up." When she turned, he latched an arm across her stomach. Holding her still, he teased a tender spot behind her ear with his lips and tongue, palming her breast and running his thumb over a pebbled nipple until she squirmed. She let out a sound of raw need as he let her go. "Consider this motivation. I've got a plan."

Chapter Twenty Nine

Exploring the ruins of San Pedro de Arlanza drained Sebastian, even though wandering through the decrepit, but beautifully gothic structure had always taken him away from harsh reality as a child. Stone walls, crumbling around the edges, towered over him, bleached and stained by the elements, yet still standing tall after centuries, were simply awesome to behold. Bringing Luke and Jami here, having them hang on to his every word as he detailed the rich history of the monastery—much like his mother had over and over until he was old enough to repeat the stories—made him feel closer to them than all the dinners and shows and outings put together. He almost forgot how cruel the midday sun could be until Jami began lagging behind. He could ignore his own exhaustion—plane trips and new surroundings often left him feeling out of sorts—but he would not ignore Jami's.

He did, however, pretend not to hear her protests when he announced that it was time to go.

"There is a Spanish tradition I would like to introduce you both to," he said as he climbed into the driver's seat of their rented car. He grinned when they both leaned toward him. "Siesta."

"Isn't that like a nap?" Luke groaned at Sebastian's nod. "Seriously? I didn't come all the way to Spain to sleep."

Jami turned in her seat to give Luke a dirty look. "Do you have to complain about everything?"

"Lately? Yeah." Luke's lips quirked. "Maybe I wouldn't have to if you weren't such a tease."

"Oh, bite me."

"I would absolutely love to." Luke trailed his finger over her bare shoulder, slightly reddened despite the liberal amount of sunscreen Sebastian had used on her. Blue eyes hooded, he moved closer to graze the flesh he'd touched with his teeth. "Should I start here?"

"Mmm . . ." Jami's tipped her head to the side as Luke stroked along her throat with his fingertips. "There's good."

"Tell me when to stop . . ."

Sebastian put his hand over Luke's, lifting his brow when Luke frowned. "She needs her rest."

"In her own bed, right?"

"Yes."

"All right." Luke sat back and pulled on his seat belt. "Fair enough."

Too easy. But Sebastian didn't say a word until they returned to the villa and he had Jami comfortably settled in bed with the air conditioner on high. He found Luke in the kitchen, gulping down water as if they'd just spent days in the desert. After Luke uncapped the third bottle, Sebastian moved in, cornering him between the granite counter and the sand colored wall.

"Enough, *niño*, you'll make yourself sick." He took the bottle from Luke, finishing it off himself. He licked a droplet from his bottom lip, smiling as Luke made a gruff sound in his throat, gaze fixed on the intentionally provocative gesture. "I know what you are trying to do, but I thought I should warn you. There will be consequences."

"I wouldn't expect anything less, Master." Luke leaned forward, sliding his smooth cheek against Sebastian's. "Enjoy your nap."

For the longest time, Sebastian lay in his bed, alone, wishing he could simply invite Jami and Luke to join him. But what had started off as a way to bring them all closer, to give them a solid foundation for the relationship, had become something more, and it wouldn't end with a brief—albeit explosive—fuck.

He knew what they wanted. But learning what they really *needed* was a little more complicated. Because neither of them could tell him, openly or clearly.

They had shown him, though. A little more every day.

Now all he had to do was wait and see what they did next.

* * * *

Ropes snaked around Sebastian's wrist, a gentle caress before swiftly tightening. Instantly alert, he wrapped his arm around a trim yet solid waist, flipping the body under him before he'd fully opened his eyes.

Luke panted, then laughed. "Shit, I wasn't fast enough."

"What exactly did you plan to do with me once you had me bound?" Sebastian fisted his hands in Luke's hair, jerking his head back so he could take his mouth in a brutal kiss. "Would you have fucked me?"

Eyes wide, pupils dilated, Luke shook his head. "You're... you... I couldn't—"

"But you want to." Sebastian ground his hips into Luke's, hissing through his teeth. "Say it."

"Fuck yes!" Luke pressed his eyes shut. "Only... I *love* having you in control. I don't want that to change."

Sebastian chuckled. "It won't. Do you think a Domme surrenders control when her sub pleasures her with his cock?"

"No."

"When I suck your dick, am I still your Master?"

"Yes," Luke said, opening eyes glazed with lust. "You're my Master. Always."

"Good, *niño*." Sebastian pushed off the bed, throwing his legs over the side to stand. He held out his hand, clasping it with Luke's and pulling him to his feet. "Where is Jami?"

Luke swallowed hard, then glanced toward the door. "Umm. Hiding?"

"*Hiding?*" Sebastian's jaw ticked as he strode from the room. After what had happened to her, letting her out of his sight for any length of time was pure hell. He'd smother her if he kept as close an eye on her as he'd like to, so he'd forced himself to come to grips with the fact that she was a grown woman and had learned from her horrible experience. But in a strange country where she didn't even know enough of the language to ask for help?

His palms dampened as he stared at her empty bed. Then reason kicked in. Jami would not leave the house. She was playing a game. Being naughty. Likely hoping to be punished.

Relax, Ramos. Sebastian counted under his breath in Spanish. Tension eased from his muscles. "Jami?"

"Polo!" Jami's giggles echoed through the villa.

"Polo?" Sebastian grabbed Luke by the front of his shirt when the *cabrón* laughed. "What does that mean?"

"Marco Polo. It's a game."

"I see." Sebastian cleared his throat. "Come out, Jami."

Another giggle. "That's not how hide and seek works, *mi Rey*!"

"Hey, you okay, dude?" Luke gave Sebastian a cheeky grin. "Did you think someone had kidnapped her to make her part of their harem?" He cocked his head. "Do Spanish guys have Harems?"

"I do." Sebastian slid his hand around Luke's throat and shoved him against the wall, shattering the composure his *niño* had temporarily regained. *So they want to play?* He bared his teeth. "Do you think my *putina* will come to save you, *esclavo*?"

"Slave?" Luke chewed his bottom lip. Then shook his head. "I won't let her."

"You do not have a choice." Sebastian dragged Luke back to his bedroom. He pointed to the floor at his feet. "Kneel."

Luke dropped hard to his knees, clasping his hands behind his neck and spreading his thighs, copying a pose Chicklet's sub, Tyler, often took at the club. Sebastian watched Luke's chest heave with rapid breaths, stared down at him until defiance faded from his eyes. He doubted submitting would ever be easy for Luke, but the internal struggle that played over his face each and every time made it even more precious when he finally gave in. He'd moved beyond needing to be forced to surrender control. There would be times when he craved the fight, craved being physically overpowered, but this wasn't one of them.

"Very good, *niño*." Sebastian stroked Luke's rumpled hair, pleased when Luke leaned into his touch. "I will restrain you. Beat you until you scream loud enough to bring her to us." He crouched down, tipping Luke's chin up to look into his eyes. "Unless you call for her now."

"I . . ." Luke blinked fast, opening his mouth as though ready to call for Jami simply because Sebastian had asked it of him. He'd sunk into submission so quickly it took him a moment to bring himself into the game. But then his eyes narrowed. He jerked back. "No. Do your worst. I'll never betray her."

"So loyal." Sebastian chuckled and straightened. "Charming, really. But I believe you will reconsider before long."

His large, leather toy bag was well equipped, and he felt Luke's eyes on him as he carried it from the closet to the bed. Luke had asked his permission to go through it once, so he knew exactly what kind of wicked tools of erotic torture it contained. Sebastian took his time laying them out on the bed, standing off to the side so Luke could see what he planned to use. He left Luke kneeling in the bedroom while he prepared a few supplies in the kitchen, then returned to attach a set of straps to the bedroom door. He retrieved two pairs of cuffs from his bag, then went to Luke and pressed two fingers to the side of his throat to check his pulse. Nice and steady, if a little fast. Excellent.

"The wrist cuffs have 'panic snaps,' so do not tug too hard unless you intend to free yourself."

Luke snorted. "Really, Seb? I can handle—"

"I know that, *semental*. But I will ask you to free yourself at some point." Sebastian took a firm hold on Luke's jaw. His tone dropped, low and cold. "And I should warn you, if you speak again, I expect you to refer to me as 'Master' or 'Sir,' or I will be forced to punish you."

"Aren't you punishing me anyway?" Luke paled slightly as Sebastian dug his fingers into his jaw. "Ah . . . Sir?"

"You know very well there is a difference between real punishment and what we are about to do." Sebastian lowered his hand to Luke's throat. "Unless you need a reminder?"

Lips parted, Luke shook his head. "No, Sir."

"Very well. Then strip. Make it fast. I will not be pleased if we bore *mi cielo* to the point that she falls asleep wherever she is hiding."

Rising with more grace than he'd shown kneeling, Luke tore at his shirt. The bottom of his T-shirt ripped as he wrenched it over his head. He tossed it aside, then fumbled with his belt. Sweat gleamed on his bare chest. His stomach muscles rippled as he unbuttoned his jeans. He paused, gulping in air before shoving his jeans down and stepping out of them. His cock jutted out as he stood at attention, like a soldier facing an interrogation, strong and proud, ready to take any amount of pain without giving an inch.

Sebastian circled him, admiring his solid, unmarked flanks, the curve of his ass, nicely rounded despite the carved muscles of his thighs and torso. Luke swam outdoors often during the summer and had done so often enough over the last few weeks to give him a golden tan. Oddly enough, the tan wasn't broken below his hips as it had been before.

"Have you been sunbathing naked, *niño?*"

"Ah... yeah. My balcony is high enough and big enough." Luke's cheeks darkened slightly. "We all do it."

"We all?"

"Me, Tyler, and Demyan."

"I see." Sebastian shook his head slowly. "I will not share you with Scott."

Luke's eyes widened. His face reddened even more. "It's not like that! Hell, I see the guys naked in the shower all the time. It's not like I'd—Hey, wait." Luke frowned. "You'll share Jami, but not me?"

Snapping every word, Sebastian spoke into Luke's ear. "I will not let anyone else fuck her. Or you. And after the way Scott treated Zach, he is not fit to suck your dick."

"Oh." Luke's brow furrowed. "But you'd let me suck—"

"If the idea has you so distracted, perhaps I should find several men to use your mouth."

"Fuck no!"

"No is not a safeword, Luke."

Luke rasped in a breath. "Red. A big fucking red. I'm not ready for that."

"Then put these on." Sebastian slammed the cuffs into Luke's chest, sharpening his tone to hide how much he liked Luke's objecting to any other man using him. That could change, and he would deal with it if it did, but for now this young man belonged to him alone. He gave Luke a stiff smile once the cuffs were in place. "Face the door."

Without another word, Luke positioned himself in front of the wide open door. Usually, Sebastian would close the door to prevent unnecessary movement, but with the door against the wall, Luke would be stable enough. And it would be easy for Jami to join them.

He secured Luke to the straps, ran a hand over his back to comfort him, then gathered a few toys and some lube to begin the scene.

The snap from the glove Sebastian pulled on made Luke flinch. He knelt behind Luke, running a lubed finger down the crease of his ass. Pressed gently against Luke's tight hole, giving his ass a sharp slap when he clenched.

"Relax. This plug is rather large. It will hurt if you fight it."

"Ugh, a plug?" Luke thunked his head against the door. "I hate butt plugs."

Sebastian's brow furrowed. "Why?"

"I was doing a scene with Chicklet once and her sub, Laura . . ." Luke groaned. "I don't want to talk about it."

"If you do not, this scene ends now." Sebastian moved his hand, then used the one without the glove to stroke Luke's thigh when he sighed. "Set the game aside and consider carefully, *semental*. Would you continue if something you did hit a trigger for Jami that she would not share?"

"No . . . but it's not a trigger. It was just . . ." Luke clenched his fists. "Uncomfortable. I wasn't expecting it, and I came and . . ."

"A straight man should not enjoy having things stuffed in his ass."

"Exactly. But . . ." Luke ground his teeth hard enough that Sebastian could hear his jaw crack. "Ugh, I hate talking about this stuff. But I get why I have to. Since it's you, it's . . . it's okay. I swear, if anything's not okay, I'll tell you."

"Thank you, Luke. Now . . ." Sebastian massaged Luke's ass cheeks, then pushed one gloved finger inside him. "Relax while I stretch you. I need to know if you can take it all."

"I can take you." Luke panted, sweat beading on his back as he opened himself to accept another finger. "Oh fuck, I don't know how long I can—"

"You do not have permission to come, so you will not." Sebastian pushed in deeper, thrusting in and out, testing Luke's control. He stopped when Luke shuddered. "Once I have the plug in, you may have your release. Thankfully, you are young enough to recover quickly. I plan to use you hard tonight."

"Jesus." Luke threw his head back as Sebastian fucked him with his fingers. "I can't—"

"Call for her, and I will stop torturing you." Sebastian pulled his fingers out, replacing them with the slim tip of the metal plug. "Otherwise . . ."

The lube on the plug made the first few inches slide in easily, but as it widened, Luke cried out, jerking his hips forward, then pushing back, as though not sure whether he wanted it or not. Sebastian drizzled more lube over the plug, working it in and out slowly. Luke took it, first only a few centimeters, then a full inch as the widest part stretched him. He moaned as Sebastian seated the plug inside him.

"You enjoyed that, didn't you?" Sebastian stood and pressed his chest against Luke's back, reaching around to grasp Luke's cock in his fist. "You are more of a slut than she is. Come for me now. You will scream. Even if you refuse to call her, she may stop hiding once she hears what she is missing."

"No!" Luke gasped as Sebastian stroked him. He quivered as he came, bowing his head as much as he could with his arms stretched over his head. "Mmph!"

Hot cum filled Sebastian's hand. He waited until Luke stopped shuddering before stepping away. Using a napkin from his bag, he cleaned his hand, letting out a sound of disgust. "You leave me no choice. Perhaps pain will do what pleasure cannot."

He chose the flogger first. Warmed Luke's flesh, hitting his back, ass, and thighs with raindrop light strokes. As the strikes intensified, he found a sharp clarity that only ever came when he felt completely in tune with his sub's needs. Delivering pain was not enough. It was the harmony, his own surrender in a way. Reading each sharp breath, sensing when to push further. And when to ease off.

Very few subs pulled him as far as Luke. Before long, he was snapping his wrist to increase the impact, drawn in by the way Luke pushed out as far as he could to meet the lick of the long leather strands.

Not enough. Sebastian could almost hear Luke saying as he tugged at the restraints, careful not to tug too hard. He traded the flogger for a tawse, running his hand over Luke's hot flesh, letting it cool before swinging back.

Crack!

"Ah!" Luke flattened himself against the door, bracing himself, his thigh muscles clenching and uncleaning to absorb the impact laid across them.

Sebastian waited until Luke's muscles relaxed. Then struck on the low curve of Luke's ass. Harder and harder, over, under, finding a rhythm that had Luke letting out a raw, low hum of pleasure.

More.

The weight of the fiberglass cane felt odd in Sebastian's hand. He had experience with it, but more for punishment than anything else. Usually five strikes across a subs ass and thighs would be enough to have them begging forgiveness for just about anything, but it would never serve as a good punishment for Luke.

Snap!

"Pleasepleaseplease! Ah!" Luke ground his dick against the door. "Don't stop!"

"What?" Sebastian tightened his grip on the handle of the cane, staring at the stark red strip cutting across Luke's ass cheeks. No blood, but any harder and there would be. A sadist would not concern himself with formalities at this point, but Sebastian needed to know Luke felt more than the pain. That he felt the connection between them. Because without it, those marks meant nothing to Sebastian. He might as well have hauled back and punched Luke in the face. "Who am I, Luke? Do you know?"

"Sir! Master! Seb, please! It's good. It's so fucking good." Luke mumbled something else, a curse, more pleas, tugging so hard at his wrist cuffs one came loose. "No! I didn't mean to!"

"Shh, I know." Sebastian clipped the cuff, pressing a soft kiss between Luke's shoulder blades. "Where are you, Luke? Can you remember the colors? Red if it is too much?"

Luke laughed. "Not red. Purple and green and gold. A really fucked up rainbow. Just a little more, Sir? I'll scream. I'll do whatever you want."

Sebastian inhaled deep. Then lifted the cane. He lashed it across Luke's ass and thighs until blood red stripes covered them. Until he had to stop or cry "red" himself. If Luke needed more, he would arrange a scene with Callahan or Chicklet. He would be there to set the limits, since Luke obviously could not, but this was as far as he could go.

He tugged at Luke's hair and hissed into his ear. "You swore you'd scream. Do it now. Call her name."

Luke sobbed. "Jami!"

"Luke!" Jami tripped into the room so quickly it seemed she had been just outside the door all along. She covered her mouth with her hands. "Oh, God! It was a game, Sebastian! Just a game! Why—"

"Do not judge him, *mi cielo*." Sebastian knew it wouldn't be Luke she would judge. He had done this to him. He moved toward her, afraid she would shy away. Then sighed with relief as she leaned against him. "His needs are not yours. Or mine. I . . . I must admit, he has pushed my limits. We may need to find someone else for this, but—"

"No, Sir." Luke slumped against the door. "Perfect. Holy shit, it was perfect."

"*Mi Rey?*" Jami took Sebastian's face between her hands. "Are you okay? You're allowed to call red too, you know."

"I almost did." Sebastian inhaled roughly. It shamed him to admit it, but he expected honesty from Jami and Luke. He could not give them any less in return. And he refused to ruin the scene with what might have been. With a sinister smile, he latched on to the back of Jami's neck. "Did you think to escape me, *puta?*"

Jami bit her bottom lip and shook her head.

"You should be naked in my presence. When I look on you again, you shall be." Sebastian made a dismissive gesture toward the bed. "Wait for me there. My *esclavo* took your punishment for you. I could use him for my pleasure, but I need a hot, wet cunt to fuck. Are you willing to spare him further abuse by giving yourself to me?"

Glancing over at Luke, Jami drew in a sharp breath, then let it out slowly. "Yes, *mi Rey*."

Her clothes hit the floor behind him with a soft wisp, but Sebastian kept his focus on Luke, first making sure that he had done no real damage. Every strike had been carefully controlled, but there was no telling how a sub would react when pushed this far. He pressed his hand to Luke's cheek, kissing him, whispering all the words he knew Luke would want to hear. He was strong. Brave. He had done everything Sebastian had asked of him and more.

"Seb, listen to me." The far-off look in Luke's eyes faded. "I'm fine. I . . . I don't have the words to tell you how good I feel. Just let me hang onto it a little longer. Go to Jami. I'll be with you in a bit. These cuffs are shit."

Sebastian barked out a laugh. "You amaze me, *semental.*"

"Hey." Luke gave him a lopsided smile. "You ain't seen nothin' yet."

* * * *

Jami squeezed her eyes shut as she stretched out on the bed. If anyone but Sebastian had left those marks on Luke, she would have lost it. Gone after them like a mad woman. But it *was* Sebastian.

And the doubt in his eyes had been more than enough to reassure her. They were both pushing his limits. Her with the party and the other men. Luke with the pain.

"*Mi Rey?*" Jami held up a hand as Sebastian approached her with a black, silk blindfold. She tongued her bottom lip. "The 'no sex' over the past few weeks has been so we can communicate better, right?"

"Yes, *mi cielo.*" Sebastian sat on the side of the bed, his face lined with concern. "I hope you will tell me if what I have done to Luke disturbs you to the point that you cannot . . . that you do not trust me."

"I trust you. Damn it, don't you ever doubt that. I didn't—fuck, I'm not ruining this by bringing *that* up." Her jaw clenched. "The point is, you've made it clear that me and Luke can tell you anything. But we need to know you can do the same."

Sebastian stood up straight, his jaw ticking as he fisted the blindfold in one hand. "I am fine."

"Right." Jami frowned at him. Damn it, weren't subs supposed to be the ones so determined to please their Doms that they had to be reminded to use a fucking safeword? "It scares me that you don't have your own limits."

Bowing his head, Sebastian nodded slowly. "You are right. *Maldita sea,* I find no pleasure in hurting either of you. But I do find pleasure in giving you what you need. The two do not always . . . mesh."

"Well, we've got to work on that. Luke's not gonna be happy when he finds out you ignored *your* triggers for him."

"So noted." Sebastian tipped his head back, staring at the ceiling for a long time before he looked at her again. Then he grinned. "You may both come up with a suitable punishment. But until then, I seem to recall you hiding from me." He combed his fingers through her short hair, and her eyes teared at the sharp pain in her scalp. "You abandoned my *esclavo* to the pain I dealt out. No matter what I did, he would not call for you. You said you were willing to serve my pleasure to spare him?"

"I'll do anything." Jami sank into the mattress, feeling more at ease since they were playing "make-believe" again. She couldn't enjoy this if it got all serious. And she'd heard Luke and Sebastian playing just fine without her. Until the *crack* of the cane on Luke's flesh had become too much for her to stay away. Right now, she was *very* happy she'd decided to stop hiding. Not because Luke needed her to step in. Because Sebastian did. "I'm sorry I hid from you. I was afraid."

Sebastian held the blindfold close to her eyes, but didn't cover them. "Afraid of what?"

"Afraid of the pleasure I feel with you. I was so innocent before you took me for the first time. I'd never experienced anything like that." She simpered, playing the innocent, virgin sacrifice. "I should save myself for the man my father gives me to. You stole me away, and I knew I had to fight you, but . . . I can't. You make me feel things. Bad things."

Placing the blindfold over her eyes, Sebastian let out a rough laugh. "You are mine. I care not who your father is. Who you once belonged to. I will make you forget any before me."

"Oh, oh, you mustn't! I'll be ruined!"

"You will be mine." Sebastian flattened his hand between her breasts. "I will kill any man who touches you without my permission."

"Any man? Even if he is your slave?"

"If he is my slave, and he pleases me . . ." Sebastian drew her arms over her head, placing the one with the cast on a pillow. "You shall be his reward."

Jami's toes curled. She hoped Sebastian would restrain her,

because she wasn't sure how much longer she could keep her hands to herself. "I live for your pleasure, *mi Rey*."

"I do not like to damage my property. So I will bind one wrist and your legs. If you fight, I will know you need more time to heal."

"I would never fight you."

Sebastian rose from the bed, finding cuffs to bind her from his black bag. The restraints attached to the headboard and footboard freed her in a weird way, because she didn't have to lie there, fully exposed, of her own will. She could immerse herself in the game, forget how her arm had been broken, let it lie on the bed as though it was restrained as well. She didn't have to be the stupid girl who'd made all the wrong choices. She could be here. Now. With no choices to make.

The blindfold covered her eyes. She bit her lip as she sensed Sebastian moving away from her. She could hear Luke nearby, his hoarse breaths coming slow and steady. Wherever Sebastian had taken him, he was coming back.

"I think this has cooled enough," Sebastian said.

Jami hissed in a breath as thick, hot liquid spilled over her breasts. A rich scent drifted up to her, but she couldn't identify it at first. She felt Sebastian's tongue glide over the heat. Another fiery line drizzled over her breasts, and her hips arched up off the bed. The heat flowed down, licking her core like sun-kissed waves rising with the tide.

Sebastian slowly licked her breasts clean, pressing them together as he laved around and around, moving up the sides, under, over, avoiding her nipples. The tender nubs throbbed with anticipation. Sebastian's weight shifted. His mouth left her.

Hot droplets hit one nipple. Then the other.

"Ah!" Jami tipped her head back, gasping as the nerves in her breasts caught fire. Sebastian's lips covered hers, and the taste of chocolate and caramel filled her mouth. "Oh . . . mmm."

"Yes, you are delicious." Sebastian chuckled, catching her chin and tugging at her bottom lip with his teeth. "Come taste her, Luke."

A wider spill, spreading too fast to be the caramel, covered her breasts and she panted as a hand lifted one breast, slipping as it gently squeezed. Licking and sucking, smearing the still warm melted chocolate down over her ribs. Another mouth on her other breast. Hot breaths over a neglected nipple. Luke let out a muffled moan. She pictured Sebastian taking his mouth hard, tasting him as they'd tasted her.

Two more hot drops. Then ice cold. She cried out, shaking as the sensations clashed.

"Our own chocolate fondue," Sebastian said.

A sweet, juicy fruit, coated in chocolate, pressed against her lips. She bit into it, humming with appreciation as the flavor of a deliciously ripe strawberry filled her mouth.

Heat alternated with cold, from her breasts, down her stomach, filling her belly button before a firm tongue dipped in. Her nipples were sucked clean, then covered again and again. She drifted into a chocolate scented cloud of pleasure, rising higher as the hard nips on her sensitized nipples threaded straight down to her clit, winding around until it throbbed and swelled. The pressure on her nipples increased. A wild current rode down the thread, shooting off sparks every which way, forcing her inner muscles to contract. The orgasm hit her hard, tearing through her like a wildfire, stealing all the air from the room. She writhed and screamed.

The blindfold fell away. Sebastian leaned over her, smoothing her hair away from her face as she slowly came down. He kissed her, smiling against her lips as Luke used a warm cloth to clean the chocolate from her body. "You are a mess, *gatita*."

Her bottom lip trembled. For some reason, even as Luke wiped away the stickiness all over her, she still felt . . .

Dirty. So fucking dirty. She choked back a sob. "When is it going to go away?"

Luke lifted his head and frowned. "What?"

Sebastian held her face between his hands and studied her face. Those deep, dark eyes seemed to see straight down to her soul. "It will take time, *mi cielo*. All those things you feel, those things which others made you ashamed of, are part of the woman I love. When you are wild and dirty, you are giving me—and Luke—all the purest parts of yourself. And that is precious. Never forget that."

His words washed over her like a heavy rain breaking through a summer smog. A fresh breeze teased her damp flesh. Crisp. *Clean.*

She hauled in a rough inhale, remembering how often he'd washed her, replacing all that was dirty and nasty with his loving touch. "I'll never forget."

"Would you like to stop?"

"No!" Jami shook her head. If he stopped, all those feelings of being ruined, tainted, would come back. They came less and less when she was with him. "I need to feel you. Everywhere. Please, *mi Rey.*"

Sebastian moved over her, kissing her throat, positioning himself between her thighs as he whispered in her ear. "Then feel me. *Si el propósito de la vida es el amor, el propósito de la mía serás tú.*"

In a smooth thrust, he filled her. She cried out into his mouth, barely managing to speak before she lost herself to him completely. "What does that mean?"

He drew almost all the way out. Tenderness filled his eyes. "If the purpose of life is love, the purpose of mine shall be you."

****

"Join us, *semental.*"

Luke dropped his hand away from his dick, swallowing as he watched Seb thrust into Jami and hold still. He found a bottle of lube in Seb's toy bag, poured a liberal amount into his palm, then used it to slick up his cock. He moved into position behind Seb, kissing down his spine, groaning as the solid muscles tensed and relaxed under his lips. He felt so out of control that he couldn't do more than press his body against Seb's. If he moved, he'd come. This was too much.

"I can't—"

"You will." Seb stroked Jami's thighs and glanced over his shoulder at Luke, his eyes hard. "It is easy to take what I give you. Now, you will give something in return."

"I want to. But this is . . . intense."

"Do not tell me, Luke." Seb gave him a dark smile, challenging him. "Show me."

Gritting his teeth, Luke sank the head of his dick into Seb, moaning as the ring of muscle gripped him. He rested his forehead between Seb's shoulders and shoved in all the way. Seb grunted, then reached back, taking a firm hold on Luke's ass.

"Hard! Fuck me hard!"

Panting, Luke pulled out, then slammed in. Seb matched his pace, meeting each pounding thrust, pistoning in and out of Jami's pussy with a hard slap of flesh on flesh. Luke threw his head back as he fought the urge to climax. Seb's tight grip on his ass steadied him, reminding him that while he might be on top, he wasn't in control. And he didn't need to be.

Seb hadn't given him permission to come. And more, he suddenly didn't want to until he'd . . . pleased his Master. Seb was right. Taking *was* easy. But giving meant so much more.

Jami screamed as her orgasm thrashed through her. Seb bent over her, grunting as Luke rammed into him.

"*Joder!*" Seb fisted his hands in the sheet by Jami's head as he came. His body clamped down on Luke like an iron fist.

Luke snarled as pleasure ripped through him, blazing from his balls to the head of his cock like a fireball. His legs gave out. He dropped to his knees, and stayed there until Seb dragged him up onto the bed to lie beside Jami.

Both he and Jami rested while Seb cleaned them, Jami half asleep, and Luke to worn out to move. He held Jami close, watching her eyelids flutter as she drifted away, smiling as Seb finally came to bed, curving his naked body against Luke's.

"She's beautiful," Luke murmured as Seb pressed his lips to his throat. "You're both . . . I don't know. Fucking unbelievable. I never thought I'd get this lucky."

"Neither did I," Seb said softly.

"*You're* beautiful." Jami's hand drifted up to Luke's face. Her fingers traced his scar. In her eyes he saw so much love, so much acceptance, that he could tell she didn't see anything ugly when she looked at him. But then she frowned. "Not that you believe me."

Seb bent over him, caressing Jami's cheek with his fingertips. "I think he does, *mi cielo*."

Luke used Seb's arm as a pillow, Jami's soft body in his arms, solid muscle at his back. This was where he belonged. The scars on his face, the ones that went deeper, were part of him. As were Jami's and Seb's. Maybe once he'd thought those scars would haunt him for the rest of his life, but not anymore. He nodded slowly.

"I do."

THE END

Visit the Dartmouth Cobras
www.thedartmouthcobras.com

Game Misconduct

THE DARTMOUTH COBRAS #1

The game has always cast a shadow over Oriana Delgado's life. She should hate the game. But she doesn't. The passion and the energy of the sport are part of her. But so is the urge to drop the role of the Dartmouth Cobra owner's "good daughter" and find a less...conventional one.

Playmaker Max Perron never expected a woman to accept him and his twisted desires. Oriana came close, but he wasn't surprised when she walked away. A girl like her needs normal. Which he can't give her. He's too much of a team player and not just on the ice.

But then Oriana's father goes too far in trying to control her and she decides to use exposure as blackmail. Just the implication of her spending the night with the Cobras' finest should get her father to back off.

Turns out a team player is exactly what she needs.

"Ms Sommerland takes us on an extremely incredible journey as we watch Oriana's master her own sexuality. She comes to realize that there is more out there that she craves and desires, than she has ever realized." Rhayne -Guilty Pleasures

"With a delicious storyline and kinky characters outside of the norm, Game Misconduct pushes you outside of your comfort zone and rewards your submission with phenomenally erotic sex. If you're a fan of hardcore BDSM, then this book is going to top your list of must reads!" Silla Beaumont - Just Erotic Romance

Defensive Zone

THE DARTMOUTH COBRAS #2

Silver Delgado has gained control of the Dartmouth Cobras—and lost control of her life.

Hockey might be the family business, but it's never interested Silver. Until her father's health decline thrusts responsibility for the team he owns straight into her hands. Now she has to find a way to get the team more fans and establish herself as the new owner. Which means standing up to Dean Richter, the general manager and the advisor her father has forced on her. The fact that their "business relationship" started with her over his lap at his BDSM club shouldn't be too much of a problem. Their hot one-night stand meant nothing! But how can she earn his respect when he sees her as submissive? Can they separate work and the lifestyle she's curious to explore?

Balancing her new life away from Hollywood, living among people who see her as the selfish Delgado princess, has her feeling lost and alone until Landon Bower, the Cobras new goalie slips into her life and becomes her best—and only—friend. The time they spend together makes everything else bearable, but before long his eyes meet hers with more than friendship, reflecting what she feels. Which could ruin everything.

Two Dominant men who see past her pretty mask and the shallow image she portrayed to the flashing cameras. A gentle attack from both sides that she can't hope to block unless she learns how to play.

But she's getting the hang of the game.

Offside

THE DARTMOUTH COBRAS #4 (Coming April 2013)

A pace ahead of the play can send you back to the start. And put everything you've worked for at risk.

Single mother and submissive Rebecca Bower abandoned her career as a sports reporter to become a media consultant with her brother's hockey team. A failed marriage to a selfish man makes her wary of getting involved with another. Unfortunately, chemistry is hard to deny, and all her hormones are dancing when she gets close to the Cobra's sniper, Scott Demyan.

Zachary Pearce 'came out' to the world last season to shift attention away from a teammate. And his one night with Scott Demyan had been unsettling. There could be more there, if only Scott was a different person. Instead, a night of sensual BDSM play with Becky leaves him wanting more, but she thinks he's gay and questions his interest. It's been a long time since a woman has attracted him both as a man and a Dom, and he'll do everything in his power to prove she's the only one he needs. Or wants. His one time with Scott was a mistake.

Scott might have forgotten what happened in his childhood, but the effects linger, and he specializes in drunken one-night stands…until he meets Zach and Becky and sees what he's missing. But neither one believes Scott can be faithful. Although he's trying hard to clean up his act to avoid getting kicked off the team, they want more from him. He's willing to make changes, but the most important one—putting their happiness before his own—means he'll probably end up alone.

About the Author

Tell you about me? Hmm, well, there's not much to say. I love hockey and cars and my kids…not in that order of course! Lol! When I'm not writing—which isn't often—I'm usually watching a game or a car show while networking. Going out with my kids is my only downtime. I get to clear my head and forget everything.

As for when and why I first started writing, I guess I thought I'd get extra cookies if I was quiet for a while—that's how young I was. I used to bring my grandmother barely legible pages filled with tales of evil unicorns. She told me then that I would be a famous author.

I hope one day to prove her right.

For more of my work, please visit: www.ImNoAngel.com

PRAISE FOR BIANCA SOMMERLAND'S BOOKS

"I just have to start by saying that this book is not for the faint of heart or the easily offended. Secondly, I have to say to the author, Bianca Sommerland, I give you a standing ovation. Deadly Captive was dark, sinister, erotic, intense, sexy and dangerous. Wow!"

–Karyl
Dark Diva Review of Deadly Captive

"My heart broke a little for Shawna. The entire set up made sense and from a personal note, I've been in the same situation. That's when I completely connected to the story and I was moved to tears."

–BookAddict
The Romance Reviews review of The Trip

Made in the USA
San Bernardino, CA
03 November 2017